Chapter 1 –

A shiver of excitement passed down (the village faded away to be replaced by the twittering of birds, buzzing of insects and the rustling of leaves; he was free! The world was his to explore, and he was going to make the most of it!

Walking briskly along, George felt the occasional rays of the warm summer sun filtering down through the tangle of branches overhead. A little further down the woodland path, two bright red squirrels chased each other before scampering up a tree and out of sight. All was peace and tranquillity; this was how it was meant to be. He hadn't felt like this since… since his dad had left.

George had not seen his father for two weeks. This was not unusual; after all, his dad was a merchant and he often had to travel the length and breadth of Britannia, buying and selling fine cloth, jewellery, pottery; in fact anything that he could easily transport and make a good profit on. He was often away for long periods, but this time it was different; this time his dad wasn't coming back! Tears began to well up in his eyes at this thought, but George blinked them away; he had done more than enough crying lately.

Approaching the edge of the wood that separated the village from the wide open lands beyond, George stepped out from beneath the trees, and was momentarily blinded by the sun's light, unhindered by clouds on this beautiful summer's day. Shielding his eyes from the glare, George turned his head to the west, where rolling green hills climbed away from him towards the darker mountains that lay beyond. Ahead of him, to the north, the dirt track descended into the valley and then climbed steeply again at the other side until it disappeared over a ridge. To the left of the ridge, a steep hill, covered in purple heather, rose upwards to a domed top, high above the path: Lookout Hill. George had been up there only twice before in his life, but the sights and feelings associated with that place had been etched on his memory. From the top you could see for miles in every direction, and on a cloudless day like today the view would be spectacular!

As George followed the dry stony track down into the valley, his mind turned once more to that fateful day, two weeks ago, when his dad had returned from his latest business venture. There had been something different about him, something distant. His father always gave George a present when he returned from a long journey, some small item that he had picked up on his travels. This time though, his gift had been a sword: a real, heavy, sharp-bladed longsword, such as a grown man would use, complete with its own leather scabbard and belt. It was too heavy for George to use yet - he had only seen twelve winters - but his father had told him it would come in handy when he was older. George had been thrilled at the time, but now he would gladly give up that sword, and everything else he owned, if he could only have his dad back!

Almost without realising it, George had reached the far side of the narrow valley. The path now rose steeply in front of him, and he started to climb with a steady pace, as once more his mind drifted away.

George lay curled up on his mat, the furs pulled over his head, trying to shut out the sound of his parents' arguing. Lying awake, listening to them, gave him a sick feeling in his stomach. "Please let them make up!" he whispered into the darkness. "Please let them make up!"

But the voices only got louder, more irate, until finally there was a moment of uneasy silence and then he heard his father, in a slightly choked voice, say, "I'm sorry."

A faint hope welled up inside George; maybe it would be all right after all.

Another awkward pause and then his father's voice again. "Take this... for the boy."

Take what? What was his dad saying? George's faint hope started to waver.

"I don't want your filthy money!" screamed his mother.

There was a loud crash followed by several strange clinking noises, and then the worst sound that George had ever heard: that of the door creaking open, and the footsteps of his father disappearing into the night.

George rose from his bed feeling numb; his mother was sobbing bitterly now. Making his way unsteadily towards her, he felt something cold and hard beneath his bare foot. Looking down, George could make out several circular objects on the ground, and as the moonlight streamed through the open door, he realised that the floor was covered in silver coins!

A sudden gust of wind brought George back to the present; he had climbed to the top of the ridge. Below him, the track zigzagged down to a wide shallow stream, where half a dozen large stepping-stones formed the path to the opposite bank. But he wasn't going that way, not yet anyhow.

Turning aside from the path, George started to climb Lookout Hill, making his way through the coarse purple heather and scrambling upwards. In places, the thick undergrowth stretched high above his head and he was forced to burrow his way through, but George kept going, gaining height all the time, until the heather became sparser and the ground more rocky.

How could his father have betrayed him like that? How could a stupid woman whom he'd only just met mean more to him than his only son? And why hadn't his mother stopped him? Couldn't she see that he needed his father around? Surely she could have persuaded him to stay. George wiped an angry tear from his eye; he wasn't going to think about it anymore. He had spent these last two weeks turning it over and over in his mind, and it had only made him more miserable. He had escaped from the village for the day in order to forget, and that was what he was going to do.

His mind back on the task at hand, George scrambled the last few yards to the top and stood gazing out across the land below in wonder. As the wind tugged at his woollen tunic, he felt like the king of the world, standing there on high surveying his kingdom, casting an imperious eye over the tiny insignificant lives of his subjects. Actually there wasn't a single person in sight, just miles and miles of rolling hills, woods, mountains and rivers.

Shielding his eyes, once more, from the glare of the sun, George followed the course of the wide shallow stream as it swept through the hills, fed by many smaller tributaries until it had become a fast-flowing river. The river disappeared into a gorge, lost from his sight, but soon emerged, cascading down in a series of waterfalls towards a wide lake with a forest of trees at its farther end. He remembered walking there with his parents last summer. Eyes misting up, George quickly turned from the lake to look to the north. Down below, just visible beyond a range of pine trees, lay the small town of Cambodonum. He had been there on several occasions with his father, who had taken him to the market where he often bought and sold his wares.

George smiled grimly to himself. It was time to start living the life his father had trained him up for, the life he had always dreamt of leading. *He was a trader, but not just any trader; he was the legendary George: merchant of great renown, saviour of the oppressed, scourge of the wicked.* George could almost hear the trumpet fanfare as he saluted the imaginary crowds, turned on his heel and strode purposefully down the hill, tripping over a jagged rock and sliding head first into a particularly prickly clump of thistles!

The sun, still unobstructed by clouds, was nearing its highest position in the clear blue sky, and George was thankful that he had remembered to fill his waterskin at the village well before he set off that morning. He took a long swig of the cool refreshing liquid before replacing the skin in his backpack and pressing on.

Below him, the inhabitants of the town of Cambodonum went about their business. "The town used to be a Roman garrison", his father had told him, "But these days nearly all the soldiers that live here are retired". The settlement was obviously of Roman construction, perfectly rectangular in shape, except for where the old fort jutted out at the northeast corner. Cambodunum had long since outgrown its military roots and spread south and west, but it had not abandoned all fortifications; a narrow stone wall encircled its extended perimeter, and beyond that lay a wide ditch. These defences continued unbroken around the whole town, save for where the main road entered it. Here there were two iron gates: one in the northeast side and one in the southwest, and George knew that halfway between the two, in the very centre of the town, was the marketplace, his destination.

Some Britons were uncomfortable with these Roman towns, and many of these same people still resented Roman rule, but without the Romans the opportunities for trade would be very limited. After all, who kept the peace that enabled trade to take place? Who built and maintained the roads, without which it would take weeks to get to the nearest town? Who imported goods from all over the world so that they were available for the citizens of Britannia? "The Romans have been good for us", his father had said, and George was inclined to agree with him.

The sun glinted blindingly off the polished helmet of the soldier who was guarding the southwest gate of the town and, despite his positive outlook on Romans in general, George felt slightly uneasy as he passed below the point of the man's dangerous looking spear. He needn't have worried however; the guard, who was slightly overweight and sweating profusely under the glare of the noonday sun, completely ignored him, and George soon found himself wandering freely down the cobbled street, staring in wonder at his new surroundings.

Ahead of him, talking loudly to one another, were two native Britons, men dressed similarly to George: both wearing brightly coloured tunics and checked trousers. Approaching in the opposite direction, an important looking Roman woman, dressed in a long flowing garment of deepest blue, swept past George without giving him a second glance. Following her at a respectful distance was a younger woman, wearing a simple knee-length tunic and carrying a basket full of fruit: obviously a servant girl.

And it wasn't just the people who were fascinating. As he walked down the perfectly straight street, George admired the houses on either side of him. Unlike the circular huts of his village, these dwellings were rectangular and had tiled roofs, rather than thatch. Some of them even had two storeys! And as he neared the centre of the town, they were becoming more impressive; he was now passing buildings constructed of hewn stone rather than timber. In George's village there were no buildings made of stone, not even the great hall!

There was no time to stop and marvel at these sights though, because now the street was busy with people and the press of the crowd forced him to move along at a reasonable pace. George was unable to see where the crowd was heading, but he could smell the pleasant aroma of freshly baked bread wafting towards him from somewhere not too far ahead, and the general noise level was definitely increasing.

At this point, George remembered the food he had in his pack; it was getting near to dinnertime. Telling himself that he would stop and eat soon, George continued down the street, approaching the largest building yet: two storeys high and spanning the road. A stone archway allowed access through to what lay beyond: the hub of the town. With the rest of the noisy jostling crowd, George passed under the arch and entered the marketplace.

To his left was the impressive basilica: a grand, many-pillared building, where the town's officials met to make important decisions and dispense justice. The remaining three sides of the square were bordered by the huge stone structure he had just passed through; he now remembered that this was called the forum.

Now that he was inside the market, George could see that the forum housed a large number of shops. To his right, he could make out a butcher's store, with several joints of meat hanging down from hooks in the ceiling. Next to this was the source of the lovely smells: a well-stocked bakery. George squeezed through a group of men, who were admiring a collection of swords displayed at the front of a weaponsmith's shop, and made his way into the square, where a couple of dozen stalls were dotted about in no particular order.

The legendary George stepped into his arena. This is what he had travelled hundreds of miles to see: the fabled market of Cambodonum. What should he purchase? Leather, pottery, dyed cloth. No - too common. He had travelled far, having heard tales of wondrous things that were to be had in this magnificent market. Silk then, or glass (made with great skill by local craftsmen). No, he must have something rare and exquisite. "Aha!" George moved towards the stall that had just caught his eye; this is what he was looking for.

Displayed on a large cart at the far side of the square, were a great number of strange and mysterious objects: necklaces made of odd-shaped teeth, bracelets made of animal bones; different colours and sizes of furs and animal skins (some with spots or stripes on), scary masks made of clay, a large wooden cage with two brightly coloured birds inside, and two huge smooth curved white horns (or at least that's what they looked like to George). And in the centre of the cart, the biggest egg that George had ever seen! It was about a foot long, and more cylindrical than oval, pale green in colour, though with a slight hint of blue, and George couldn't take his eyes off it!

"Hey!"

George looked up. Standing behind the cart, looking down at him with a disapproving expression, was a fat man with a darkly tanned face, dressed in brightly coloured flowing robes.

"Move along, little boy", he said, in a condescending tone. His voice was surprisingly squeaky for such a big man, and his accent sounded funny to George. In fact, the silly man wasn't at all intimidating, and George decided he wasn't leaving.

"Excuse me", he said in his most grown up voice, "But I may be wishing to make a purchase."

"This is quality merchandise!" exclaimed the merchant indignantly. "Each item on this stall is worth more money than you have ever seen!"

Undeterred, George cast his eye casually over the contents of the cart, carefully concealing his wonder at the fantastic curiosities on display. "I doubt it", he said in sceptical tones. "My father is a rich merchant; he has enough gold to buy your cart and everything on it!" This was a bit of an exaggeration, but the fat stallholder wasn't to know.

"If your father is so rich, why doesn't he bother to clothe you properly?" asked the merchant, looking George up and down disdainfully.

"Err..." George wasn't prepared for this question. Glancing down, he noticed that his green tunic had indeed become rather faded, and his patchwork breeches did have one or two more holes in them than was absolutely necessary.

Recovering himself quickly, George replied, "I'm not bothered about clothes, and neither is my dad." Then thinking quickly he added, "He is bothered about rare animal... err... merchandise though."

The trader had a look of uncertainty on his chubby face; maybe he was starting to believe the story. Now was his chance! George gave the merchant what he hoped was an offended look, and turned on his heel, taking a step away from the cart. Without realising it, he had shut his eyes and clenched his fists tight.

"Wait!"

It had worked; George opened his eyes.

"Forgive me", continued the overweight merchant, his voice sounding even squeakier. "I see you are an enlightened young man."

George wasn't sure what that meant, but it sounded complementary, so he turned around and took another look at the strange and wonderful selection. He was desperate to find out about the giant egg, but he remembered his dad saying that a trader shouldn't show too much interest in anything he was hoping to buy, so he gestured towards the brightly coloured birds instead.

"They're parrots", stated the man, in answer to his question. "Beautiful aren't they? They're clever too; it is said that the goddess Minerva was so impressed with their bright plumage that she gave them the gift of speech."

Here the merchant started making strange clicking and whistling sounds, apparently in an attempt to get the parrots to demonstrate their rare talent. Unfortunately, the brightly coloured creatures seemed intent on keeping any divine gifts they might possess to themselves and so, with a cheeky smile on his face, George interrupted the slightly flustered trader and asked about the two white horns.

"They're elephant tusks", replied the merchant, giving the parrots a withering look.

"Tusks?" The only animal that George had seen with tusks was a wild boar. He tried to picture a boar with tusks that size! The monstrous image charged through the woods of his imagination, knocking down the occasional tree that blocked its path!

"How big is an err…?"

"Elephant", supplied the merchant. "Oh it's huge, bigger than a… a… horse", he finished rather lamely.

George waited for something more.

"A big horse!"

Not good enough. George suppressed a grin and tried to look disinterested; he was running rings around this fat fool and thoroughly enjoying it. By the look on his round face, the trader was rapidly losing patience; the legendary George had him right where he wanted him!

"So, what's that egg?" He asked as casually as he could.

"It's an ostrich egg", replied the merchant, hiding his growing annoyance with difficulty. "The largest bird in the world!"

"How big?"

"Bigger than you", snapped the trader, letting his temper get the better of him.

"How can it fly if it's so big?"

"It can't, it just walks or runs", answered the stallholder triumphantly.

"How much are you asking for it?"

The trader's expression altered; George had uttered the magic words. "100 denarii", he said, smiling shrewdly.

8

George didn't know much about money. In his village, if you wanted something, you offered something else of similar value in exchange for it; money wasn't required. Of course as a trader, his father had handled it regularly, and shown George the various coins that were in use throughout the Roman Empire. Denarii were the silver ones, he recalled, but as to how much they were worth… Not that it really mattered, since he didn't have enough silver in his pack to buy a duck egg, never mind an ostrich egg!

"Get serious!" he replied, with a confident air. "Ten denarii are all it's worth".

"Ten?" spluttered the merchant, obviously outraged, or at least pretending to be. His round face flushed a deep purple and he seemed to be having trouble articulating anything further. Fortunately, before the trader could translate his anger into words, a large lady interrupted.

"Do you have any of those leopard skins in my size?"

George doubted that any animal skin would cover this lady's imposing bulk, and from the look on the merchant's face, he seemed to be thinking the same thing.

"Maybe a cape would suit you better, madam."

This comment did not go down very well at all, and as the imperious woman vented her anger on him, the unfortunate trader cowered behind the cart, frantically rummaging through his stock of animal skins.

Seeing that the stallholder was distracted, George tentatively reached out a hand towards the gigantic egg, and moments later his fingertips touched the shell. He had expected it to feel cold, hard and perfectly smooth, but instead it had a slightly rough surface with a strangely leathery texture. George cast a cautious glance in the trader's direction, but the poor fellow was still bearing the brunt of the woman's anger and wasn't paying him any attention. Fervently hoping that this state of affairs would continue, George reached out and lifted the egg gingerly with both hands. The huge thing weighed even more than George had expected.

"WHAT ARE YOU DOING?" shouted the merchant suddenly, nearly causing George to drop the egg in his shock and dismay at being discovered.

Recovering himself with difficulty, George replied in an almost steady voice. "You d… don't expect me to buy without handling the goods, do you?"

Once more, the large woman came to his rescue. She didn't like being interrupted, and she hadn't finished with this rude stallholder just yet.

"Well, have you got a leopard skin in my size or not?"

The trader stammered some sort of apologetic reply, but George wasn't listening: he was staring, transfixed by the awesome treasure within his grasp. If only he had enough money to buy it; if only he could take it back to the village and show his friends.

"Oh George, you're such a hero!" echoed Silvia's voice in his head as, in his mind's eye, he finished telling his tale to an awestruck group of youngsters and produced the egg from his pack with a flourish.

That happy image had hardly finished floating around in his mind when a new thought entered George's head, an outrageous idea; one that shocked him: he was going to steal the egg!

Chapter 2 – Thief!

He couldn't just steal it; that would be wrong. But as he stood there cradling the wonderful treasure in his arms, the idea started to seem more and more reasonable. After all, the merchant obviously had plenty of other items, and George was sure that charging 100 denarii for an egg amounted to attempted robbery anyway; so he would only be doing to the trader what the trader would happily have done to him.

Glancing about him, George noted that there were three archways leading out of the marketplace: one in the centre of each of the forum's sides. The nearest was only a few paces beyond and to the left of the stall and, unlike the arch he had entered by, it was reasonably clear of people.

The merchant was still on the receiving end of the fat lady's sharp tongue; this was his chance. Giving himself no time for second thoughts, George sprang into action, sprinting around the cart at full speed, the trader's high-pitched cry of "THIEF!" ringing in his ears.

With both arms out in front of him, protecting the egg, George dodged right and left through the thinning crowd, narrowly avoiding a group of chattering women and an angry looking man with a bushy moustache, who attempted to grab him as he rushed past. Reaching the edge of the square, George sprinted through the stone arch, away from the crush of the market and the merchant's angry shouts.

Risking a quick glance over his shoulder, George was dismayed to find that he was being pursued, and not by the overweight trader, but by a trim younger man with bronzed skin and dark brown hair. The egg suddenly felt much heavier!

Reaching a crossroads, he swerved to his right, down a side street, and almost collided with a horse! The frightened animal reared up on its hind legs, and George had to jump sideways to avoid being kicked! This sudden change of direction caused the boy to lose his balance and, spinning out of control, he hit the side of the cart to which the horse was tied, grazing his knuckles on the wood in the process.

George was somewhat fortunate because had the cart not been there he would certainly have fallen. As it was, he found himself leaning against it, clutching the egg tightly to his chest, his nose only a few inches away from one of the many barrels that stood on the back of the wagon.

At that moment, a sudden idea struck him. Knowing that he couldn't hope to escape whilst encumbered with this heavy burden, and with no time to stop and think, George lifted the egg onto the cart, wedging it into a gap between the nearest three barrels and the wooden side panel, and then he was away, accelerating into a sprint.

Even as he set off, George was conscious of heavy footfalls pounding the cobbled street behind him. A hand grabbed hold of his backpack. This was it: he was caught! No, he wasn't going to give up now! George dropped to the ground, changing his momentum from forward to downward in a heartbeat. The next moment, he was hit hard from behind, as with a cry of surprise, his pursuer fell over George's prone form and rolled head-over-heels, landing heavily on his back.

George leapt to his feet and turned, only to see the outstretched arms of a second pursuer, a stockier man with green eyes, heading straight for him. Ducking under the new arrival's reach, George surged left, down another street, adrenalin pumping through his veins.

Once again, George weaved in and out of the bemused inhabitants of Cambodonum, sprinting down the road, spurred on by fear, the fear of being caught and then... What was the punishment for stealing? A flogging; having his hand cut off; crucifixion?

A wave of panic washed over George and, as he reached the far end of the road, he frantically jostled his way through the dense crowd of people blocking his path. It was no good, however; the press was too great and after receiving an angry remark and a shove in the back, he resigned himself to being carried along with it. Everyone seemed to be heading in the same direction, towards a large building with a familiar looking archway... He was heading back into the marketplace!

As the crowd passed out from beneath the stone arch, they dispersed in various directions, and George once again found himself with the freedom to choose his own destination. Now that he had this opportunity, he found himself hesitating. He had entered through the third archway: the one directly opposite the basilica. And between him and that imposing building, was the stall he had just stolen from. He had to somehow get out of the square without being seen by either of the two men who were after him or by the fat stallholder! Forcing his legs to move, George skirted right, around the edge of the market, quickly pushing his way into the midst of a group of people, so as to keep out of sight.

Everyone seemed to be moving agonisingly slowly, stopping to view items of clothing, examining pieces of pottery or jewellery, that were on display at the various stalls, or picking up fruit and vegetables, that were being sold from shops built into the stone forum that surrounded the square.

George kept casting furtive glances over his shoulder, but he saw no sign of his pursuers. After what seemed like an age, he reached the side of the square nearest the cart that he had just stolen from. As he inched past, George tried hard to keep his gaze anywhere but on the stall full of mysterious objects, but he couldn't help himself, and in this brief lapse, caught a momentary glimpse of the merchant pacing up and down, an angry look on his face, before quickly averting his eyes, hoping desperately that he hadn't been seen.

Quickening his pace as the crowd thinned, George made for the archway he had recently charged through with the egg, all the while expecting to feel a restraining hand on his shoulder or to hear the dreaded cry of "Thief". Mercifully, however, these fears were not realised and so, glancing behind him, at regular intervals, to make sure that he wasn't being followed, George hurried away from the market; it seemed that he'd got away with his crime. A feeling of relief came over him, as if a great weight had been lifted from his shoulders, and he broke into a jog; he still had a job to do.

Reaching the crossroads, George turned right and then stopped dead in his tracks. He looked around; this was definitely the place. He recognised the inn on the corner with its painted sign depicting a boar's head, but the horse and cart were no longer here: the egg was gone!

George wasn't going to give up now, not after he'd risked so much; the cart couldn't have got far. Turning, he headed up the road in the direction that the horse had been facing, confident that he would soon track down the missing vehicle and reclaim his prize.

George's confidence had worn off somewhat by the time he had passed the next two crossroads, with still no sight of his quarry. If only the streets had been dirt tracks like in his village, instead of these stone cobbles, he would have been able to follow the wheel ruts and find the cart easily. Turning right, George jogged along a quieter road, lined with poorer houses, his hope diminishing with every stride. He was starting to tire too; perhaps it was time to admit defeat. Reaching the end of this street, George looked left: nothing, and then right. There it was! He could just make out the barrels over the heads of a few wandering town inhabitants.

Forcing himself to speed up, despite the heaviness in his legs, George raced down the road in pursuit. Thankfully, the vehicle was travelling slowly, no doubt due to the overcrowded streets, and he soon overtook it. Jogging alongside, he scanned the rows of barrels, but couldn't see the precious egg. What if it had dropped off and smashed? No, it couldn't have done; he had wedged it in next to the side panel; it must have rolled over.

George moved closer to the large wooden wheels, keeping up easily, and then he spotted it; the egg had indeed rolled over, but it looked undamaged. Retrieving the treasure, however, was going to be tricky. The thing was so big it needed both hands to grasp and, because of the position of the barrels, he could only do this whilst standing sideways on to the cart, certainly not while running. Maybe he should wait until the driver had stopped, but when might that be? He couldn't very well follow it along the road out of town; he was sure to be noticed! He had to act now. Throwing caution to the wind, George grabbed the side of the cart and pulled himself up, leaning over the panel and bending his knees to keep his feet away from the road. Letting his stomach support his weight, he reached for the egg with both hands and grabbed it.

"OI!"

George tumbled backwards off the cart with a cry, and landed hard on his backside, the enormous egg clutched to his chest. Scrambling to his feet in some discomfort, he saw the driver dismount, an angry look on his red face.

"What do you think you're doing to my cart?" he demanded.

Feeling sure that the explanation would not help in the least, George turned to run.

"THERE HE IS!" A deep, booming voice rang out, causing passers-by to stare. This time it wasn't the driver, it was the merchant's guards: they had tracked him down!

Doubling back, George dodged around the cart, avoiding the irate driver, and sped off down the road, swerving right, into a side street. Reaching the end of this road, he turned left and then right again. George's lungs felt like they were on fire, his legs ached and he was sure that his backside would be a deep purple colour in the morning. In addition, his arms were getting tired; the egg was heavy.

Halfway along this new street, George spied a grand building supported by many stone pillars. Wide stone steps led up from the street to the large open doors, and a queue of people stood on them, waiting to enter. It was a temple, but to which of the many Roman deities it belonged, George didn't know, nor did he care; it was a perfect place to hide. Concealing himself behind one of the pillars, he slumped down, taking in large gulps of air.

With one eye on the street, George removed his backpack, unfastened the leather straps, and stuffed the large egg in as far as it would go. He knew that it would squash his bread and cheese to pulp, but he didn't care; he would have gladly sacrificed a week's worth of meals to win this fabulous prize.

There was still no sign of his pursuers, and George's breathing had returned to normal; now would be an excellent time to leave. Shouldering the bulging pack with some difficulty, George heaved himself to his feet and stepped back out into the street.

Picking up the pace again, he jogged to the far end of the road, where there was a T-junction. Having completely lost his bearings by this point, George made a couple of turns at random before spying a large stone archway some distance ahead. He backed up; there was no way that he was heading in that direction! At least now, though, he had a pretty good idea where he was; Roman towns were nothing if not predictable.

Turning left, George jogged down the street, carried on straight ahead at the crossroads and then turned right at the next junction. He then continued at speed to the next left turn, where he slowed to a walk. Was he right? He had to be right. *Please!* Looking left, George saw what he had been desperate to see: the open gate he had entered by!

Freedom beckoned, and George was going to answer its call. He sprinted down the road, swerving in and out of people who seemed to be milling about in a frustratingly aimless fashion. As he approached his destination, however, George slowed, realising how suspicious it would look to the guard if he tried to run out of the town.

Hardly daring even to breathe, George walked up to the gate, his eyes to the ground, desperately hoping that he would be ignored.

"Hey, lad."

George froze; his heart seemed to stop beating, and a sick feeling welled up in his stomach.

"Aren't you a bit young to be travelling on your own?"

George looked up at the soldier. It was a different man to the one who had ignored him on the way in, although similarly dressed: with gleaming helmet, breastplate over his knee-length tunic, greaves (leg armour), sturdy boots and a long-shafted spear.

Despite the man's imposing appearance, he had a kindly face, and George managed a nervous smile. "I... I... I've s... seen tw... err... fifteen winters", he stammered.

"Winters must come often in this cold country!" laughed the guard. "You had better get home quickly before it starts to snow!"

George didn't need to be told twice and, without a backward glance, he hurried away, his heart still beating like a drum.

"STOP, THIEF!"

George's blood turned to ice in his veins. He knew that deep booming voice, and it wasn't the guard's. He tried to run, but his legs didn't seem to want to do what his brain was telling them. "Come on!" he urged his tired limbs, forcing them to move.

The path climbed steeply uphill into the wood, but George sprinted up it with a speed born of fear. If they caught him out here in the open... it didn't bear thinking about.

George could tell, from the shouts, that his pursuers were still a good way back, but his pack was starting to weigh very heavily on him, and his legs felt like jelly. At least the thick covering of branches overhead gave him relief from the relentless glare of the sun; it was almost cool in here, and quiet. Were they still following him? George strained his ears, but all he could hear was his own panting breath and the dull thud of his footfalls on the pine-needle carpet underfoot. He held his breath, but moments later it forced itself out with a loud exhaled blast. It was no good; he would just have to stop and listen, but not yet. The ground had levelled out now and the going was much easier; he would stop at the foot of the next rise.

Soon the ground grew stony underfoot and rose steeply once more. George's breath was coming in painful gasps now, and there were pains in his side and his back; he had to stop. Coming to a sudden halt, George instinctively leaned forward, hands going to his knees as he exhaled sharply. Next moment, the great weight on his back had overbalanced him and his legs gave way as he pitched forwards, exhausted.

For a long time, George just lay there, face-down on the soft earth, filling his lungs with cool fresh air. Presently, as his breathing slowed, he became aware of other noises around him: the call of a bird, the scampering of a small creature in the undergrowth. In the distance, he could hear the roar of running water, and closer to there was a faint rustling and the snap of a twig. Startled, George scrambled to his feet, his eyes scanning the surrounding woods. What had made that sound? A man's shout confirmed his fears: they had found him!

George turned to run once more, his hope of escape almost gone. He had nothing left; his legs felt like lead weights, and he stumbled forwards, scrambling on hands and knees to climb the steep slope. Reaching the top of the little hill, George was almost blinded by a sudden shaft of light; he was out of the woods. Even as the ray of light spread a ray of hope into his heart, it was snatched away: George had reached the edge of a gorge. Thirty feet below him was the source of the now deafening roar: the foaming white water of the river. He was trapped!

A sense of panic descended upon George as he stood looking down at the fast-flowing river. Turning his head, he looked up and down the gorge; he had to get to the stepping-stones. Which way were they? Hesitating for what seemed like an age, he forced his weary legs uphill, right along the top of the gorge.

Without warning, the tall man with bronzed skin and dark brown hair raced out of the trees, cutting him off. Skidding to a halt, George turned and fled downhill, only to find his way barred by the shorter stocky man with flashing green eyes. In desperation, George turned to head back into the trees, but both men moved quickly to intercept, forcing him towards the gorge.

The stocky man spoke in his deep gravelly voice: "Give us the egg."

The taller man just grinned evilly and drew a knife from his belt.

George's mind was racing; what were they going to do with him? Would they really kill him if he didn't hand over the egg?

Looking into the shorter man's cold green eyes he got his answer: 'yes!'

Turning to his other foe, standing there grinning, his knife pointing steadily at George, another question popped into the boy's frightened mind: would they kill him even if he gave them what they wanted?

Whilst thinking these unpleasant thoughts, George had been unconsciously backing away; now he found himself standing right at the edge of the gorge.

"Give us the egg now!" The stocky man's voice was raised, so that he could be heard over the roar of rushing water, and he was striding purposefully towards George.

All at once, George's mind was made up. Spinning around, he let out a cry and, before the two men could grab him, he jumped into the gorge!

Yelling and swinging his arms wildly, George plunged towards the foaming water at a terrifying speed, and then with a painful slap, his feet struck the surface and he was sinking down, down, down into a strange echoing underwater world. George fought to overcome the sense of panic that was threatening to engulf him; he was rising quickly now and, with a gasp, he broke the surface and immediately got a mouthful of water.

Spluttering and coughing, he struggled to get his breath and went under again. The roar of the water filled his ears and the strong current dragged him along, coughing and splashing. Forcing his head above the surface, George caught a glimpse of a large rock just ahead, before the water rushed over him again. Gasping for breath, he plunged his hands into the water, trying desperately to swim against the current, but it was no good; he was pulled relentlessly onwards.

The white foam obstructed George's view as he rushed headlong down the rapids. His left arm collided with something solid, and he spun around before plunging backwards over a dip. George's feet scraped along the bottom and water went up his nose. Rising rapidly above the surface, he spluttered wildly, trying to fill his lungs with air, only managing a quick gasp before he bobbed under again.

As George re-emerged, he was struck on his outstretched right hand; this time it didn't feel like a rock. George tilted his head back, but water was in his eyes and he couldn't see a thing. Something pulled at his hair, and he cried out in pain, swallowing more water in the process.

Coughing violently, he emerged again, but on this occasion succeeded in keeping above the surface long enough to catch a glimpse of his surroundings; he was out of the gorge now and near the right hand bank of the river. Low branches were jutting out over the side, almost down to the water, and it was these that were striking him on the hands and head.

The wild river bore George swiftly along beneath the overhanging branches. He was no longer bobbing up and down like a cork, nor did there seem to be any rocks in this part of the river; in fact the water was clear blue here, and not foaming white. But George was still helpless in its grasp even though he was managing, for the moment, to keep his head above water.

Now that he wasn't being continually plunged beneath the surface of the river, the rushing water that had filled his eyes and ears drained away, giving him chance to look about. There was certainly no sign of the two men, nor would he see them again, George was sure of that: no one would risk those rapids unless they had absolutely no choice.

As the mighty currents swept him effortlessly on, George began to notice that the ever-present roaring in his ears was growing steadily louder. Up ahead, the course of the river swung sharply left and disappeared around a tree-lined bend.

George's mind flitted back to the river he had seen from the top of Lookout Hill, the one that had flowed through a gorge and then down a series of… He gave a cry of fright, and struck out for the near bank, but he could make little headway; the trees were whizzing by! Kicking and splashing wildly, George fought against the currents. Water once more obstructed his view; he must be nearly to the bank by now! Suddenly, a large bough struck the top of his head, forcing him under. Spluttering and thrashing, George broke the surface and groped for the unseen branch; several more whipped at his hands, but he couldn't grasp them.

The thunderous roar of the river pounded away at his ears; it was by now the only sound that he could hear. Desperately trying to wipe the water out of his stinging eyes with the back of one hand, George spotted a great clump of leaf-covered branches sticking out just ahead, and next moment he was flinging both arms skywards, grasping at the green mass.

George's right hand closed over a medium sized bough, his arm jerking painfully as the river sought to tear it from his grasp. His grip started to fail; then his left hand found a nearby branch, strengthening his hold. The river tugged at George, as though angry at his attempts to escape, the force of it lifting him to a near horizontal position with water cascading over him violently. Clinging on for dear life, he eventually managed to swing one leg over a thicker branch, hidden by the clump of leaves, and slowly hoisted his bruised body out of the water.

After struggling along several slender swaying boughs and through a mass of tangled branches, which scratched at his flesh and pulled at his hair, George finally picked his way to a small patch of relatively dry ground, just beyond the overhanging trees, and flopped down completely exhausted. He didn't move for a long while, but just lay there, his bruised and battered body warmed by the healing rays of the afternoon sun.

Much later, when George did finally get up, he reached for his soggy pack and pulled it off his back, laying it out on the wet grass. His food would be mushy and inedible by now, but at least the egg… The egg! Where was it?

"NO!" George screamed at the top of his lungs, venting his anger on the roaring river that had almost killed him and, worse than that, had stolen his prize!

Chapter 3 – Night of the Wolves

"The young man's breath came in painful gasps; his legs ached, his side hurt, and his heart was beating so fast he felt sure it must burst. He couldn't go on… but he had to; to give up now would surely mean a violent death! The thunderous footfalls of his nightmarish pursuer were getting closer and closer. The exhausted youth looked wildly about him, desperately seeking for some way of escape. To his left stood a large oak tree with low-hanging branches and, with no time to hesitate, the young man stumbled towards it, slipping on its exposed roots, before hauling his athletic frame up onto the lowest bough."

"Knowing that he was still far too near the ground for safety, the nimble lad scrambled higher, almost losing his grip in a frantic attempt to get out of reach of his foe. Finally gaining a secure perch, some twenty feet above the ground, the dark-haired youngster looked down. The sight that met his eyes chilled him to the core: below him, puffing and blowing like an enraged bull, was a terrifying giant!"

"The giant's arms and legs were like tree trunks and his chest like a huge barrel; he had terrible green eyes and wild black hair, including a huge shaggy beard that fell almost to his waist. As frightening as this was, it was not his enemy's appearance alone that had frozen the brave lad's heart (he was made of sterner stuff than that!) No, it was the huge axe that the giant now held in his mighty grip, and the evil glint in his eye; the giant was going to cut his tree down!"

"The great tree shuddered under the first savage swing; then there was another and another. The terrified youngster clung on as the oak shook with the repeated blows of the axe. This was it; he was going to die! Then, just as all hope had left him, a shout rang out and the thudding stopped. The angry giant bellowed a challenge in reply, and the young man craned his neck, peering down through the branches, trying to get a glimpse of the new arrival. A shadowy figure stepped into view; it had what looked like dark wings and a hideous horned face: a demon!"

"No… it couldn't be… As the thing came closer, the youth saw that what he had mistaken for wings was actually a dark cloak, billowing in the wind, and the monstrous head was really a full-length, horned helmet, covering the mysterious man's face. The stranger, who was clad in black from head to foot, stood defiantly facing his enormous opponent, gloved hands on hips. The enraged giant gave one final fierce bellow and strode towards the dark figure, swinging his axe. Instantly, as if by magic, two gleaming swords appeared in the helmeted man's hands, and there followed the ringing sound of metal on metal as he parried the mighty blow."

"The two combatants circled each other, lunging and parrying, whilst the giant blew hard and cursed often. The mysterious stranger, however, made no sound. Leaning dangerously forward to get a better view of the battle, the young man saw the dark-clad figure get in a blow on his foe's mighty arm. With an awful cry, the giant fell back, giving ground steadily, until he had his back to the oak tree, his shaggy black head directly below the youngster's perch, but before the mysterious swordsman could strike the killing blow, the fierce giant kicked out with a huge hobnailed boot, knocking the helmeted man to the floor."

"The youth gasped; the giant gave an evil chuckle and raised his axe for the kill. With no time to think, the brave youngster gave a wild cry and jumped out of the tree. His feet collided with the giant's shaggy head, and he heard an angry grunt as he tumbled backwards, landing painfully on his right shoulder. Dazed and disorientated, the confused lad scrambled unsteadily to his feet, only to find the angry giant towering over him, a fierce look on his red face, his axe held high, poised to split the boy in two!"

"Gritting his teeth, he waited for the blow to fall… but instead, the giant let out a strange gurgling sound and toppled sideways. Behind him stood the mysterious stranger, one sword covered with the giant's blood; the battle was over! But what would this ferocious warrior do now? Was he friendly?"

George paused for breath, letting the suspense build, keeping his listeners hanging on. He made eye contact with each one in turn; this didn't take very long, he noted with disappointment. There had been a time when all the children in the village had flocked to hear his stories. After his legendary tale of the stealing of the ostrich egg, he had been treated like a hero for weeks, but now, four years later, only a handful would sit and listen and, except for the two orphans, Catherine and Tristan, these were all young children.

Setting his disappointment aside, George continued the narrative. "The masked man bent down, wiped his bloody sword clean on the grass, straightened, and then sheathed the blade, holding out his black-gloved hand in friendship. The young man shook it and thanked his mysterious saviour, who in turn thanked the youth and handed him the other sword. 'Take it as a token of my gratitude', he said, in a deep booming voice."

George glanced over at the group of young men and women who were sitting nearby, laughing and joking together. He tried to catch Sylvia's eye, hoping that she was secretly listening, but she was deep in conversation and didn't seem to be paying any attention to him at all.

"Is that the end?" asked a small boy with a shrill voice.

"No", replied George, turning back to his audience. "You may be wondering who that young man was, and how I know about his encounter with the giant and the mysterious stranger."

George paused once more; he had come to the exciting climax of his tale. Reaching under the green travelling cloak that lay in front of him, he grasped the hilt of his sword, the sword his father had given him before he'd gone away. With one swift dramatic movement, he drew it out and rose to his feet, holding the blade aloft. "Wonder no longer!" he exclaimed.

There were gasps from two or three of the younger children, but these were quickly drowned out by raucous laughter coming from the nearby group.

"You got that sword from your father!"

It was Sylvia; she had been listening after all. Looking up at her, George felt his cheeks grow warm. How did she know where he'd got the sword?

"Before he ran off and left you", she finished, nastily.

Now George remembered; he had boasted to her about the sword not long after his father had walked out.

"How tall was the giant, George?" enquired Dean, a fair-haired lad who was sitting dangerously close to Sylvia; it seemed that they'd all been listening.

"Nine feet", replied George, confidently.

"Nine feet? That's nearly as tall as your story!"

Some of the older boys began to laugh. Even some of the young boys joined in, although George was sure they wouldn't have understood.

"And who was that masked man?" asked Dean, in a voice that almost sounded sincere.

"Captain Helm", replied George, trying to sound dramatic. "Captain Helm?"

All the older boys were laughing now, and the girls joined in too.

"Who's next week's hero? Sheriff Sword? And the following week, watch out for George's continued adventures as he comes face to face with the mighty Emperor Breastplate and his trusty lieutenant, Shoulder-guard!"

The whole group was nearly crying with laughter now.

"George is the best storyteller in the village!" exclaimed Catherine, the blonde orphan girl, jumping to George's defence.

"He's the best liar!" countered Dean, sending the other lads into hysterical laughter once again.

"Stories are for children", added Sylvia, sticking her nose in the air. "If you want to run around with children like George, that's up to you; I prefer men." She put her arm around Dean, and gave Catherine a haughty look.

George turned away; the sight of Sylvia with her arm draped around Dean hurt him more than all the laughter and taunts. Getting to his feet, he picked up his sword and started walking, ignoring the fresh bursts of laughter and snide comments directed at him. He was going to show them all. After today there would be no more talk of him being a child; he was a man now and soon they would all see it.

George allowed himself a faint smile as the sounds of laughter faded in his ears. It was all set up so nicely, he might have thought up the plot himself. Today was the festival of Samhain, something lots of the villagers got excited about, especially the old druid. It was the day that the village celebrated the end of the harvest and prepared itself for the onset of winter, and it was said that on this day, which belonged neither to the old year or the new, the dead visited the living! George shivered; it was all rubbish of course, but that didn't matter. The important thing was that the village Games were held as part of the festival; not the sort of games that children play, but running, wrestling and javelin-throwing: games that were popular with men throughout the Empire. He had watched for the last three years, but now that he was of age, George could finally take part, and he felt sure that after his performance, the whole village would recognise him as a man, and a better man than most, certainly better than that idiot, Dean.

George had entered the running event, supremely confident of his chances; no one in the village did more running than he did. In fact, most of the villagers spent all their time within a mile of their homes, whereas George spent hours roaming the hills, running and climbing; he was bound to win.

It was early afternoon on this, the last day of October by Roman reckoning, and traditionally for Britons, the last day of the year. All the villagers had gathered together in the large meadow that lay to the west of the village, just beyond the animal enclosures. Normally, the sheep and cattle would have been roaming free in this area, under the watchful eye of a shepherd, but today they were kept penned up so that everyone could take part in the festivities. As usual, Caradog, the village sheriff (as he liked to be known) felt the need to give a long and boring speech. The Games had been his idea in the beginning; he loved everything to do with Roman culture and practices, and had introduced the Games to the traditional festival of Samhain, which the village had celebrated every year for as long as George could remember. George, who was sitting on the grass next to Tristan and Catherine, and well away from the rest of the village youth, had switched off after Caradog's opening line, and was in the middle of a daydream.

With a burst of speed, George surged past Dean and strained towards the finish line. The exhausted Dean stumbled and, unfortunately, fell headlong into something a relieved cow had left by the side of the track earlier that day.

"And now, let the Games begin!"

George opened his eyes; Caradog's long-winded introduction had come to an end. It was the moment he had been waiting for, his big chance to prove himself in front of the whole village.

Now that the Games were actually beginning, George realised that he wasn't quite as confident as he had been in the days leading up to it. He began to feel an uncomfortable sensation in his stomach. Trying to ignore it, he walked over to where the javelin contest was about to take place.

George had never thrown a javelin in his life, but this did not stop him from commenting on various aspects of the throwers' technique that, in his opinion, could be improved. Tristan listened attentively to this commentary whilst clapping and cheering whenever a well-thrown javelin thudded into the ground. Catherine stood with them, watching with polite interest. *But then she is a girl,* thought George, *and they seem to have a limited understanding of such contests.* He hoped that she would show a bit more concern when it came to his event. Scanning the crowd, he caught a glimpse of Sylvia; she seemed to be enjoying the spectacle, and was laughing and clapping quite enthusiastically. The queasy feeling in his stomach returned.

Too soon, the javelin-throwing competition was over; it was time for the running event. This was it; George stood nervously behind the line scraped out in the mud, and stared at the large oak tree at the far side of the meadow. He had to pass it on the right, turn, pass it on the left and get back to the start, crossing the line before anyone else. He glanced around at the other competitors, suddenly conscious of his youth (he was the youngest of about twenty runners) and the distance to the oak: it seemed a lot further now than it had yesterday.

George looked towards the tall thin figure of Caradog, who was standing to one side of the course, a little way ahead of them. The mousy-haired sheriff was holding a piece of bright red cloth in his hand, which contrasted violently with his flowing white robes. Out of the corner of his eye, George spotted Dean, a serious look on his face for once. Gritting his teeth, George turned his attention back to Caradog; whatever happened he was going to beat Dean.

Caradog held one arm aloft. Everyone was quiet now, and George could hear his heart hammering away in his chest, as he crouched, waiting to explode into action as soon as the cloth was released. George held his breath; time seemed to stand still, and then, with a flutter of red and a sudden burst of noise, they were off.

George was jostled in the mad scramble to get to the front. Stumbling slightly, he soon found himself towards the rear of the group. A feeling of panic started to arise from within. *Just keep up a good pace,* he told himself, *and you'll be all right.* Getting into a steady rhythm, George lengthened his stride and, breathing easily, he soon passed a struggling competitor on the outside.

A gentle breeze ruffled George's hair as his feet sprang lightly over the short grass. Overtaking two more runners with ease, his confidence soared. He could do this; he was moving up towards the leaders and he still had plenty left for a sprint finish.

The ground started to dip slightly as the oak tree loomed large, and George began to bear right. To his left, the front-runners had just rounded the gnarled trunk and were headed back towards the finish. Suddenly, his self-belief began to falter; maybe he had left it too late to catch up! Accelerating, George rounded a small group of runners as he passed the oak, and cut across sharply, stretching out after the leaders. Then, without warning, something gave in his left leg and it buckled beneath him, sending him sprawling. Desperately, George tried to get to his feet but, as he did so, he felt a stab of pain and collapsed once more, holding the inside of his leg, tears of frustration running down his cheeks. It was over; everything that mattered to him was gone!

George sat alone, his back against a tree, inconsolable. Catherine and Tristan, having tried, and failed, to cheer him up, had gone off to collect wood for the bonfire. His mother, along with the other women in the village, would be preparing the food for the feast, while the men would be busy carrying out tables from the great hall, and setting up the log benches that everyone would be sitting on. Everybody seemed to have some role to play, except him.

Wisps of smoke drifted above the trees that sheltered George from the rest of the village; they must have lit the bonfire. He had been sitting here, moping, longer than he had thought. George wrinkled up his nose in disgust as the aroma of burnt goat invaded his nostrils. The sacrificing and burning of a goat was an intimate part of the festival of Samhain; he supposed it was done to ward off the dead. George held his nose; if the dead still had any sense of smell, they certainly wouldn't be hanging around here! He wondered what it would be like to be dead. If you really only got one day each year to visit the living, and then some druid wafted burnt goat at you, it didn't seem to be much of a life... err... death.

An owl hooted from somewhere high above, and George jumped. It was not good to think of such things when you were sitting all alone on the edge of a dark wood. He had not realised just how dark it had become; the sun had long since disappeared below the horizon and even its faint pink tinge had now gone from the sky. George wrapped his cloak around him; it had become cold too. Should he go to the feast or just head back home? If he went home he would not have to spend time around anyone, but on the other hand he hadn't eaten since noon and there was going to be loads of delicious food at the feast.

As he pondered this choice, George became aware of faint noises, like whispering voices, coming towards him. A shiver ran the length of his spine, and he scrambled to his feet. What was making that noise? All the villagers would be at the feast, and there were no other living souls for miles. *What about souls that aren't living?* A cold sweat broke out on his brow. The owl hooted again, and George whirled around.

"There you are, George!"

George nearly jumped out of his skin before he realised it was only Tristan.

"Don't do that!" he shouted; his heart was beating like a drum. "It's the night when the dead walk the earth, and you're sneaking about like some kind of… of…" Words failed him.

"The dead don't walk the earth; they are judged, and then they either go to eternal happiness or eternal torment."

George jumped again. This voice belonged to Catherine, whom he had not noticed in the near darkness.

"Sorry, George", said Tristan, looking crestfallen. "We just wanted to know if you were coming to the feast."

As if on cue, a low rumbling sound suddenly emanated from George's stomach.

"We'll take that as a 'yes' shall we?" said Catherine, chuckling. Tristan laughed too and even George joined in briefly. For a moment the gloom lifted, but then the events of the day rushed back into his mind and his laughter died.

"I suppose so", George muttered, his voice heavy with resignation.

The feast was magnificent. There were nine large wooden tables, spread with sides of pork, joints of beef, several roast pheasants, mountains of freshly baked bread, a great variety of cheeses, fruit pies, scones, biscuits and an assortment of huge cream cakes. The tables were arranged in a horseshoe shape around the central bonfire, which crackled and blazed, giving out much needed heat on this cold, clear night. George was seated on a log, next to the two orphans, at one end of the horseshoe (the place where all the sparks were landing, he observed), but neither Catherine nor Tristan complained, and since it was his fault that they had been the last to arrive at the feast, he didn't mention it either.

Just visible on the far side of the fire, was the high table, where the champions of the Games sat in places of honour: Cunobelinos, the village blacksmith, and father of Sylvia, a huge bear-like man with black hair and a neatly trimmed moustache, who had, as usual, triumphed in both the wrestling and javelin; and next to him, the winner of the running event: a smug looking, Dean.

George turned away, bitter regrets flooding into his head. *Of all the people to win, why did it have to be Dean?* Grabbing a crusty loaf, he ripped a large piece off and began to get to work on the feast, trying to take his mind off the day's events. Despite his intense focus on eating though, George couldn't help noticing that, somewhere over to his left, the word 'helm' was coming up in conversation more than it had any right to.

When most people had had their fill of food (George was still going strong), those villagers who had brought musical instruments produced them, and the sound of music filled the air. A drum boomed out a steady beat, and the cheerful chirping of flutes and gentle strumming of lyres supplied the melody, with occasional harmonies thrown in. After listening for a while, people started getting up and moving around the tables towards the fire.

"Let us dance around the fire and ward off the spirits of the dead", shouted the druid in his croaky voice and, with a vigour that belied his considerable age, he led the jig, chanting strange words as he leapt and twirled around the flames, his bushy white beard bobbing up and down in a most comical manner.

Most of the villagers had joined this ritual procession. Aside from George and the two orphans, only the elderly, the very young, and those caring for them, remained seated. George had participated in this activity in previous years, but after the day's disasters, he didn't feel like dancing. As for the orphans, George knew that they never took part in any of the village's religious traditions. Unlike the majority of village inhabitants, they had not lived all their lives here, but had been brought to the village after their parents had both died suddenly of plague. They worshipped a different god: one named Janus, or something like that.

After a short while, the druid collapsed back onto his log, panting and wheezing most alarmingly, and the dancing became more civilised. The chanting had ceased now and the participants were now merely engaged in enjoying themselves rather than frightening away the dead.

Catherine got to her feet. "Would you like to dance?" she asked George shyly.

"No", he answered abruptly.

Catherine opened her mouth to reply, but then apparently thought better of it. "What about you, Tristan?"

George watched as Catherine and Tristan made their way into the circle of dancers, between the tables and the fire. He looked on as they took one another's hands and jigged about, laughing together. *They shouldn't be enjoying themselves*, George thought to himself, not while he was miserable. He watched as they disappeared behind the leaping flames, troubled by a slight feeling of regret. He shouldn't have been so harsh with Catherine; maybe he should even have said 'yes'; at least then he wouldn't be sitting alone staring at other people having fun. George wondered briefly if that was what it felt like to the dead: always having to look on from the shadows whilst those in the land of the living enjoyed themselves.

Once again forcing his mind away from this disturbing subject, George reached for another slice of cream cake. His hand was halfway to his mouth when somewhere in the distance there was a harsh cry, as if from some huge bird. The cake remained a few inches from his mouth. There it was again; it didn't sound quite like a bird. It had a deeper quality to it and seemed to linger in the night air; it made George shiver. Next moment there was a horrible bloodcurdling howl; the cake dropped from his hand. George froze; two more howls followed in quick succession. Startled, he looked around. Where were the sounds coming from? He would expect such noises to be coming from the woods; wolves had been known to visit them at night. But George was almost sure that the noises had been coming from somewhere behind him, across the meadow.

Everything was quiet now. It took a moment for George to register that the music had stopped; it was as if the whole village was holding its breath, waiting to see what would happen.

There was another, louder howl. It sounded much closer than the others had been. George jumped to his feet and whirled round, straining his eyes as he stared into the inky blackness. It suddenly occurred to him that he was on his own; most of the villagers were standing by the bonfire. He could hear the pattering of footsteps now as something scampered towards him. George turned to run but found his way blocked by one of the feast tables. From somewhere not far behind him, a snarl filled the air, causing his heart to skip a beat.

Letting out a frightened yelp, he launched himself over the table. Even as he did so, George felt a stab of pain travel up his left leg and, instead of clearing the table, he found himself crashing down on top of it, before rolling off, scattering food and plates. George landed on his back, with a bone-jarring thud, on the opposite side, and instinctively clutched his injured leg. Next moment, a dark shaggy creature bounded onto the table and flew over his head, landing inside the fire-lit circle. As it sped away, cries and shrieks broke the silence, sounds of panic. What was going on? Wolves might take a sheep every now and then, but they never ventured near humans if they could help it!

George lay still, not daring even to breathe. Another wolf entered the circle and hared across the open ground, scattering villagers left and right. George could hear the sounds of more scampering feet, mixed with an occasional snarl coming from beyond the tables, but it seemed that most of the wolves were steering clear of the fire. They seemed to be making for the woods on the far side.

Without warning, a great snarling beast landed heavily on the table just above George. He stared up at its evil red eyes, reflecting the fire's light. The wolf seemed to pause, its long snout twitching left and right, and then its gaze alighted on the terrified figure cowering below it. George lay on the ground, paralysed by fear. A voice screamed in his head, pleading with him to get up, to run, but his legs wouldn't obey. Time seemed to stand still as those fearful red orbs bored into his skull. Looking up into those eyes George saw no hope, only death! The wolf bared its teeth and prepared to leap.

As George looked into the animal's snarling jaws, the wolf's shaggy coat burst into flames! He stared in disbelief as the horrible apparition was licked by tongues of fire, like some demonic beast from the depths of the underworld! George opened his mouth to scream, but no sound came out. Then, with a hideous shrieking howl, the monster leapt. A wall of heat passed over George as, reflexively, he covered his head with his hands, expecting to feel teeth and claws rending his flesh. When he did not, he cautiously opened an eye. The demonic creature was gone. In its place stood Tristan, holding a burning branch, plucked from the fire.

It took several moments for George to work out what had happened. Finally it sank in: Tristan had just saved his life! Shaking, George rose unsteadily to his feet, acutely aware of the sword, dangling at his side. What was he doing? He had had the chance to be a hero, to fight the wolves, and what had he done? He had cowered like a frightened child while the little orphan had saved the day! George turned, hoping that no one had seen his cowardice. Maybe he could make amends; perhaps a wolf was still inside the circle and he could chase it off.

"George!" shrieked his mother, from somewhere close by, "Are you all right?"

Moments later, she arrived at his side, an excitedly chattering bunch of villagers at her heels.

"I'm okay", grunted George, trying to fend her off.

"I saw the whole thing!" yelled someone in the crowd. "The orphan boy saved his life!"

George groaned inwardly.

"Well done, Tristan!" bellowed Cunobelinos in his rich, deep voice. "You're a hero, boy!"

There were various murmurs of agreement. A small voice somewhere inside George's head was whispering, *'Thank you Tristan'*, but the words wouldn't make their way to his lips. George felt sick; he wished he were on his own; he wished the wolf had eaten him!

"Hey, George!" Sylvia's voice cut through George's thoughts; he looked up. "Since he's a hero, why don't you give that sword to Tristan?"

"Yeah", agreed Dean. "Then it wouldn't trip you up the next time you're running away!"

There was scattered laughter from the other young people in the group and then, finally, the crowd began to disperse.

George just stood there, looking down at his feet. What a day! He had been beaten at running, humiliated, upstaged by little Tristan, and the whole village thought he was a coward; it couldn't get any worse than this!

As the other villagers moved away, George's mum started to fuss over him again, tugging at his cloak, checking for signs of injury: tears in the cloth or blood on his clothes.

"George, you're all sticky!" she exclaimed, her voice unnecessarily loud. "You've got cake all over your bottom!"

Chapter 4 – Bear Hunt

George lay on his back, head resting on a bundled up cloak, and stared up at the night sky. He never tired of staring up at the stars, of trying to see patterns in the arrangements of the countless twinkling lights. Yawning sleepily, George mused that perhaps 'never tired' wasn't quite right. The warm fire was making gentle crackling noises and his eyelids were growing heavy. *I'll just close my eyes for a moment.* The stars would still be there when he opened them again.

He had just got nicely comfortable when he was disturbed by the sound of feet approaching: Tristan had returned from checking the far enclosures. George ignored him, hoping the orphan boy would take the hint and let him rest. Tristan took this whole 'night-watch' thing far too seriously. Yes, they were supposed to be looking after the village animals whilst the rest of the villagers slept, but there was no need to get up and check them all the time. It was not as though Taranis was paying them well for their labours. A few eggs, some goats' milk, and the odd fleece at shearing time were hardly generous. For that, he was lucky they bothered to stay awake at all!

At least the nights were short during the summer; it would be the solstice tomorrow. George wondered what the village was going to do about solstice this year. The druid, who had led the village in all such religious festivals in the past, had mysteriously disappeared last winter and no one had seen anything of him since!

"George", whispered Tristan, disturbing him once more.
George opened one eye and glared at his fellow watchman.
"Did you hear that?"
"What?"
"That noise, sort of a creaking sound?"
"No, it's probably the wind."
"Maybe it's a wolf?"
George sighed heavily. "Wolves don't creak, they howl. Besides, no one's seen a wolf in these parts since..." He had been going to say *since those wolves attacked us during Samhain*, but he didn't want to think about it. That had happened almost two years ago and he still had nightmares! George closed his eye, indicating that the conversation was over.

CRACK! George sat bolt upright, all thoughts of sleep gone. A cacophony of bleating and yammering assaulted their ears; something had spooked the animals! Tristan grabbed a branch from the fire and, holding this torch aloft, headed over to the nearest enclosure. Reluctantly, George got to his feet and followed, his right hand shaking involuntarily as it grasped the hilt of his sword.

Tristan fumbled with the rope that secured the gate to the pen. From within, the noise of pitiful bleating was mixed with a ripping sound: the snapping of wood, George realised.

"Hold this", Tristan insisted, sounding scared.

Passing George the torch, he tugged at the rope with both hands, finally managing to release the gate. There was a frantic stampede as a number of animals charged towards them, sensing a way out, and the little orphan was almost knocked to the ground as he fought to enter! George followed, pushing the terrified sheep backwards, and struggled to shut the gate before any could escape. His heart was beating like a drum now. What was going on?

Tristan tied the gate securely behind them whilst George drew his sword from its sheath. He didn't like this one bit; by preventing the sheep from escaping they were trapping themselves with whatever had made those terrible ripping noises. Reclaiming his torch, Tristan advanced boldly into the centre of the enclosure. George followed, frantically searching the darkness for a sign of their enemy. The bleating and yammering of the sheep had been joined by lowing from the next pen; a loud crowing erupted from somewhere behind them. George spun round, nearly decapitating his friend in the process; the village rooster had decided to join in! The resulting racket was deafening; no one in the village could be sleeping through this!

Suddenly, all the sheep in the enclosure changed direction, charging wildly to the right; the two lads were bumped and buffeted as the white, woolly, tide surged across them. Above the thunderous din of many hooves on the hard turf, the boys could just about discern a different sound, a horrible crunching noise. George whirled round again, sword held out in front of him, desperately trying to pinpoint the source of this new and terrifying sound. There was something in here with them, something dangerous!

Tristan cautiously made his way across the grass, George following, staying within the circle of light, his feeling of unease growing with every step. As his companion waved the flaming branch from side to side, casting light into the dim corners of the enclosure, George's right hand shakily gripped his sword hilt, all his senses on heightened alert.

Tristan gasped, George stiffened. For a moment he couldn't work out what was wrong, and then he saw the gap. The fence was constructed of wooden stakes, about seven feet high, and woven between these were roughly hewn branches intertwining to form a solid mesh that kept the animals in and supposedly kept predators out. By the light of Tristan's torch, they could both see that one of the poles had been torn out, leaving an empty void several feet wide! Tristan held his torch nearer to the breach and pulled a strand of wool off one of the branches. George swore loudly; they were going to get a roasting for this!

"Wolves are eating my livestock and you're just sitting there and watching it happen!" yelled the enraged farmer, his face going an alarming shade of red.

"It wasn't wolves", interrupted George, trying to defend himself. "A wolf couldn't have made a hole that size in the fence!"

"Well something ate my sheep!" exploded Taranis, "And that's three in the last month!"

"Not all of them on our watch", replied George.

"No, but you're winning! And it's not just the sheep; I've had complaints from the other watches. You've consistently turned up late; they've found you sleeping after the early watch; I've found you sleeping after the late watch!"

George opened his mouth to say that Taranis had only ever found one of them sleeping, but since that one had always been him, he decided that it would be wiser not to comment. Instead, he tried a different tack: "Maybe a bear has been taking your sheep."

"There aren't any bears in these parts", snorted the farmer.

"Maybe it was a human thief", suggested Tristan, choosing to enter the conversation at last.

"I don't care if my own mother stole the sheep!" roared Taranis, his patience exhausted. "It's your job to stay awake and protect them, and you've failed once too often!" He glared at the two boys; George knew what was coming next. "So don't bother to turn up tomorrow night; you don't work for me any more."

There was a stunned silence, broken, to George's surprise by Tristan. "I n...need this job sir!" he stammered, his voice squeaky with desperation.

"I'm sorry", replied their former employer, his voice gentler but resigned. "This conversation is over."

George and Tristan made their way through the village in silence, both deep in thought. Initially, George had not been too worried at losing his job; at least he wouldn't have to get up in the middle of the night any more. But now that he thought about it, guarding the animal pens had been pretty easy, requiring very little effort from him. What if he now had to do something that meant working all day? When would he go off adventuring? And what if he had to get a proper trade, something that required intense concentration and no daydreaming? George shuddered; he needed his old job back.

As they passed the great hall, the large building constructed of heavy wooden beams that stood in the centre of the village, the two lads parted company. Tristan mumbled "Goodnight", in a very subdued voice, and George grunted in reply. The sun was shining brightly now and most villagers were up and about, busying themselves with various chores before the day's work began in earnest.

George made his way back to his home, completely oblivious of the activities going on around him. A plan was forming in his mind: a scheme so brilliant that when successfully completed it would not only get him and Tristan their jobs back, but would make him the hero of the village!

Pulling back the wooden board that served as a door, George entered his hut. His mother was already hard at work with needle and thread; a big pile of rather tattered looking clothing lay before her. A good proportion of the village came to her when their garments needed mending. She would be busy sewing up tears and patching up holes for the rest of the day. It was hard work; George certainly didn't want to do that for a living!

Looking up from her labours, his mother smiled at her son and asked him how the night watch had been. A pang of guilt welled up within George; the thread she was using had come from the fleeces he had brought home during the last sheep shearing. Now there would be no more wool from that quarter.

"Okay", he replied, his voice shaking slightly. Then, putting on a yawn, George kicked off his boots, undid his sword-belt, threw himself down on his mattress, and pulled the blanket over his head. It would only make his mother anxious if he told her he'd lost his job, and anyway, if his idea worked he would have it back by tomorrow night, so there was really no point in him mentioning it. Convinced of this reasoning, George lay awake for a while, putting the finishing touches to his plan, before slipping into unconsciousness.

George awoke to the delicious smell of stew, drifting in through the open door. It was a fine, warm day, so his mother had lit a fire outside, rather than in the middle of the hut, where only a small hole in the roof could let out the smoke. Yawning loudly and rubbing the sleep from his eyes, George pushed his blanket aside and pulled his boots on. Getting to his feet, he made his way out of the hut, to where his mother was stirring the pot that hung suspended over the small fire that she had made. Seeing George, she greeted him warmly and handed him his wooden bowl, into which she ladled a generous portion of stew. It tasted as delicious as it smelled and there was enough for a second bowlful.

His mother chattered away while George, nodding and grunting in the appropriate places, savoured the thick chunks of tender chicken and the generous quantities of carrots and beans. Many of the other villagers were also sitting outside their huts, cooking or eating food, and conversing lazily. The sweet sound of birdsong filled the air and the pleasant summer sun gently warmed his back. Just at this moment, life seemed idyllic. Then, before he could stop them, the events of this morning flooded back into his mind, and George felt that pang of guilt again. Why was it that every time he felt happy there was always something waiting to spoil the day?

Patting his belly in appreciation, George handed his bowl and spoon (both licked clean) to his mother.

"Just off to see Tristan", he said.

She smiled at him; George couldn't help thinking that she wouldn't be in such a good mood if she knew what had happened that morning. *But that won't matter soon*, he told himself. It was time to put his plan into action.

George walked past several huts, all of which had villagers sitting outside them, but no one greeted him or acknowledged him in any way. George didn't care though; he was on a quest. At the eastern edge of the village, he came to a slightly crooked hut, with an untidily thatched roof. Tristan sat outside it, busily scrubbing out pots with a cloth.

"Come on", said George without preamble, "Adventure beckons!"

Tristan started to say something about chores, but George silenced him.

"Never mind that. Do you want your job back or not?"

The young orphan boy stared at George, wide-eyed and open-mouthed; he clearly very much wanted his job back.

"Come on then", repeated George, and started walking.

He smiled to himself as he heard the jangling sound of pots being quickly stowed. *The legendary George strode onwards, his loyal servant in tow. His quest: to track down and slay the ferocious bear that had taken the sheep and, by so doing, to rescue his friend from poverty, reinstate his own honour, and thus set all to rights.*

George led the way past the orphans' hut and into the wood that lay beyond; he did not wish anyone to see what they were up to just yet. After skirting the north of the village, the two lads emerged from the trees and crossed the meadow, passing a herd of grazing sheep, and arrived at the far side of the enclosures without encountering another soul. Locating the gap in the fence was a simple task; someone had hammered the stake back into the ground, but the branches that were supposed to be woven around it were still a mess.

George bent down and surveyed the ground. Tristan, who had only now caught up, asked the obvious question: "What are we doing?"

"Searching for bear tracks", replied George, enigmatically, and knelt down to examine a muddy patch, close to the breach. Satisfied that he had found what he was looking for, George backed away from the fence, still staring intently at the ground.

"Have you ever seen a bear's tracks?" enquired Tristan, hesitantly.

George grunted dismissively; the question wasn't worth the bother of answering. His father had told him tales of huge black bears that roamed the countryside in the wilder lands to the north. Such a large creature would be simple to track, and besides, to tell Tristan that he had very little idea what a bear looked like, never mind what tracks it made, would hardly inspire his young friend. *A hero must always be confident; he must never show uncertainty even for a moment.*

"There", said George, pointing at the muddy stretch of turf. "See that? The bear obviously crossed the meadow in…" He paused, straightened and pointed to the southwest, "…that direction."

Tristan regarded him with an expression of awe. He scanned the ground trying to glimpse the clues that had led his knowledgeable friend to this conclusion.

"That looks like blood!" he exclaimed, spotting a darker shade amongst the green.

George looked over at the patch of grass that his companion was indicating.

"And here's some more!" Tristan's excited voice caused a nearby sheep to bleat loudly and scamper away. "There's some marks over here!" he continued, striding away from the bemused George.

George slowly wandered over, putting on an appearance of disinterest. As he cast a sceptical eye over the marks, though, he realised that Tristan had indeed found a footprint, or paw-print. The print consisted of three or four (it was difficult to make out) furrows in the turf, fanning out at slight angles to one another. Dropping his disinterested air, George rushed ahead, spotting another fairly distinct print.

"I knew it!" he exclaimed. "This way", he shouted to Tristan, pointing in the direction of some low-lying hills to the northwest.

His young companion seemed about to open his mouth, but then closed it again, and George could have sworn the innocent orphan boy gave him a wry smile before following him across the meadow.

The two hunters reached the far side of the open ground and entered the thin band of trees that bordered it. George hoped they were still on the right trail, but neither of them had seen any further evidence of the bear's passing. Thorny bushes snagged at their tunics and breeches as they made their way through the wooded area, but there was no sign of wool. *Surely, if the bear had dragged the sheep through here, there would be white threads everywhere!*

Hope was flagging by the time George pushed through the tangle of branches and emerged into bright sunlight. Ahead of him, gently rolling hills, with occasional craggy rock formations, rose up to the blue sky. Puffy white clouds drifted lazily across the wide blue expanse. On another day, he would have found a soft piece of ground and lain down in the warm sun, drinking in the glorious views, but today this peace and tranquillity only frustrated him.

Lengthening his stride, George forged ahead up the first of many hills. He had no idea where he was going, only a vague notion that the more ground he covered, the more likely he was to come across some clue to the bear's whereabouts. He didn't really have much hope though; the trail had gone cold. Tristan followed obediently, panting in the hot sun, as they clambered over rocks, slithered into gullies and meandered across the trackless hills in no particular direction.

Fording a shallow brook, some while later, George finally saw something of interest; there were muddy prints leading up the bank on the far side. He splashed his way across and stepped onto dry ground, bending down to investigate closer. The prints weren't as distinctive as the ones in the meadow, but something large had definitely passed this way. George turned his head and shouted to Tristan, who was lagging some way behind, and then he hurried up the bank, eager for further evidence of their quarry.

The trail led along the far side of the brook and then abruptly disappeared. Dismayed, George stopped, scanning his surroundings for any clue as to which direction the bear might have taken. A close investigation of the bushes to his right, revealed what he was looking for: a number of torn and trampled leaves. He was getting good at this.

"George", called Tristan weakly, breathing heavily as he struggled to catch up. "We've been this way before!"

George looked back at the brook; it did look vaguely familiar now that he thought about it. He wondered why they hadn't noticed this trail before. Then it dawned on him; he had been tracking his own footsteps!

George kicked at one of the thick bushes in frustration, but this only served to injure his foot and cause him to yell out in pain. What a waste of an afternoon! He was going to have to tell his mother about the loss of his job after all. Dejectedly, George turned back the way he had come.

"It's no good", he complained, as he rejoined Tristan. "We'll never find the beast now; the trail's gone cold."

Tristan didn't argue; it was plain from his expression that he had reached this same conclusion some time ago. The two disappointed trackers splashed back across the brook and trudged off in the direction of the village. Neither of them spoke as they walked; Tristan was too tired and George was too angry and frustrated. It was too hot, there was no breeze at all, and the flies that continually swarmed around his head did nothing to improve his mood.

After walking for a couple of miles, they reached the edge of the woods that lay between them and the village fields. As they passed beneath the boughs of a particularly large oak, Tristan finally broke the silence.

"What's that?"

"What?"

"There's something shiny over there!"

George followed his companion's finger and caught the glint of metal in the sunlight. Tristan was already moving towards the object. He bent down to examine it, and suddenly let out a strangled cry. George rushed to his side, heart beating wildly; what had his friend seen?

The object had a short curved blade with what looked like a gold handle. It took a moment for him to register what it was.

"The druid's sickle!" George exclaimed.

Tristan didn't reply; he wasn't looking at the sickle. He was looking at…

"By Belenos!" George swore by one of the many 'gods' of his people. "Those are human bones!"

Chapter 5 – Into the Darkness

At the base of the oak tree, half covered with leaves and twigs, lay a tangled mound of ripped cloth and several weathered bones, many of them broken or gnawed. They had found the missing druid, or what was left of him; something had picked his bones completely clean of meat!

George turned his face away; he had never seen anything like this before. Feeling a little queasy, he stared back out of the woods. Through the trees he could just make out the mouth of a cave, a dark opening in the rock, at the foot of the nearest hill.

"Mistletoe!"

George whirled round, staring at Tristan uncomprehendingly.

"He was looking for mistletoe."

George followed the orphan's gaze, noticing patches of the green shrub twined around several of the oak's branches. The white berries were no longer in evidence, but there was no mistaking it. Held in highest honour by all druids, the mistletoe that grew on oak trees was rare and valuable, and was traditionally harvested in wintertime with a golden sickle. Their druid had gone out searching for mistletoe and never returned, and now they knew why: he had found the sacred plant and the bear had found him; it was a man-eater!

George walked slowly back into the bright sunlight. Almost without realising what he was doing, he made his way towards the cave entrance. He wasn't sure what he expected to find there, but something about that dark opening in the rock made him feel uneasy. As he drew nearer, he felt a tingling sensation at the back of his neck; not five feet from the dark entrance lay a sheep's skull.

George stared into the yawning mouth, feeling cold even though the afternoon sun beat upon his back. His right hand moved to the sword at his side; this was it. The bear was inside, he was sure of it; the cave made a perfect den for the man-eating beast.

In his mind, George had already drawn his sword and was walking boldly into the inky blackness, but his body wasn't having any of it! He stood stock still, his limbs shaking slightly, his mouth open, beads of sweat breaking out on his brow. *Go on, you coward! No, it's suicide; the bear would kill me before I could even see it! So light a fire and get a torch. I can't face a bear on my own; it'll rip me to pieces! Then take Tristan with you. What use would that be? He's not even armed! If you back out of this now, you'll always be a coward!*

"Hey, George!"

Tristan's shout echoed back at him from the walls of the cave. George's heart was in his mouth; what if that noise had woken the bear? He staggered backwards, away from the forbidding entrance, then whirled round, silencing his foolish companion with a furious glare.

Relieved to be away from the cave mouth, George backed away still further until he was level with the fair-haired orphan. For a while, he didn't speak, thinking furiously, trying desperately to reconcile the two voices in his mind. Then he had it: they would return to the village and fetch his tinderbox to light the fire, and he would find a sword for Tristan. George had a pretty good idea where he could get one; he'd have to borrow it without permission, but it was in a good cause. The trick would be in concealing this 'borrowing' from Tristan. George knew that both orphans had strict ideas about honesty; if Tristan found out the sword was stolen he would probably refuse to use it, and that would ruin the plan.

"The bear's in there", said George, pointing towards the dark opening and then turning to face his young companion, whose eyes widened with shock and maybe a trace of fear. "We're going to need fire". Tristan opened his mouth to say something but George cut him off. "…and a sword for you."

The little orphan's eyes were almost bulging out of his head now. "Where am I going to get a sword from?"

"I have a second sword at home", George lied.

"You have two swords?"

The look on Tristan's face was so comical that George almost laughed. "One given to me by my father before he left, and the one from Captain Helm."

George broke into a violent coughing fit, hoping to distract his friend and somehow hide this blatant fabrication; the Captain Helm story was starting to sound silly even to him now.

The frown on the fair-haired lad's face told him that Tristan was far from convinced, but George wasn't about to give him time to voice his doubts. Before the confused boy could object, George launched into his plan, words rushing out of his mouth so fast that he left no opportunity for question or comment.

"We're going to have to be quick: we need to get back to the village, eat; get our gear; hurry back here; light a fire; go in there; kill the bear, and get home before sunset with the beast's head, as proof of our mighty deeds."

With that, George turned on his heel and strode back into the woods, a faint smile on his lips: he'd got away with that one.

As George passed the oak tree, a thought struck him; he bent down and picked up the golden sickle. When he marched into the great hall, triumphantly carrying the bear's head, this valuable token would leave nobody in any doubt as to what his trophy signified: that the druid's death had been avenged.

For the second time that day, George finished his bowl of soup, handed it to his mother, and headed towards the orphans' hut. This time, however, he carried his tinderbox with him, and he had a job to do before he called for Tristan.

Reaching the great hall, George casually wandered up to the large wooden door. The sound of voices and laughter within drifted out into the mild evening air. Being of age, George was entitled to enter the hall and join the nightly gathering of men, but that wasn't why he was here. He had tried it once and hadn't enjoyed it; just a lot of fat men swilling beer and talking about subjects that were of no interest to him. He had tried a mug of beer, but had been surprised to find that, though just about all the men in the village raved about it as though it were the nectar of the gods, it actually tasted foul.

George glanced from side to side to check that no one was watching and then, brushing his loathing for the place aside, silently pushed on the door. Opening it a fraction, George strained his ears, checking for any lowering of the noise level. Cautiously, he opened the door a little more, hoping that his presence would continue to go unnoticed. Heart in his mouth, George finally poked his head inside and saw what he had come for: behind the door, in a little porch area, separate from the main room, lay a small pile of weapons. (It was the village rule that all weapons be left at the door of the main hall. This was in case a fight broke out amongst the beer drinkers: a common occurrence. The drunken brawl would then result in nothing more than sore heads and broken noses, rather than widespread killing and maiming.) The pile included three knives, a couple of staffs, an axe and one shortsword. George leaned around the door and grasped the hilt of the sword.

"OI!"

Startled, George grabbed the sword and ran, cursing his luck. Glancing over his shoulder, he caught sight of his pursuer rounding the hut he'd just passed; dressed in flowing purple robes it could be only one man: Caradog.

George's heart sank: he was in big trouble now! Gasping for breath, he rounded the last hut and sprinted, head down, for the woods. Caradog had nearly caught him; the sound of his breathing filled George's ears. The combined weight of the two swords he was now carrying was slowing him too much; he wasn't going to make it. A hand grasped his sword-belt and George swerved, desperately trying to avoid capture. As he did so, his feet went from under him and he fell, landing with a thud on the hard dry ground.

Caradog stood over him, a triumphant look on his red face. "You're going to regret this, thief", he said, between short gasps for breath. "Did you really think that you could…?" He broke off suddenly, seeing something in the grass. Bending down, he picked it up.

"The druid's golden sickle!" The village leader stood there, holding the treasure, a look of shock and incomprehension on his face. He turned back to George, a fierce glint in his blue eyes. "Where did you get this?"

Anger bubbled inside George; this arrogant, pompous fool was ruining everything. His one chance to be the village hero had gone; he would have to hand over the stolen sword, would probably have his own sword confiscated, and would be forced to tell Caradog about the bear. Then, no doubt, a group of older men would be sent to kill the bear, and George's achievement in solving the mystery and finding the cave would be forgotten. Feelings of frustration and bitterness consumed him, and without realising quite what he was doing, George swung the shortsword at the older man.

Caradog leapt back with an oath. George got to his feet and swung the weapon again; he was not aiming to hit the sheriff, just to scare him away. He had played this game often with Tristan, swinging his sword over the orphan's head, cutting it down a few inches to his left, then stabbing to his right. Caradog staggered backwards, fear in his eyes, as the sword whipped past his ear.

"I'll see you rot in jail for this!" he screamed, quivering with anger. Then as the sword swished through the air, missing his head by inches, the sheriff turned to run. George watched with amusement as he sprinted away, purple robes billowing out behind him.

As the fleeing figure disappeared between two huts on the outskirts of the village, George's amused smile faded. What had he done? Would the sheriff really bring this matter before the government? George didn't know much about the Roman justice system, but he knew that Caradog had connections with the Cambodunum town council. He was the one who organised the annual collection of taxes for them. This didn't do much for his popularity amongst village folk, but it had established him as a leader and, since the druid had vanished, he was the only leader the village had. George had never really considered why people should put up with this arrogant, bossy, Roman boot-licker. Now he realised that it was because people feared him, or rather they feared his powerful friends. Could he really go to jail? Jail: the place that the Roman authorities put undesirables when they wanted to forget about them. Most that went in never came out, or so he had been told.

It suddenly dawned on George that, whilst deep in thought, he had been standing still. Caradog would be back at the great hall by now. Any moment, he would be leading a group of well-armed men to this very spot! Forcing his legs into action, George sprinted for the cover of the woods.

As he ran, George's anxious thoughts turned back to his plan. If he could return to the village with the bear's head, surely everything would be all right. A lot of the villagers owned livestock and they would be grateful that the sheep-stealer was out of the way. Also, many people had been devastated by the disappearance of the druid, and although his followers would be unhappy knowing that he was dead, they would doubtless be glad that his murder had been avenged. With these two sizeable groups hailing George as a hero, the sheriff would be forced to let him off, especially because he had only borrowed his sword to safeguard a fellow villager.

Convinced by his own arguments, George picked his way through the tangle of branches and thorny bushes, emerging from the woods within sight of the orphans' hut. A few moments later he caught sight of Tristan, waiting expectantly for him at the door of his home.

Seeing his friend, the fair-haired lad called out a greeting. Alarmed, George quickly gestured for quiet, and worriedly glanced around at the neighbouring huts to see if anyone was watching them. Apart from a group of children playing 'hide and seek' nearby, there was no one in sight.

Just then, Catherine emerged from the hut, a garment in one hand and a sewing needle in the other. "What are you two up to?" she enquired, a suspicious look in her grey-green eyes.

Knowing the orphan boy's annoying tendency to tell the truth in all situations, and feeling that Tristan's big sister wouldn't approve of the potentially lethal task he was being encouraged to embark upon, George quickly spoke up:

"We're off adventuring."

"Adventuring doesn't put food on the table, you know?" replied Catherine, a disapproving tone in her voice.

"We'll see", countered George, with more confidence than he felt.

"Make sure you two adventurers are back by sunset", she added.

"Yes mother", replied the two lads in unison.

Catherine laughed and disappeared back into the hut. George couldn't help smiling despite his predicament; there was something about Catherine that made him feel good, that gave him confidence. They were going to succeed; everything was going to work out. Motioning to Tristan to follow him, George made his way back into the woods.

For a while, the only sounds to be heard were the rustle of bushes, the snapping of twigs underfoot, and the occasional chirrup of a bird, as the two adventurers trekked quietly through the wood. Eventually Tristan broke the silence:

"Did you remember to fetch your second sword?"

It was a silly question, George thought; the orphan must have seen the shortsword in his hand. No doubt Tristan just wanted to hold it. Well he could; it was getting heavy. George handed the weapon to his eager friend. Tristan let out a low whistle; he was clearly impressed and started to chatter excitedly about the blade. George just grunted in reply; he was in no mood for talking. As they neared their destination, a sense of foreboding was growing in his mind; he felt cold despite the warmth of the evening sun.

Emerging from the trees to get his bearings, George noted that they were almost at the northwest corner of the meadow. They had only to walk back into the wood and continue through to the far side and they would be at the cave. He almost wished it wasn't so easy, that they still had five miles to go, or even that they were lost and couldn't find it at all.

All too soon, the adventurers found themselves at the northern edge of the wood, where the druid's grisly remains still lay exposed at the foot of the large oak tree. George wondered briefly if they should try to bury him, but there wasn't much left to bury and, in any case, they were there for all to see should Caradog demand further proof of the druid's demise.

Stepping out from beneath the trees, George stared apprehensively at the dark opening in the hillside. He wiped the sweat off his brow with his sleeve before reaching for the tinderbox. *I'm not scared*, George told himself, *it's just a very warm evening*. Overhead, grey clouds moved across the sun, threatening rain. The air was still, heavy; it felt like a storm was brewing.

Tristan had already gathered a small pile of kindling from the woods, and George crouched over it, trying to spark the fire into existence. His hands were shaking and, after several failed attempts, George handed the flint to his companion.

"See if you can get it going", he grunted, furious with himself. "I'll go and find some torches."

The orphan quickly got a small fire started, and George found two thick, dry branches. Setting them in the fire, they soon had a lighted brand each. With torch in one hand and sword in the other, the two lads approached the cave entrance.

George's legs were shaking, and he had a sick feeling in the pit of his stomach. Now that the moment had come, his earlier confidence was melting away faster than snow on a warm spring morning. Every fibre of his being protested at the stupidity of what they were about to do. There was every chance that neither of them would return from that cave alive! Yet the alternative was to return to the village as a criminal, and maybe face a long slow death in a Roman jail. It was as if the gods had decreed this end for him; there was no way out!

As they reached the yawning mouth of the cavern, Tristan put out a hand to stop George. "I'm going to pray", he said, in a slightly shaky voice.

At any other time, George would have laughed, told him that speaking into the air wouldn't help. But staring death in the face, he wasn't laughing; if there were any gods listening, George desperately wanted their help.

Tristan bowed his head. "Great Father in heaven", he began, and as he continued his voice grew in strength and purpose. "Our lives are in your hands. Protect us from evil; go with us into the darkness, and strengthen our hands so that we may bring your justice upon the beast that lies within. We ask this in Jesus' name."

George was astonished; the shy little orphan seemed almost to have grown in stature as he prayed. Now, as he walked forward into the dark, his face set with determination, Tristan had become the leader, and George had to follow, sincerely hoping that the orphan's God had been listening.

Inside the cave, all was dark and cold. George stood there shivering, waiting for his eyes to adjust to the change. At first he could see very little apart from the bright yellow flames flickering in the inky blackness. His nose took much less time to adjust; the stench in here was overpowering! George held his breath, straining his ears for any sound of movement from the depths of the cavern, but all he could hear was the thump, thump, thump of his own heart, and the constant drip, drip, drip of water from the damp ceiling above. He could see the cave walls now; they looked smooth and slimy. The rock beneath their feet was also smooth: limestone.

As the two would-be heroes made their way deeper into the hillside, the flickering torchlight cast eerie shadows on the walls. Suddenly, out of the darkness above them, a hideous visage appeared, a gaping maw with foot-long sharp teeth dangling like spears! George let out a cry of terror, jumped backwards, slipped and landed on his backside, nearly setting his hair alight with the torch. Tristan let out a yelp and swung his sword wildly. There was a dull clang as the steel struck rock.

"It's just stalactites!" exclaimed Tristan, letting out a loud sigh of relief.

"Shush!" cautioned George, getting to his feet, his rear end and his pride both smarting. Looking up at the rock formation now, it was hard to imagine how he could have thought it was a living creature. His relief was short-lived however; between them they'd just made enough noise to waken the dead. If there was a bear in this cave it was sure to have heard them.

The two adventurers moved cautiously forward, torches held aloft, ears alert for any sound of danger. The tunnel continued deeper, turning to the left and then back to the right, dropping slightly as it went. They passed several cracks and openings in the walls that were wide enough for them to enter, but the passage they were walking down was easily the largest (wide enough for them to walk side by side and high enough for George to walk upright without fear of banging his head) so they carried on down this main way.

If anything the smell was getting worse. George was just beginning to wonder if the tunnel would ever come to an end when, suddenly, the passage opened out and the ceiling rose upwards into the darkness; it looked like they were just about to enter a large cavern.

George froze; he had just heard a low rumbling noise.

"W…what was that?" asked Tristan, in a small hollow voice.

A wave of fear crashed over George; he couldn't speak, he couldn't move. In the awful silence that followed the orphan's question, they could both hear the sound of claws clicking over the smooth stone floor; something large was approaching. At the edge of the torchlight, a dark shape loomed, then suddenly, before either of them could react, an ear-splitting roar echoed around the cave and a blast of air issued up the tunnel. The boys staggered backwards, almost losing their footing. For a brief moment the flames from the torches streamed out over their shoulders, and then the fire sputtered and died; they were in complete darkness!

With a shriek of terror, George dropped the now useless piece of wood, turned, stumbling over his companion, and fled blindly back up the tunnel, arms out in front of him. Almost immediately, his left hand collided with a wall of rock and George spun around, dropping to one knee as his foot slipped on the smooth surface. As he tried to get back to his feet, something hit him from behind, bowling him forwards into the wall. Crying out in pain, George got back to his feet and staggered onwards, not waiting to see whether it was Tristan or the bear that had collided with him. Behind him, he could hear sounds of scrambling and heavy breathing; it must have been the orphan.

I must keep ahead of Tristan. It was selfish, but this was a matter of life and death. As long as the orphan was between him and the bear, George knew he was safe. In the pitch dark, his outstretched sword struck the cave wall and was nearly ripped from his hand. The ringing of metal on rock echoed strangely down the tunnel and was answered by another thunderous roar. It sounded very close; George could almost feel the claws on his back and the jaws clamping onto his skull!

A solid wall of rock blocked the path. George moved to his left, sword scraping along the stone as he desperately searched for a way through. Finding none, he hurriedly changed direction. *The passage can't be blocked; we came through this way!* George was almost crying with frustration. Footsteps rang out from somewhere close behind him; Tristan was catching up... or was it the bear?

At last, the probing sword found the narrow gap it was searching for, and George staggered onwards, his arms spread wide, feeling for the sides of the tunnel. The sounds of pursuit were growing steadily louder; he started to run, eyes tight shut (not that this made any difference), teeth gritted, knowing that at any moment he might collide with solid rock. Catching his left foot on a snag in the uneven rock, George pitched forward, landing heavily, his sword clanging loudly on the cave floor. He could taste blood in his mouth, and the knuckles of his right hand hurt horribly, but he scrambled to his feet, fear lending him speed.

"George!" It was Tristan's voice, and he sounded desperate. His footsteps rang in George's ears, mingled with the bear's snarls and heavy tread. They were nearly on him now!

Careering off the sides of the tunnel, George stumbled forwards in a blind panic. He had to get out; he had to escape! Ahead, he could just make out a patch of light: the cave entrance! Hope rekindled, George lengthened his stride. Even as he strained towards the exit, a savage snarl erupted from somewhere not too far behind him. This was followed by a terrible scream, which echoed all along the passage, ringing in his ears, making his hair stand on end. Then came the most terrifying sound yet: a horrible crunching noise! With an awful finality, the scream choked off, until even the echo had died away.

Chapter 6 – Never to be Forgiven?

"NO!"

George's anguished cry filled the air as he sprinted out of the darkness into the light. Squinting, his eyes full of sunlight and tears, he blundered on, not slowing his pace until he had reached the comparative safety of the trees, where the fire that Tristan had lit was still burning. Only then did he stop and turn to face the cave, breaths coming in ragged gasps.

Everything was blurred. George rubbed his eyes to remove the tears that were welling up, and then wiped his nose on his sleeve. He stood there, numbly, staring into the black mouth that had swallowed up his friend, waiting, refusing to believe that Tristan was gone. A single raindrop landed on his head, followed by another and another. Soon, the rain was falling heavily and water was streaming out of his hair, down his nose, into his ears and eyes, and yet George didn't move a muscle. The fire had gone out; still there was no movement from the cave entrance, and yet he continued to delay, sword hanging limply from his right hand.

There was a distant rumble. For a moment George's eyes widened in fear, and he stared even more intensely at the cave mouth, then he realised that the noise was thunder. Finally roused into action, he tore his eyes away from the dark opening and headed into the woods.

By the time that George reached his village, the last light of evening had faded. Soaked to the skin, covered from head to toe in mud and blood, limping slightly, and thoroughly exhausted, he had never wanted his bed so much, and yet, hovering outside his hut in the pouring rain, the bedraggled figure could not bring himself to go in. There were going to be questions, hard questions that he didn't want to answer just now. Maybe Caradog had already been to see his mother; maybe George would have to go to the great hall and explain to the whole village why he had attacked the sheriff, and why Tristan would never be coming home again.

George stifled a sob: never was a very long time! He couldn't go in, couldn't face any more. Hadn't he suffered enough today? Where could he go? There were only two people in the village, in the whole world, whom he could call friends. *No, just one!* With a lump in his throat he set off, once more, for the orphans' hut.

As he arrived at his destination, there was a loud crack and the night sky was lit up as clear as day. All the hairs on the back of George's neck tingled; it was as if the gods were angry with him for surviving the terrors of the cave, and wanted to finish the job.

George hesitated, taking deep breaths; this wasn't going to be easy. Catherine would cry; he knew that. He felt like crying himself. Maybe they could both cry together and somehow make everything better. With one final deep breath, George pulled open the door, stooped, and entered the hut.

"George!" Catherine exclaimed. She was sitting by a small fire that was burning in the centre of the hut; the smoke rose upwards and out of a small hole in the roof, which was letting in more water than it should.

"What happened to you?" And then before he could answer that one: "Where's Tristan?"

George couldn't speak; he didn't have any idea how to say what he needed to say. His expression told the story for him.

"Where is he?" Catherine was almost hysterical now; she had got to her feet and had grabbed her cloak.

"He… he's…" Tears began to well up in George's eyes. He tried again: "He's d…d…dead!" he managed, through a broken sob, and then stared up at the roof, trying to get his emotions under control, blinking back the tears.

There was a stunned silence. George waited for Catherine to say something or to start crying, but she remained dumbfounded. He looked into her eyes, but they just stared through him, sightlessly, as if she couldn't see him.

"Dead?" she repeated, seeming not to comprehend the meaning of that awful word.

"We were hunting a bear", started George, feeling that he owed Catherine some sort of explanation. "The one that killed that sheep last night", he continued, words spilling out at a furious pace. "We found a cave… Well, we found the druid's bones first."

George wasn't making much sense and he knew it, but he had to get it all out. "So we lit torches and went in, and then the bear roared, the torches went out, and we ran for it. I got out and Tristan…" George choked, unable to finish his sentence, but he had said enough.

"You ran and left my brother to die?"

"No." George was startled; he hadn't expected this. "We both ran."

"You coward!" screamed Catherine. "You took him with you on this mad, stupid hunt, and now, thanks to you, my brother is dead!" She started to sob uncontrollably.

"No", repeated George, pain and desperation in his voice. "You don't understand."

"I understand", replied Catherine, through the tears. "I thought you were Tristan's friend; I thought you cared about him. But now I see; you've never cared for anyone but yourself. Get out!" She pointed to the door, "And never come back!"

George staggered backwards, reaching for the door. This was almost worse than what had happened in the cave. He couldn't understand why she was acting like this. As he stumbled back out into the rain and the darkness, George turned to Catherine, his eyes imploring her to listen, but the anger in her face caused the words to die on his lips.

"May God forgive you for what you've done", she shouted into the night, "Because I never will!"

Then she was gone and George was alone, all alone with no one to turn to. What was he going to do now? He stood and stared at the crooked door of Catherine's hut as the rain lashed down. He had nowhere left to go now but home, but what if his mother reacted in the same way? And how could he go on now, having lost both his friends in one night?

George blundered through the village, his tears mingling with the driving rain. Passing the great hall, he came to a sudden halt; there were voices coming from within. It sounded like the entire population was inside, all the men anyway. George couldn't tell what was being said, but he knew what they must be discussing: *They're deciding what to do with me when they find me.*

Ducking behind a nearby hut, George ran, his feet slipping on a path that was rapidly turning to mud. As he slid to his knees, another flash of light split the sky, and the air exploded with a ferocious boom! Pulling himself upright once more, George peered anxiously in all directions. Was that a shout he had heard mixed in with the thunder? Had he been seen? He stood motionless, ears straining for any further sound. But all he could make out was the steady pattering of rain and, in the distance, another threatening rumble.

Scampering from hut to hut, George arrived beneath the thatched roof of the dwelling that faced his own. He had managed to cross the village unnoticed, but now he was going to have to face his mother. What would she say when she found out her son was responsible for an attack on the village sheriff and the death of a friend? *No, I'm not responsible for his death! We both ran; there was nothing I could have done!* But George couldn't get Catherine's words out of his head: *"thanks to you, my brother is dead!"*

As George stood staring across at his home, summoning the courage to go in, the door opened unexpectedly. His mother stood in the doorway; George stiffened, desperately hoping she wouldn't look in his direction. He couldn't see her face; the hood of her cloak covered it. She turned, shut the door behind her, and headed along the path, the path that led to the great hall. She was betraying him!

George watched his mother vanish into the darkness, before making his way, numbly, towards the door of his home: he had nowhere else to go. Inside, George flung himself onto his bed and wept, the blanket muffling the sound of his sobs. He had never felt so alone! *What am I to do?*

As the storm raged outside his hut, a fiercer storm of emotions raged within George. Everything that had meant anything to him had been swept away in this one ill-fated day. His life, as it had been, was over. A choice now lay before him: to give in to exhaustion and sleep, or to gather what few belongings he had and leave before his mother returned. His body ached all over and, although wet through, George felt comfortable on his mat; his eyelids were getting heavy. *Don't be a fool; it won't take Caradog long to find you in your own hut! You'll have plenty of time to sleep in prison or...* Did the dead sleep? George shivered.

When, a few moments later, he arose from the bed, eyes rimmed red, George was thinking more clearly; he knew what he had to do. Firstly, he was going to need supplies. Rummaging around in the dark, George eventually located a couple of carrots, and part of a loaf of bread, in a small sack. He stuffed these into his pack, along with a spare tunic and some socks that he found lying about; then he started for the door.

Even as George's hand grasped the wood, a wave of hopelessness washed over him. *How long do you think you'll last on two carrots and half a loaf?* George had no answer, just a sick feeling in the pit of his stomach. Then, almost as if he were receiving a message from the gods, an image appeared in his mind, an image of silver coins shining in the moonlight.

Of course! There was only one place they could be. George quickly moved across to his mother's mat, picked up the bundle of bedding and shook it. Nothing silver fell out; there were no clinking noises. Where was the money? Had she spent it all? His mum had spent some of it, George knew; she had not wanted to at first, but with the little she earned for mending clothes and the little he earned for watching animals, they didn't have enough to buy things like clothes and shoes, so once every year, she would go down to the market in Cambodonum, and buy what was needed.

His mother was always very careful not to overspend: surely there would be some money somewhere. Then he saw it: in the faint reddish glow of the fire embers, George could make out a piece of leather on the floor, where his mother's bedding had been. On closer inspection, it turned out to be a pouch sitting in a small hole in the ground. It was the moneybag and, from the weight of it, there was still plenty of silver inside. As George dropped the pouch into his pack, he felt a twinge of guilt. After all, he was stealing from his own mother! As if to counter this feeling, the last words he'd heard his father say flooded into his mind: *"Take this for the boy."* No, it wasn't stealing; the money was really his. With only one mouth to feed, his mum wouldn't need it anyway. And George would pay it back one day, when he was a rich and famous trader. With that comforting thought, George shouldered his pack, opened the door, and vanished into the night.

George was pretty sure no one had seen him leave the village; no one but he would venture out into this storm tonight. Making his escape into the woods at the dead of night, with lightning flashing across the sky, had provided a thrill of excitement. For a while, he had almost forgotten the awful events that had led up to this desperate action. Now, chilled to the bone by the driving rain, stumbling over tree roots and whipped by flailing branches, George's spirits were somewhat dampened. He wasn't even sure that he was heading in the right direction; it was pitch black except for the occasional flash of lightning. He was making for

Cambodonum, but right now he might as well be heading for the moon!

George had just stumbled into what must have been the twentieth tree trunk, when there was a thunderous boom, the loudest one yet. A flash of blinding light ripped the sky in half, and George jumped, slipped on an exposed root, and tumbled backwards with a yelp. As he lay there, petrified, the distinctive smell of charred wood invaded his nostrils, then came an ominous creaking. Where was it coming from? George gritted his teeth and held his breath; something very bad was about to happen. The creaking turned to an awful splintering noise. George scrambled to his feet; he had to get out of there. He turned to run, but it was too late; something unseen struck him on the shoulder, and a great weight bore him to the ground! There was a cracking, crunching sound, an earth-shaking thud and then silence.

George lay there, eyes tight shut, not daring to move. He was going to die. He had just been hit by a thunderbolt from the gods! Why were they so angry with him? He couldn't have saved Tristan; it wasn't his fault that the little orphan had died. *Please don't let me die; I didn't mean for any of this to happen. I'm sorry. Please, I'm not ready to die!* Was anyone ever ready to die? Tristan wasn't, was he? All George knew for sure was that he wasn't. He supposed that an old person who'd lived a long and fulfilled life might be ready, but his life had been neither.

Please spare my life... and I promise to... What was it the gods wanted? George had never even considered this before. He frantically racked his brain, searching for anything that might appease these angry gods. No, not gods: God. He vaguely remembered Catherine and Tristan telling him that this notion of many gods was false, that there was only one true God. But what was it this God wanted? If only he'd paid attention. *Whatever you want of me... I'll do it.*

George was suddenly conscious of the rain, still hammering down upon his skull, and that his mouth was half full of mud. He spat, and cautiously opened one eye. This didn't really make much of a difference, since it was still pitch black. He tried to get up, but his legs wouldn't move. Panicking, George struggled wildly, eventually succeeding in wriggling his body free from beneath the unseen obstacle.

As he pulled himself to his feet, another flash of lightning lit up the sky, revealing the thing that had almost crushed him: a fallen tree! The great trunk was hanging precariously above the spot he'd just vacated, its downward progress halted only by the tangled branches of its neighbour.

Scrambling away from this hazardous obstacle, George was surprised to find that a strange calm had descended over him. Although the violent storm showed no sign of abating, and his situation had not improved (he was still fleeing imprisonment and death, with no clear idea of where he would end up or what he would do when he got there), George knew that his cry in the dark had not gone unanswered; something had been set in motion, this night, that would change his life forever.

Chapter 7 – The Boar's Head

When George blearily opened his eyes, the first thing he noticed was that his back ached; he had been lying in an uncomfortable position. He rolled over and stretched, and knocked his arm against… a tree. Where was he? Then it all flooded back to him; a knot started to form in his stomach, and a tear appeared in the corner of his eye. He wiped it away with the back of his very grubby hand. *I thought you liked adventures? Well you're in one now, so pull yourself together!*

George hauled himself to his feet, discovering several more aches in the process, and also that his clothes were damp and covered with a layer of dried mud. He had a vague memory of the storm dying down last night, and of feeling so exhausted that he just wanted to slump down in the first dry place he came to. It looked like he hadn't made it! Taking stock of his surroundings, George discovered his pack lying discarded at the base of a large yew tree; he picked it up before sneezing violently. Something small and furry scurried away into the undergrowth, frightened by this sudden explosion of sound.

George had no idea where he was. Last night he had just wanted to escape from the village, and he had had no clear idea of where he was heading, not that it would have made a big difference in that storm! *I must have walked miles last night, but in which direction?* George looked around him again; he had to get out of these woods. Spying what seemed to be a thinning of the trees, some distance to his left, he shouldered his pack and trudged off in that direction.

A short walk brought George to what was indeed the edge of the woods. Out in the open, the ground was damp and the sky overcast. A cool breeze rustled the leaves overhead and left him feeling slightly chilly. As he glanced around, he got a nasty shock; a narrow valley lay before him, and on the far side of it stood the unmistakeable mound of Lookout Hill: he was less than a mile from the village! He had been going round in circles!

Something stirred in the bushes to his left, and George whirled around, hand flying to his sword hilt, but it was only a rabbit. Nervously, he peered back through the trees. He was too close to the village; they could be out searching for him right now. He mustn't be caught! There was no time to lose; he had to get as far away from home as he possibly could. *Home? Not any more. Will I ever return?*

George tried to put these thoughts out of his mind; he had no time to ponder them at the moment. Scrambling through the long wet grass, down the steep side of the valley, he reached the bottom of the first dip and turned his head to look back in the direction of the village. There was no one to be seen, but George wasn't taking any chances; rather than making for the path, he forced his way uphill through dense shrubs and thick grass, hoping that this would cover his tracks and make it difficult for anyone to spot him from the other side of the valley.

After a lot of effort and a few fresh scratches, to add to the growing collection on his arms and face, George gained the ridge and was able to look down on the wide stream below. The heavy rain had swollen it somewhat, but the stepping-stones were still visible above the waterline. Although tired from the climb, George was unwilling to stop even to catch his breath; he was still far too close to the village for comfort. Keeping up this relentless pace, he crossed the stream and forged uphill to the pine forest beyond. Only when surrounded on all sides by a dense cover of trees, did he finally stop, sinking onto his haunches and breathing deeply.

Where am I going? Cambodunum seemed to be the only choice for the moment, but he couldn't stay there, not for long anyway. They would find him there eventually. He had to disappear, far away. *The merchants:* he could join up with a merchant caravan and head south, maybe even as far as the great city of Londinium[1]. *Will I return?* Yes, one day, when he had made his fortune. He would return bringing expensive gifts for his mother and for Catherine, and then maybe everything would be forgiven and he could live in the village again; or perhaps he would choose to dwell in a grand villa with lots of servants to cook and clean for him and to take care of his land, while he went off hunting or fishing, or riding one of his many horses.

Buoyed by these pleasant daydreams, George made his way swiftly through the pine forest and was soon overlooking the bustling town of Cambodunum. From up here, it appeared much the same as it had on his last visit, six years ago. George had not been back since the incident with the egg. He had had the opportunity to

---

[1] London

go; his mother had gone occasionally, with some of the other men and women of the village, but George had avoided the place, fearing that someone might recognise him. George stroked the untidy stubble on his chin; he had changed a lot in the intervening time; surely no one would mark him out as the little thief that had fled the town with a stolen treasure in his pack.

The little Roman town grew steadily larger as George made his way down the steep track to the bottom of the valley and headed towards the southwest gate at a brisk pace. The sun had still not put in an appearance and there was a chill breeze in the air, but George was sweating profusely as he approached the guard at the gate. The Roman soldier, who was dressed in full armour, with a pilum (a short spear) in his hand and a large square shield at his side, let him past with no questions, however, and a very relieved George made his way through the cobbled streets towards the centre of town.

It felt strange to walk these roads again after all this time; it was as if those six years had never been, and here he was again: a fugitive from the law.

Cambodunum did not seem as busy as he remembered, and it didn't take George very long before he was entering the market square. To his left stood the basilica, the huge stone building with marble pillars supporting the roof at its impressive entrance. Around the edges of the square, the forum, with its array of shops and eating establishments, was doing steady business. He recognised the butcher's shop with its joints of meat hanging from hooks, the bakery, which still emanated such wonderful smells, the weaponsmith's with its array of swords, spears and axes. George looked about him, watching people milling about in the square, going about their business. Something was different about this place, but what? He shook his head to clear it; some things were bound to change in six years. The only thing that mattered was that he join a merchant caravan and… Suddenly George realised what was different: the market square was completely bereft of stalls; there were no merchants!

George wandered aimlessly around the town, with one question buzzing in his brain: *What do I do now?* He felt sapped of energy, without purpose. As the daylight faded, he found himself in a place that seemed vaguely familiar; he was outside a large two-storey building which sported a painted sign, depicting a slightly faded boar's head. Then it came to him: it was outside this inn that he'd nearly collided with a horse, whilst escaping with the giant egg. George smiled wanly to himself; those had been the days. He had been happy then, with not a care in the world; things were different now.

As he stood in the road, feeling sorry for himself, a large man, dressed in a white knee-length tunic and sandals, walked past George and entered the inn. Before the door banged shut, sounds of laughter and delicious smells wafted out onto the street. George squinted up at the sun, which had finally deigned to grace the poor mortals below with its presence; the heavenly orb was very low in the sky. He knew that the gates of the town would be shutting soon, and he would need somewhere to spend the night. After a few moments hesitation, George steeled himself and, stepping forward, pushed open the heavy wooden door.

Crossing the threshold, George was immediately engulfed by a mixture of happy conversation and pleasant aromas. The large room was laid out with several oak tables surrounded by people sitting on benches, tucking into huge platefuls of delicious food. At its far end was a long wooden bar, behind which stood a short, stout man with a round smiley face: obviously the innkeeper. He was pouring a drink for the big man who had just entered.

As George waited for the innkeeper to spot him, he noticed an open door to the right of the bar. The sound of meat sizzling, the clanging of pans, and the smells wafting from this entrance told him that it led to a busy kitchen. George began to feel very hungry indeed; he had only had two soggy carrots all day (the loaf of bread had been ruined by the storm), and his growling stomach was reminding him of this.

"What can I do for you, young sir?" enquired the innkeeper in a cheery voice.

"I need a place to stay", replied George nervously. He had never been in an inn before and wasn't sure what you were supposed to do.

"Certainly", replied the smiling patron, reaching under the bar and handing George a small iron key. "Room six is free."

"Really?" George had expected to have to pay for his accommodation.

"That'll be seven denarii for the night."

George gave the little man a confused look and then opened his pack, fumbling for the leather bag. This must be some use of the word 'free' that he had not previously come across.

While George counted out the silver coins, the innkeeper continued: "I expect you could do with a hot meal. We're doing roast peacock, tonight, in a delicious creamy herb and apple sauce."

"Yes please", replied George enthusiastically. He had never had roast peacock before, at least he didn't think so, but the way his stomach felt right now he could have devoured one raw, feathered tail and all!

"Very good", smiled the stout landlord, "May I take your sword?"

George hesitated for a moment and then unfastened his sword-belt, handing it to the innkeeper. It seemed that the same rule applied here as in the great hall in his village.

Finding a seat in what he hoped would be a quiet corner, George waited patiently for his meal to arrive. He had not been sitting long when two middle-aged women, deep in conversation, wandered across and deposited themselves on the opposite bench. The women seemed to have an intense dislike of silence, and continued their dialogue apace, able to talk, drink, and listen in to other people's conversations, all at once. By the time his huge plate of smothered roast peacock was brought in from the kitchen, George had learned more than he would ever need to know on the subject of weaving, and practically every word that Quintus had said to his wife that week, not to mention all the best places to buy a stola. As a stola turned out to be a type of long dress, this information was not going to be of much use to George, however.

The roast peacock was certainly well worth the wait, and George savoured every mouthful, washing it down with a mug of wine, which he found, to his surprise, that he quite enjoyed. As the evening wore on, he ordered another mug-full and sipped it slowly whilst eavesdropping on a group of grey-haired old men, who were recounting their heroic deeds on the battlefield. The wine made George feel all warm and cosy, and he smiled to himself as he listened to the retired soldiers, who seemed to have routed an entire army of vicious axe-wielding barbarians between the four of them!

It was getting late; George's eyelids began to droop. Leaning back against the stone wall, and folding his arms, he made himself comfortable; he would just rest his eyes for a few moments.

Someone was nudging him in the side. Startled, George opened his eyes and looked about him.

"Time for bed, son", smiled the innkeeper, as he began collecting up empty mugs and bidding goodnight to the few patrons who were still around.

George got unsteadily to his feet, yawned loudly, stretched, and wondered where the bedrooms were. *They must be on the upper storey*, he thought, but how to get up there? George had never been in a building with two storeys before; he supposed that there must be a ladder around the back that enabled you to get up to the second level.

Wandering across the room, feeling slightly light-headed, George exited the inn, and was immediately met by a rush of cold night air. He was feeling wide-awake now, but could see no sign of a ladder, or of any steps at the back of the inn that would take you to the upper storey. After a while, the innkeeper came out, gave him a funny look, and directed him back into the inn.

"Up you go, lad", he said, opening a door on the left that George hadn't noticed. "I think you may have overdone it with the wine."

Through the doorway, George could see some wooden steps leading upwards. *So that's how they do it.* He climbed the stairs and reached the landing. At the top was a narrow hallway, dimly lit by oil lamps, with several doors leading off it. *Room six: that's an 'I' and a 'V'.* Feeling proud of his knowledge of Roman numerals, George opened door number 'IV'. Inside, he was startled to see the large man that he'd followed into the inn earlier. The muscular figure was doing some kind of exercises, dressed only in a loincloth, and didn't seem at all pleased to see him.

"Oops, wrong room", said George, smiling weakly, and hastily shut the door. "VI, idiot!" he exclaimed aloud, berating himself for his stupidity.

He quickly found room 'VI', knocked, just in case, and pushed the door: it didn't open. George scolded himself again, as he fished around for the key and eventually, after several attempts, worked out how to open the door.

Inside, he was relieved to find that the room contained nothing but a bed, a small table, an unlit oil lamp and a wooden cupboard. The bed was made of wood and raised on four legs, which surprised George, as he had only ever slept on the ground. He contemplated pulling the blankets off it and making his own bundle on the floor, but he was too tired and, discarding his dirty clothes, he slumped onto the mattress, wrapped the blankets around him, and fell fast asleep.

George awoke the next morning feeling stiff. He rolled over, as he normally did, and tumbled to the floor with a loud crash. This newfangled notion of sleeping in raised wooden beds would never catch on! Massaging his bruised head, he pulled on his rather dishevelled clothes and, yawning loudly, opened the shutters of his window, letting in daylight.

Looking down from his vantage point, George could see people milling about in the streets below. Gazing upwards he saw that the sky was, once more, overcast, but it was certainly mid-morning; he had overslept.

George made his way rapidly down the steps and was, once again, met by an assortment of delicious aromas. Unable to resist them, he ordered a breakfast of bacon and eggs; he was getting the hang of life at the inn.

"Will you be leaving today?" asked the innkeeper.

"Yes", replied George, confidently, handing over the key to his room.

"Then you'll be needing these." The stout landlord reached under the bar and passed him his sword and belt. "May God be with you", he added as George turned to leave.

"Err thanks", mumbled George, not sure how to reply, and with that he marched out of the inn, heading for a new life of exploration and adventure.

George's pace slowed. He was almost at the market square. *What if there are no merchants there?* He stopped in his tracks; his chest felt tight and he was breathing heavily. He was almost too afraid to look. *Please God, if you are there, let there be merchants in the marketplace today.* Inhaling deeply, George strode forwards and peered over the heads of two women who were just ahead of him.

His heart sank; once again there were no market stalls, just the usual traders in the forum. He stood motionless, hands hanging limply at his sides. Small knots of people wandered past him in either direction, but George stood stock still, staring into space. *Why? Why does nothing ever go right in my life? What have I done to deserve...?* George wiped an angry tear from his eye; he knew the answer to that question: he was responsible for Tristan's death and now he was paying for it. *What do you want me to do? Hand myself over to the authorities? Or maybe I should just go back to the cave and let the bear eat me!*

George stood there defiantly; he wasn't going to give up so easily. Turning on his heels, he headed back the way he had come.

"Back so soon?" enquired the innkeeper, as George re-entered the Boar's Head.

"God wasn't with me", he replied wryly. "Don't the merchants visit this town any more?"

"Certainly they do; a caravan came through here the other day. What with being on the trade route between Deva[1] and Eburacum[2], we get traders every two or three weeks during the summer."

Two or three weeks! Did he have enough money to stay at the Boar's Head for that length of time? He tried to work it out: *It cost me seven silver coins for the night, three for the roast peacock, and two more for breakfast. Wine is one coin per mug. If I just drink water from the town well from now on that'll be... err... twelve silver coins each day... but I'll need another meal... say fifteen coins a day. It's lucky I'm good with numbers. So, fifteen coins a day for, say, two weeks, is... err... um... a big pile of silver! I'd better count it.*

George found an empty table in the corner of the inn, away from the few patrons who were still taking their time over breakfast, and opened his money pouch. He glanced around cautiously, to make sure no one was watching, before beginning to count his silver.

Counting a large amount of silver coins, in a public place, without drawing attention to oneself, is a difficult skill, and George soon found himself knocking over one of the small piles he had made. There was a very obvious clinking sound, and as he shielded the coins with his arms, one of them dropped onto the floor and rolled away. This was retrieved almost immediately by one of the women whose conversation George had endured last night.

"You dropped this, dear", she said, returning the denarius, and casting an enquiring look at the piles of money in front of him.

---

[1] Chester
[2] York

"Thanks", mumbled George, casually trying to conceal the other coins by leaning forwards.

The nosey woman hovered a little while longer, as if waiting for an explanation of what the lad was up to, but when she saw that no information was forthcoming, returned to her table. George waited until he heard the sound of her bench scraping on the stone floor, and then began again. He had just reached fifty-eight (or was it sixty-eight?) when a small cough startled him: an elderly man with wispy white hair had managed to sneak right up to his shoulder without being noticed.

"If I were you, son, I wouldn't count my money in public. You never know who could be watching!"

"Yeah, well I need to count it now; I'll risk it", replied George, through gritted teeth, keeping his composure with great difficulty; inwardly he was a cauldron, steaming and bubbling, threatening to boil over at any moment.

He waited for the white-haired man to leave, which the old fellow did eventually, but not before muttering something about young people not having the sense they were born with, which did nothing to improve George's mood.

He shuffled around on the bench, presenting his back to the old man and the nosey woman and, with a sigh, started to count again. This time he was startled, almost immediately, by a firm hand placed on his shoulder.

"Forgive my intrusion", said a familiar, cheery voice. "Is there anything I can do to help?"

George let out the breath he didn't realise he'd been holding, with explosive force. "You could leave me alone to count my money! Or no, why don't you just count it yourself? You could get some of your friends to count it too; they seem very interested in my business!"

George stared up defiantly into the innkeeper's face, expecting an angry retort. To his surprise, the man's smile didn't falter for a moment, in fact it seemed to grow broader, and finally a chuckle escaped his lips.

"I was thinking more along the lines of offering you a job."

George opened his mouth to speak, and then shut it again with a loud snap; he didn't know what to say.

"I couldn't help noticing that you have financial concerns", continued the stout landlord. Seeing George's nonplussed expression, he added: "You're worried about money."

George nodded, unsure of quite what was coming next.

"I've been short-handed here since my elder son started his apprenticeship with the blacksmith. You need a job; I need a helper. What do you say?"

"Erm…" George wasn't sure. A job would solve some problems, but he couldn't stay in Cambodunum for long; he wasn't safe here.

"It would only be a temporary arrangement", added the innkeeper, as if he had read George's mind. "As soon as a merchant caravan arrives in town, you're free to go."

"Okay, I'll do it", replied George, his remaining difficulties answered. "When do I start?"

"This afternoon. You'll need time to smarten up first."

George stroked the hairy growth on his chin and looked down at his mud-splattered breeches and torn tunic; he was a bit of a mess.

"A change of clothes and a visit to the baths should do it. Get yourself a shave while you're there."

Chapter 8 – Discovered?

George returned, shortly before midday, dressed in a brand new pair of yellow and green striped trousers and wearing a sky blue tunic. He was clean-shaven, sweet smelling, and only slightly traumatised by his visit to the Roman baths. The idea of bathing indoors, and in a public building, what's more, was a disturbing one to him. To George, bathing was a strictly private matter, and doubtless what God had created rivers for: rivers with trees on the bank, which hid your body from prying eyes.

"That's much better", declared the innkeeper, on seeing the new, clean version of George. "Now, get yourself some food in the kitchen and then we'll put you to work."

After a meal of bread and fish, George helped Aidan, Caddy's younger son, to serve food to the inn's customers. This wasn't as easy as it sounded: he had to collect trays of food from the busy kitchen, carry them past the noisy crowd quaffing ale at the bar, weave his way through the chattering throng making their way to the bar, and arrive, with tray and food intact, at the far end of the room, where the hungry patrons were seated at long oak tables.

Unfortunately, George seemed to have picked up a cold, either from his recent night out in the storm or from his visit to the baths, and had to make frequent stops en route to wipe his nose. He was finally relieved of this food serving duty after sneezing violently into a bowl of tomato soup!

George spent the rest of the afternoon in the kitchen, washing the seemingly endless supply of dirty mugs, plates and bowls. The taps fascinated him, the way you could just turn one and water would flow straight out! It seemed almost magical to George, and certainly beat fetching it from a well. *And how do they get it to come out hot?*

After the first hundred or so pieces of crockery, though, George's fascination with Roman plumbing had waned somewhat, and his mind began to wander. His thoughts strayed to Tristan, and he immediately shut his eyes tight, hoping to banish the awful vision of the little orphan being savaged by the hateful bear. Shaking his head, as if to clear it of these thoughts, George returned once more to the business of washing up. However, it was not long before he was daydreaming again; this time it was Catherine's face that appeared in his head: *"May God forgive you for what you've done, because I never will!"* With a great effort, George forced the image from his mind and focused on the pan he was scrubbing.

After a hastily gobbled tea in the kitchen, it was back to the sink for more of the same. George felt awful: his nose was sore, his head was pounding, the muscles in his back ached and, no matter how hard he tried to concentrate on his job, disturbing images kept popping into his head.

"Well done, lad!"

It was the innkeeper, whose name, George had discovered, was Cadeyrn (or Caddy for short).

"That's enough for today. You'd better get off to bed; it'll be an early start tomorrow."

With a grunt, the Boar's Head's newest employee dragged himself up to his room and, too tired to undress, flopped down on the mattress. But despite his near exhaustion, George found it frustratingly difficult to drop off; he just couldn't get comfortable, and his aching head was still buzzing with unpleasant thoughts. Finally, in desperation, he piled his blankets on the floor and made a makeshift bed on the ground, where God had surely intended man to sleep!

Something was gently nudging his shoulder. George pushed it away and rolled over. The thing, whatever it was, nudged harder, and a sound slowly filtered through the dim recesses of his mind. The sound seemed to be repeating itself over and over. *Were there words buried within this strange noise?* George struggled to comprehend its meaning. It seemed to be getting clearer.

"Wake up, George. Wake up."

"Oh no!" groaned George, and opened his eyes blearily.

Without preamble, Caddy led him down into the cellar for his first job of the day. The innkeeper set his lamp on a hook in the wall, casting light around the dingy room. Down here were several wooden barrels, some large jars (which Caddy informed him were called amphorae), and a sizeable pile of logs. After finding George a small axe, the landlord left him to chop the wood to make a fire.

"The better the job you do with this fire, the more hot water you'll have for washing up later on", called the smiling innkeeper enthusiastically, as he departed.

If this comment was meant to encourage George in his work, it failed miserably. The promise of further washing up, added to the thought of chopping all that wood, on top of feeling cold, tired and generally washed out, was almost too much to bear.

George struggled with his tasks until teatime, when he found that he couldn't even manage to eat his food. At this point, Caddy took pity on him and sent him up to his room, where he tumbled onto his customized bed and lay there, exhausted. On reflection, it had been one of the worst days of his life, but George didn't want to reflect on it, and quickly slipped off to sleep.

"Mind the bar for a bit, would you George? I've got a delivery of ale to see to."

With that, Caddy pushed open the heavy oak door, with a creak, and stepped out of the inn. George was in charge. His gaze swept around the room and alighted on a table in the far corner, where two old men were quaffing ale and complaining loudly to one another about the way society was going, and about how different it had been in their day. Other than these old-timers, the building was empty, so he wasn't actually in charge of very much at all. But still, a lot of things had changed over the course of the week he had been employed at the Boar's Head.

Mercifully, his cold had vanished and he'd been allowed to wait on tables as well as sharing the washing up with Aidan. Also, he'd got so quick at chopping firewood that Caddy had no need to get him out of bed so early, and he was sleeping much better now that he was lying on the floor. Caddy's wife, who spent most of her time cooking in the kitchen, and who George knew only as Mrs Caddy, was full of praise for his hard work. The longstanding customers of the inn were also very complementary, and many of them now greeted him by name. Even the lady into whose soup he had sneezed, had stopped muttering darkly whenever he passed. All in all, George decided, he quite liked his new job, and although it had not made him forget his recent grief, it had numbed the pain a little.

Roused from these pleasant thoughts by the creaking of the inn's front door, George looked up to see who had entered, only to find that the room had emptied. It was the quiet part of the afternoon; things wouldn't start getting busy for a while yet.

Unexpectedly, the door began to open again; someone was coming in this time; a tall thin man with mousy brown hair, dressed in long flowing purple robes: Caradog! George froze as the familiar figure held the door open for an unseen colleague. There was nowhere to run; in a moment the sheriff would turn and see him. What could he do?

In desperation, George did the only thing he could think of, he ducked behind the bar and waited, holding his breath.

There was a thud as the inn door closed, and George could hear Caradog's monotonous drone, which contrasted with his companion's deep resonating voice. *Cunobelinos!* The voices were growing louder; the men were approaching his position. Why hadn't he nipped into the kitchen? It was too late now; the two men would see him the instant he moved from behind the bar.

"Innkeeper?"

They haven't seen me; maybe they'll just go away.

"Ho, innkeeper, there's two thirsty souls here!"

Go away. Please go away.

There was an ominous creaking.

Not more customers!

"There you are, landlord. I was just telling Caradog here what good service you get in this inn; you're letting me down."

Caddy! Now what do I do?

"George, where are you?" called the bemused innkeeper.

George kept silent, beads of cold sweat forming on his brow. He daren't reply, he would be caught, but when Caddy reached the bar he would be discovered anyway. *There's no way out of this one!*

"You have a servant named George?" enquired Caradog, suspiciously.

George peeped around the bar; the sheriff and the blacksmith stood only a few feet away, but they had both turned to face the stout innkeeper.

"A helper", corrected Caddy. "I only hired him last week. Why the interest?"

"There's a boy from our village, named George, who ran away a week ago", replied Caradog, speaking slowly and deliberately. "He vanished at the same time as another boy, who we fear is dead. He was also involved in the mysterious death of the village druid."

"There are a few questions that we want him to answer", added Cunobelinos, menacingly.

On hearing this, George shot from behind the bar, yanked open the door to the kitchen, and launched himself through it.

"GEORGE!"

Ignoring Caddy's yell of surprise, George slammed the kitchen door behind him. He had to get out of the inn. A surprised Aidan looked up from the vegetables he was chopping.

"What's the matter?"

George didn't answer; he rushed to the exit in the far corner that led out of the back of the inn, to freedom. He grasped the handle; it was locked!

"Here he is", announced Caddy, a short while later. "Is this the boy you're looking for?"

George held his breath and shut his eyes tightly.

"No", replied the two men, sounding disappointed.

"Well then, George, I don't know what you thought you were doing running away, but you can get these two gentlemen their drinks."

Opening his eyes, George risked a deep breath; the deception had worked. From his vantage point behind the kitchen door, he could hear the clink of mugs as Aidan, now answering to the name of George, poured their drinks. It seemed that he'd made it into the kitchen before either of his fellow villagers could get a good look at him. Aidan was slightly shorter than he, and his hair was a shade lighter, but neither Caradog nor Cunobelinos had noticed the switch.

George stayed cooped up in the kitchen for what seemed an age, until the sheriff and the blacksmith had finally gone. After that, the inn began to fill up, and he was kept busy fetching and carrying food from the kitchen, and doing a mountain of washing up, but he knew from the significant look that Caddy gave him that this wasn't over.

It was after the last customer had gone, and he and Aidan were busy tidying up, that George felt a heavy hand on his shoulder, and turned to find the stout innkeeper behind him, a grim expression on his face.

"As God is my witness, I've tried to be an honest man", began Caddy, his voice lowered just enough so that Aidan, who was sweeping at the opposite end of the room, couldn't hear. "I've raised my sons to be truth tellers. And now, today, I've deceived two strangers and involved my youngest son in the plot! Why, George? Why were they so keen to find you? What have you got to do with these mysterious disappearances they were talking about? Tell me I haven't made the wrong decision!"

"The wrong decision?" George blurted out, staring disbelievingly at Caddy, who was waiting for his response, hands on hips, a determined look on his round face. "Do you seriously think that I killed the village druid and then, having got a taste for it, murdered my best friend in cold blood and hid his body?"

He stared defiantly back at the innkeeper, whose look of grim determination had wavered to one of uncertainty, even regret. George wondered if he was being too hard on the mild-mannered landlord. Caddy had covered for him, after all; he deserved some kind of explanation.

"The village druid, and my best friend, were both killed by a bear", he stated flatly, keeping his voice steady with some difficulty. "The other villagers all think it was my fault."

"A bear?" The innkeeper's expression had changed again, this time to a look of stunned disbelief. "In these parts?"

George nodded slowly, hoping that Caddy would leave it at that and let him go to bed.

"But that's terrible!"

George was suddenly aware of Aidan, who had stopped sweeping and was listening in, open-mouthed. His father noticed him too.

"Off to bed now, son", he commanded sternly.

Aidan headed obediently for the door. George made to follow, but the innkeeper's podgy hand gripped his arm.

"I'm very sorry about your friend", continued Caddy, as the heavy oak door closed behind his son. He shook his head sadly. "But why are they blaming you? And what's this business about the druid?"

It was no good; he just wasn't going to let it go.

"All right", conceded George, "I'll tell you the full story, but don't say I didn't warn you!"

Settling himself onto the nearest bench, George began the tale. The words poured out of him, like blood from a recent wound, bringing back the pain, but also, in a strange way, relief. It was as if the wound was gammy and, in reopening it, he was cleansing it of the infection.

Caddy sat opposite George, his mouth opened wide in an identical expression to Aidan's, listening intently as the young Briton recounted the sequence of events that had led to him being wanted in connection with two murders.

When the story had been told in its entirety, George turned away from the innkeeper, hiding the tears he could no longer hold back. A heavy silence descended upon the room, during which he tried to compose himself, drying his eyes and wiping his nose with the back of his hand. Some part of him had needed to tell that story, but what would Caddy think of him now? George turned to look him in the eye.

"Did you make the wrong decision?" he asked, still defiant.

"That depends", replied Caddy, thoughtfully. "Do you regret any of your actions in the story you've just told me?"

"All of them!" replied George, his voice heavy with emotion.

"Then no, I made the right decision."

"Does God ever forgive?" The question burst out of George before he could stop it. It had been tormenting him for days, ever since he had parted from Catherine on such bitter terms; for some reason her words had hurt him almost as much as Tristan's death.

"Yes of course", replied Caddy, his tone back to its usual chirpy, assured state. "But you mustn't take him for a fool; he will know whether you are truly sorry or not."

"But how do I know?" George was slightly taken aback by the innkeeper's certainty on a question that he had thought unanswerable.

"Well", answered Caddy, giving the question some thought. "If you are really sorry for something, you will do everything in your power to avoid repeating the offence again."

George pondered these words as he made his way up the wooden staircase to his room. He wasn't likely to get the chance to repeat his offence; he didn't seem to have any more friends to leave to die. Even as that thought crossed his mind, George dismissed it with a shake of his head; he had only known Caddy for a week and already considered the kindly innkeeper a friend and, besides, that wasn't what Caddy had meant. There was a great deal more wrong with the 'old' George than that one act of cowardice; there were a lot of things that he didn't want to repeat.

Unlocking the door of room 'VI', George slipped in and undressed ready for bed. As he lay down and reached for the bundle of blankets, a thought struck him; in his mind, he pictured the little orphan, at the cave entrance, his head bowed in prayer. Getting up again, a tear in his eye and a firm resolve in his heart, George bowed in a similar fashion.

"Great Father in Heaven", he began, repeating Tristan's words, "I'm sorry for… for… leaving Tristan to die." There, he had said it; he had finally admitted it to himself. "And… I'm sorry for… everything. Please forgive me…" George's words trailed off. Tristan had ended his prayer with a particular phrase, but George couldn't remember it. There was a warm glow in his heart though, and he felt sure that it didn't really matter.

"George, George."

It was Caddy's voice. George opened his eyes to see the innkeeper beaming at him from the doorway.

"You've slept in."

Startled, George quickly threw off his blankets and scrambled to his feet.

"It's all right, I've made the fire", the innkeeper continued, "And I've got some good news: a caravan of merchants have arrived; they're setting up in the market square."

George didn't know what to say; he didn't know what to think. All his plans rested on joining up with a group of traders, but now that they were actually here, he didn't feel excited or relieved, or anything like he had expected to feel; in fact, he just felt a bit sick.

"Breakfast is porridge and fresh bread", continued the smiling innkeeper. "Just one final chore before I let you go: put the blankets back on the bed will you? I'm trying to run a civilised establishment here!"

Chortling to himself, Caddy closed the door, leaving his former employee to tidy the room.

George ate his breakfast without relish; there was nothing wrong with the food, he just didn't feel hungry.

"Eat up, George." It was Mrs Caddy, the round, smiling, female equivalent of the innkeeper.

"I will", he replied rather flatly, taking a mouthful of the now lukewarm porridge.

"There's a good lad", she chirped.

She had an infectious smile, and George couldn't help but return it, despite the uncomfortable feeling in the pit of his stomach.

"Now, you be careful out there in the big wide world." She put a reassuring hand on his shoulder. "I'm sure it will all work out all right for you. And next time you're passing through Cambodunum, pop in and see us won't you. You know you'll get a decent feed."

With that, she bent down and kissed him on the cheek. George's face turned a bright pink and he suddenly found the pattern of wood grain, on the table, very interesting. Smiling once more, Mrs Caddy returned to the kitchen.

It took George a long time to make his way through the rest of the porridge in his bowl. Regular customers of the Boar's Head kept interrupting him, slapping him on the back and wishing him all the best. Strangely, the more people wished him well, the worse George felt. At that moment, he would have very much liked to put the whole thing off until tomorrow, but now that everyone had said 'goodbye', it would look silly if he didn't go.

At last, he could stall no longer: his bowl was empty, only crumbs remained of the bread roll, and it really was time to leave. George headed slowly towards the bar where his newfound friend, Caddy, was waiting for him with a familiar grin.

"You'll be needing these", gestured the innkeeper, handing George his sword and belt, "And this will probably help", he added, pressing a number of silver coins into George's hand. "Don't count them until you're alone, eh!" Caddy gave a little chuckle and continued: "I don't know how we're going to cope without you. I'm going to have to do the washing up until I can find someone else." The innkeeper grimaced at the thought of this.

"Thank you", replied George a little awkwardly. The words didn't seem adequate after all the kindness that the innkeeper had shown him.

"Now be off with you", said Caddy in a kindly voice, "And when you've finished travelling the world, I dare say the Boar's Head will still be here." He paused and then, winking at George, added in conspiratorial tones: "And if you acquired an amphora or two of Gaulish wine on your travels, I could put them to good use."

Chapter 9 – Never to return?

George made his way down the, now familiar, cobbled street that led from the Boar's Head to the market square. The knot in his stomach and the feeling of apprehension were also familiar, unpleasantly so. If he could just join up with this caravan of merchants, everything would be all right: he would be away from the village and the possibility of arrest, and all the ties to his old, unhappy life would be severed. But how did you go about becoming a trader? George hadn't really given any thought to this; his mind had been fixed on this course of action since he'd fled the village, but his thoughts had always been of what to do and never of how it was to be done. The knot in his stomach tightened. *You handled that trader no problem when you were twelve, surely you can do it now!* But that had been in a different life, a life where everything was a game. That life was over; it had ended nine days ago with Tristan's death. Things were serious now, deadly serious.

George's thoughts trailed off; the crowd in front of him had slowed and compressed, like sheep being herded through a narrow gate and out into the field beyond. In a few moments he would enter the marketplace, and then… Part of him almost hoped that the merchants wouldn't be there, and then he could just go back to the inn and forget about this whole thing. But it was a forlorn hope; he had only once before seen the streets of Cambodunum this crowded, and that was six years ago, when the market had been full of traders. And anyway, he couldn't forget about leaving; he had survived one close encounter with Caradog, but Cambodunum was too near to his village; it was only a matter of time before he was found. If the sheriff convinced his Roman friends that George was guilty of two murders… It didn't bear thinking about.

All at once, the people in front of George fanned out to the left and right, and he saw what he had been both longing and dreading to see: merchants; dozens of them, each with their own brightly coloured stall, invitingly laid out, enticing the crowd to part with their silver. Everywhere he looked, money and goods were changing hands; people were swarming round the stalls like bees around honey: running their fingers down silk garments, examining highly decorative pots and jugs, admiring intricately crafted gold and silver jewellery, and marvelling at the exotic artefacts collected from far-away lands.

George approached the nearest stall, a cart covered with red cloth, upon which was set out a large quantity of necklaces, brooches, bracelets, rings and any number of other pieces of expensive looking jewellery. He stood for a moment, gazing at the precious stones sparkling in the morning sun: rubies, diamonds, emeralds, sapphires…

"Can I help you?"

George looked up, startled. The merchant: a short, slender man, with tanned skin and a twirling black moustache, was eyeing him with suspicion. Evidently the trader wasn't expecting a teenage lad to buy expensive trinkets!

"Err… I want to be a… a… merchant", stated George, stuttering slightly in his nervousness.

"Pardon?"

"I want to be a merchant", he repeated, loudly and firmly, pronouncing his words carefully, in case the trader couldn't work out his northern accent.

A burst of laughter erupted from his right. George instinctively turned his head to see three men, all with dark hair and moustaches, leaning against the wall of the basilica; they were apparently laughing at him.

"And I want to be Caesar", quipped the largest of the three.

His two cronies, one on either side, snorted loudly at this, and George felt his cheeks burn.

"So, what do you have to sell?" enquired the stallholder.

At first, George had difficulty comprehending this question and stared blankly at the merchant's moustache.

"What can you sell me?" repeated the trader, seeing the glazed look in the boy's eye.

"Err… nothing."

At this, another round of guffawing issued from the three hairy-lipped spectators.

"A merchant with nothing to sell!" exclaimed the ringleader of the three. "Who else, here, thinks that's not going to work?"

The other two henchmen fell about clutching their sides, forcefully reminding George of Dean and his friends from the village. He was beginning to feel very foolish indeed.

The trader turned to the men, leaning against the wall, and silenced them with a stern look.

"You have money, yes?" he enquired, turning back to face George.

"Yes", replied the Briton, indignantly.

"Then to be a merchant, you must obtain merchandise." The trader gave George a shrewd smile. "Allow me to recommend some items of jewellery; they never lose their value. A necklace, perhaps, or some of these silver brooches: they're only five denarii a piece."

George hesitated; this was not what he'd had in mind at all. Sensing uncertainty, the stallholder pressed his advantage:

"That is how I began", he added conversationally. "I acquired a few pieces of jewellery, sold them for a profit, bought more and sold them, and eventually..." He gestured to the impressive array of jewellery on display.

It sounded so simple, but George had a vague idea that he was being conned somehow.

"So what do you say?" continued the merchant, not letting up. "Buy a few brooches today, maybe some rings: from only eighteen denarii for solid gold, and thirty for a topaz or amethyst, you'd be a fool not to; and then tomorrow, when we've moved on, you can set up stall here and sell them to all the pretty girls who missed their chance today." The merchant was in full flow now. "I'm having to sell them cheap today; it breaks my heart, but what can I do? I have to compete with all these other traders. But tomorrow, you'll be here on your own with no competition. You could sell them for double what you pay me, easily!"

The cunning stallholder paused for breath, eyes fixed on the young man before him, waiting to see whether his patter had succeeded. If he could have looked inside George's head at that moment, however, he would have been most disappointed, because the only phrase that had really registered, throughout the whole of the sales pitch, was: *"tomorrow, when we've moved on..."*

Tomorrow would be too late; he had to join the caravan today, and buying brooches and necklaces wasn't going to achieve that! But how could he achieve it? It seemed impossible. He'd been such a fool, thinking he could just stroll into the marketplace with no merchandise and expect to become a merchant!

A pair of giggly women, with enough jewellery between them to set up in competition with the trader, had just arrived on the scene, and George took this opportunity to mutter something inconsequential and drift away towards the other stalls. He was still inwardly berating himself for his stupidity as he approached a smaller cart, displaying an assortment of clothing of varying materials: everything from coarse cloth to fine silk.

George had no idea what he was going to do next, only that he had to somehow join up with this merchant caravan today. There was no way of knowing when the next one would come along, if at all, and anyway, he would have no more idea of how to tag along with that caravan than he did with this one! Had it just been an impossible dream all along? Caddy had believed it; he had waved him off, fully expecting not to see him again for a long time, if ever. Or had he? A doubt entered his mind; was the stout innkeeper laughing away at George's naivety, knowing that he would be back in his employ by nightfall? Were the Boar's Head regulars taking bets on how long it would take him to realise his stupidity?

No, Caddy is a good man; he wouldn't do that! So, how do you join up with a caravan of merchants without being a merchant?

The question buzzed around George's head like an annoying fly, one that never settles in one place long enough to be swatted. The young Briton looked around him, searching for inspiration, and spied the three moustached jokers, who were still leaning lazily against the basilica wall.

They're part of the caravan and they're not merchants. I could stand around doing nothing and making stupid comments! In fact I could stand up straighter and make better stupid comments than them!

"Can I help you?"

The trader's gruff voice startled George, who without realising it had moved right up to the front of the clothes stall.

"Erm... I'm just looking..." he replied, uncertainly. *Why is it that you can never browse at merchandise without being pestered?*

"For whom?"

Surprised by the question, George looked up to see a large bald man staring at him with one eyebrow raised in an enquiring manner. Lost in thought, he had not registered what the merchandise was; now that he was actually paying attention, he saw that all the items on display were women's clothes: richly ornamented robes, long flowing dresses, undergarments. George's cheeks flushed a deep red.

"For... for..." He searched through his brain, frantically trying to recall why he had approached this stall in the first place. "...for a job", he finished lamely.

"What?" The bald man was evidently confused, and his tone was impatient; he didn't seem the sort to mess around with.

"I'm looking for work", clarified George, his thoughts struggling to catch up with his tongue. "As a..." *What kind of worker would a merchant need? Someone to carry his stock, feed the horses that pulled his cart, count his money?* "Horse counter." That hadn't come out right! Feeling flustered under the merchant's glare, he tried again: "Horse carrier." No, that wasn't it either!

Looking into the bald man's incredulous face, George decided to try one final time before he died of embarrassment: "Horse feeder."

"I can feed my own horses, thanks", replied the stern-faced trader curtly. And that was the end of that.

George made a hasty withdrawal, heading for the far corner of the marketplace, his head full of colourful and insulting adjectives that summed up his performance very well. After composing himself, he decided on a new strategy: *Work out what you're going to say in advance and then approach a stall!*

Now that he was no longer under pressure, it quickly occurred to him that the most important kind of work that a purveyor of expensive merchandise required was that of guarding his valuable stock from thieves, which was obviously what those men had been doing six years ago when he himself had been the thief! In fact, it was so obvious that George had already thought of several more insulting adjectives before he realised that this wasn't helping. So, instead, armed with some well thought out lines, George set out to become a guard.

His next attempt at gaining employment was less embarrassing, but no more successful: the man selling glass bottles of various shapes, sizes and colours, wasn't hiring guards today. The man selling soft cushions and feather pillows wasn't either.

Sixteen merchants later and George's confidence had drained away. It wasn't his fault, George told himself; his performances had become increasingly polished: his tone was now respectful and assured and he stood straight, chin up, chest out, being careful to draw attention to the sword at his side. But all to no avail, no one was hiring today.

Despondently, George pushed his way through the jostling crowd; it seemed as if everyone from the surrounding villages had converged on Cambodunum for today's market! Fighting his way through to the wide stone steps of the basilica, he paused; despite his predicament, George couldn't help but admire this impressive feat of Roman architecture. A large stone portico jutted out over the steps, supported by huge stone pillars; statues of various dignities and war heroes stood proudly between the pillars, overlooking the square, and beyond these a pair of double doors, embossed with red lions, opened into the main body of the building. He was, by now, quite familiar with the Roman style, repeated in several other buildings within the town: the baths and the many temples, but he still couldn't get over how immense they were; and this was the biggest structure of the lot: each pillar was easily three times the height of a man!

"Hey, it's the merchant!"

Startled, George spun around to see the three moustached guards he had encountered earlier, still leaning against the basilica wall; in fact, they didn't seem to have moved at all from that spot all morning!

"Hey, Caesar", he responded resignedly.

"Not bad", replied the leader of the three, twirling his moustache. "It's 'Ave, Caesar' though, and you need to salute." He raised his hand to demonstrate.

But George wasn't paying attention; he'd just caught sight of a familiar face: a tall, broad-shouldered woman with long blonde hair. It was Hazel, the wife of Cunobelinos, the village blacksmith, and she was staring right back at him!

George instinctively turned his head away, heart thumping in his chest. Had she recognised him? Moments later, he risked another glance; she wasn't looking in his direction any more, but as he watched her melt back into the crowd, a feeling of impending doom came over him. *How many others are here from the village? Is Caradog here again? I can't afford to wait any longer; I've got to leave now!*

Glancing around in desperation, George spied the nearby jewellery salesman whom he had first spoken to.

"Excuse me!"

"Oh, it's the merchant."

A familiar chorus of laughter wafted across from somewhere by the basilica wall, but George ignored it.

"Have you given some thought to my suggestion?" the trader asked hopefully, picking up an ornate silver brooch and holding it out.

"Err yeah", replied George distractedly, "But I really need a job now. Could you use another guard? Because I'm a hard worker and…"

"Sorry, kid", cut in the merchant. He gestured at the three jokers. "As you can see, I'm already paying too many people to stand around doing nothing!"

"Make yourselves useful, eh!" he shouted in their direction. "Go and buy us some dinner."

The three men sloped off, muttering dark words.

"Thanks a lot, amigo!" spat one of Caesar's cronies, as he passed.

George wasn't sure what an 'amigo' was, but it didn't sound very complementary.

"If you want a job, try Justus", said Caesar, unexpectedly, as he headed off into the marketplace. "He takes in waifs and strays."

"Which one's Justus?"

"The silver-haired Roman. Tell him you know Caesar, and he might even hire you!"

George watched the three men leave, chuckling heartily once more. He wasn't sure Caesar's comment about the Roman merchant had been serious; it was hard to take a man with a moustache that long and droopy, seriously! He wasn't even sure Caesar was capable of being serious, but George was desperate; if there was a merchant out there who might hire him, he needed to find them right now.

George searched frantically, among the crowded market, for a merchant matching Justus's description. He was sure he'd spoken to most of them in his quest for employment, but couldn't recall any silver-haired Romans. *Is this just a sick joke?* His stomach felt like it was being wrung out like a damp cloth. Every shopper was a potential Caradog or Cunobelinos; he would catch sight of a familiar hairstyle here, overhear a familiar voice there. The whole village could have piled into Cambodunum for all he knew!

Finally, George spotted him: not Caradog, nor Cunobelinos, but Justus, or at least a trader with silver hair and a Romanesque nose. His heart skipped a beat; this was it, the last chance to escape from this ever-tightening snare.

The trader was busy with a customer, so George stood in line, glancing nervously around, heart beating like a drum and hands shaking like leaves in a chill breeze. An array of plates, pots, jugs and jars met his gaze, stacked neatly on a cart: some of clay, some of bronze or silver; one or two even looked to be made of glass! At least the man wasn't selling women's undergarments!

"What can I do for you, young man?"

It took a moment for George to realise that the merchant was addressing him. The man's voice was deep and rich: the sort that you could listen to for hours, and his tone was kindly enough.

"I was told that you take in… err… I mean that you might be looking for someone to… help with guarding your stuff… err pots… valuable items of pottery and…"

George's voice tailed off; he had messed up. Involuntarily, his shoulders slumped and he closed his eyes. *Why now? Why couldn't I just say, "I heard you were looking for a guard"? Why?*

"You seem to be well informed; I do need another worker."

George opened his eyes, barely able to believe what he was hearing.

"You… you do?"

"Yes. Although you must be aware that if you wish to work for me, you will have to travel a long way from home. A very long way."

George opened his mouth to speak, but unsure of what to say, shut it again. The merchant continued.

"I assume you live locally?"

"Yes", replied George. He needed to assert himself, convince the man that he wanted the job, but nothing was coming to his mind.

"Then working for me will cause a certain upheaval in your life. In fact, I would say it would forever alter its course."

That's what you want; you want your fortunes to change. Tell him. But all George could manage was a weak nod.

"I live in Cyrenaica." Noticing George's nonplussed expression, he added: "That's in Africa", and then continued. "I expect this to be my last visit to these shores. I'm not retiring just yet, but your country is at the extreme northwestern edge of the empire - it has taken me four months to travel here - and the army is having increasing difficulty defending its borders. If the troubles with the northern barbarians continue, I fear that Britannia will soon become isolated."

George was staggered: he couldn't conceive of a country so far away that it took four months to reach it!

"So, do you still want the job?"

George hesitated; he wanted the job very much, but the thought of never returning home was a hard thing to digest. Right now, he wanted to be as far away from the village as possible, and Africa was certainly that, but never to return?

His brain worked feverishly, assessing the options. He could take this job, go to Africa and never return, or he could stay in Cambodunum and wait for Caradog to find him, have him arrested, and either thrown into prison or executed; he didn't have any options!

"Yes", he replied. "I've left home."

"Well, if you're sure", said the Roman, doubtfully. "The job will entail keeping watch through part of the night."

George was on firm ground here: "I've worked as a watchman before, guarding sheep and cattle."

"Excellent, you should have no problems with that then. I see you have your own sword."

George beamed proudly; the interview was going well.

"Have you had much cause to use it?"

The old George would have given the merchant an emphatic 'yes', and would have gone on to relate various stories of fierce battles he had had with thieves, wolves, bears, giant two-headed fire-breathing monsters (if he thought he could get away with it!) each of which he had emerged from victorious by dint of his extraordinary courage and consummate skill with the sword. But the 'new' George hesitated. *I'm not going to lie. Right, so you're going to tell him that you've never fought off so much as an angry dog with it! I can learn on the job. You won't have a job if you tell him the truth!* George was in turmoil; what should he do? By telling the truth he could be losing his last chance to escape arrest. *One little lie; that's all it will take and, after you're out of here, you can be as honest as you like. But one lie leads to another and another, and I'm not going back to that!*

"I have practised with it, but I've never needed to use it to defend myself."

The words were his, but it seemed to George almost as if someone else were saying them. They sounded weak; he couldn't believe that he was meekly surrendering his last chance of a decent life. Unwilling to meet the Roman's gaze, he stared down at the cart between them, as if studying the fine detail on the beautifully crafted clay pots, and awaited the verdict.

"An honest lad!" exclaimed the merchant. "Skill with arms can easily be taught, but honesty is a rare commodity."

Looking up in surprise, George saw that the Roman's good-natured face was split by a wide grin. He moved out from behind the cart and placed a hand on George's shoulder, as if about to perform some sort of initiation ceremony.

"What's your name, son?"

"George."

"Well, George, welcome to my little travelling family!"

The young Briton didn't quite know how to respond to this display of warmth and affection from a man he'd only just met, but managed a heartfelt "Thank you, sir", his relief spreading into a broad grin of his own.

"My name is Justus."

"I know", replied George, before he could stop himself.

"You are well informed, aren't you?" Justus chuckled. "Now, where are the other members of my family? Ah, here they are!"

George turned slightly apprehensively, following the direction of Justus's gaze. Three men were approaching, and whatever he had been expecting it wasn't this. All three wore Roman garb: knee-length tunics with belts, and sandals on their feet, but George was pretty sure that none of them was Roman. One was slightly built with brown skin, not merely tanned but a deep brown; another man, similar in height to the first but far stockier, had bright red hair, tied back in a pony tail, and a neatly combed moustache; and the third was tall and muscular, with untidy blond hair. This last man was carrying a huge joint of meat in his arms.

"You'll be pleased to know that I have hired another worker", announced Justus, as the three men stopped in front of the cart and surveyed the Briton with interest. "This is George."

"Excellent!" exclaimed the red-haired man in a thick accent, "Another brother to share the load, just as Hercules bore the weight of the world for a brief time whilst the titan, Atlas, rested."

George, who didn't have the first idea what the man was talking about, just stood there trying to look friendly and hardworking and professional all at the same time.

"I am Hector de Massilia."

"George", replied the Briton, suddenly feeling that his name was somehow inadequate.

Before he knew what was happening, Hector had embraced him, planting a kiss on each cheek. George's face turned a rosy pink colour and he looked about awkwardly.

"It's all right, he's a Gaul", explained the tall blond man. "They insist on doing that. It's a bit embarrassing, but you've got to humour them. I'm Brennos, by the way."

Hector gave Brennos a dark look and seemed about to say something, when the brown-skinned man stepped forward.

"Your humble servant, Juba."

"Thanks", mumbled George, who didn't know how you were supposed to reply to a greeting like that.

"Well", said Justus, before the situation could become any more awkward, "It looks like your first task is to help them eat a whole pig for dinner!"

"If I'd have known you were hiring, I would have got a bigger one", grinned Brennos.

"There wasn't a bigger cut of meat in the whole shop!" exclaimed Hector. "Unless you were planning on eating the butcher!"

Chapter 10 – Heroes & Villains

The two combatants stood facing one another. Between them, they could boast a hundred fights, a hundred victories; they had fought side by side, triumphing over impossible odds, each saving the other on numerous occasions. But now they faced one another, their friendship irretrievably broken, no warmth between them, only cold steel, and this time for one of them there would be no victory, only death!

On one side stood the giant southern barbarian, a veteran of many campaigns, whose strength and ferocity had always been more than a match for his foes; at least they had been up till now. On the other stood his most accomplished pupil, the tough northern warrior, a legendary swordsman in his own right, whose agility, skill and endurance had kept him alive when death had seemed more likely. A distant rumble of thunder signalled the start of this final conflict, master against apprentice; who would make the first move?

The northern warrior watched his former master, the man who had taught him everything he knew. Everything? He had only one chance to overcome his mentor: he had to grow, move beyond his old tutor; do something unexpected. Resolved, the apprentice hefted his blade and swung hard and low, but his mentor had anticipated this, and parried the attack. The northerner was forced to jump backwards as the barbarian aimed a swipe at his gut. This was followed by a thrust, which the legendary swordsman turned aside before swinging his sword in a wide arc towards the giant's throat. The southerner blocked this attack with reflexes that belied his size, and as the two swords clashed, he threw all his considerable weight behind the blade, forcing his young apprentice backwards. The agile northerner somehow kept his footing on the wet grass, regaining his balance just in time to sidestep the barbarian's sudden lunge, and then, unexpectedly, he spun on the spot, his sword gleaming in the sunlight as it arced towards…

The narrative playing in George's mind was suddenly interrupted by his own cry of pain.

"What was that, George? I'm teaching you to fight, not dance!"

George opened his mouth to reply, but all that came out was a muffled groan. The muffling was due to his lying facedown in thick grass; the groan was due to the blow that he'd just received from Brennos's sword. It may only be a wooden training sword, but it was still a hefty implement and he would have a nasty bruise.

"Leave him alone, he was doing well", interjected Hector, reproachfully.

"He was until he decided to do that silly pirouette in the middle of the fight!" replied Brennos, in a tone of disbelief. "I've no idea what he was trying to achieve?"

"You're just jealous because he's better than you!"

"I'm not the one sniffing the daisies!" snorted Brennos.

"Well, you're definitely a better swordsman than me, George", encouraged Juba, adding his quiet and thoughtful tones to the argument, and helping George, gingerly, to his feet.

"Yes, but so is my grandmother!" retorted Brennos. "As I was going to say before I was mobbed by your fans" – he waved his sword accusingly at Hector and Juba – "You are getting good, but you can't afford to lose concentration and do something foolish like that; good and dead is still dead!"

"I was trying something different", mumbled George, rubbing his aching back with his left hand.

"It was certainly different! The only thing you'll accomplish by spinning around like that is to make yourself dizzy and off-balance, plus you'll doubtless get a sword in your back for your trouble, as I just demonstrated. Remember, you need to concentrate on your opponent, work out what they're going to do next. If you can see in their eyes what they're preparing to do, or if you can tell from their stance, the way they shift their weight, then blocking or dodging the blow, when it comes, will be easy. Let's try again."

George sighed heavily and raised his wooden weapon once more.

Several bruises later, George was sitting outside the recently erected tent, the appetising smell of stewed rabbit wafting across from the campfire. Brennos was stirring the pot whilst Hector added various bits of grass, which he claimed to be herbs, without which the stew would only be fit for "a barbaric Briton". Nearby, Juba lay on his back staring up at the white clouds in the beautiful blue sky. Justus was in the large crimson coloured tent, reading from a collection of precious scrolls that he carried with him, and would doubtless emerge shortly, when the food was ready.

Life was good, bruises not withstanding. George was learning a lot: he could tell the difference between coarse and fine ware pottery, and was able to distinguish between pewter, a material that at first glance looked like silver, and the real thing. He was learning the art of sword fighting, how to hunt and skin wild animals, how to light a fire (properly); he was growing fitter and stronger too, able to walk the twenty miles or so, that the caravan covered each day, without difficulty (Justus had explained that Roman soldiers measured marching distances using what they called a 'passus'- a double pace, which was equivalent to five feet. A Roman mile was a measurement of a thousand double paces, so twenty miles was… a lot of hard walking!)

George had been on the road for less than a month, but even in this short time Justus, Brennos, Hector and Juba had indeed become like family. His old life in the village already seemed like a distant memory, like a dream that he had awoken from; his thoughts seldom dwelt on the past any more, and his dreams were no longer haunted by screams, or visages of ferocious fang-toothed bears.

"Come and get it!"

Brennos's shout stirred George from his reverie, and he quickly got to his feet and headed over to the campfire. A few moments later, Justus emerged from the tent, still clutching a scroll in his hand. As was his custom, the Roman said a prayer of thankfulness to God for the food, and then Brennos ladled it into wooden bowls for everyone (as Justus had told him, the clay ones were for selling, not for eating from). The food was delicious and there was plenty of it, as there usually was when Brennos had anything to do with the quantities.

Justus had rolled up his scroll now, and was giving the stew his undivided attention. George, however, was not; he had a question that he had been meaning to ask the Roman for a while and, plucking up the courage, he decided that now was the time.

"Justus, when you pray you always say 'in Jesus' name', but who is Jesus?"

Justus, who had just spooned in a particularly large chunk of meat, was unable to reply straight away, so Brennos answered for him.

"He was a Jewish rabble-rouser, who lived over two centuries ago, and was crucified by the Romans for his radical teachings."

"He was much more than that", interjected Justus, his mouth now emptied of stew. "He was, or I should say is, God incarnate. Without the sacrifice of his perfect life, no one could enter paradise."

Brennos rolled his eyes, but said nothing and ladled himself another helping of stew; it was clear that the two men did not see eye to eye on this subject.

George pondered what the merchant had just said; he was fairly sure that Catherine had once told him something similar. Even as the thought went through his mind, he felt a lump in his throat; it was better that he didn't think about his old life, it was all too painful.

"Some of this grass you put in is almost edible", remarked Brennos to Hector, although he winked at George as he said it.

"You are too kind", scowled the Gaul. "I'm just trying to liven up your bland British tastes."

A smile on his face once more, George quickly polished off the last of his stew, washed his bowl in a nearby stream, and sat down with the others, around the campfire, for the nightly ritual of storytelling. He loved these times when he could just sit back, relax after a hard day's walking, and drink in tales of far away and long ago. All around him, others were doing the same thing; a hush seemed to descend over the entire camp, and then, one by one, individual voices broke out until the noises mingled together like a babbling brook.

Justus began with an ancient tale, borrowed from the scroll that he had just been reading. It concerned an Israelite named Samson, whose birth had been foretold, and along with this prophecy had come the strange command that his hair must never be cut. The merchant described how, as a young man, Samson had been set upon by a lion, and had torn the creature apart with his bare hands! With great enthusiasm, the Roman had gone on to describe other mighty deeds that this hero of old had performed: how Samson had caught three hundred foxes, tied them in pairs, tail to tail, fastened a lighted torch to each pair, and set them loose in the corn fields of his enemies, the Philistines. How, when the Philistine army had come out to capture him, he had struck down a thousand soldiers with a donkey's jawbone, and how, when trapped by his enemies in a walled city, the mighty man had wrenched the great gates off their hinges and escaped, carrying those same gates on his broad shoulders, in triumph, to the top of the hill that faced the city!

"But, in the end, this mighty hero was brought down by a woman", continued Justus in a sad tone. "He fell in love with a Philistine woman, named Delilah, and revealed to her the secret of his great strength. As he slept, the conspiring woman had his head shaved, and when Samson awoke from sleep, his strength had left him. Delilah, who was in the pay of the Philistine leaders, had summoned soldiers to the house, and they seized Samson, gouged out his eyes, bound him with bronze shackles, and set him to grinding in the prison."

"And the moral of the story is: if you have a secret, and you want it to stay secret, never tell it to a woman", Brennos cut in.

"I haven't finished yet", protested Justus, with a chuckle. "Sometime later, the Philistines held a great celebration in honour of Samson's capture; thousands gathered in their largest temple, including all the dignitaries and nobles, and they called for Samson to be brought from prison so that he could perform for them. But Samson's hair had grown again whilst in prison."

The Roman merchant paused, letting the significance of this last line sink in, building the suspense.

"As Samson was guided towards the centre of the temple, he asked the servant, leading him, to place his hands against the two central pillars. Bracing himself against these supporting columns, Samson called upon God to give him strength for one last deed, and then he pushed with all his might and the great pillars gave way, bringing the whole structure crashing down. And thus, with one act of final sacrifice, Samson killed thousands of his foes and set his people free from the tyrannical rule of the Philistines!"

In the silence that followed this dramatic conclusion, George surreptitiously wiped at a damp patch in the corner of his eye. The story had awoken strong emotions within him; he had a sudden longing to fight, to perform some great feat of strength and endurance. At that moment there was nothing he couldn't do. *What a story! And what a way to go! When I die I want it to count for something.*

"It's always sacrifice with you Christians, isn't it?" remarked Brennos, bringing George back to reality.

"I suppose it is", replied Justus, looking thoughtful.

"An excellent story", complemented Hector, and there were murmurs of agreement from Juba and George. "And it reminds me of another heroic tale, that of Hercules."

"Don't tell me", interrupted Brennos, "Roman mythology".

"Greek mythology, I believe", countered Justus.

"May I?" enquired Hector, one eyebrow raised.

"Please do", replied Justus, with a nod, and the Gaul began.

Hector told of how, after killing his own children in a senseless rage, Hercules had been forced to atone for his crimes by completing twelve impossible tasks. George listened intently as the Gaul recounted the hero's victories over lions, boars, bulls; birds with armour-piercing beaks, flesh-eating horses, and a tribe of savage warrior women. He was particularly fascinated by the Lernean hydra: a monster with nine snake-like heads, which grew two more for every one that Hercules cut off.

It was a long tale. Justus went to bed after Hercules had completed his tenth task, bringing back the cattle of Geryon, a strange three-headed, six-legged monster from the world's end.

"Let me know how it turns out", yawned the Roman, as he lifted the tent flap and disappeared from view.

George stifled a yawn of his own; he was keen to make it through all twelve tasks. Besides, he was on first watch, so he would have to stay awake for several hours anyway.

Hercules' next labour was to pick apples from the legendary garden of the Hesperides, nymph daughters of the Titan, Atlas, whose job it was to hold up the world on his shoulders. Hercules persuaded Atlas to pick the apples for him, while he bore the weight, but after the Titan had picked them, the Greek hero tricked him into holding up the world once more, and returned in triumph with the apples.

"The twelfth task was to prove the hardest of them all!" exclaimed Hector, theatrically. "In order to complete this final test and win his freedom, Hercules had to capture Cerberus, the three-headed hound of Hades!"

The Gaul went on to describe, in dramatic tones, the mighty Greek's journey through the shadowy regions of the underworld, climaxing in his terrific struggle to overcome the immortal hound and wrestle it back to the surface.

"Thus", concluded Hector, "The mighty Hercules, having atoned for his crimes, finally earned his freedom, and took his place as possibly the greatest hero the world of mortals has ever seen!"

There was a short pause as the storyteller waited for the appreciation his epic deserved.

"Justus's story was better", began Brennos after some consideration. "I almost believed that one."

"Mythology isn't supposed to be believed, it's meant to entertain", countered Juba, and then, seeing the scowl on Hector's face, quickly added: "And that tale was certainly entertaining."

"Very", agreed George, who had enjoyed the story immensely, and believed none of it.

"Speaking of entertainment", added Brennos, in conspiratorial tones, "I was chatting with one of the town watchmen earlier, and I reckon they'll let us in. There's a little place I know in the west quarter where they have plenty of it."

"Of what?" George enquired.

"The three 'W's."

"Wine, women and err, why not?" exclaimed Hector, jumping to his feet.

"You can't go into Verulamium[1]", objected Juba, his normally quiet voice raised for once. "Brennos is on first watch with George."

The Briton seemed about to argue, but then clapped his hand to his head. "By Juno, you're right!"

"Pluto's beard!" cursed Hector, a frustrated look on his face, but George noticed an odd twinkle in his eye.

"Goodnight then", said Juba, looking suspiciously at the two of them.

"Goodnight", they replied in unison.

"Goodnight", added George.

With that, Juba stepped into the tent, disappearing from view.

George sensed that something was up, and his suspicions were confirmed a few moments later when Brennos got to his feet.

"We'll see you later, George."

"I thought we were on first watch", replied George, puzzled.

"You are", replied his mentor. "I feel the time has come for you to take your own watch."

"You're definitely ready", added Hector.

"Undoubtedly", agreed Brennos. "No need to mention this to Justus though", he added in an undertone, "He tends to be a bit overcautious; treats us a bit like little children sometimes. No need to worry him is there?"

---

[1] St. Albans

With that, the two conspirators turned and silently headed away from the firelight, towards the town gates, in search of further entertainment.

George watched them go with mingled feelings of resentment, nervousness and excitement. It was the first time he had stood guard on his own; even when he had been working for Taranis, he had had Tristan for company. Swallowing hard, he got to his feet. This was the job he was being paid for and he would do it to the best of his ability; he was indebted to Justus for the faith the Roman had shown in him; now it was time to start repaying that debt.

George surveyed the area he was to guard: the large tent, the horses tethered to a stake nearby, and the cart, with its hide covering, protecting the precious items within from inclement weather and thieving hands. He glanced towards the high stone walls that encircled Verulamium; he could no longer see his two companions; it seemed they had managed to gain access.

The sun had set a short while ago and the moon was shining brightly in the star-spangled heavens. George stared up at them for a while, wondering briefly if they would look the same in an African sky. Finding that these thoughts were doing nothing to allay his anxiety, he got to his feet and started pacing backwards and forwards in front of the fire.

At least I won't have that long to wait before I'm relieved, he thought. The Roman system split the night into four equal watches, rather than the two he was used to - The Romans seemed obsessed with dividing up time. Justus had explained to him how they broke up each day into twelve equal hours, beginning at dawn and ending at dusk. Why anyone needed to know what time it was to that degree of accuracy was a mystery to George. And even on a clear day, he still had trouble working out which of the twelve hours they were in (Brennos could tell the time, even in thick fog, just by listening to the noises of his hungry belly!) Things were easier once the sun had gone down, though; George had long known how to keep track of the passing of time during a night watch; it was a simple matter of locating the constellation known as 'The Serpent' in the evening sky, and following its progress as it rotated slowly on its circular course.

George's eyes strayed back to the town gate. The serpent in the sky would tell him exactly when his watch was over, but he had a feeling that Hector, who was supposed to follow him, would have better things to do, right now, than stare up at the stars. He could be in for a long night after all.

Turning his head back to face the cart, George stiffened; was it just the wind rustling the hide covering or had he heard something else? Standing stock still, he strained his ears for any small sound that might be out of place. There it was again; it seemed to be coming from somewhere over by the cart. George felt suddenly cold and alone; all those heroic tales he had been listening to seemed somehow silly and far removed from reality now. He remained motionless, trying to imagine all the completely innocent things that could be making such a noise. Surely no one would try to steal their merchandise while someone was standing guard?

There was no mistaking it this time; the loud ripping sound he had just heard could mean only one thing: a thief was attempting to cut through the cover! George's hands hung limp; his heart was beating fast. *Come on you coward, this is what you're being paid to do; if you don't do your job now, you might as well go home!*

He took a tentative step towards the cart, his right hand shaking uncontrollably as it moved towards the hilt of his sword. He took another step and another, each one seeming to take an enormous amount of effort, as if he were battling against a gale. George tried to ease the blade from its sheath without making a noise, but his trembling fingers slipped, causing the sword to slide back into the scabbard with a harsh rasping.

He froze; the thief must have heard that, they would have to be deaf not to, but there were no sounds of panic or retreat. Was the villain standing there, silently, hoping that he hadn't been detected? Or perhaps, waiting to ambush the one who had discovered him as soon as they turned the corner?

Unable to stand this tension any longer, George swung around the side of the cart, sword out, and stopped short. There, less than ten feet away, was the thief! His nose, mouth, and the lower half of his face, were obscured by a piece of dark cloth; in his right hand he held the object responsible for the eerie noises: a wickedly curved, serrated knife. One corner of the cart cover was flapping wildly in the gusty breeze; it seemed the villain had already succeeded in cutting a large hole through the hide. But the man wasn't cutting now, and he wasn't running either; he stood facing George, knife pointing threateningly in his direction, dark eyes flashing evilly.

The two men stared at one another; both were of similar height and build, but in contrast to his adversary, the masked robber appeared quite at ease. Unnervingly so, given that he had just been caught red-handed and was now being threatened with two feet of cold sharp steel. George stood motionless, staring, unsure of what to do next; he had expected the thief, once discovered, to flee back into the shadows or, if he felt cornered, to attack, but this man was just standing there, looking back at him. In fact, he didn't even seem to be looking directly at George; his gaze was fixed on a point behind the Briton, somewhere over his right shoulder.

Too late, George realised what was happening. He whirled around, flailing wildly with his sword, but the other thief, the one he hadn't counted on, was already within striking range. George cried out in pain as his opponent's hurried sword thrust bit into his shoulder, and then saw his assailant double up, clutching a hand to his side, where George's own blade had caught him.

There was a sudden muffled cry of rage, but not from the man he had just wounded. George spun around again, just in time to see the first thief hurtling towards him, the curved blade held high above his head. Instinct kicked in, and George's sword swung upwards, blocking the knife thrust inches from his face, before the momentum of the charge threw him backwards. There was another yell as the struggling pair crashed into the man behind, knocking him off his feet. George tumbled over the prone form, landing with a bone-jarring thud on his back, forcing a gasp from his lips and loosening the sword from his hand. Next moment, the charging thief landed on top of him, knocking all the remaining breath out of his body.

Gasping for air, George struggled to free himself from the tangled mass of arms and legs. As he hauled himself out of the melee, a sharp pain shot up his left arm, then a flailing elbow made contact with the side of his head, causing him to slip sideways onto his injured shoulder. It was as if he had been stabbed again; George howled in agony, but the adrenalin coursing through his body kept him from collapsing, and somehow, the young Briton managed to stagger to his feet. But where was his sword? It was too dark, he couldn't see it, and there was no time, the uninjured thief was upright, once again, and closing in.

The serrated knife arced down towards his throat. George reached up and grabbed the man's forearm in mid swing, once more halting the blade inches from his face. The robber lashed out with his free arm, but George gripped that too, wincing with pain as he did so. Now the two combatants were locked together in a life and death struggle for the knife.

His adversary was winning; the pain in George's injured shoulder was almost more than he could stand. He could feel blood flowing freely down his left arm as the evil blade moved inexorably towards his throat. In desperation, he kicked out, his right foot making contact with his opponent's kneecap. With a yelp of pain, the thief staggered sideways, and George shoved him to the ground. Now was his chance to get away; if he could wake Justus and Juba, he would be saved.

Turning to run, George registered a sudden movement to his right and swerved; he had forgotten the other thief! There was a flash of steel, followed by a sharp intake of breath; the swing had missed by inches!

George backed up, keeping out of range whilst glancing around fearfully. Where was the first man? Something solid struck him squarely on the jaw and, reeling from the blow, he lost his balance and collapsed into the side of the cart.

Coloured lights flashed before George's eyes as he slid to the ground. Groggily he fought to bring things back into focus, but it was too late; by the time he had regained full consciousness the two masked robbers were standing over him. One, his mask askew, revealing the corner of a snarling mouth, was unarmed; the other, however, held his shortsword menacingly above George's head, ready to split his skull.

"Kill him!"

These words chilled the young Briton to the core; this was it. Was he ready? He wasn't sure, but he didn't seem to have much choice – or did he?

The sword flashed down upon him.

Chapter 11 – Bad Blood

George cried out in pain as he rolled sideways onto his injured shoulder, and under the cart, just as the thief's killing blow struck the turf where he had been lying.

As he lay there in the blackness, clutching his bleeding wound, George heard a shout, and then – oh the relief of it – the robbers were running away!

"Brennos, George; where are you?"

It was Justus's voice; he was emerging from the tent.

George opened his mouth to answer when, to his surprise, he heard Brennos reply. His mentor sounded out of breath, as if he had been running.

"What's going on?" the Roman wanted to know. "I heard shouting."

"That was us."

This time it was Hector speaking; he also sounded out of breath.

"We scared off a couple of thieves", added Brennos. "They look to have torn a hole in the side of the cart cover; I don't think they got anything though."

"Where's George?" There was a note of anxiety in Justus's usually calm voice.

"We got separated", replied his mentor, after only a short pause.

You lying toad!

George slid himself painfully out from underneath the cart. "I'm here", he announced, in a voice that sounded hollow and drained.

"George! What happened to you?"

"Are you all right?"

"'Course he's not all right!"

George just lay there while his friends rushed about fetching water and bandages. Justus propped him up against one of the cartwheels and lit a lamp to inspect the injury.

"Deep but not dangerous. If it had been a little further across, though…" He left the sentence purposefully unfinished.

As Brennos began cleaning the wound, Justus plied George with questions about the attack. The young Briton was suddenly

100

faced with a dilemma: should he tell the merchant about his mentor's absence, or should he try to cover for him?

He deserves to be dropped right in it; thanks to him I could have been killed! Looking up at the man busily bathing his shoulder, George saw a pleading expression on the normally arrogant, self-assured features, and grudgingly made up his mind to try to keep his mentor out of trouble. *But I'm not going to lie for him.*

The task of retelling the night's events truthfully, without mentioning Brennos's absence, was a difficult one, especially with his mentor watching him closely, as he bandaged the cut, and flashing him meaningful looks whenever Justus turned away. When George accidentally let slip that he had been alone when the second thief had ambushed him, Brennos tugged the bandage tightly, causing him to wince in pain, at which point his mentor smoothly interrupted: "I was circling around from the other side to cut off the thief's escape route; we had no idea that there were two of them."

Justus frowned at this explanation and opened his mouth to ask another question, but then seemed to change his mind.

"Try and get some sleep, George", is all he said.

The two men retreated to their respective corners of the tent, and George slumped down on his travelling cloak, pulling a bundle of clothes under his head, to serve as a pillow. He was exhausted, and longed for sleep to cover him like a soft blanket, to take him away, far away, to a land where pain was but a distant memory. But it didn't; he just couldn't get comfortable. His left shoulder still hurt horribly, his jaw ached, and on top of this, although it had never really occurred to him before, George now realised that he always slept on his left side. Trying to get to sleep on his other side just didn't feel right, and lying flat on his back wasn't working either.

His mind would not shut down; it just kept replaying the night's events over and over. He tried to think about something else, anything, but it was no use, each time his thoughts would quickly return to the attack. And it wasn't just pictures in his head, he would revisit the emotions too: the fear he had felt when approaching the cart, the pain and horror he had experienced when being stabbed, the desperation as he had fought to stay alive, and the sudden pang of helplessness as he heard the terrible words: *"Kill him!"*

George was finally starting to doze, when he heard a noise coming from outside the tent; someone was fumbling at the door flap. He sat bolt upright, heart missing a beat. The flap opened, and a dark figure was silhouetted against the stars; it slipped inside and made its way silently across the floor, stepping over the prone form of Justus who, oblivious of this intrusion, was snoring gently; then it stopped and bent down by the side of another sleeper. George, who by now could feel beads of cold sweat on his brow, opened his mouth to give a warning shout, but the cry never came.

"Juba, wake up, it's your watch."

The voice was Hector's. George slumped back down, a wave of relief washing over him, and closed his eyes. *Why am I so jumpy?* But he already knew the answer to that; it hadn't left his thoughts all night: he was a coward. He had been so sure that he'd changed: he worked hard, he told the truth, he even bathed once in a while, but deep down, underneath all these layers, he was still the same boy who had left Tristan to die so that he could save his own miserable hide. He was a coward and he would always be: tonight proved it.

Juba, now wide awake, left the tent to take his turn on watch. Hector settled down in his corner, and George tried, once more, to get to sleep. He had already been awake for half the night; now there was only Juba's watch, Justus's, and then it would be morning!

George must have dozed off eventually because he found himself waking to the dawn chorus of twittering birds. It was still dark outside, though and, groaning, he turned over to get back to sleep. His resultant yelp of pain echoed around the tent; he wasn't going to roll over like that again!

"Are you all right, George?" enquired Brennos, yawning.

"Not really", muttered George, bitterly. He hadn't forgiven his mentor for leaving him alone on watch.

"Justus might be able to get you some herbs to help with the pain", interjected Juba, trying to keep the peace as usual.

"I could do with some of those for my head", moaned Hector.

The tent flap opened and Justus entered. "Since you're all wide awake, we might as well get an early start."

A chorus of groans filled the morning air.

The early start meant that they were amongst the first to arrive in the marketplace, and Justus was able to secure a prime position, right at the edge of the square, where everyone entering the market would have a fine view of his merchandise. The Roman organised the others to set up the stall for business, while George kept an eye on the horses. As his companions scurried about, arranging the many and varied pots, jugs, jars and bowls, he watched the other merchants arriving in dribs and drabs, manoeuvring their wagons into the rapidly decreasing market floor space.

Presently, an argument broke out between two merchants who both wanted the same plot of ground, and there was some pushing and shoving. Engaged in this disturbance, George didn't notice the approaching cart until it pulled up beside him, and he was a little taken aback to be addressed by the round-faced man driving it.

"I hear you fended off two thieves last night."

"Err yeah", replied George hesitantly, unsure what was coming next.

"Good for you. There have been too many thefts from this caravan over the last few months; I've lost some valuable stuff myself. It's good to know that justice prevailed this time."

"Err yeah." George didn't know quite how to respond to this statement either.

"Well, keep up the good work."

With a smile, the merchant flicked the reins and his horse clip-clopped forward, as he made his way across to a vacant plot in the market.

As he watched the cart go, George, still slightly flummoxed by the compliments he had received from a total stranger, was startled by an angry tirade. Looking around him, he saw that the nearby argument had drawn in a couple of other stallholders. Seemingly, one of the horses had sought to spice up the conflict by relieving itself right where the two merchants were proposing to set up stall; both had then had second thoughts about the position's suitability, but were now caught up in a row over who was going to clean up the mess.

"So George, I hear you're a bit of a hero", called out Brennos, mockingly.

"Not yet fully fledged, but nevertheless he has started down that glorious path", added Hector, with slightly more sincerity.

"And what did the legendary George have to say in victory, as the laurel wreath was placed upon his noble brow?" Brennos paused for effect and then, putting on a vacant expression, answered his own question: "Err yeah".

He imitated George's voice well. Hector and Juba laughed; George blushed, realising how stupid he must have seemed to the kindly merchant.

"Better work on that acceptance speech, George", his mentor finished.

At that moment Justus cut in. "I need a word with you, Brennos." He sounded grave.

"I'm not a hero", George muttered, turning away, his cheeks burning.

"Are you sure?" questioned Juba, smiling broadly. "I think you have another admirer."

"Caesar!" he exclaimed.

"Those who nearly died defending their cart, I salute you", replied Caesar, grinning behind his droopy moustache.

It had been a strange morning for George; he must have talked to more total strangers in the past few hours than ever in his life before. After Caesar had left, a steady stream of merchants and guards had approached him to offer their congratulations on his victory over the thieves. The young Briton had tried to convince them that it wasn't really a victory – he'd lost the fight, after all – but, for some reason, this explanation had only served to enhance his hero status.

"I'm not a hero", he repeated to Juba, when the latest of his fans had departed.

"No one seems to agree with you", laughed the African.

But George wasn't laughing; he felt a fraud. He couldn't just sit back and take all this adulation; it was wrong.

"If I'm such a hero, how come I was so afraid?" he burst out. "I was scared when I went to see what was making the noises behind the cart; I was scared when I saw the thieves; I was scared to death when I thought I was going to die!"

"So?" Juba was still smiling, his teeth standing out brilliant white against the darkness of his skin.

"So, I'm not a hero, I'm a coward!" exclaimed George, frustrated. It hurt him to admit to his cowardice, but he just wasn't getting through.

"Do you think a hero is someone who is never afraid? Do you think that courage is about never being frightened of anything?"

George didn't answer; that about summed it up in his mind. Juba was no longer smiling; his face now wore an expression of earnestness, almost desperation, so intent was he on making his point.

"Courage is about being afraid of doing something, but overcoming that fear and doing it anyway. Fear attacks both the brave and the cowardly; it's how we react that shows which we are. The coward fears and runs; the courageous fear, but stand their ground."

Before George could respond to this, his elbow was jogged. Turning, he saw Hector, a fierce expression on his face, and a mysterious rounded light brown object in his hand.

"Eat it", commanded the red-haired Gaul, savagely.

George wondered what the matter was; he had never seen his friend like this.

"Go on", insisted Hector, brown eyes flashing dangerously.

George looked down dubiously at the thing in Hector's hand: it had something like hair sprouting out of the top of it, and looked far from appetising. He glanced at Juba for help, but the African just shrugged.

Hector had thrust the brown hairy ball right under George's nose; the Gaul was muttering under his breath and seemed about to explode! He had no choice; George took the 'whatever it was' and bit into it. The thing had a strong taste, and he was having difficulty swallowing the papery skin.

"You don't eat the skin", grunted Hector.

George opened his mouth to protest that his comrade had not mentioned this at the best time, but Hector didn't look in the mood for complaints, so instead, he picked the pulp out of his mouth, and took another bite of the white interior. Tears began to stream down his face, although the Briton couldn't understand why: he wasn't sad or in great pain. He wiped his eyes with the back of his free hand. *What is this thing? Is this some kind of test?*

Determined to finish his task and not give in, George peeled off the remainder of the skin and took a large bite of the strange food. His eyes were watering so much he could hardly see, but he kept going doggedly. The thing was obviously some kind of vegetable, but one that he'd never tasted before; he would definitely have remembered this taste! Stuffing the last piece in his mouth,

George rubbed his eyes. They were stinging now, but he stared back at the Gaul, defiantly through the tears.

"What was that all about?"

"It is a custom of my people; when someone does something really stupid", replied Hector, underscoring these words with venom, "We give them an onion to eat."

"Why?" enquired George, completely perplexed by this whole episode, "What have I done?"

"You know what you have done, Brutus!" And, with that, the red-faced Gaul turned his back on them and strode away.

George stood there watching him storm off, bewildered and also a little angry and upset. Why had Hector treated him like that? What stupid thing was he supposed to have done? What was that thing he'd just eaten? And who on earth was Brutus?

He put this last question to Juba, in the hope that the African might be able to shed some light on this whole mystery.

"Let me think; I'm sure I've heard that story", Juba replied, his brow creasing. "Oh yes. Brutus was a friend of Julius Caesar, a great Roman emperor."

Juba paused and stared upwards, as if the story was hovering above his head, somewhere just out of reach. George waited.

"He was asked to join a conspiracy against Caesar to save the people of Rome, I think, and he betrayed his friend; he ended up stabbing him to death!"

"So what's that got to do with me? I was the one that got stabbed!"

"If Hector is comparing you with Brutus", pondered Juba, speaking his thoughts out loud, "He must believe that you have betrayed a friend."

"I haven't betrayed anyone!"

George stared indignantly into his friend's dark face. As he did so, an expression of dawning comprehension greeted him, replacing the puzzled frown.

"Brennos went into town last night, didn't he?"

George nodded.

"That must be what master Justus was speaking to him about earlier; he must have found out that Brennos left his post."

"And Hector thinks I've told Justus?" George's voice was raised in anger. "Do you think I told Justus?" he added, looking accusingly at Juba.

"Did you?"

Juba's tone was calm, quiet; his dark brown eyes were fixed on George's face. It was a simple question, not an accusation.

"No!" George was unable to keep the anger out of his voice.

"Then no, I don't believe you told master Justus", replied Juba, earnestly.

"Then tell them that!"

George lay on his mat, staring blankly up at the tent roof. It was raining outside, and the sound of the water drumming rhythmically on the leather wasn't helping him cope with the throbbing pain in his shoulder or the sense of injustice he felt at the way his comrades were treating him. It had been a thoroughly miserable afternoon: neither Brennos nor Hector had wanted anything to do with him. The Gaul had muttered dark words whenever he had come too close, and the one time that George had tried to communicate with his mentor, all he got was, "Your breath stinks!"

As he lay there, his thoughts strayed to his old life: to Tristan and Catherine; and to his mother, sitting at home, wondering what had become of her son. A tear came to George's eye; he had not had these feelings for weeks. Everything had been going so well; he had been busy working, learning, making friends and having fun, and now it was all unravelling. He had escaped from one miserable situation; what was he going to do if this turned into another?

George's moment of self-pity was interrupted as the tent flap opened, and his bedraggled companions trooped in. With them was a man he recognised as Flavius, another Roman merchant, and a close friend of Justus.

"Ah, last night's hero", began Flavius, brushing a tangle of sodden curls out of his eyes and smiling broadly down at George.

George returned the smile weakly, staring at his toes, doing his best to avoid eye contact with Brennos or Hector.

"That's right", agreed Justus, proudly. "Not bad for an apprentice, eh?"

If George could have burrowed his way out of the tent at this point, he would have; he could almost feel his companions' angry gazes boring into the back of his head.

"Justus tells me you're having trouble sleeping", continued Flavius, oblivious to the tension he was creating. "I have some medicine that can ease pain and induce sleep."

These words didn't have the positive effect that Flavius was expecting. George had heard tales of Roman medicine, how they cut off damaged limbs and burnt the stumps to prevent wounds from going bad. He had grown quite fond of his left arm over the years and didn't think that life would be quite the same without it.

"May I have a look at the injury?" enquired the Roman.

Hesitantly, George rolled up the sleeve of his tunic, and Flavius proceeded to unwind the bandage and inspect the wound. George gritted his teeth.

"You're not going to cut my arm off are you?"

"I wasn't planning on that, no", chuckled the Roman.

Somebody, probably Brennos, snorted; George felt his cheeks flush.

Flavius held out a small clay pot. "This contains somniferum, or poppy milk, as it is more commonly known", he explained, as George eyed the container with suspicion. "It is extremely potent and must only be taken in very small doses, and only before sleep. A small dose makes one very drowsy; a large dose could kill you!"

Flavius uncorked the jar of poppy milk and took out a pinch of the brown gummy substance, which he held between forefinger and thumb. Rubbing the two together produced a powder which the Roman let fall into a cup of wine that Justus had just poured.

"The wine will take away some of the taste", remarked Flavius, swirling the cup to further mix the powder. "It will still be very bitter though."

George reluctantly took the cup from the knowledgeable Roman. *So it tastes foul and it could kill me, and this is supposed to make me feel better?* Everyone was watching him closely; the young Briton imagined that this must be how a gladiator felt as he walked into the arena, the crowd looking on, eager to see what grisly fate awaited him. George put the cup to his lips and, after a brief hesitation and a fervent prayer, took a large gulp.

Flavius had been right: it tasted vile! George made a face.

"That's right", encouraged the Roman. "As my friend Gaius, the doctor, says: 'If it tastes good, it's bad for you, and if it tastes bad it must be doing you good.'"

"We've no worries with your cooking then, Hector", quipped Brennos who, despite his bad mood, could never resist the chance of an insult.

With encouragement from Flavius and Justus, George managed to force down the rest of the bitter medicine, and then, feeling exceedingly light-headed, he sank down onto his bedding and closed his eyes.

"Wake up George; everyone else is having breakfast. That poppy milk must be good stuff!"

George blearily opened his eyes and saw Justus's smiling face beaming at him from the entrance. The early morning sun shone in through the open flap, illuminating a tent that, save for him, was completely empty. He had slept right through the night; *the poppy milk was good stuff!*

After a rapidly eaten, and unusually quiet, breakfast, George stood around, feeling useless, while the others packed up the tent and their belongings, loaded them onto the cart, and hitched up the horses. When all was ready, he climbed up beside Justus, who gave a flick of the reins, and they were off.

The journey south to Londinium[1], largest of all British towns, was exceedingly dull. None of his companions seemed in the mood to talk; even Justus was oddly quiet, not giving his usual commentary on the virtues of Roman engineering and architecture. George wondered whether the merchant was upset with him too, or was it because of that onion he'd eaten the day before; he could still taste the wretched thing now!

It was about the ninth hour when they finally arrived at their destination. Justus sent Brennos and Hector into town to buy food, while he helped Juba to pitch camp. Once again, feeling like a spare part, George watched his fellow servant as he attended to the horses.

"Master Justus has told Brennos that he won't be travelling with us to Gaul", stated the African, as he hammered an iron stake into the hard earth.

"What?" George turned to face Juba, completely taken aback by his friend's sudden revelation. "Why?"

"Master Justus said it was because he could not trust him any more."

---

[1] London

"Because he deserted his post once?" George was incredulous.

"I do not think that is the real reason", replied Juba, quietly, as he tethered the first of the coal black steeds to the stake.

"Then what is?"

"Master Justus knows that Brennos lied to him."

"One lie and that's it?" exclaimed George, his shocked tones rising above the general hustle and bustle of the camp.

"One lie is all it takes to break trust", countered Juba, wisely.

"But what about a second chance? What about forgiving?"

"You cannot forgive someone who does not admit their guilt."

Juba's sage words were only serving to infuriate George. He wasn't exactly getting on well with Brennos at the moment, but he didn't want him to lose his job, and he couldn't believe that there was no way to avoid this unhappy conclusion. He was just about to voice this complaint, when the object of their conversation returned, armed with several large silver-scaled fish.

As Hector cooked the fish over the campfire, George raised the subject of his mentor's banishment once again.

"Surely Justus would keep Brennos on if he admitted his crime?" he whispered.

"I am sure he would", agreed Juba, in an undertone. "Why don't you talk to him?"

"Talk to him?" replied George, a little too loudly, and then lowering his voice added: "He'd sooner take advice from a carthorse!"

George ate his fish without relish; it tasted decidedly dodgy, and he wondered briefly if Brennos had put something in it to poison him. Electing not to stay up for the storytelling, he went to bed shortly after the meal, taking his daily dose of poppy milk before settling down.

As he waited for sleep to take him, images of his mother, Catherine, Tristan and Brennos flashed before his eyes. Each figure was pointing an accusing finger at him, and their expressions were dark as stormy skies. An angry tear slid down George's cheek as he drifted into unconsciousness.

George opened his eyes, but it didn't make any difference, he couldn't see a thing: it was still the middle of the night. He had a strong urge to relieve himself, but it was nice and cosy in the tent and it would be cold outside, so he fought hard to suppress it. He lay there trying to think about something else, anything at all, but it was no good, he was becoming increasingly uncomfortable. Finally, able to stand it no more, George threw off his cloak, and groped his way out of the tent.

Outside, the campfire was burning brightly in the pitch-blackness. By its yellow light, George could make out the watchman sitting nearby, staring up at the myriad of stars overhead. The silhouetted figure looked around, hearing the rustle of the tent flap, and then, seeing him, turned away again: it was Brennos. George hurried away into the dark: he had no wish to speak to his mentor; he had far more pressing business to attend to.

A short while later, feeling considerably relieved, George returned to the tent. He hesitated at the entrance; Juba's words were nagging away at him. *Juba should talk to him,* George told himself, and reached for the tent flap, but it was as if an invisible hand held him back. *He won't listen to me.* The nagging voice wouldn't be silenced. *All right, I'll try, but it won't do any good.*

With a sense of foreboding, the young Briton turned and made his way slowly towards the campfire.

"I have nothing to say to you", spat Brennos, before his fellow watchman had taken more than a couple of steps.

George spun on his heel. He'd been right; Brennos just wasn't going to listen. As he marched back towards the tent, anger boiled up inside; he'd had enough of this whole situation, of listening to stupid advice, of being ignored, of dark mutterings when his back was turned, of being blamed for something he hadn't done. All at once, George made up his mind: he was going to finish this once and for all.

"I have something to say to you!" he exclaimed, angrily, turning back towards the firelight. "I know you think that I told Justus what you did, but I didn't!"

"He knows", replied Brennos simply. "You got what you wanted. So I didn't stay and hold your hand, so what? Four years I've been working for Justus, I've travelled with him to the ends of the earth, risked my life to protect him and his livelihood; he's been like a father to me and I've been like a son to him, and now he's abandoning me! Why?"

Brennos's voice was filled with pain, though there were no tears in his eyes. No doubt, he would see tears as a sign of weakness.

"Justus prizes truth above all things", answered George, restraining his anger with difficulty. "He said so when he gave me this job. You lied to him and broke his trust; you have to say sorry."

George dropped his gaze; he had a feeling that these words might not be well received. He was right.

"You expect me to take advice from you? You back-stabbing coward!"

This was too much for the young Briton. "Well you're a... a..." George searched his mind for the most insulting word he could think of. Suddenly it popped into his head; he didn't even know what it meant, *but it must be pretty offensive:* "...you're an amigo!" he finished.

Brennos stared at him, nonplussed, and then, after a few moments, began to laugh. This was neither the response that George had expected nor wanted.

"What's so funny?" he snapped.

"Amigo is Spanish for friend", chuckled his mentor, when his laughter had finally subsided enough for him to speak.

Feeling angry with the big Briton for calling him a coward, and peeved that his insult had backfired, George stormed away from the fire, heading for his bed.

"Fine, laugh!" he called, on reaching the tent. "You won't be laughing when we sail to Gaul and you're left behind; and all because you were too proud to admit you'd left your post. You need to eat a whole sack full of onions for that!"

Chapter 12 – Across the Mare Britannicum

The sun shone almost blood red as it sank low in the western sky, painting the clouds pink, and giving the evening sky a purple tinge. George sat with his back to a silver birch tree and watched the sunset, lost in the wonder and beauty of it. For the first time since the attack, he felt at peace. A warm, cosy feeling enveloped him, shielding him from the harsh realities of this world, and transporting him somewhere else, somewhere safe; and in that moment, George knew that the one who was painting the sky with glorious colours, had everything under control, even the chaotic circumstances of his little life.

"GEORGE!"

The Briton whirled around, heart in his mouth, peace shattered.

"Brennos."

George started to let out a sigh of relief, but there was something wrong. His mentor had a strange expression on his face, one that George had not seen before, and he didn't like the look of it.

"You're responsible for the circumstances I now find myself in", stated Brennos, pointing an accusing finger at his young companion. "And now I'm going to give you your reward."

George watched in horror as his mentor reached into his belt and pulled out a dagger. Before he had registered what was happening, the weapon had been launched. For a moment, time seemed to slow down; the knife almost hung in mid-air as it arced towards him, yet George was unable to react; he sat rooted to the spot.

THUD. Time caught up; the dagger hit the trunk of the silver birch. He turned to look at it; the blade had missed his head by about a foot.

"Had you there!" crowed Brennos, as George's head snapped back to face him. For the first time in three days, his mentor was smiling.

"You'll be needing this as well."

The big man lobbed a leather sheath into George's lap. It appeared that the dagger was a gift.

"Reckon I owe you something for your words of wisdom", Brennos explained. "Old Justus just wanted me to admit I'd lied to him. Lucky guess of yours, but still…" He winked at George. "I expect Hector will speak to you again now, but never mind, you can't have everything."

George smiled up at his fair-haired friend; everything was all right with the world again. With a nod that confirmed this assessment, Brennos turned and walked back towards the camp, leaving George to yank the dagger out of the silver birch. The sun was just dropping below the horizon, and he watched it until it disappeared from sight, the warm glow inside him matching the orange glow in the sky.

"Thank you", he whispered into the night air, and turned to follow his mentor.

It had been four days since George had caught his first ever glimpse of the sea. He had marvelled at the vastness of it then, a body of water that stretched unbroken to the horizon. But now, standing by the quayside in Portus Dubris[1], looking out across the dark blue expanse, towards the distant shore of Gaul, it made him feel somehow small and insignificant. He had heard tales of the sea ever since he was a young boy, but he had never thought that one day he would be crossing it, bound for distant lands.

"It's so wide!" he exclaimed, almost to himself.

"Wait till you see the Mare Internum[2]", laughed Justus. "This is a mere stream by comparison."

George's eyes opened still wider. "There is a greater sea than this?" he asked incredulously.

"It will take us a matter of hours to cross the Mare Britannicum[3]", explained Justus, gesturing towards the water lapping rhythmically against the stone quay. "To travel from one end of the Mare Internum to the other will take us more than a month!"

George stared out across the deep blue expanse, suddenly feeling apprehensive. Until a couple of months ago, his world had ended at Cambodunum; now his little world was about to get a whole lot bigger. He glanced across at the boat that was soon to broaden his horizons: a Roman merchant ship with one huge square sail fixed to a central mast, and a smaller sail set forward in, what Brennos referred to as, the bows. In the aft quarter, two huge

---

[1] Dover
[2] Mediterranean Sea
[3] English Channel

steering oars reached from either side of the high stern, down into the dark water below. It was certainly an impressive vessel, large enough to transport the whole caravan in one trip, but when compared with the Mare Britannicum, it was just a small stick in a wide river.

"That's the lot", called Justus, as Juba and Brennos carried the last few pots up the gangplank and onto the ship. "We might as well get on board."

George followed the merchant uneasily, not used to walking on things that moved up and down. He stepped unsteadily into the boat, and immediately tripped over a coil of rope, only just managing to right himself by grabbing the arm of a portly sailor. The sailor spun round and spat an angry tirade at him, which fortunately, due to the thickness of the man's accent, George caught very little of.

Muttering a hasty apology, the young Briton turned and gingerly made his way along the deck, head down so as to avoid eye contact with anyone who might have seen this embarrassing event, and also so that he could check for further stray coils of rope. In this way, he soon arrived in the bows of the boat, where he found Hector leaning out, staring reverently at the bronze figurehead on the prow of the ship, and mouthing silent words.

Slightly surprised at his friend's behaviour, George watched the eccentric Gaul until, a short while later, he stepped down from this precarious position and, finally, noticed that he was not alone.

"The twin gods: Castor and Pollux", he said, pointing back at the figurehead.

If Hector thought that by this he would remove the puzzled expression from his companion's face, he was mistaken. If anything, George looked more bewildered now than he had before.

The Gaul tried again. "Castor and Pollux: sons of Jupiter, or rather, sons of Queen Leda. Castor was actually the son of King Tyndareus, whereas his brother was the result of the union of Leda with Jupiter, who was disguised as a swan, and Leda gave birth to an egg, from which sprang the twins."

George tried to comprehend the meaning of Hector's words. He felt sure that his friend was genuinely attempting to make sense, but he was failing spectacularly.

"He's not been kissing statues again, has he?"

Brennos now joined them, with Juba in close attendance.

"I have been praying to the twin gods, patrons of sailors", replied Hector, indignantly. "It is dangerous to voyage across Neptune's kingdom without their protection."

"It's dangerous to kiss statues", countered Brennos. "You lean out to plant a smacker on the bronze figurehead, overbalance, and, next thing you know, you're swimming with the fishes!"

George and Juba laughed at this, while Hector turned a nasty shade of purple. But, thankfully, before he could vent his feelings, there was a loud shout of command, and the ship's crew began hurrying to and fro, untying knots and throwing ropes.

"What did he say?" enquired George, nervously staring at the portly sailor with whom he had collided earlier, disconcerted to find that the man was, in fact, the captain.

"Cast off", translated Brennos.

"That's all?" replied George, puzzled. "I'm sure he said more than that!"

"Look lively you bilge rats, cast off you land-lubbers", revised Brennos. "I used to be a sailor", he added. "They have a language all there own."

"What's a land-lubber?" George wanted to know.

Without warning, the boat jerked forward and the young Briton, caught by surprise, tumbled backwards.

"You are", grunted Hector, grabbing a handful of George's tunic, and thus preventing him from an untimely meeting with the deck.

George clasped the side of the ship as it pitched up and down; he couldn't get the hang of 'rolling with the boat', as Brennos had put it. The others weren't having the same problems; they seemed to be able to walk around on the undulating deck, quite happily, without the need to hold on to anything.

As he clung to the side of the boat, George turned his head in the direction of the stern. Through the gap beneath the bottom of the billowing sails, and the heads of those on deck, he could see the white cliffs of Portus Dubris, already starting to grow smaller. His stomach was beginning to feel a little queasy. Turning around once more, he faced the direction they were sailing in; the shores of Gaul still seemed a long way off.

"Are you all right, George?" asked Juba in concerned tones.

George was far from all right. Every time the ship rose on the crest of a wave, his stomach seemed to drop inside him, and when the prow dipped moments later, it felt like it was shooting up towards his mouth.

"I used to get the seasickness too", sympathised Hector. "I find that eating an apple, a green one mind you, not the red ones, cures the problem."

"Have you got one?" gasped George, desperately. He didn't know how much more of this constant rising and falling he could stand.

"I'm afraid not", replied the Gaul, unhelpfully. "I don't get the seasickness anymore."

"I'll see if I can find one for you", offered Juba, obligingly.

While the African went in search of a green apple, George tried to take his mind off the churning of his stomach, by listening to his friends' continued discussion on the dangers of sea voyages, and the merits, or otherwise, of divine assistance.

"I heard an old sailor tell of how his ship had encountered a sea serpent", Hector was saying. "It stove in the starboard bow with one blow of its mighty tail, and picked several men from the wreckage with its huge jaws, before Neptune, himself, arose from the water, bearing his mighty trident, and summoned the monster back to the deep."

Brennos snorted. "It sounds like he'd encountered an amphora of strong wine! I was at sea for more than eight months of the year, for three years, on various ships, before I joined Justus; I've sailed from one end of the Mare Internum to the other, and I've never seen a sea serpent. The greatest danger you can face at sea is bad weather", he insisted knowledgeably. "I was once serving on a Spanish galley that was overtaken by a storm, en route to Carthage. We were blown ahead of it for ten days and nights, without any respite, and hardly any sleep! The sails were torn to shreds, the main mast was snapped in two; we lost a couple of men overboard. We ended up throwing most of the cargo over the side to keep the boat from shipping too much water! Eventually the storm broke, but it still took us nearly two days to row our battered vessel to the nearest port. We never made it to Carthage."

"Don't worry, George", reassured Hector, misinterpreting George's sickly pallor for anxiety. "There's no danger of a storm like that on the Mare Britannicum."

"There's pirates though", added Brennos enthusiastically. "Plenty of those in these waters. We'd be a nice prize for a band of cut-throats, with all the expensive merchandise we're carrying."

"Don't say that", chided Hector. "It's not wise to tempt the Fates."

"The Fates?" questioned Juba, arriving back at that moment with a large bag of green apples.

"The three goddesses who weave the threads of destiny that control our lives", answered Hector.

"Don't encourage him, Juba", interrupted Brennos. "Have you got enough apples there?"

"I had to buy in bulk", explained Juba. "They wouldn't sell me just one."

George gratefully accepted the proffered fruit, biting into it at once. He really didn't feel like eating anything, but if this was going to cure his sick stomach, it had to be done. He took another bite, chewing the apple slowly, willing the nausea to pass.

"Perhaps I should tell you the tale of Jason and the Golden Fleece", suggested Hector to George. "Maybe it will keep your mind off the seasickness."

"Please no!" exclaimed Brennos, butting in. "I've had enough mythology to last me a week! Give him an apple, Juba; it might shut him up for a bit."

His friends continued with their banter, but George no longer heard the words; he just stood clinging onto the side with his left hand, the half-eaten apple held loosely in his right, as the waves sloshed against the hull, and the prow dipped and then soared upwards, dropped down again and then rose swiftly once more. He closed his eyes, but, if anything, this only made it worse. Groaning, he lent forwards.

The background noise was growing louder; the friendly banter had turned into an argument. For a moment, Brennos's raised voice broke into George's world of continuous ups and downs.

"If you say one more word about mythology, I'll take Neptune's trident and ram it up your…"

George vomited violently over the side.

It was with great relief that George had set foot on Gallic soil. The voyage across the Mare Britannicum had not been the worst experience of his life, but it was up there! Now, two weeks later, he was adapting well to life in a new country. Gaul wasn't really that different to Britannia, except maybe a little warmer. The Gauls lived in Romanized towns, just like the Britons; they even spoke a similar language, and George found that he could understand quite a lot of what the locals were saying, even when they didn't use Latin.

One noticeable difference was that Gauls seemed less content with life than their British counterparts; Roman rule was faltering. The 'Gallic' empire that had broken away from Rome, less than a decade before, was becoming less and less stable. More and more troops were being sent to reinforce the northern borders, and rumours that Gothic tribes were breaking through and sacking Gallic towns abounded. Unlike in Britannia, most of the towns here in Gaul were unwalled, and this perceived vulnerability only served to fuel the anxiety and unrest.

Despite their general discontent with the authorities, the Gauls seemed to have been more influenced by Roman dress and customs than the Britons, however. Most people wore sandals and the long tunics, fashionable in Roman society, leaving their legs bare. Up to this point in his journeys, George had stubbornly stuck to his shorter tunics and breeches, worn among the men of his village (with the exception of Caradog) on the principle that he didn't want to "dress like a girl". But, following a particularly gruelling twenty-mile trek, through baking heat, to reach Paris, a town built on a river island, George finally took the plunge and purchased a light blue knee-length tunic and some sandals.

Dressed in his Roman outfit, George felt very self-conscious as he walked through the streets of Paris with the rest of the merchant caravan. He wasn't used to having bare legs; it made him feel almost naked, and he became increasingly worried when the wind started to get up as they crossed the second bridge, the one that linked the island with the far side of the river. It didn't help that Brennos and Hector insisted on wolf-whistling at his legs at regular intervals.

As the caravan made its way ponderously down the crowded streets, Justus gave his usual commentary. According to the knowledgeable Roman, the town had, at some point in the past, outgrown the heavily fortified island and spilled out onto the southern bank, where large buildings such as the baths, theatres and amphitheatre were now situated.

"That's the Lutetian arena", Hector added, pointing in the direction of a huge semi-circular structure, built into the hillside, some distance to their left. He was obviously keen to show that he knew as much about his home country as the Roman.

"Lutetian?" repeated George, puzzled.

"Lutetia was the old name for this town", explained Hector. "That's one of the largest amphitheatres in the whole of Gaul", he added impressively.

"Is that where they race chariots?" enquired George, who vaguely remembered hearing that this was a favourite sport of the Romans.

"No", replied Gaul and Roman in unison.

"Chariots are raced in circuses", explained Hector; "Long oval buildings. Amphitheatres are for gladiatorial games."

"Games are a poor title for what happens in those evil arenas", contended Justus bitterly. "Slaves are made to fight to the death to satisfy the crowd's bloodlust. Many Christians have been slaughtered too", he added, his voice wavering slightly.

"Why?" George asked, taken aback.

"Because Christianity is against everything that Rome stands for", replied Justus. "Rome seeks its own pleasure and wellbeing, Christ sought the good of others."

There was an awkward silence. George opened his mouth to ask another question, but it never came. Instead, his mouth opened wider and wider as he goggled in amazement at the procession heading their way. It was led by a huge creature, the like of which George could never have imagined, even in his wildest dreams. The beast had what looked like a thick grey snake protruding from its face, flanked by two huge curved horns. It had enormous flaps on the side of its head and, supporting its vast grey bulk, were four thick, tree-trunk legs. Perched about ten feet above the ground, was its rider, a dark-skinned, well-muscled man, who would have been at least as tall as George, but looked tiny next to his gigantic mount.

As the great grey creature plodded by, George's wide eyes followed it down the street until they were drawn to another strange sight. Behind the grey beast, came two oxen pulling a large wheeled cage that held a couple of enormous spotted cats. At least that's what they looked like to George, though they were so much bigger and sleeker and fiercer than any cat he'd ever seen that the description hardly fit.

Two more ox-drawn wagons completed the strange procession, each surrounded by wooden bars, no doubt to keep the vicious animals within from escaping. The floors of these cages were covered with straw, and at first, George couldn't make out what they contained. Then he noticed a golden coloured something lying among the yellow stalks of the penultimate wagon; it looked like thick wool. Was this the legendary Golden Fleece that Hector had mentioned? Then, as the last wagon passed in front of him, something stirred. A huge cat-like beast, larger even than the spotted felines in the first cage, moved to the bars, and George saw that the woolly stuff was not a fleece, but the creature's shaggy mane of hair.

The lordly animal let out a savage snarl, and George leapt backwards in surprise, stepping heavily on Hector's foot.

"YOU STUPID…" started the Gaul.

"Amigo", concluded Juba, neatly.

When the laughter had died down, George had a list of questions that he could not contain. He was soon informed that the huge grey creature was an elephant (the name seemed somehow familiar, but he couldn't think why); the giant spotted cats were leopards, and the enormous cat, with the shaggy mane, was a lion. And they were all being transported to the Lutetian arena to kill and die for the entertainment of the crowds.

"Do the animals ever escape?" asked George, looking nervously after the retreating wagons.

"When I was a boy, there were stories of escaped lions roaming the countryside around Massilia[1]", Hector informed them.

"I heard of an elephant that escaped from its captors on the way to the Flavian amphitheatre[2] in Rome", Justus added. "It rampaged through the streets, trampling several bystanders before they managed to corner and kill it."

"Is the elephant the biggest animal of all?" George wanted to know.

"There are larger creatures in the sea", replied Brennos, "Or so it is said. But there is nothing bigger on land."

Juba shook his head. "Back home in Africa, there are greater animals even than the elephant", he announced.

"Name one", snorted Brennos.

---

[1] Marseilles
[2] Colosseum

"Dragons", Juba continued, undaunted.

Brennos laughed derisively. Juba might have blushed but with his dark skin it was difficult to tell.

"What's a dragon?" asked George, interestedly.

"There are many different types", the African explained. "Some walk on four legs, some on two, some eat plants, some eat meat. They all have tough scaly hides and long powerful tails."

"And how big are they?" George asked.

"My grandfather once told me that he had seen a dragon feasting on an animal carcass; he insisted that the beast was at least twice as tall as a man and as long as three camels in a row!"

"And you believed him?" chuckled Brennos, obviously highly amused by this topic.

"My grandfather would not lie to me", replied Juba, sounding hurt.

"And how come your granddad has seen a dragon, when the rest of the civilised world believes them to be a myth?"

"There is a big chunk of Africa that is not part of what you call the 'civilised world'. My people, the Berbers, have travelled deep into Africa; they have seen sights that no white man ever has."

"Well", shrugged Brennos. "If this white man ever sees a dragon, he will eat his own loincloth!"

Chapter 13 - The Bulls of Hades

It was a beautiful September day in southern Gaul, and George ambled along happily, drinking in the sights and sounds of the pleasant river valley that they were passing through. For the first time since he had joined the caravan, Justus's wagon was at the head of the procession, giving George an unobstructed view of the lush green countryside.

The weather, of late, had grown unbearably hot, turning George's skin brown, and making him feel like a piece of meat sizzling over a campfire, but today a gentle breeze provided welcome relief from this scorching heat.

To his left, the peaceful sound of clear flowing water, to his right, the twittering of birds in the treetops. His surroundings were idyllic, yet George had a vague sense that something wasn't right. Of course, there was the growing threat of invasion - not a day seemed to go by without them encountering well-armed troops, all heading for the troubled northern border. *Yes, that must be it*, he decided.

Putting these disquieting thoughts from his mind, George returned to the marvellous views unfolding before him as they rounded a bend in the valley. Somewhere close behind him, Hector was rambling on about some girl he had met last night in Tolosa[1]. Recently, girls seemed to have overtaken mythology as the Gaul's favourite topic of conversation.

"I heard something strange last night", the Gaul was saying.

"Yes, sorry about that", interrupted Brennos. "I think it was those beans you put in the stew."

"Strange news", continued Hector, shaking his head at the Briton. "A lady of Tolosa told me that there were two fell beasts roaming this valley. She said they were known locally as the Bulls of Hades", he finished, his voice tailing off in a dreamy sort of way.

"What were they like?" asked George, turning to face the Gaul, his interest piqued.

"Soft, warm, sweet smelling…"

"The bulls!"

"Oh those", started Hector, aroused from his daydream.

---

[1] Toulouse

"Huge and red, with three horns, I think. I was a little distracted."

"More than a little, I'd say", interrupted Justus, who had been listening in from his vantage point up on the cart. "But I heard something similar from a local potter."

"I thought it was the three-headed hound of Hades, not the three-horned bull", snorted Brennos.

Hector shrugged. "Hades must be a big place; who knows what Pluto's got down there?"

"There are no bulls in Hades, only sinners who never made their peace with God", stated Justus, forcefully. "Still, there must be something behind this story. A few of the other merchants wanted to turn back, head towards Aginnum[1] and follow the road up through the mountains to Lugdunum[2] and then down to Massilia[3] that way. But if the Goths do invade, that will take us too close to the fighting for my liking, not to mention adding about three weeks to our journey!"

"We can't afford to lose that much time!" exclaimed Hector. "It'll be winter before we sail for Africa!"

"We won't make it to Africa", voiced Brennos. "No one will risk a sea voyage that late in the year."

"Exactly", agreed Justus. "And besides", he added, winking mischievously at George, "We'd miss out on these giant three-horned bulls; where's the fun in that?"

"Is that why we're at the front of the caravan and some of the carts in the rear are lagging behind?" enquired Brennos, looking back over his shoulder.

Before the Roman could reply to this, there came a sudden wild cry and, looking up, George saw a lone rider on the road ahead, galloping towards them at a great pace, rocking precariously from side to side, obviously struggling to control his horse. Immediately, Justus jumped down from the cart and began unhitching one of their own horses. The rider was rapidly closing on them, and his cries could now be easily discerned:

"Help! The Bulls! The Bulls!"

Wide-eyed with terror, long black hair whipping at his face, the hapless rider thundered past them. With a speed that belied his age, Justus wheeled around on the free horse and gave pursuit, his

---

[1] Agen
[2] Lyons
[3] Marseilles

chestnut mount eating up the ground between them. Justus rode hard and straight and, before the frenzied rider had passed the last cart in the caravan, the Roman had pulled along side, reaching across for the reins, supporting the other rider with his right shoulder. He had done it; the two horses were slowing now, coming to a stop.

Brennos turned to George. "Bring the wineskin", was all he said, and then he set off at a run in Justus's direction.

George obediently grabbed a wineskin from the cart and followed his mentor.

"It was the Bulls!" the dark-haired man ranted, as George arrived on the scene. "They trampled Tertius and Apollos, and I'm the only one left!"

George passed the wineskin to the man, who took it with trembling hands. He was shaking violently, and his unkempt appearance spoke silently of the horrors he had witnessed. Finally managing to uncork the skin, he drank deeply from it. As the stranger stood gulping down the fortifying beverage, a crowd began to form. The whole caravan had come to a halt! Everyone was eager to find out what this commotion was all about. Realising that he had an audience, the wild-eyed man stopped drinking and looked about him.

"Don't go that way!" he implored them, pointing back down the road in the direction from which he had come. "It leads to Hades, and you won't escape, any of you!"

They could get nothing more from him and, after taking another swig from the wineskin, the desperate stranger remounted his horse and galloped away. The bewildered crowd stared after him as the rider sped on his way, diminishing in size until he rounded a bend and vanished altogether. Ignoring the mutterings of the other merchants, Justus mounted his own horse and, motioning for Brennos and George to follow him, rode it back to the head of the column and hitched it up, once more, to his wagon.

The caravan rumbled on through the valley as it had before, but now something was different; there was tension in the air. An eerie silence seemed to have descended over them; no one was speaking; even the birds had stopped singing. The horses' hooves echoed loudly in the quiet surroundings and, up ahead, dark clouds were gathering. Everyone, merchants and servants alike, stared down the long straight road apprehensively. They were about to reach a point where the narrow valley opened out. If there was anything to see, they would come upon it all too soon.

With every step he took, George could see more and more of the land ahead. His heart began to beat faster, his breathing quickened. So far all he could see were grass and trees.

"Bulls of Hades!" exclaimed Hector, fear in his voice.

George gave a yelp of surprise and followed the Gaul's pointing finger. There they were: two huge horned beasts, some distance to the right of the road. Wild cries from behind told him that the following group had also seen what they had. There was a loud whinny from one of the horses.

"Easy", spoke Justus, in a voice of forced calm, patting the creature on its haunches.

One of the Bulls moved lazily towards them. It was a dirty orange colour and had two spear-like horns protruding menacingly from above its tiny red eyes. The third horn was shorter and thicker and situated on the creature's nose. The huge head was made even more imposing by a large bony shield that surrounded it, protecting the beast's thick neck. As it lumbered forwards, George gawped at it with a mixture of terror and amazement. The monster was roughly the size of their horses and cart put together, but almost certainly a great deal heavier!

"What do we do, master?" Juba sounded scared, and with good reason.

"We keep going and don't alarm them", whispered Justus, patting the horses as they neighed uneasily.

"Don't alarm them?" exclaimed Hector in a loud whisper. "What about us?"

"Quiet", warned Brennos, putting his finger to his lips. There were no sarcastic remarks now.

The other Bull wandered over to its mate. The great beasts stood glaring at the tiny humans who had dared to invade their territory. The first Bull snorted angrily; the bony frill around its neck was changing colour, growing darker. Soon it was no longer a dirty orange but a bright red. It was easy to see why those who had seen these monsters had described them as supernatural; there was something about them that seemed not of this world. The huge monster pawed the ground, there was a loud shout from somewhere behind, and suddenly the Bull charged.

The ground shook as the enormous creature bounded towards them. Justus's cart shot forwards, out of the monster's path, as the horses bolted. Cries of terror erupted from the following group, who had unwittingly become the new targets of the Bull's wrath, and moments later the monster collided with their wagon. There was a horrible splintering sound, a loud whinnying, and the heavy cart was overturned, scattering necklaces and brooches all over the road. George watched in horror as the angry Bull shook itself free of the wreckage and turned to view Justus's retreating wagon.

"JAVELINS", shouted Brennos, chasing after the cart.

Justus was desperately trying to get the horses under control. The wagon veered to the left, rumbled through the drainage ditch, at the side of the road, and headed across the grass, in the general direction of the river. George raced after his mentor, in hot pursuit of the runaway cart. Ahead, it lurched right, back towards the road. Behind, everything was confusion; George heard another splintering, crunching sound but didn't look back. The valley rang with the angry snorts of the Bulls and the wild cries of the men under attack.

Brennos reached the wagon first with George just behind him. Justus had managed to bring the horses to a stop, but now the cart was stuck: one wheel lodged against a large rock and another jammed in the roadside ditch. *It's a sitting target!*

"Help me get them unhitched", grunted the Roman, jumping off the cart and landing heavily in the grass.

The horses wouldn't keep still. Hector and Juba had joined them now, and the Gaul climbed onto the wagon, pulling out a bundle of javelins from inside the hide covering.

As soon as the first horse was free, Justus swung himself onto its back, grabbed a javelin from Hector, and headed for the fray. Brennos mounted the second horse, which immediately reared up on its hind legs. George jumped backwards to avoid the frenzied steed, but a moment later his mentor had got the animal under control and, spear in hand, galloped after Justus.

George stood and stared, uncertain of what to do. The two great beasts were charging about, clearly maddened by all the noise and panic. Besides Justus and Brennos, there were another couple of men on horseback also carrying javelins. George watched as one of the iron-tipped weapons clattered into the shield of bone that surrounded the huge three-horned head of the nearer Bull. The projectile just bounced off and landed on the ground, its wooden shaft snapped in two. *We're in trouble!*

There was a thunderous bellow; another javelin had struck the Bull, this time in the right flank. This one stuck fast, but far from felling the gargantuan, it just seemed to enrage it further. The beast charged again. George saw Justus's horse rear up, and watched in horror as, with a cry, his master tumbled backwards and crashed to the ground. The earth shook as the Bull rumbled past the spot where the Roman lay, unmoving in the short grass.

George let out a gasp; his master was about to be trampled to death, and he was standing there looking on helplessly! The young Briton hesitated; he had to do something. His brain had shut down, but his legs seemed to bypass this obstacle and started moving forwards on their own. Between him and the prone form of his master were two gigantic charging monsters and three spear-wielding horsemen, but George was going to reach Justus or die trying!

Entering the fray, George was forced to swerve almost immediately to avoid one of the galloping horses. The ground shook as one of the Bulls peeled off to the left, in hot pursuit of the rider, passing within a few feet of the startled Briton. The other charged off to his right, heading towards the abandoned wagons. Taking advantage of this opportunity, George raced through the middle of the battleground, stopping to avoid a second rider, before sprinting the remaining distance to his master.

At first he thought the Roman was dead, but then he saw his chest rise slightly; he was still breathing. George heaved him into a sitting position.

"Come on Justus!" he grunted in desperation. There was no reply.

George hauled the unconscious body upwards with all his might. Stumbling backwards, with the effort, he almost dropped him, just recovering his footing in time. He heaved again, this time managing to get the comatose Roman onto his knees.

"Come on Justus!"

There was another angry bellow, and George looked up in alarm. One of the Bulls of Hades was staring straight at him, pawing the ground with a huge forefoot as it gave an intimidating snort. The bony frill around its head was flushed a deep red, mirroring its mood. A javelin protruded from the great beast's back, goading the creature still further. With a superhuman effort, George hauled Justus onto his feet and held him there, both arms around the Roman's chest. What was he going to do if the beast charged? *Leave Justus to die or die with him? What a choice!*

George was suddenly conscious of the noise of hooves; a horse was galloping nearby.

"GEORGE". It was Brennos. "LIFT HIM ONTO MY HORSE."

Brennos leaned over the side of his mount, right arm outstretched, left arm grasping the reins. George's knees started to buckle; the ground was shaking again. The Bull was charging!

"NOW!" screamed Brennos, above the thundering of giant footfalls.

George dragged the dead weight of Justus's body and heaved it upwards. The Roman groaned; he was coming to. The snorting grew louder; the ground shook more violently. *Get out of there! It's over; you can't save him!*

Gritting his teeth to block out the voice that screamed in his head, George hefted Justus off the ground and then felt him being yanked from his grasp; Brennos had got him. The noise of the charging beast had reached a crescendo; there was a sudden rush of air as the great Bull bore down on him. With a cry, George let go of his master and dived to his right.

The rampaging Bull surged past, missing him by a hair's breadth. George looked up, from the patch of grass he'd landed on, in time to see Justus dangling from Brennos's horse; he was safe, at least for the moment. Scrambling to his feet, George glanced around him; there was nothing safe about his position. The Bull was turning, its huge squat tail swinging behind it. It faced him again, snorting its displeasure. George drew his sword from its sheath, holding it out in front of him. The Bull charged again.

George stood rooted to the spot as the gigantic creature thundered towards him. His sword suddenly seemed very short and flimsy, as the great beast loomed large. *You'll be impaled on those horns before your sword even reaches the beast!*

At the last moment, George hurled his weapon at the oncoming monster and dived sideways once more. There was a clanging sound as his sword struck the great bony skull, and once more the Bull swept past, narrowly missing him. George struggled to his feet once again, clutching the old injury on his left shoulder after having landed awkwardly. He had to get out of there fast!

George sprinted for the comparative safety of the line of immobilised wagons, narrowly avoiding a spear-wielding horseman heading in the opposite direction. He could see the Bull with the javelin protruding from its flank; the beast was charging after a rider some distance to his right. But where was the other Bull? George kept running, his breath coming in painful gasps; he was nearly there. Ahead of him, scared faces were peering out from behind the line of wagons that were being used as a barricade against the giant Bulls.

Someone shouted a warning; George felt the ground moving under him. The other Bull was on him! Summoning everything he had left, the Briton sprinted for the nearest gap in the line of wagons. He could almost feel the hot breath of the beast on the back of his neck as it snorted loudly; almost feel the sharp horn that must plunge into his back at any moment.

A javelin, aimed at the pursuing monster, flew over his head as he reached the gap and flung himself through it. Behind him, there was a bellow of rage and a loud crunch followed by an ominous creaking. George turned, pulling himself painfully from the ground. The wagon immediately behind him was toppling. Desperately, he leapt forward, collapsing on the grass as the covered cart came crashing down on the patch of ground that he had just vacated.

In the space left by the ruined wagon, there loomed the enormous Bull. It now had three spears sticking from its sturdy hide, but showed no sign of slowing. Advancing purposefully, it trampled what remained of the wagon under its huge clawed feet. George scrambled to his feet once again, urging his tired limbs on. But the beast was too fast; he wasn't going to make it! Exhausted, George tripped on a stone and fell forwards, arms outstretched. The ground shook, the snorting was deafening; he had nothing left.

Suddenly the air was filled with a hideous bellowing. George turned his head in time to see Brennos, on horseback, veering away from the huge creature, his javelin deeply embedded in the beast's neck. The great Bull stumbled, swaying sideways, and fell, letting out a long low moan as it crashed heavily to the ground. The red colour slowly drained from its bony frill as life slipped away from the monster. The moan was answered by a mournful bellow from the other Bull. This beast had stopped charging and was moving slowly away from its tormentors, all the fight driven from it.

George got wearily to his feet. He could see Hector moving out from behind one of the wagons to meet him. The enthusiastic Gaul flung his arms around him and kissed him on both cheeks.

"You're a hero, you crazy Briton!" he exclaimed.

Brennos dismounted and came over to them.

"And you did okay too", continued Hector, reaching out to hug Brennos.

Brennos held him at arm's length. "I've made it a rule", he stated, "Never to let myself be kissed by anyone less attractive than my own mother."

Hector snorted. "I don't think you can afford to be so fussy."

At that moment they were joined by Juba, leading a slightly dazed looking Justus.

"Did I just see you slay one of the Bulls of Hades?" asked the African, grinning broadly.

"A divine beast", replied Brennos, holding his arms aloft in triumph. "Hercules himself would have been proud of such a feat!"

"One of those javelins was mine", grumbled Hector, wanting some of the credit.

"But the killing blow was undoubtedly mine", added Brennos. "Heroic Brennos, the mighty Bull slayer!"

"You're both heroes in my book", praised Juba. "And so is George, for saving Justus's life."

"He's more than that", interrupted Justus, colour rapidly returning to his pale face. "He's a hero of the faith – a saint!"

"Saint George", repeated George to himself. "That has a nice ring to it."

Chapter 14 – A Land of Mysteries

The eight teams of horses galloped down the back straight, pulling their chariots behind them. The drivers furiously jostled for position as they neared the bend. Fifty thousand pairs of eyes strained towards the turning post, the stone tower that marked one end of the spina (the circuit's central barrier), eager to see who would turn first.

The White team's chariot appeared first, having taken a tight inside line around the bend. Immediately behind him came the lead Blue charioteer, urging his four magnificent black horses on with frantic cracks of the whip. Next came the two drivers for the Red team, side by side, their horses eating up the ground between them and the leaders. High above the competitors, the last of the seven ornate dolphin markers fell, signifying the final lap of the race.

The thunder of the horses' hooves on the sand of the circus track could no longer be heard, drowned out by the baying of the crowd. One of the Red chariots pulled alongside the Blue team, the furiously spinning wheels dangerously close to colliding. The Blue driver tried to fend him off, pulling out as they approached the far turn, forcing Red wide. As he did so, the other Red driver sneaked up on the inside, squeezing his chariot between Blue's and the spina wall. Suddenly, realising his danger, Blue attempted to close the door on this new challenge, but he was too late; the all-important inside line had been stolen from him, and they had reached the far turning post.

As the three chariots rounded the bend, a huge roar went up from the crowd; the Blue chariot and the outside Red chariot had collided. It was a mess! The two teams of horses had become entangled, two of the animals were down, one of the chariots had overturned, and the driver was in grave danger of being trampled by his own horses.

Seemingly unconcerned by the mayhem he had just created, the remaining Red team driver raced down the back straight, his horses in full flight. "PRIMUS, PRIMUS", chanted the Red section of the crowd, as their man bore down on the leader. "TALUS, TALUS", responded the White support, defiantly.

Talus's horses were tiring now, Primus had nearly caught him, but there was only one more bend to go. Had Primus left his charge too late? The wall of noise built towards a crescendo as

Primus's horses pulled level. The two chariots were so close that the drivers could have reached out and touched one another. They were approaching the turning post; could Talus hold on?

The crowd erupted as the inside chariot hit the central barrier and flipped! Talus, entangled in his reins, was being dragged along the track by his four horses, which continued to gallop at full speed!

Primus rounded the final turn and raced to the line, his supporters going delirious with delight. Everywhere George looked, fans were jumping up and down or hugging one another. Even Brennos, who rarely got excited about anything, was applauding and cheering enthusiastically.

"I told you Primus was good!" shouted Justus, above the noise of the crowd, grabbing George's shoulders and shaking him in his excitement at the outcome of the race. "I've seen him win many times at the circus in Cyrene[1]."

Justus had told George that "Primus was good", several times. He had been enthusing about the charioteer from the moment they arrived in Leptis Magna and discovered that he would be competing here today, at the calends of November (Calends was a Roman term for the first day of the month). George now knew that the twenty year-old Roman, Marcus Leonius Primus, owned a villa in the town of Cyrene, only a short distance from Justus's home in Silene; that he was the best charioteer in the entire province of Cyrenaica (at least according to Justus), and that he had raced for two years with the Cyrenaican Reds, during which time he had already amassed sixty wins – sixty-one now. How Justus knew all these things, given that he had spent the last eight months travelling the world, George could not fathom; he supposed the acquisition of pointless information must be a curse of old age. *And the curse of youth is listening to it!*

George, now free of Justus's joyous embrace, surveyed the scene down on the track below. At the finish line, Primus had dismounted from his chariot and was being presented with his prizes: a laurel wreath and a palm branch. As the wreath was placed upon his brow, the victorious charioteer raised the branch aloft and received the adulation of the crowd once more.

Turning his head, George peered over towards the final bend where, unnoticed by most of the crowd, a battered and broken Talus

---

[1] Shahhat

was being loaded onto a wooden stretcher. Moments ago, thousands had been chanting his name, now no one seemed to care whether he lived or died: it was a cruel sport. George continued to watch as the stretcher-bearers carried Talus from the arena.

"I'm just going down to see if I can get a word with Primus", said Justus, excitedly. "Round up Hector and meet me at gate three, will you?"

George looked around, roused from his melancholy contemplations. "Where is Hector anyway?"

"I don't know", replied Brennos, "But when I catch up with him, he'll be fifteen denarii poorer; I'm up by five races!"

"Does Justus know you've been betting?" enquired George, knowing the answer already.

"I thought we'd left Juba looking after the cart", came the reply. "I could have sworn I'd just heard his voice."

"Here's Hector", interrupted George, as the Gaul emerged from the crowd.

"You haven't seen me", stated Hector in a loud whisper, as he reached them, pushed past, and disappeared into a group of men further along the row.

George looked up inquisitively at his mentor, eyebrows raised, but before he could say anything, a gruff voice interjected.

"Which way did that red-haired barbarian go?"

Startled, George turned to see a large, thick-set, Roman with a red face and an expression like thunder. Two even larger men, who appeared to be his bodyguards, flanked the angry individual.

George, unsure of what to do, looked to his mentor for help.

"Are you referring to a runty Gaul with a moustache?" asked Brennos, casually.

"Yes", replied the red-faced Roman, belligerently, "He was flirting with my fiancée!"

"Unbelievable!" replied the Briton, affecting a shocked voice. "I caught him meddling with my sister during the third race."

"Where did he go?" The irate man's face was growing redder by the moment.

"I haven't seen him since then", lied Brennos. "He ran away before I could give him the beating he deserved. But if I do catch him, he'll have to do all his flirting in the doctor's surgery", reassured the Briton, feigning anger.

Convinced by this show of outrage, the Roman grunted something to his bodyguards and moved off.

Brennos waited till the posse had moved out of earshot and then shouted along the row: "You can come out now, Hector."

Hector emerged a few moments later, looking slightly more crumpled than normal.

"Cheers, Brennos, you saved my life; I owe you."

"That's right", replied Brennos, a smug look on his face. "Fifteen denarii for the races plus whatever your life's worth: better make it twenty."

George stood in the bows of the Alexandrian ship, surveying the Cyrenaican coastline for signs of their destination. He had come a long way since his first, unhappy, voyage to Gaul. He no longer needed to cling onto the side, while fighting to keep his breakfast down. George was gently swaying with the motion of the ship, as it cut through the clear blue water, and his stomach felt fine. He could happily go through the rest of his life without seeing another green apple, but at least his experiences of life at sea were more comfortable these days.

"Over there!" exclaimed Juba, pointing enthusiastically. "Apollonia.[1]"

George stared in the direction that his dark-skinned friend was indicating. Along the rugged coastline, a little rocky bay had just come into view, with a wooden jetty projecting into the water. Further inland, various buildings could now be discerned, partially hidden by trees. Houses, built into the hillside, overlooked the bay, peeking out from between the greenery at various levels, giving the impression that the town had been constructed on a set of giant steps: it was a beautiful setting.

The Alexandrian ship was towed into the port by two small oared vessels, and then it was time to disembark.

"This port will be shutting down for winter soon", remarked Justus. "The weather conditions, at this time of year, make travel by sea too dangerous. This ship will carry on to Alexandria and then winter there."

"Is that it then?" enquired George. "Is that our last voyage?"

---

[1] Sousa

"No", laughed the Roman, "I'm a merchant; I'm not going to sell my wares sitting in Cyrenaica. But don't worry, George, there'll be no more sailing until the end of February."

The year had been a decent one for Justus: the stock that had required a large covered wagon to transport across Britannia and Gaul, had now dwindled to such a low level that the Roman only needed to hire one donkey to carry it all.

Justus and his travelling family (as the Roman often referred to them) refreshed themselves with an early lunch of bread and fish, in a shaded grove, before they set out up the steep road that led to the larger town of Cyrene. The sun was shining, there wasn't a cloud in the sky, and the temperature was just right: not too hot and not too cold. George imagined what the weather would have been like if they had been taking this walk back in Britannia: probably cold, wet and miserable. As they climbed the hill, he turned his head to drink in the scenery. Behind him, the sea pounded endlessly against the rocky coastline; ahead, the hills stretched to the horizon, dotted about with small, dark green, many-branched trees, along with a scattering of taller, thinner trees that were also dark green in colour.

"The smaller ones are mastic trees", explained Justus, "And the others are junipers. You can see why I wanted to live here, can't you?" he added. "I once thought that all Africa was dry and barren, and then I came to Cyrenaica and fell in love."

"My people say that there is a hole in the sky over this part of the country", said Juba, in a dreamy sort of voice. "That's why the rain gets through here and makes everything green."

The afternoon sun shone down on the little group, as they climbed towards the plateau, on which stood the impressive town of Cyrene. The hillside below the town was honeycombed with dark openings into the rock, and George was curious to know what they were.

"That's the Necropolis", began Justus.

"The city of the dead", translated Brennos.

George wished he hadn't asked. In his mind, he slipped back to the worst day of his life, as he stood in the pouring rain, staring at the dark opening, which had swallowed up his friend. He closed his eyes, shaking his head to clear the memory.

"You have no need to fear the dead, George", reassured Juba, laying a hand on his shoulder.

"Those caves are just full of empty shells", agreed Justus. "Their human spirits have left this world."

"And, as a Christian, you have no need to fear the afterlife", added the African.

"The caves you need to fear are deeper within the Green Mountains", said Hector, his voice low and mysterious, "Lest you become food for the trolls."

"Trolls?" enquired George, relieved that the subject had changed. "What are they?"

"They are giants, descended from the Titans of old, but cursed by the gods to live in darkness. They hide from the sunlight during the day, and then leave their caves, at night, to hunt for meat, preying on unwary travellers."

George looked doubtfully at the Gaul, and turned to Brennos, expecting a sneer or a derisive comment. To his surprise, the Briton nodded his agreement at Hector's outrageous story.

"He's right, if you give him the usual poetic license with his mythology", qualified Brennos. "I've seen them."

"What were they like?" asked George, fascinated.

"Huge figures, hunched and misshapen."

"How huge?" George wanted to know.

"I was some distance from them, and it was dusk, but I reckon… about… seven, maybe eight feet tall."

"Come on boys, we need to pick up the pace", interrupted Justus. "Silene is three miles beyond Cyrene, and I don't want to be walking the last mile in the dark."

Four men, and one donkey, climbed steadily up to the gates of Cyrene. The heat of midday had subsided, the autumn sun had been joined by a number of grey clouds, and a chill breeze blew on their backs, hastening them into the town.

Cyrene was a fairly large settlement but, even so, it seemed to have a disproportionate amount of temples within it. Everywhere George looked he saw impressive stone pillars and beautifully carved statues of the many gods or goddesses. The buildings ranged in size from small shrines of minor deities, to the huge temple of Jupiter, on the eastern outskirts, which could be seen towering over the surrounding structures.

As Justus led the way into the forum, George noticed some commotion in the marketplace. A dark-skinned man, dressed only in a loincloth, and with a bronze disk fastened to a chain around his neck, was running in their direction, a look of fear on his face.

"STOP HIM!" someone shouted, from across the square.

"No", countermanded Justus, as Brennos moved to intercept the man.

The bare-chested fugitive sprinted past them without a word. A few moments later, two well-dressed men, both a little stout, hurried after him, cursing loudly.

Justus ignored them and, quickening his pace across the market square, he exited the forum, leaving the others trailing in his wake.

"What was that all about?" George wanted to know, as he struggled to keep up with the speeding Roman.

"That poor man was being sold as a slave", explained Juba. "The bronze disk around his neck was engraved with the name of his master."

"Does the Roman Empire allow slavery?" George asked, surprised. He had heard of people being sold as slaves, but had assumed that this only happened in barbaric countries, far away from the civilised world.

"The Roman Empire encourages slavery", replied Juba, a trace of bitterness in his voice that George had never heard before. "I was taken from my people and sold as a slave."

George was shocked; he had always considered Juba his equal, a paid worker just like himself. He couldn't believe that the kind Roman, who had given him so much, would own a slave.

"I'm not a slave any more", continued Juba, seeing the confused look on George's face. "There's no bronze disk around my neck; I get paid the same as you do."

"More, if there's any justice", interjected Brennos.

"Justus bought me in the slave market, and then set me free", the African continued.

George had just thought of something. "So why do you still call him master?"

"Should I have less respect for him now that he has set me free?" asked Juba, rhetorically, his voice becoming high pitched, as it always did when he was in earnest about anything.

They had reached the western edge of the town by now, where a number of grand looking Roman villas stood. Justus slowed his pace slightly so that Hector, who was struggling with the donkey, could catch up, and then pointed to the nearest one.

"That's where the church of Cyrene meets", he said.

"I thought those buildings were all houses", replied George, a little puzzled.

"They are", agreed Justus. "That is Simon's home, but it is also the home of the church."

George wondered why, in a town so full of temples, Christians had no special place to worship their God.

"Ironic isn't it?" mused Justus, as if reading George's mind. "The gods of stone, superstition and man's wild fancies, have ornate temples, but the God who holds all our destinies in his hand, isn't welcome here."

The journey from Cyrene to Silene began pleasantly; the cobbled road ran along the top of the plateau, and the view from there down to the sea was spectacular. Overhead, though, the clouds darkened and, presently, the companions were treated to some squally rain.

"Remind you of home, George?" laughed Justus, as George struggled to retrieve his travelling cloak from his pack.

The shower didn't last long though: after about half a mile, the rain had stopped and the sun was out again. Stowing his cloak away in his pack, George continued to drink in these new surroundings; it was just beginning to register with him that this was going to be his new home. After travelling for so long, it was going to seem strange to live in one fixed place again; he had got used to life on the road, and he wasn't sure what life in Silene was going to be like.

George soon got his first glimpse of Silene: the village was a peaceful country retreat, little more than a collection of Roman villas, each one with its own plot of land; away from the hustle and bustle of town life, but close enough so that the market, baths, theatre and circus of Cyrene were easily accessible.

As they neared the gates of Justus's villa, George spied two figures approaching them from the house: one was a girl, younger than he, with shoulder length black hair, wearing a long white tunic that reached down to her knees. The other was an attractive middle-aged woman with long brown hair, clothed in what George recognised as a stola, a long overdress, over which she had draped a deep blue shawl.

On seeing them, Justus burst into a run and, with a happy shout of greeting, embraced them both in a huge bear-hug. The others entered at a more leisurely pace, unwilling to intrude on this joyous family reunion.

George stared at his new home; it was in stark contrast to his one previous dwelling. The property was protected by high stone walls, the gate they had entered by was the only way in or out; lining the walls on either side were various outbuildings, one of which seemed to contain hens, judging by the clucking sounds emanating from it. Midway between the gates and the house itself, were four small trees, each loaded with strange little purple fruit, oval in shape, which, like a lot of things George had seen on his travels, were unfamiliar to him. Between the trees and the archway that led into the house, was what looked like a small vegetable garden.

George was staring at the sloping tiled roof of the villa, and marvelling at the size of the whole property, when he felt Justus's hand on his shoulder.

"George, let me introduce you to the two women in my life."

George turned to face the two smiling figures.

"My wife, Julia, and my daughter, Cassia. And this, ladies", he continued, turning to look at George, "This is George, the newest member of my travelling family. And one who rescued me from the Bulls of Hades", he finished impressively.

George blushed and mumbled a greeting, which Julia and Cassia wholeheartedly returned.

"You've not been putting yourself in danger, I hope", chided Julia.

"I'll tell you all about it later", replied Justus, winking at George. "It's an excellent story."

"Can I show him the fire drakes, mummy?" asked Cassia, smiling up at George, and turning pleading eyes towards Julia.

Julia looked up at the sky, frowning. "It's not long till dusk, dear."

"Please, they're nesting really close."

"I bet they are", cut in Justus. "They'll be after the hens."

"Please, daddy", persisted Cassia, turning her pleading brown eyes on her father.

"All right", conceded Justus. "But tomorrow I want them chased away; I'm not raising hens just to feed a bunch of drakes!"

Cassia led the way, an excited spring in her step; George followed, intrigued as to what a fire drake might be. Brennos was busy unloading the donkey, but Juba and Hector took the opportunity to walk with them.

Cassia marched quickly across the fields that were attached to the villa. At the edge of the last piece of cultivated ground, they came to a dip and a steep banking that ran down and then up again at the far side. With a whoop of excitement, Cassia charged down the bank and up the slope. The others followed more sedately, although George was tempted to let out a joyful noise himself; he was enjoying his new surroundings.

On the opposite side of the ditch, the country became wilder, dotted here and there with prickly shrubs and sprawling trees. At the foot of one tree that seemed to have two trunks, Cassia stopped and looked up. George followed her gaze, searching the twisted mass of leaf-covered branches for some sign of their quarry.

"There", she whispered, pointing to the topmost branches.

George craned his neck back, straining to see what she could. He didn't have to struggle for long, though, because, presently, a bright yellow creature glided down from the top of the tree and perched in a branch just above their heads, as if wanting to get a good look at the odd humans who were staring up at it.

The fire drake was like nothing that George had ever seen: it had membranous wings like a bat, a relatively small body with tiny legs, and a long thin tail that ended in a diamond-shaped tip. Its head was nearly as long as its body, with two large eyes and a long thin jaw, containing wickedly curved, needle-sharp, teeth.

George stared at this strange creature, transfixed. It stared back for a while, showing no fear of these large flightless two-legged animals that had disturbed it, and then it gracefully unfolded its wings, caught the gentle breeze, and soared away.

George watched it silently until it disappeared into the foliage of another tree some distance away, before turning to Cassia.

"Why is it called a fire drake? Can it breathe fire?"

Cassia giggled. "Of course not."

"It is the bright colours", explained Juba. "You see yellows and oranges, even reds occasionally."

"This kind are pretty harmless", added Hector, "Unless you're a hen. But if you're up in the mountains, you'd better watch out for thunder drakes."

"Thunder drakes?" George lifted his eyes up, following the range of aptly named 'Green Mountains' as it crossed the country from west to east, reaching down to the coastline beyond Apollonia.

"They are black as night and, when they take flight, their dark wings block out the sun", struck up Juba in a singsong voice. "The sky drums beat when their wing tips meet, and when they rest the storm is done."

"I like that!" exclaimed Cassia, enthusiastically.

"It is a song we used to sing as children", said Juba, wistfully.

"We had better be getting back", added the Berber. "The sun is sinking fast."

As they turned back towards Silene, Cassia put her soft warm hand on George's shoulder.

"What do you think of Cyrenaica, George?" she asked.

George looked down into her pretty brown eyes, and quickly turned away again, looking towards the setting sun, which had turned a deep orange. *What do I think of Cyrenaica? A land under a hole in the sky, where there are cities for the dead; a land of trolls and dragons and drakes...*

"George?"

"It's a land of mysteries", replied George, thoughtfully. "And I can't wait to explore them."

Chapter 15 - An Evil Lurks

Claudius's fine tunic emporium was closed for business. Inside, the shop was dark except for in one corner where a small olive oil lamp burned low, illuminating the garment on which the girl was working. It was late and she was tired, but this tunic was for one of the town magistrates and had to be finished by the morning.

Wearily, she examined the dyed purple threads that she had woven into the garment. All was in order; the slender bands of colour would leave an observer in no doubt as to the rank and office of the wearer. Now all that remained was to sew the front and back pieces together.

Outside, the wind howled ferociously. Thankful for the thick stone walls of the shop, that kept the winter elements at bay, she reached into her sewing box. Locating the needle, she threaded it expertly and began methodically stitching the two pieces of garment together.

It wasn't a bad living, she mused, continuing her sewing action almost subconsciously; Claudius was a good master. His wages were fair, if not extravagant, and it had been kind of him to let her have the room above the shop. It was true that he didn't need it, having a more than comfortable villa on the outskirts of the town, but his action had shown a good deal of faith in her. He had given her sole responsibility for his property, and if living on the premises meant that she occasionally had to work after everyone else had gone, she was happy to do it to repay that trust.

The young woman paused; she had heard something above the swirling of the wind. There it was again: a knocking sound; perhaps one of the shutters was loose. Rising from her seat, she picked up the oil lamp and made her way across the room.

Before she had walked three paces, there was another knock. This time there was no mistaking it: someone was banging on the door. *But who could it be at this time of night?*

Anxiety rising within, the girl fumbled with the key before turning it in the lock and cautiously edging the door open.

"Drusilla!" she exclaimed, recognising her friend and fellow seamstress in the lamplight. "What's the matter?"

"Oh Catalina", sobbed her windswept, and obviously distressed, friend. "I don't know who else to turn to."

Drusilla was swiftly ushered in out of the chill November night and the door firmly shut against the howling gale.

"Can I get you anything?"

"No… I… My father… He's gone!"

Drusilla broke down and began sobbing uncontrollably. Her friend put a consoling arm around her heaving shoulder.

"There, there, Drusilla. What do you mean gone? Where has he gone?"

"I'm s…sorry", sniffed the seamstress, pulling herself together with difficulty. "He's been out fishing down by the lake again. I told him not to, warned him that strange things have been happening around there, but he wouldn't listen, and now he's disappeared!" she finished with a great raking sob.

"Have you been over to the lake to see if you can find him?"

"I daren't. You know the stories that people are telling: they say the lake's cursed, that demons walk its shores at night!"

"That's superstitious nonsense! Some people should try speaking with their mouths instead of their backsides!"

"But, Catalina, what about that beast my father caught? I saw it with my own eyes!"

"The strange little creature, you told me about, with the pointed tail?"

"It was like nothing I've ever seen; it walked on two legs like a man!"

"I admit that is pretty strange", conceded Catalina, "But this world is full of strange and wonderful creatures; that is how God made it. And besides, you told me the little beast ate fish."

Her friend nodded.

"Demons don't eat fish; they are not of this world, they don't need physical food like we do."

Drusilla did not look entirely convinced by this argument, and anyway none of this was helping to locate her missing father.

"But, Catalina, what am I going to do?" she implored, helplessly.

There was only one thing for it. "We'll go and look for him together."

The biting wind whipped at the cloaks of the two women as they struggled over the brow of the hill. Below, concealed by the darkness, lay the mysterious lake that had lately been such a source of scare-mongering in the town. Holding their flickering lamps aloft, they began the descent. The body of water was surrounded on all sides by rolling hills and, as they drew nearer, this higher ground provided them with some relief from the relentless battering they had been subjected to.

"I d…don't l…like this", stated Drusilla unnecessarily, her teeth chattering in the bitter cold.

"Neither do I", agreed her friend, "But it'll be all right; we'll find your father."

Catalina moved to give Drusilla a reassuring pat on the arm and then realised that she couldn't, not with a lamp in one hand and a hatchet in the other.

"Your h…hatchet won't s…save us from demons!"

"No, but it'll be pretty good against beasts or bandits", replied Catalina confidently, "God will protect us from the demons."

Now that the blustering wind no longer filled their ears, the two women became aware of various other noises: the lapping of waves against the lake's sandy shore, the rustling of leaves in the trees nearby, at its western end, and the hoot of an owl. All things considered, Catalina had preferred it when the blustering gale had drowned out everything else; it had been easier then to shut out worrying thoughts and fears. Now though, every sound was magnified and terrifying. Noises that would have seemed innocent, or even gone unnoticed during the day, summoned up visions of monsters stalking them through the inky blackness.

"W…what was that?"

"What?"

"That creaking and groaning sound. There it is again! Oh, Catalina, I can't bear this!"

"It's just branches swaying in the wind", replied her friend, forcing herself to stay calm though her heart was thumping like a blacksmith's hammer. "Come on; let's move away from this wood. We'll follow the shoreline."

Hearts pounding and lamps shaking in trembling fingers, the two women started to circle the lake. As they walked, their heads moved from side to side, anxiously searching for any sign of Drusilla's father, but every so often one or the other would peer fearfully into the darkness behind them, hearing a rustling or scuttling noise from just beyond the circles of light.

Hurrying along the shore, the two women soon reached its eastern end, which was bordered by a steep rock face. From beneath the outcrop, water foamed and churned, as the energetic currents of an underground river mixed with the stagnant waters of the lake. Between the sheer rock and the cold dark water, a narrow ledge jutted out uninvitingly. Hesitantly, Catalina edged out onto the smooth rocky shelf, beckoning her reluctant friend to follow. The stone had been well polished by the elements and was as slippery as ice, but despite a few anxious moments, the two women managed to reach the far side without mishap.

"What's that?" whimpered Drusilla, her lantern picking out a ghostly white shape moving amongst the bushes on the far bank.

Both women turned their lamps upon the strange sight but neither ventured any closer. The thing was long, thin and scaly.

"Is it a snake?"

Catalina continued to watch silently. If it was a snake it was surely a dead one: the outline wasn't smooth, but rough and ragged, and it wasn't really moving, merely swaying in the breeze. Laying her hatchet on the ground and stepping forward tentatively, she reached out a hand.

"Catalina, no!"

Ignoring her friend's warning, she closed her fingers around the strange scaly substance.

"It's all right, it's just some sort of skin."

Catalina's voice was almost steady but her heart continued to pound. The skin, if that was what it was, was thick and leathery and, as she tugged on it, a sizeable bundle unravelled from amongst the surrounding bushes by the water's edge. There was a lot of it; whatever had left this behind was large!

Stepping back from the bushes, the young woman bent down to retrieve her hatchet and stopped motionless, frozen like a statue. The handle was resting in what she had taken for a hollow in the ground, but the light of her lamp had just revealed it for what it was: a footprint in the soft mud. It had a round heal and only three toes, each of which were as wide, and almost as long, as her whole foot, but it was a footprint none the less. *But what kind of animal could make those?*

"W…what are you l…looking at, Catalina?"

Drusilla's voice was shaking badly; it wasn't going to make her feel any better to know that there were monstrous footprints on the lake's shore.

"I'm looking for signs of your father", she replied, as truthfully as she could. "Nothing yet."

Catalina picked up her hatchet and gripped the oak handle tightly, her lips silently mouthing a prayer.

The two women continued their agonising search of the shore, one greatly fearing what they might find, and the other now more worried about what might find them. The unnerving creaking of tree boughs had returned; they were nearing the wooded end of the lake.

"Father's boat!"

Drusilla rushed towards the small wooden craft that was resting on the shingle, half out of the water, waves gently lapping against its stern. Two oars lay within, along with an empty net, but there was no sign of the owner.

"What could have happened to him?" Drusilla asked, her voice desperate.

"We don't know that anything has happened to him", replied her friend, attempting to calm her. "We don't even know for sure that he was here today; an empty boat proves nothing."

"Yes we do", interrupted Drusilla, with a little sob. "If he hadn't been here, the boat would have been at the other side of the lake, nearer to home."

It was a good point; Catalina had no answer to this. Drusilla began to sob again, running her hand tenderly over the bow of the little boat, as if this somehow connected her to the father she could not find.

The boat smelled vaguely of fish, which was not surprising really, but there was another scent on the night air, something more pungent. *But what…?*

Further along the shore, at the very edge of the lamplight, something dark lay across the smooth pebbles. Leaving her grieving companion, Catalina walked towards it. The smell was growing stronger now, and so was her dread. She didn't want to move any closer to this ominous dark object, but yet she was drawn inexorably towards it.

"Catalina, what is it?"

What was it? A bundle of rags? *But what are those white things? Sticks? And what is that awful smell?*

"No!"

"Catalina, what's the matter?"

For the first time that night, Drusilla had heard panic in her friend's voice. She rushed to her, a feeling of dread welling up inside.

"No, Drusilla don't…"

But it was too late. Drusilla let out a despairing howl; she had seen what her friend had at first mistaken for rags: the mangled body of her father! The corpse had been picked almost clean, and was no longer identifiable, but it had been human, the tattered remains of clothing bore testimony to that. And there was his abandoned boat, a matter of feet away.

Catalina watched in horror and pity as her friend fell to the ground, sobbing her heart out, wanting to touch her father, as she had so recently caressed the bow of his boat, but unable to fight off the revulsion that she felt at the sight of his grisly remains.

The sound of wailing seemed unnaturally loud in these lonely surroundings and, after a short while, Drusilla subsided into quiet sobs. Catalina placed comforting arms around her and, for a while, the two women sat by the lake, holding each other close.

After the pair had sat grieving together for a short while, Catalina became conscious of movement in the darkness behind her. They were not alone; something was out there, something large. Drusilla stopped crying; she had heard it too. The women both turned, staring inland, and listened intently, not daring to make a sound. Somewhere, just outside the glow of their upraised lanterns, a large dark shape loomed. There was a loud crunching as the thing stepped from the muddy bank onto the shingle.

"HELP!" screamed Drusilla, dropping her lantern with a crash, and setting off down the shore at a run.

"GET IN THE BOAT", her friend screamed back, sprinting after, her lamp jangling at one side, and the hatchet swinging freely at the other.

Drusilla reached the boat first, but hesitated, unsure of whether to keep running.

"GET IN!" yelled Catalina decisively, certain that any delay would end in disaster.

The crunching sounds were growing louder; the thing was gaining on her. Fighting the urge to look back at her nightmarish pursuer, she sprinted the last few strides to the boat, dumped her belongings in it, and pushed the bow with all her might.

There was a harsh scraping sound as the wooden keel slid reluctantly over the pebbles, and then the boat glided smoothly into the water. The little craft rocked precariously as Catalina clambered over the side to join her huddled, terrified, companion.

"It's going to eat us!" whimpered Drusilla hysterically.

"Grab an oar!" yelled her friend, ignoring this statement, and rooting around in the bottom of the boat.

There was a huge splash, and the boat shot away from the shore. Both women screamed; Drusilla pitched forward, thrown from her seat in the stern, and landed on top of her friend, who had been scrabbling about looking for the oars.

"We're going to die!"

Catalina fought her way out from underneath her panicked companion. She, herself, was sopping wet, bruised, and badly scared, but she wasn't resigning herself to death just yet. Her hand closed around a wooden handle, not the oar that she had originally reached for, but her hatchet.

As Catalina struggled to her knees, the boat tipped at the bow end, causing her to topple forward, bashing her elbow on the wooden boards as she attempted to regain her balance. Something had gripped the front of the little craft and was now attempting to empty out its contents!

Catalina could make out very little of their attacker, since the only surviving lamp was now somewhere underneath a prone Drusilla. All that could be seen was an ominous dark shape overhanging the bows. The thing was weighing down the front of the boat so much that the stern had almost completely cleared the water. With horror, Catalina found herself sliding forward as the angle increased still further.

Desperately, she swung her hatchet at the dark shape. There was a snarl, a splintering sound, and the weapon was almost yanked from her grip. The stern of the boat dropped back into the water and Catalina tumbled backwards, once more finding herself in a tangled heap, though this time on top. Scrambling over her whimpering friend, she finally located an oar and began to paddle furiously, firstly on one side of the boat and then the other.

With virtually no light to see by, and shaking violently with cold and fear, Catalina had little idea of which direction she was paddling in. She might be taking the boat back towards the bank, and the waiting monster, for all she knew.

"Drusilla, the lamp", she pleaded.

Her friend seemed, at first, unable or unwilling to move. She just cowered in the bottom of the boat, shivering, and ignoring all Catalina's entreaties.

"Drusilla, the lamp, NOW!" she cried, becoming more insistent, anxiety gnawing at her insides.

After what felt like an age of fumbling, Drusilla managed to retrieve the lantern, which amazingly was still lit, and hold it up with shaking hands. As she did so, she let out a gasp.

Catalina looked around, terrified that the shadowy creature had returned, but then her eyes fell on the sight that had shocked her friend: propped up at the side of the little boat lay her hatchet or, to be precise, the hatchet's handle. Just above the place where the hand would grip the shaft, the wood had been completely split. There was no sign of the metal blade; something had bitten it clean off!

Chapter 16 – The Wager

"Hurry up, George, we're going hunting", called Cassia, standing at the entrance to the kitchen, where George was busy peeling carrots.

"I've nearly finished", he replied, adding another freshly peeled vegetable to the growing pile.

"That's all right, George", assured Julia, without looking up from the pan of sauce she was stirring. "You can go; I'll finish that."

George put down the knife that he'd been using, thanked his mistress, and trailed Cassia out of the kitchen. The delicious herby aroma of the sauce followed them as they walked through into the atrium. The small rectangular pool of clear water, in the centre of the large airy room, mirrored the clear blue sky visible through the opening in the roof above; there would be no rainwater collecting in it today.

Outside, Brennos, Hector and Juba had already saddled the horses, and were eager to get going.

"How long does it take to peel a handful of carrots?" Hector wanted to know.

"George doesn't peel, he sculpts", laughed Cassia. "Each one is a work of art."

Brennos handed George a javelin. "In the Roman army, soldiers have to be ready to mount their horses while holding a weapon", he stated.

"Like this?"

George, spear in hand, vaulted onto the back of his mount, landing squarely, if not gracefully, in the saddle.

"By Neptune!" exclaimed Hector, "He's getting good at that."

"Shame", agreed Brennos, shaking his head. "Remember the first time he tried it?"

"He landed right on the corner of the saddle", chuckled the Gaul.

"And when you asked him if he was all right he said…" Brennos paused for effect.

"Not really", finished Hector, in a high squeaky voice.

"Are you two mighty hunters ready?" enquired Cassia. "We'll see who's laughing when George catches the first gazelle."

George smiled across at Cassia; he could always count on her to stand up for him.

"That sounds like a challenge to me", replied Brennos, urging his horse forward.

Cassia gave George a conspiratorial wink, and followed at a brisk trot. He and Cassie had hit it off from the day he had first arrived at her home, and the four winters they had spent in close proximity had only cemented that friendship. She had changed a lot in that time though, George mused. The girl he had been introduced to had grown into an attractive young woman.

The five friends set off riding at a canter, heading for the gentle green rolling hills that began where the cultivated land ended. The morning sun beamed down upon them, but a pleasant breeze kept the heat from becoming unbearable, and ruffled the wheat in the golden fields, on either side, as they passed. The barley harvest was over and the wheat harvest would soon follow, bringing with it a lot of hard work for Justus's household. This could well be their last hunting trip for some time.

Reaching the dip at the edge of the wheat field, each of the companions, in turn, eased their horses down the steep bank and negotiated the far slope with practised skill. George reined in his horse as they neared the twin trunks of the mastic tree that had previously been home to several fire drakes. There were no drakes nesting in its branches this year, but the group often used the spot as a meeting place.

As the horses snorted and stamped their hooves, eager for the hunt to begin, George became conscious of another sound, the distant thunder of galloping hooves on dry ground. Looking up, he saw four horsemen, riding among the trees a little way off. As he watched, the leader pointed in his general direction, and all four riders turned and headed down the gentle slope towards him. Each of the men had a javelin in his hand, just as George did, but were they just out hunting or did they have some darker purpose? George felt a knot tighten in his stomach.

As the tall, dark-haired, leader of the mysterious horsemen approached, George had the distinct impression that he had seen the man somewhere before.

"It's Primus!" exclaimed Hector, moving out from under the boughs of the mastic tree.

"You have me at a disadvantage", replied the famous charioteer, as he pulled alongside, his entourage flanking him protectively.

"Hector de Massilia", stated the Gaul, impressively.

"And whom have we here?" enquired Primus, turning his attention to Cassia.

"Cassia Justa."

"The gods must be smiling on me today!" exclaimed the charioteer. "That I should happen upon so fair a maiden."

Cassia blushed and looked down. George felt a sudden surge of annoyance at this intrusion; he didn't like this pompous Roman.

"And what brings you out into the wilds on this glorious day?" continued Primus, addressing Cassia once more.

"We're hunting", answered George, abruptly, and moved protectively to her side.

"In my household, servants do not speak before their mistresses", rebuked Primus, sharply.

"In the household of Justus, everyone is free to speak", replied Cassia.

"An interesting notion", mused the charioteer, raising one eyebrow. "We, too, are hunting, and I fear that being in competition with us, you may return home disappointed."

"I wouldn't worry about us", chimed in Brennos, entering the conversation. "We'll leave you a fennec or two."

Primus glared at the Briton. George smiled to himself; the fennec was a small sandy coloured fox with large ears, and wouldn't be much of a catch. They were after gazelles.

"You know I am a man who likes competition", stated Primus, looking at each of the companions in turn, as if he were an orator at a theatre production. "I will wager one aureus that we are the first to return to this tree with a captured gazelle."

"An aureus?" exclaimed Hector, before he could stop himself.

An aureus was a solid gold coin, worth more than a month's wages. George had managed to save up quite a number of the silver denarii that Justus paid him every month, but he knew that these coins weren't solid silver; they contained a small amount of silver mixed in with base metal. He would need around 500 denarii to exchange for a single aureus. George doubted whether, between them all, they could match the Roman's wager, even if they wanted to.

"Forgive me", said Primus, insincerely. "I forget that for all the rights of free speech that the household of Justus affords, you are still paid as servants."

George glared at the charioteer; his dislike for this rich, arrogant man was growing fast.

"Let me propose a fairer wager", Primus continued. "If you win, I will give you an aureus; if I win…" He paused, his brow creased in thought; then smote his forehead as a sudden idea came to him. "If I win… then the lady Cassia must give me the pleasure of her company for the rest of the day."

"No!" exclaimed George, unable to contain his indignation at the Roman's audacious request. He looked round at the others: Juba was shaking his head, obviously unhappy with the idea; Brennos and Hector seemed to be weighing things up. George looked sideways at Cassia; to his surprise she was smiling.

"Agreed", she said, mischievously.

George was dumbfounded; what was she doing? How could she even contemplate going off with that odious Roman? But it was too late; the deal had been done.

"Good hunting", called Primus, and in an instant he whisked his horse around and rode off, followed by his three attendants.

"Bravely spoken", congratulated Hector, as he beamed at Cassia. "You remind me of Antiope, queen of the Amazons."

"Less talk, more action", Brennos cut in, practical as ever. "We need to split up, about a hundred paces apart. Juba and George: start to the east, Hector and I will head west, and Cassia, stay in the centre. When you've reached your positions, head south. If you spy a gazelle, make the cry of an eagle and the rest of us will join you."

"May Diana, goddess of hunting and the moon, go with us", called Hector, as they separated.

"If you don't stop using your mouth and start using your eyes, we'll see the moon long before we get anywhere near a gazelle!" was Brennos's harsh reply.

Primus's team were already fanning out some distance to their right, and Hector and Brennos moved off in that general direction. Juba had already started out towards the morning sun, and George followed the Berber at a trot. He was determined not to lose this contest; the thought of Cassia spending the afternoon with Primus made his blood boil.

When they had travelled about a hundred paces from the twin trunks of the mastic tree, George swung around and headed south. Looking right, he could see Cassia sitting astride her light brown mare, a javelin in her right hand. *What possessed her to agree to this wager?*

Shaking his head, George refocused on the ground before him; he had to concentrate on the task at hand. The land around was dotted with bushes, trees and shrubs: any amount of cover for a slender gazelle.

Without warning, the harsh cry of a bird of prey filled the air. George gripped the reins of his mount tightly. *Which direction did that come from?*

After hesitating for a moment, George squeezed his knees against the flanks of his chestnut mount, and the horse quickened its pace to a canter. He was fairly confident that the signal had come from somewhere a little way off to his left, but he'd seen nothing to confirm that yet.

Rounding a particularly dense patch of bushes, George startled a small brown speckled bird of prey that had been perched on a dead tree. The bird, probably a kestrel, gave a squawk and launched skywards. The noise sounded sickeningly similar to the one he had heard a few moments before. George groaned in frustration, pulling on the reins to return to his original track. He could almost hear Brennos's disapproving tones: *Eagles don't sound anything like kestrels.*

"Not to other eagles, perhaps", he muttered out loud to himself.

It was slow going; the sun had risen to its zenith, its sapping rays beating down mercilessly on George's sweating back. His stomach had begun to growl too; no one had said anything about suspending the competition for a lunch break, nor of what time to call off the hunt if they didn't find any gazelles.

Spotting movement up ahead, George put thoughts of food out of his mind; raising his spear to shoulder height, he nudged his horse forward. Ahead, a small cluster of trees provided a possible source of cover. Pushing his way through the low-hanging branches, George peered into the undergrowth; nothing stirred. Moving on, he came to a place where a thick patch of tangled bushes sprouted up between several large rocks. Once again, George tensed, drawing back his right arm in anticipation, but once more he was disappointed. A hare emerged from behind a rock. On another day he would have gone after it, but today George ignored the animal and pressed on. Had he imagined the sudden flurry of movement?

No, there it is again! Something was hiding among the trees to his left. Moments later, to George's surprise, and delight, out sprang a gazelle, directly in front of him! It was slightly built with pale legs and rump, and a darker streak of brown along its back. Its slender horns curved back and then rose to needle-sharp points, high above its head.

George was about to move in when he remembered that he was supposed to make the signal. He opened his mouth to 'cry like an eagle', but only managed a pathetic croaking sound. *My throat's too dry!* George spat on the ground and tried again; this time he succeeded in making a loud high-pitched squawk, which promptly caused the gazelle to scatter for cover.

"Oh, that's great!" muttered George, kicking his horse into action. "A signal that frightens off the prey. Let's just shout 'boo' next time!"

George pursued the swift gazelle, dodging in and out of the thick bushes, trying to keep pace with this prize. The slender creature vaulted a tangle of thorny plants that blocked its path, and George urged his mount on, landing firmly on the far side of the obstacle. Up ahead, the gazelle had paused, unsure of which way to run; this was his chance. George took careful aim and hurled his javelin at the hesitant animal.

"COME ON!" screamed George, but it was in frustration rather than triumph. His spear had landed well to the right of his intended target.

The gazelle darted off to the left. George would have to dismount, pull the javelin out of the ground and then remount before resuming the chase, by which time his quarry would have disappeared back into the undergrowth.

No. He had found this gazelle and he wasn't going to let one of Primus's men bag it first. George pulled on the reins to manoeuvre his mount into position, and then urged the horse into a gallop. Bending low over the neck of his steed, George stretched out his right hand to grasp the shaft of the spear. As his fingers closed over the wood, he yanked hard and… found that the javelin was more deeply embedded in the ground than he had thought. Next moment, George's world was turned upside down as he tumbled helplessly out of the saddle!

George tried vainly to extricate himself unscathed from the centre of the thick thorny bush into which he had fallen. He had been fortunate to have such a soft landing, but he was in less than grateful mood by the time he had escaped its tangled clutches. The sharp spines had torn his clothes, and numerous small cuts covered his arms and legs. At least no one had seen him fall.

"You aren't taking this very seriously are you?" called a lilting voice from somewhere nearby.

I'm not taking it seriously? George couldn't believe it. *Here I am risking life and limb for your honour…* But before he could get the words out, Cassia had whisked around and vanished between the trees.

Before George had time to dwell on this injustice, the sound of galloping horses filled the air. Looking round, he caught sight of Brennos, his black stallion in full flight. Not more than a couple of lengths ahead of him was one of Primus's cronies, and three or four lengths in front of him was another gazelle, different to the one George had been chasing; the horns were shorter, probably a female.

George looked about frantically for his horse, and spotted the chestnut stallion a short distance to his left. He gave a loud whistle and waved his arms to attract the animal's attention.

"Come on, Gideon!"

But his horse gave a snort and looked away, as if it had had enough of his foolish antics.

"Come on you useless nag!" cried George, in frustration, as he charged towards the apathetic creature, spear in hand.

Gideon reared up on his hind legs and whinnied loudly, seemingly fearing that George was going to attack.

"Easy, boy", reassured George, trying to keep the frustration out of his voice, as he grabbed the reins and patted the horse's neck rapidly.

By the time George was in the saddle, Brennos was out of sight, but the sounds of the pursuit were still audible, so he set off at a gallop in that direction. It didn't take long before George had sighted his mentor again; he had caught up with the other man and they were now riding neck and neck. George hadn't really taken much notice of Primus's lackeys (the charioteer had a knack of drawing all attention towards himself), but now that he was getting a close-up of this Roman, he realised what a colossus he was. Brennos was a big man, but his opponent was significantly taller and broader even than he.

George looked on, almost spellbound, as the fleet-footed gazelle led both men a merry dance, zigzagging around dense patches of undergrowth and passing under low-hanging tree boughs in an attempt to lose its pursuers.

Unexpectedly, the frightened animal doubled back on itself. Brennos, reacting the quicker, cut inside his opponent with a sharp turn. Pulling his right arm back, he took aim, but just as his arm whipped forward, the huge Roman lurched across, barging into him from the side, causing the spear to fire wide of the elusive gazelle. As the missile hit a patch of stony ground, there was an ominous sound of splintering wood. George looked on in horror: the shaft of the weapon had broken near the point; Brennos was out of the hunt. With a cry of triumph, the Roman hulk charged after the fleeing animal; one good spear throw and it would all be over. *Only one man stood in his way: the legendary George.*

George, desperate to prevent this foul, cheating, pig of a Roman, from winning the day, swerved to intercept him. The panicked gazelle changed direction again, forcing both men to alter course. George was now only a length behind and steadily gaining ground on his opponent, whose bulk must surely be slowing his horse somewhat. Suddenly the gazelle, that had shown no sign of tiring thus far, faltered. The man-mountain drew back a mighty arm to propel his spear on its way. George had to do something, *but what?*

Leaning forward in the saddle and reaching out with his own spear, George just managed to clip the shaft of the bulky Roman's javelin as he released it.

"WHAT IN JUPITER'S NAME ARE YOU DOING?"

The throw had gone wildly wrong, and the irate Roman was none too impressed with George's interference. They were riding side by side now; the gazelle was dead ahead, an easy target. George took aim and... something struck him in the chest. With a cry, he toppled sideways.

The ground rushed up to meet him and, with a bone-jarring thud, George landed hard on the dry turf, tumbling over and over.

Through a haze of pain, blood and sweat, George stared up at the sky. The trees at the edge of his vision were spinning, the ground swayed beneath him. He tried to inhale, but he couldn't draw any air into his lungs; coloured lights flashed before his eyes; everything around him began to grow dim. A sense of blind panic began to well up within him; he tried to rise, and toppled sideways, collapsing among the dry tufts of grass.

"George, what's the matter?" Cassia's concerned tones broke into his world of pain and anxiety.

George finally managed to gasp a lungful of air, and sat up, wide-eyed. Cassia dismounted from her mare and put a hand on his shoulder.

"What happened?" she asked.

"I was pushed off my horse in mid gallop! What does it look like?" snapped George, gulping in fresh supplies of air.

"Well if you've finished rolling around, I've got something to show you", replied Cassia, playfully.

"I've got to help Bren", countered George, getting unsteadily to his feet.

"That doesn't matter now", continued Cassia, undeterred.

George glared at her, his face red with anger. "Yes it does matter, Cassie. This isn't a game; you're the one who's not taking it seriously!"

With that, George staggered across to where his javelin lay in the grass, picked it up, and surveyed the scene. The big Roman was just remounting his horse, having recovered his own javelin; Brennos was some distance to his right, still pursuing the gazelle on horseback, though armed only with a hunting knife. The pair of them, hunter and hunted, were heading his way.

George stood, spear at the ready, as the gazelle sped towards him. *This is it; this is my chance to end this.* George drew back his arm to throw but, as he did so, the darting creature changed direction. Readjusting his stance, George readied himself once more, only to see the frightened animal alter course again. It was no good, the tiny beast, less than three feet high at the shoulder, was moving too fast and getting further away with each turn. The chances of him hitting it from this distance were very slim indeed, but he might as well have a go. George pulled back his arm for the third time and…

"GEORGE, SPEAR."

Startled, George looked up to see Brennos galloping straight towards him, left arm outstretched. It took a moment for the Briton to register what was required of him, then, as the black stallion halved the distance between the two men, he lightly tossed his spear in the air, and his fellow countryman caught it neatly, his left hand closing over the centre of the shaft.

George watched in admiration as his mentor deftly switched the spear to his right hand and closed in on his prey. His arm went back, the spear went forward, and the gazelle collapsed in the dust; the hunt was over!

George's loud cry of triumph was interrupted in mid flow as he spied a struggling Cassia, dragging a gazelle carcass across the grass towards him.

"If you want to win this 'oh so important competition', you'd better help me get this gazelle to the twin-trunked tree", she said, crossly.

George looked at her sheepishly. "I didn't realise… Bren's caught one too."

"I seem to remember that the competition was to catch the first gazelle, not the most", replied Cassia, caustically. "If you'd have followed me when I asked, we'd have been back at the tree by now. Well?" she gestured, glancing down at her trophy and then looking meaningfully back at George.

Apologetically, George hefted the gazelle over his shoulder and followed the slender, raven-haired figure back towards her mare, which was waiting patiently in a cluster of small dark trees not far to their left.

A trio of horses made their way, at a brisk trot, across the wild scrubland above Silene. On the right rode Brennos, his gazelle draped over the shoulders of his broad-backed stallion; to the left rode Cassia, a triumphant gleam in her eyes as she cradled her catch in front of her. At the centre of the party was George, bloodied and battered, his blue tunic torn in various places, his emotions torn between disappointment, at his lack of success, and pleasure, at his team's victory. And as for his feelings towards Cassia, he could hardly begin to make sense of them himself. Was it grudging admiration, jealousy, anger, a sense of betrayal, or a confusing mixture of them all?

They were nearly there now; once they had reached the top of the next rise they would be able to look down from the top of the gentle slope to the twin-trunked tree. It would feel good to place the two gazelles in its shade and wait for Primus's arrival. George couldn't wait to see the look on the arrogant Roman's face. It didn't really matter that he, George, hadn't caught a gazelle. He was part of the winning team. He had shed blood for it, he had stopped the other team from making the killing blow, and if it wasn't for his help, Brennos wouldn't have got his trophy and, come to think of it, Cassia wouldn't have found her catch either, since he was pretty sure it was the male that he had first flushed out of the undergrowth. All things considered, he had played a major part in their victory.

Feeling a little more satisfied with his morning's work, George galloped the last part of the journey, eager to reach their destination first. He could just about make it out now: two thick trunks with branches jutting out at all angles, covered in a dense mass of green, and at its foot the strange twisted merging of the two, beside which stood... *No!*

George yanked on the reins, halting Gideon in his tracks. All the colour drained from his face, all the joy vanished from his day, for standing beneath the boughs of the mastic tree was the tall figure of Primus, and at the feet of the triumphant Roman lay the carcass of a freshly killed gazelle.

"A valiant effort, my friends", he called out. "But I don't like finishing second!"

Chapter 17 – Losing Cassie

"Your turn, George", insisted Hector as he passed him three dice.

The young Briton looked down at the polished ivory cubes; he had lost track of the game. Normally, George enjoyed this Roman pastime, but tonight it just wasn't holding his attention. Absent-mindedly, he rolled the dice across the tiled floor.

"Twelve", stated the Gaul. "That's too many; have another stone."

George moved his wooden game piece twelve spaces around the board, a beautifully carved miniature of a Roman circus, and Hector handed him a shiny black pebble that he resignedly placed beside the two he already had.

The object of the game 'Circus' was to complete three laps of the track before your opponents, by rolling one, two or three dice, and moving your 'chariot' according to the total. The track was demarcated with black and red lines; crossing two red lines qualified you for a penalty stone, and once you had three stones you could no longer choose to throw three dice.

"Tired horses and it's only the beginning of the second lap", commented Brennos; "Even Primus would struggle to win from your position."

"Don't use that filthy language in front of George", chided Hector, as George glared at the older Briton. "You'll offend his sensitive Christian nature."

George glanced over at Hector, noticing a mischievous glint in his eye; they were trying to provoke him. They were succeeding too; the mere mention of the charioteer's name was enough to push him into a foul mood. It was bad enough that the arrogant Roman had triumphed over them, worse that Cassia had actually consented to go off with him, but it hadn't stopped there. The day after the hunt, while they had been hard at work harvesting in the wheat fields, George had caught sight of a lone horseman galloping up to the gate of the Justus family villa. A little later on, he had spied Cassia riding off side by side with the man, who turned out to be none other than Primus. The day after, a similar thing happened, and this morning Primus had shown up again.

"Six: just what I needed", crowed Brennos, interrupting George's dark thoughts. "I'm ramming you off the track, Hector."

George glanced at the board, attempting to banish all thoughts of Primus from his mind. Brennos had moved his game piece up to Hector's, putting him in position to 'ram' the Gaul. This meant that Brennos would choose how many dice Hector was to roll.

"Three", stated the Briton, confidently.

Hector went through an elaborately superstitious routine, kissing the dice and closing his eyes, as if uttering a silent prayer, before shaking the cubes vigorously in his clenched fist.

"Seven! How lucky is that? Not even a stone!" exclaimed the disappointed Briton.

"The Fates must be with me", smiled Hector. "Here you go, George."

George took the two dice that were offered to him, without relish.

"He's got it bad", said Brennos, looking from Hector to George.

"Got what?" asked an irate George.

"Well, let me see", began Hector, pausing for thought. "Irritable, wandering mind, can't focus on anything…"

"He left half his dinner too!" interrupted Brennos, obviously appalled that anyone who wasn't dieing of plague could do such a thing.

"Loss of appetite", continued the Gaul, counting off the symptoms on his fingers, "And, I'm willing to bet, a stomach that feels as if you're on a boat in a stormy sea."

Hector looked at George, pity in his eyes. "George, you're in love."

"Or you've got the trots", added Brennos, helpfully.

"I am not in love", retorted George, fiercely, throwing the dice a little too hard. "Curse it!" he added, as he moved his piece a meagre three spaces.

"That's right, let it all out, George", chuckled Brennos, gathering the dice from where they had come to rest, by the far wall, and rolling them himself. "Flames of Venus, these dice are warped!"

Hector handed Brennos his second stone, rolled the dice nonchalantly, and moved his game piece into the lead. As he passed the dice to George, he looked at him with a knowing smile. "Tell her, George."

"Tell who?"

Looking away from the smug Gaul, George rolled the dice. They both knew whom he meant.

"Four; unlucky, George", commented Brennos. "That puts you right before the turn. If I can just roll… thirteen!" he exclaimed as the dice came to rest. "Your hide is mine, George!"

"It's the moment of truth", remarked Hector, finishing his move and winking mischievously as he, once more, passed the dice to George.

"All three, George", crowed Brennos, anticipating triumph. "More than ten and you're gone!"

George took the three dice; he was almost certain to cross two red lines in this turn, but there was also a good chance that he would cross a third, resulting in a 'crash', and the end of the game as far as he was concerned. He let the cubes fall from his outstretched hand… a two, a three and a six.

"Bye bye, George", waved Brennos, an annoyingly broad grin on his face.

George got to his feet. He didn't care that he'd lost the game; in fact it was better that way. He needed some time alone, free from annoying comments and prying questions.

As George reached the archway that led into the atrium, Hector called him back.

"Tell her, George", he said, earnestly. "Don't fight Venus's flames; you'll get burned."

Without replying, George turned and left the room.

What do they know about my feelings? I'm not in love; Cassie and I are good friends. I just don't want her hanging around with Primus, that's all.

In the atrium, Justus and Julia were sitting on one of the stone benches, hand in hand, talking softly together. Feeling awkward, George quickly passed through and headed out into the cool evening air. Once outside, he leaned his back against the stone wall of the house and looked away west towards the setting sun.

As he sat there contemplating the awesome beauty of the heavens, two words were floating around in George's head: *"Tell her."* At first he tried to shut it out and think about something else, but his mind kept returning to them. *Tell her. Tell her what? That I love her? Do I?* George pondered the question for a while; how could you tell when you really loved someone? He could tell that Justus really loved Julia by the amount of time they spent together, when Justus was at home, and the way they so obviously enjoyed each other's company. *I love to be with Cassie.* This was certainly true: Cassia was great to be around; laughter and fun seemed to follow her wherever she went. She had helped him to settle in to this strange new country, this new way of life. He couldn't imagine life at the villa without her. *But that's what's going to happen if Primus gets his way! Not if I can help it! Then tell her.*

His mind made up, George re-entered the house, walked up the narrow entrance hall, passed swiftly through the atrium, where Justus and Julia were still deep in conversation, skirted the tablinum, where the household finances and records were kept, and walked into the peristylium: the open courtyard garden at the rear of the villa. The idea of having a garden inside your house still seemed a strange concept to George, but he had to admit that it looked picturesque, with a fountain at its centre, a covered portico, supported by elegant columns, around its perimeter, and a tasteful assortment of dark green shrubs and delicate pink flowers at each corner.

Right now, though, George wasn't here to admire the flora. Looking between the columns to his right, he could see that the partition curtain was pulled across Cassia's bedroom. Should he disturb her? What he had to say was very important. What was he going to say? *"Cassie, I love you. Please stop going off with Primus and go off with me instead."* No. *"Cassie, I've been thinking about how I feel about you and I've decided I love you."* No. *"Cassie, I don't know how to say this but…"* Too right, I don't know how to say it! I need to think about this; I'll tell her in the morning.

Feeling slightly relieved, George strolled back through into the atrium, bid Justus and Julia goodnight, and entered the room that he shared with Juba. Juba's bed was empty; come to think of it, he hadn't seen much of the quiet Berber lately. Wondering what his friend could be up to at this time of the evening, George undressed, pulled the blanket off his bed, spread it on the tiled floor, and slumped down on it. Julia insisted that each member of the household had a bed and "treat their room as a bedroom, not a barn", but George, who had never been able to understand this Roman custom of sleeping on furniture, had given it up after a couple of bad nights, and always slept by the side of his bed, replacing the blanket on it every morning so as not to annoy the mistress of the house.

George lay awake for a while, trying to decide on what to say to Cassia, but he made little progress and soon drifted off to sleep.

George was still planning his opening line at breakfast the following morning. Fortunately, there was no sign of Cassia yet. So far, only the servants had appeared, not that George really felt like a servant. Both Justus and Julia treated him, and each of the others, as if they were a special part of their family. Opposite him, Brennos was explaining to Hector that the Gaul's 'Circus' victory of the night before was due to blind luck rather than skill, and that at some point even 'the Fates' must bow to the weight of reason and logic. To his left, Juba was conversing with Cahina, a slender, dark-skinned young woman from one of the nomadic Berber tribes, whom Justus had also freed at the slave market. Over to the right, lounged the slightly rotund figure of Publius, the man responsible for the smooth running of the villa, including its farmland and livestock. With one hand, he was tucking into a large hunk of bread, smeared with a generous amount of honey; the other hand held a stylus, with which he was making marks on a wax tablet, doubtless a list of tasks that required his attention.

George was becoming increasingly agitated; he had only one task that mattered, and he needed to carry it out before breakfast was over and another day of harvesting began.

Soon, Publius began chivvying them along in his usual annoying manner. The stout Roman couldn't abide anyone sitting around idling when there was work to be done.

"Come on George, take some dates with you if you haven't finished. Time is flying", insisted Publius, in his squeaky voice.

George slowly raised himself from the couch that he had been reclining on during breakfast (Lying down to eat was another crazy Roman notion that he'd had to get used to). Just at that moment, Cassia breezed into the room, dressed in a beautifully embroidered lilac tunic.

After a chorus of "good morning" and various complementary remarks about her outfit, people started to file out of the room. George hovered, unsure of how to begin.

"Err... are you going out somewhere?" he enquired.

"Yes. I'm going to the theatre with Primus. There's an interesting new production that he says I must see", enthused Cassia, smiling at him.

"George, are you waiting for a special invitation? Come on!" called an impatient Publius.

"Well... err... enjoy yourself", finished George, awkwardly, and hurried after the annoying little Roman.

As he headed for the wheat fields with the others, George tried not to let his frustration and disappointment show. *What was I thinking? Enjoy yourself? What happened to 'He's an arrogant, selfish, idol-worshipping bully. Don't go!'*

George continued to inwardly berate himself all the way to the second field, the one that they were due to finish harvesting today. As he started into the golden sea of wheat, swinging his serrated sickle, he pictured Primus's arrogant face and resolved to wipe the smile off it. As he worked, grasping the stalks with his left hand and cutting them down with the sharp blade in his right, George began to formulate a plan.

Tomorrow Justus, Julia and Cassia, along with all those servants in the household who were Christians, would go to Simon's house in Cyrene, where they would be joined by the other members of the little church. Christians throughout the Roman Empire met together on every seventh day, corresponding to the first day of the Jewish week (This was despite the fact that the Roman week actually consisted of eight days). This meant that for a couple of hours or so, George would be in Cassia's company with no possibility of Primus appearing to steal her away. It could be his big chance to win her back. George gritted his teeth in determination; he wasn't going to mess this one up!

After a hard day in the field, George's shoulders and back were aching from repeated exertion, but as soon as he returned to the villa, the first thing he did was to go in search of Cassia. He found her sitting by the fountain in the peristylium.

"How was the play?" he asked, merely to open the conversation. Secretly, George hoped that it had been a complete disaster.

"It was a tragedy", she replied.

George turned away from Cassia to conceal his glee at this announcement.

"I thoroughly enjoyed it", she continued. "The story was very moving. The man who played the lead has a great voice; the song he sings after he finds the body of his beloved made me weep like a child."

"But I thought you said the play was tragic?" interrupted a confused George.

"A tragedy: a story of unhappy events", clarified Cassia, shaking her head in disbelief. "Oh George, sometimes I wonder if you live in the same world as the rest of us."

Smarting slightly from being made to feel stupid, George considered leaving Cassia alone and forgetting his plan. *Maybe this is a bad time. No, this could be my only chance!*

"Cassie, do you want to go riding with me tomorrow, after church?"

There, he had said it. Now he waited, nerves jangling. The words had sounded silly, as if he was a slave begging a favour from his mistress, not as a simple invitation to a friend. *We've been riding together loads of times over the last four years; why is this suddenly such an ordeal?*

"If you want", replied Cassia, looking at him with a curious expression on her pretty face.

"Great", beamed George, a feeling of triumph spreading through him, as if he had just completed some Herculean task.

George generally loved meeting with the Christians in Cyrene. Simon, the man in whose house they met, was the jolliest, friendliest and most generous man you could imagine. He treated each one who passed through his door as if they were a long lost friend. And those who met in his house were such a diverse crowd: wealthy landowners, politicians, craftsmen, soldiers, farmers, slaves. All were treated with equal kindness and respect. Then there was the incredible book that they read from at each meeting: containing the words of God! At times it seemed to him that those words opened a window into his very soul, and at others it was as if he were catching a brief glimpse of heaven.

Today, however, everything seemed dull and dry, mostly because he wasn't really listening. All he could think about was what he was going to say to Cassia on their afternoon ride.

At last, the meeting was over and people began to mill about. George waited for what seemed like an age while Cassia chatted away with a group of girls, who seemed to find something highly amusing. When this giggling group had finally dispersed, he hesitantly approached his master's daughter.

"Are you ready to go?"

"Go? Oh yes, I suppose so", she replied, seeming a little preoccupied. "Where are we going?"

"We can go to the theatre if you like."

"The theatre? On the Lord's Day? You heathen, George", she laughed, then after a moment's thought she added: "No, you wouldn't like it; it's all about feelings and emotions. I don't even think you would understand most of it."

This comment stung George a bit, although he was secretly relieved that she had not taken him up on his offer. He knew that love involved making some sacrifices, but enduring a couple of hours of the theatre was pushing his limits!

"So what do you want to do?" enquired George.

"Let's just ride home", Cassia replied, and then as George's face fell: "We'll take the scenic route."

Leaving Cyrene by the west gate, Cassia and George followed the road for a while and then branched off to the left, heading across the wide-open plateau. The afternoon sun beat down on them without mercy as they trotted across the yellow grasslands. Several juniper trees were dotted about, but spread too thinly to offer any shade. To George though, the most oppressive thing was the silence. *Why is it that now, when I need to talk to Cassie, I can't think of anything to say?*

"Over there! What are those things?" asked Cassia, finally breaking the silence.

George reined in his horse and looked in the direction that she was pointing. There, only a short distance to their left, lying in the short grass, were a number of round white objects.

"Ostrich eggs!" exclaimed Cassia, dismounting from her mare.

George followed, eager to get a closer look at the find. There were half a dozen large white eggs lying in a slight hollow in the ground; each one was oval in shape and about half a foot long.

"These aren't ostrich eggs", challenged George. "They're too small."

"They look pretty big to me", replied Cassia curtly. "What do you know about ostrich eggs?"

"I stole one from a market stall once", answered George.

"Stole?" questioned an incredulous Cassia. "When?"

"When I was a young lad."

"Well, I expect when you were a little boy everything seemed bigger", continued Cassia, "Because these are definitely ostrich eggs."

"Perhaps", conceded George. He wasn't convinced, but the last thing he wanted right now was an argument over the size of ostrich eggs!

"You must tell me all about your life as a thief", implored Cassia, sounding intrigued. "But first let's see if we can fit all these eggs into our saddlebags."

"Why?"

"So we can eat them later, of course. Just one of them will provide a meal for the whole household!"

George helped Cassia to cram the huge eggs into the saddlebags, all the while keeping a close eye on the surrounding countryside. He was a little anxious that the ostrich might return; any creature that laid eggs that size was not to be trifled with! According to Cassia, ostriches feared humans and rarely came anywhere near civilisation (she had only seen them on a couple of occasions) but her description of an eight-foot bird that could outrun a horse did nothing to allay George's fears.

Despite George's misgivings, the eggs were soon stowed safely away and they were able to continue their journey. As they rode across the grasslands, George related, as requested, the story of his theft. Cassia listened spellbound throughout the entire tale, not interrupting once; the Briton couldn't believe his luck!

As George concluded the account with the tragic discovery that, after all his efforts, he had lost the egg, Cassia sighed.

"That was a great story, George. I had no idea you had such a chequered past."

"I expect there's a lot about me that you don't know", risked George. He had just sighted Silene; time was almost up. "If you went out with me instead of Primus, who knows what you might discover?"

George could hardly believe that those words had come from his own lips, *but how will she take it?*

"Are you jealous, George?" crooned Cassia.

How were you supposed to respond to a question like that?

"Yes", he answered, honestly.

They were approaching the villa now, and both riders slowed their steeds to a gentle pace, walking side by side. To George's surprise, Cassia reached across and touched him on the shoulder. A shiver went down his back.

"If you want me, George, you're going to have to fight for me. You know Primus doesn't like finishing second."

Chapter 18 – To the Death?

Hector had been right; admitting to Cassia how he felt about her had lifted a great weight from George's shoulders. The sullen awkwardness that had plagued him for days had gone, replaced by the feelings of contentedness that had been characteristic of his time in Silene.

The perceptive Juba had noticed it first, commenting on his unusual cheeriness when they rose at dawn. Then Hector must have noticed the change because he kept winking across at George during breakfast. George even winked back, although when he saw Cassia looking across at him, he started to rub his eye as if he had got something in it. This caused Brennos to let out a chuckle, which the big Briton quickly turned to a fit of coughing as Cassia turned her head in his direction.

At that moment Publius walked in. "Marcus Leonius Primus is here to see you, mistress Cassia", he stated in the formal tones he always used with the blood members of Justus's family.

George's good mood evaporated like a small puddle on a scorching summer's day. He suddenly realised that he'd been foolishly celebrating victory without making plans as to how he would defeat the enemy.

Cassia acknowledged the message and then flashed a meaningful look at George, who suddenly found the pattern on the tiled floor very interesting. *What am I supposed to do?*

Seeing that George wasn't going to make a move, Cassia tutted loudly before leaving the room, heading for the atrium, where Primus would be waiting.

George sat up on the end of his couch. He had seemingly failed to do something that Cassia expected of him, *but what? I can't exactly throw Primus out of the house!*

"The rest of you need to be finished and out", ordered Publius, imperiously. "We've lost a day so we need to work twice as hard today to catch up."

It was clear that Publius didn't approve of the practice of resting one day out of every seven, Lord's day or not.

George was the first out of the room, but not because he was keen to get back to harvesting grain; he wanted to overhear what was going on in the atrium. The atrium, with its stone benches and rectangular water pool, was the largest room in the house, not including the inner garden, and was roughly 'T' shaped. Several rooms led into it, including the dining room, which was situated on one of the wings of the 'T'. This meant that anyone leaving the dinning room was out of sight of most of the atrium for a few steps, and it was in this space that George positioned himself.

He had been hoping to hear raised voices, an argument, even an emotional speech from Cassia about how she could no longer continue a relationship with Primus. Instead all he could make out were low voices followed by giggling, hardly a sign that Cassia had taken his words to heart.

George was acutely conscious that Publius would soon be herding the others in this direction, and his eavesdropping, such as it was, would be discovered. A fresh bout of merriment broke out from around the corner; he was going to have to confront Primus, there was no other way around it.

With no plan in mind and no idea what he was going to say, George stepped forward into plain sight, causing Cassia to look up at him from the bench that she and Primus were occupying. There was an awkward silence as he took in the disturbing scene. Cassia was sitting far too close to the charioteer for George's liking and, worse still, his muscular arm was draped around her narrow shoulders.

"Is there something you wish to say?" enquired Cassia, slightly frostily, George thought.

There were lots of things that George wished to say but, as a Christian, he didn't feel that it was appropriate to use that kind of language, and anyway, he didn't want to start a fight with Primus, a fight he was more than likely to lose.

"Well?" If Cassia had been frosty, Primus sounded positively frozen!

George was feeling distinctly uncomfortable; he couldn't think of anything to say, and Primus's angry glare was unnerving him. He suddenly became aware of footsteps behind him.

"There you are, George. Come along." It was Publius, leading the way in his businesslike manner. Behind him, the rest of the servants followed at a slightly more leisurely pace.

George hesitated for a moment and then fell into line. There really was nothing else he could do.

"Mistress Cassia", greeted Publius, bowing slightly.

"Have a productive day", she replied.

"Primus", added the stout Roman, nodding to the charioteer.

"Publius", he acknowledged unenthusiastically.

And with these formalities completed, Publius led the way out of the atrium.

George avoided looking either Primus or Cassia in the eye. He had failed and now he was leaving with his tail between his legs, like a dog that had been kicked by its master. Even as he trudged out of the room, a voice was shouting in his head: *Leave like this and you lose Cassie!* But what else could he do? He'd had his chance and he'd blown it!

The harvesters trooped out of the villa and headed for the nearest outbuilding, the one containing the farming equipment: ploughs, spades, hoes, and sickles. George was at the rear of the procession, hanging back, wondering what to do. Suddenly he turned on his heel and raced back inside. *I've got to say something; I'm not losing Cassie to Primus!*

George charged into the atrium, disturbing Primus and Cassia once again. This time he didn't give them chance to speak. "You've got to choose, Cassie", he blurted out, "Between me and Primus."

There was a short pause. George expected Primus to react angrily to this statement, but he didn't, he just laughed long and loud. Cassia's expression was difficult to read, she didn't look angry though.

"It is a difficult choice that is offered to you my lady", said Primus, laughter still evident in his voice. "A free man or a servant? Wealth or poverty? A winner or a loser?"

"Someone who loves you or someone who loves himself?" interjected George, venomously.

Cassia actually laughed out loud at this, but quickly restrained herself as the pompous Roman's expression became as dark as a thundercloud.

The next moment this fierce look was gone, replaced once more by a confident smile.

"Brave words", began Primus, speaking slowly and deliberately. "But are you man enough to back them up with deeds?"

George knew what was coming next: the situation he had hoped to avoid.

"We will fight for the lady Cassia's honour."

"W…where?" stammered George, trying to fight the feeling of panic that was welling up inside him.

"You are harvesting today?"

George nodded, not trusting himself to speak.

"Meet me in the farthest of your master's fields at the twelfth hour."

George marched towards the far wheat field silently, head bowed like a condemned man. In his arms he carried his sickle and his travelling cloak. Even at this early hour it was too hot for a cloak, but bundled up inside it was his sword, and he dare not reveal that. He knew that Justus would never approve of duelling, and the snivelling Publius would doubtless report to his master anything amiss in the conduct of his under-servants.

Reaching the farthest field, the one they were to begin harvesting today, the group, made up of Justus's household and a number of hired hands, got to work. The men rhythmically swung their sickles, cutting through the ripe stalks of wheat, and the women followed at a short distance picking up the stalks and bundling them into sheaves.

The manual work was physically demanding, but not mentally taxing. Try as he might, George couldn't keep his thoughts from the crisis that faced him. Was Primus a good swordsman? He seemed to be good at everything else. Would this fight be to the death or was the idea to wound or disarm your opponent? George was beginning to feel slightly nauseous. *Why am I feeling like this? I took on the Bulls of Hades; they were much scarier than that pompous fool, Primus.*

Publius called a halt to proceedings at about the sixth hour, and the harvesters sat down to enjoy a well-earned rest and some much needed bread and water. George sat by himself; he didn't feel like talking. When Juba came up to ask him if he was all right, George just grunted and continued with his meal. As much as he wanted to confide his troubles with his friend, George knew that Juba would never agree with his decision to duel. *Decision? Some decision!* Between Primus and Cassia he'd been backed into a corner; there was nothing else he could have done.

"What's on your mind?" asked Hector, seeing George lost in his thoughts.

George quickly weighed up what he should say. He needed to know about duelling, but would it be safe to tell the Gaul what he was up to?

"Err… I was wondering whether… you've ever fought a duel?"

Hector looked a little puzzled by the question. "I've done plenty of fighting when I was a boy", he said. "But that was with my fists. If you mean duelling with swords, then no."

"You're not thinking of duelling with Primus are you?" interrupted Brennos, who had obviously been listening in.

"I was just asking", replied George, trying to sound innocent, although inside he realised his question had been too obvious.

"Don't even think about it!" continued the Briton, unconvinced by George's response. "Primus is a trained athlete: he will have spent many hours running, wrestling, boxing and lifting weights to get into perfect physical condition. You wouldn't have a chance!"

George seethed inwardly. *I'm fit and strong too, and what about all the training in swordplay that you've given me?* How could Brennos say he had no chance? George bit his lip; he was not going to admit to the duel. Especially not now he knew his friends' thoughts on the matter.

"And don't think that a fight to first blood is safe", added Brennos.

"First blood?" questioned George, pricking up his ears.

"It's where you fight until one of the combatants draws blood", clarified Hector.

"First blood can be an eye, or your throat, or a stab to the heart!" stated Brennos, gruesomely emphasising the dangers of duelling.

"It sounds to me", cut in Publius, "That you've finished eating, so you can all get back to work."

There was a chorus of groans.

"Do you notice any difference to when you were a slave, Juba?" Brennos shouted across to him.

"I'm getting paid", chuckled the Berber.

"Good point", agreed Hector, getting to his feet.

Soon everyone had reluctantly returned to harvesting. George was almost glad to get back to work; he had no wish to be lectured further. With Brennos, you either got comedy or utter seriousness, never anything in between. George scythed through the golden stalks with grim determination. *We'll see who hasn't got a chance!*

As the day wore on, George's defiance began to ebb away and fear gnawed at his belly once again. His arms were tired from the continual exertion of swinging a sickle; his thighs and back ached too. Primus would doubtless be fresh and focused for the task. Maybe Brennos had been right; maybe he didn't have a chance. *What am I going to do?*

George wiped away the sweat that was stinging his eyes. The sun was getting low in the sky; it was about the eleventh hour. *What if Primus shows up before the reaping is done? Even if he doesn't, how do I stay behind for the duel without the others knowing?* It was clear from Brennos's comments that there was no way that his friends would allow him to fight this duel. But that was what he wanted wasn't it? If they intervened he wouldn't have to fight? *"If you want me, George, you're going to have to fight for me."* He had to fight; there was no way around it: *fight or lose Cassie.*

Finally, Publius called the day's work to a close, and with relieved yawns, and much stretching, the group of harvesters gathered their things together and began the short walk home. George moved towards his travelling cloak, lying bundled up at the side of the field, but before he reached it a sudden thought struck him. Leaving the cloak where it lay, George turned on his heel and caught up with his friends.

When they were nearly halfway home, George stopped abruptly, causing his friends to look enquiringly at him.

"I've left my cloak", he said. "I'll see you back at the villa."

He turned to head back the way they had come, hoping that no one would suspect anything.

"Be quick, George", exhorted Juba, "Or there will be no food left for you."

"Except egg", corrected Brennos, with a groan. "There's always egg, thanks to you and Cassie."

Hector, Juba and Cahina all chuckled. George just kept walking; his plan was working.

By the time George had made it back to the spot where he had left his cloak, all his companions had vanished. He was alone. *No, not alone, God is with me.* Or was he? God had been with him when he had rescued Justus from the Bulls of Hades; God had been with him when he had fought off the thieves, but this was different: this time, George was choosing to fight. Would the God who exhorted his followers to love their enemies, protect him when he was bent on harming his foe? This time he really was alone.

George looked over at the sun, sinking towards the horizon. Soon it would be dusk; perhaps Primus wasn't going to show. Even as this comforting thought entered his head, George's ears picked up a faint rumbling sound. He turned eastward, his heart sinking faster than the great yellow orb behind him. There was no mistaking it now, the steady drumming of hooves on dry ground, and soon he could see two riders heading down the gentle slope towards him. In the lead, a tall dark-haired man, sword dangling at his side; following at a swift gallop, a smaller, slenderer figure, with equally dark hair: Primus and Cassia.

The two riders slowed as they approached the ditch that separated the cultivated land from the wilds beyond. Both negotiated the obstacle with no difficulty and dismounted at the corner of the recently harvested wheat field.

"I see your little servant friend is true to his word", remarked Primus to Cassia, eyeing George with a relaxed air. The Roman seemed completely at ease, as if the duel he was about to fight was some sort of game. George, in contrast, was very conscious of sweating palms and shaking knees as he stooped and lifted his sword from under the weatherworn cloak.

"For your honour, my lady", stated Primus, drawing his blade smoothly from its sheath and saluting Cassia with it.

George didn't trust himself to say anything, but made a clumsy salute in Cassia's direction with his own sword. She smiled back, sitting calmly astride her light brown mare. *How can you sit there so coolly? I could die!* George felt like screaming, his heart was pounding, his limbs were shaking and the sword felt strangely cold and heavy in his hand.

"Good luck", called Cassia, but whether she was wishing this on him or Primus, George couldn't tell.

The duel had begun. Primus moved assuredly towards him, sword pointing at George's throat. Suddenly, the Roman lunged forward, taking him by surprise. George leapt backwards, flailing his blade wildly in a desperate attempt to block Primus's attack. George avoided the lunge but his ill-directed swing had thrown him off-balance and he was forced to give more ground as the Roman followed up his advantage with a couple of quick swipes. The first came within a handbreadth of George's left thigh, and the second, he just managed to block before it could bite into his shoulder.

The clash of steel on steel rang out as Primus continued his assault. Another quick move forced George to back up, attempting to parry a high slash followed by a low sweep. His defence was just about holding, *but for how much longer?* His breathing was laboured, his legs weary, and every blow that he blocked jarred his aching right arm.

Knocking the latest thrust aside, George, desperate to start an attack of his own, swung his sword in a wide arc towards the Roman's midriff. Blocking this with ease, Primus countered with a feint to the left and a lunge to the right, which, once again, caught George off-balance, forcing him to stagger backwards in order to avoid being disembowelled.

"Is this the best you can do?" goaded the Roman, as George clumsily fended off his latest attack.

George didn't have the breath for a reply. He was struggling to keep up this pace, and Primus knew it, but spurred on by the Roman's taunts, he hung on, dodging a low sword thrust and replying with a counterthrust that forced his opponent to take a step backwards for the first time in the duel. He was into this fight now; fear had been replaced by determination. He could almost hear Brennos's words: *"You need to concentrate on your opponent, work out what they're going to do next."*

Rather than following up his attack with another quick swing, George hesitated for a heartbeat. Seeing this, Primus stepped forward, planting his left foot firmly, preparing to strike. But George had seen this move before. Gambling that the Roman was feinting left and preparing to lunge to the right, he swiftly stepped to Primus's left and jabbed with his blade. Surprised by this move, Primus's lunge went astray, and George felt his sword make contact.

A cry of surprise and pain rang out from the Roman. He staggered backwards clutching a hand to his chest. A patch of blood could be clearly seen through his torn white tunic; the wound was about halfway between his shoulder and his heart.

Now it was George's turn to cry out, but in triumph rather than pain. He had done it; he had beaten the famous charioteer! George looked over at Cassia, who was just dismounting from her horse, a look of concern on her face. George turned to face his opponent once more.

"A valiant effort, my friend", he said, mimicking the Roman. "But I don't like finishing second!"

Something seemed to snap inside Primus. With a yell of rage, he lunged forward, his sword swinging straight for his opponent's neck. Caught completely off-guard, George barely had time to leap backwards as the blade whistled through the air, missing him by a fraction.

"Fool!" yelled Primus, surging forwards and swinging his sword again. "We fight to the death!"

Cassia let out a scream. There was a violent clash of steel and George was thrown backwards by the full force of Primus's charge. Landing on his back amongst the wheat stalks, the Briton frantically attempted to struggle to his feet before the next blow fell. But he was too late; with another ferocious swing, Primus knocked the sword from his grasp. George lay there, defenceless, staring up into his opponent's hate-filled eyes as the Roman's sword danced at his throat.

Chapter 19 – Consequences

"Don't kill him!" shrieked Cassia, rushing towards them.

George saw death in Primus's eyes; he knew what his enemy was going to do, but even with that realisation he felt no fear, only anger.

One moment Primus's expression was blacker than the evening sky, the next his arrogant sneer was back. "I won't kill him so long as he yields."

"Yield? I won and you know it!" George couldn't help himself; he was livid.

"You have lost this duel and, if you do not yield, you will lose your life." Primus underscored these last words with menace; his tone was icy, and the murderous expression was once again forming on his face, like a dark cloud crossing in front of the sun.

"No!" cried Cassia, her voice desperate. "Stop it!"

Primus turned as she reached him, his sword point momentarily shifting from George's throat. Acting purely on instinct, George rocked forward and grabbed his enemy's sword arm just below the elbow. Before the distracted Roman knew what was going on, George had hoisted himself to his feet using his opponent's arm as a lever.

Cursing loudly, Primus pivoted round, hoping to dislodge his right arm from George's grip so that he could take a swing at him. George hung on grimly, trying desperately to prise the Roman's fingers from his sword hilt, but Primus was too strong. With an almost bestial snarl, he wrenched his arm free, overbalancing as he did so.

As he saw his foe tumble backwards, sword grasped firmly in his fist, George began scanning the area for his own weapon. Cassia screamed, but the Briton didn't look up, focused only on finding his sword. He had only a few moments; failure meant death!

There, a few feet to his left, something metal was glinting in the last light of the setting sun. With a roar, Primus leapt to his feet. George dived sideways, his outstretched hand reaching for the hilt of his sword.

Even as his fingers tightened around the grip, his enemy was upon him, weapon held high. Scrambling to his feet, George flung his arm in the air and somehow blocked the killing blow with the recovered blade. The force of the attack sent a shock up George's arm that almost jarred the weapon loose from his grasp, but gritting his teeth against the pain, he held on.

Primus swung left and right, his ferocious onslaught forcing George backwards once more. Instinct had kicked in now; there was no time for thought or strategy. George's sword moved left and right, high and low, faster than his brain could register. The evening air was filled with the ring of metal on metal, punctuated with various grunts and snarls from the two combatants.

George was vaguely aware that Cassia was no longer screaming at them to stop. Next moment, he heard the sound of galloping hooves; she had fled the scene. It didn't really matter though; this wasn't about Cassia anymore, this was about survival and justice!

The two blades crossed once more, the adversaries locked together in a life and death struggle. George stared across the wall of steel at his snarling opponent, summoning hidden energy reserves, desperate to keep his feet firmly planted on the dry soil. But the Roman's greater weight and strength prevailed: with a sudden heave, George was thrown backwards.

George plunged his arms out wide to break his fall, but the ground wasn't where he had expected it to be. He tumbled backwards, landing hard on the down-slope of the dip at the edge of the field, and began rolling head-over-heels.

Managing to halt his downward momentum, George staggered groggily to his feet. His head was spinning, his stomach felt like it was doing somersaults, and his sword was no longer in his hand. Looking blankly up the slope, he could see two Primus's staring triumphantly at him. Then as the two figures merged into one, the Roman gave a battle-cry and raced down the bank towards him, his sword pulled back, ready for a mighty swing.

Dazed and defenceless, George could only watch as his enemy charged down the slope, screaming wildly, death in his eyes. At the last moment, George swung his legs out from under him and dropped onto his belly, his outstretched arms breaking his fall. Primus's blade whistled by, inches above his head, and George heard the Roman give a cry of rage as he fought to halt his downward momentum.

Primus cried out again, this time in surprise and pain, as he tripped and slid head first down the remainder of the bank. George scrambled to his feet: this was his chance. *Where's my sword?* Once more, the Briton found himself in a race against time to locate his weapon. It was darker now though; the sun had sunk below the horizon. *Come on!*

There it was, a few feet off to his left. George scrambled across the steep slope and retrieved it, keeping one eye on Primus, who was just now getting unsteadily to his feet.

Throwing caution to the wind, George surged down the bank, hoping to catch his opponent off-guard before he had had chance to recover. Down in the dip, Primus turned, raising his sword; he looked slightly dishevelled, torn tunic covered in dirt and blood, but he still seemed pretty alert. Too late, George realised his error: charging out of control down a steep bank, straight towards an armed opponent!

Pointing his sword directly towards Primus, George hurtled towards the Roman, who had drawn back his blade, ready for another mighty stroke.

"DIE!"

Primus screamed and swung with all his might; George pulled his sword back, out of range. The Roman had mistimed his stroke, the blade cutting through the air rather than the onrushing Briton. But before George could readjust and get in a blow of his own, he collided with his bedraggled foe. There was a sickening crunch, and both men dropped to the ground.

George fought to draw breath; it felt like he'd just run into a stone wall. *Get up!* George's brain screamed at his limbs to move but, despite the danger, they seemed unwilling to obey. He started to crawl up the far slope on his hands and knees, still gripping his sword hilt. *If I can just gain the higher ground...* Out of the corner of his eye, George saw movement: Primus was getting up.

With a grunt of determination, George struggled to his feet and turned, just in time to see his opponent draw back his arm for one more swing. Primus was about three feet below George, in the lowest part of the ditch. There was a clang as his weary stroke was parried by the Briton's vertical blade, at shin height, and then with a speed and ferocity that seemed to come from nowhere, George kicked out with his right leg. This sudden, unexpected attack caught Primus right on the chin and, with a cry of pain, he toppled backwards holding his face. George, almost as surprised as his opponent, took a moment to register what he'd just done. The

Roman lay on his back, left hand cradling his jaw, right hand holding his sword up limply.

George swung ferociously at his opponent's outstretched blade, knocking it from his weakened grip. Now it was his turn to dangle his sword at Primus's throat; he had won; the duel was over.

But it wasn't over. George looked down at his fallen foe, staring into his hate-filled eyes. There was fear there too. George stood, breathing heavily, sword still pointed at his enemy.

"Do you yield?" he asked, because he couldn't think of anything else to say.

"You'll pay for this", hissed the Roman.

"Not if I kill you", replied George, anger rising from within.

"You're not a killer", sneered Primus, but George detected a hint of doubt in his tone. "You're a Christian, aren't you?" he added.

George didn't reply; that last question had caused a flood of guilt to wash over him.

"You are." Primus answered his own question; the arrogant, self-confident air was starting to creep back into his voice. "What would your God say if you were to murder me, now, in cold blood?"

George remained silent, thoughtful. His God had preserved his life through the duel, but He hated murder, George knew that for sure, and He hated the anger that, under the right circumstances, led to murder, the anger that was present in George's heart even now.

"Christians are weak", sneered Primus scornfully, preparing to rise as George's sword point dropped slightly.

The anger flared up within George once more, like a pot coming to the boil, ready to bubble over at any moment. He took a half step forward, forcing the Roman back into a sitting position. *Kill him now*, screamed the angry voice in his head. *No, murder is evil! If you don't act now then Primus will be back for revenge!* The choice was clear: let Primus go, and live in fear of his retribution, or murder him, and live in fear of God's judgement. As he mulled over this unhappy choice, a verse sprung into his mind: *"Do not be afraid of those who kill the body but cannot kill the soul. Rather, be afraid of the One who can destroy both soul and body in hell."* It was no choice at all really: Primus's retribution could not follow him beyond the grave, God's judgement would.

"GEORGE!"

George jumped, startled by the sudden shout, and looked up. At the top of the bank stood Justus, with Cassia by his side; the reinforcements had arrived.

"Put away your sword at once!"

George quickly sheathed his blade. He could barely make out his master's expression in the gathering gloom, but the tone of his voice left him in no doubt that Justus was angry, very angry.

"Brawling like common criminals? I would have thought better of you, Primus! And as for you, George, you've let me down. And, more importantly, you've grieved the almighty God! What have you to say for yourself?"

"He was trying to kill me!" answered George, indignantly.

"And were you not trying to kill him?" retorted Justus, his voice still quivering with anger.

"It was a duel of honour", interjected Primus. "A duel that I won. But as I was conversing with your daughter, this cowardly dog attacked me without provocation!"

"You liar!" shouted George, incensed. "You were the one who…"

"ENOUGH!" roared Justus, cutting across the bickering. "Primus, get off my land and never return! And George", he added, looking straight into the Briton's eyes, a look of utter disappointment on his face. "As from sunrise tomorrow, you no longer work for me."

"You're dead!" whispered Primus as he moved slowly past George.

George, still reeling from Justus's ultimatum, had a sudden urge to draw his sword and finish this right there. *You've got nothing to lose now!* His right hand strayed to the hilt of his sword. *No, I'm not a murderer!*

George followed his enemy, dejectedly, back up the steep slope, and watched as Primus mounted his horse and rode away. Then he trudged home, behind Justus and Cassia, in silence. The only noise was the thudding of horse hooves on the dry ground; Justus had said all that he wanted to say, and Cassia was doubtless feeling too guilty to speak up.

When George awoke the following morning, he was at first puzzled as to why his body ached all over. Then, as he emerged gingerly from his mound of bedding, the events of last night flooded back into his mind, and with them a bitter sense of injustice. It was just beginning to sink in that he would never sleep in this villa again, that he would probably never see his friends again.

George threw his blanket back on the wooden bed for the last time. There was no sign of Juba; he must already have gone to breakfast. George quickly dressed, and gathered his few possessions together. They didn't amount to much: a cloak, a couple of tunics, a small pile of loincloths, his sword and belt, the dagger that Brennos had given him, and his money pouch.

Fastening the sword-belt around his waist, along with the sheathed dagger, George bundled the rest of the gear into his faded green travelling cloak, rolled it up and slung it over his shoulder. Emerging into the atrium, he was met by a sombre looking Juba.

"I heard what happened last night", the Berber began awkwardly.

"And I suppose you agree with your master, that I shouldn't have fought Primus", snapped George. "Don't worry, master Primus", he continued, mimicking Juba's voice. "You can have Cassia. I'll just wait at the back of the queue until a woman comes along who's so boot ugly that nobody else wants her!"

Before Juba could reply to this, Hector rushed into the room, looking uncharacteristically flustered.

"George, don't go yet! Brennos is trying to pour healing balm on the wounds. If you come with me and apologise, I'm sure Justus will be merciful."

"Be merciful for what?" replied George, angrily. "What have I done? I'm paid to be a bodyguard; am I not allowed to guard my own body when someone's hacking at it with a sword? And what about: 'Don't fight Venus's flames, George'?" he asked, putting on a Gallic accent this time. "What am I supposed to do after I've 'told her how I feel'? Pray to the gods of wishful thinking, and dumb inactivity, that Primus will fall in love with someone else?"

For possibly the first time since he'd met him, Hector was speechless. George stormed out of the house.

"Wait, George!" cried a desperate female voice. He paused and looked over his shoulder; it was Cassia.

"Don't leave!" she panted, running up to him. "My father loves you like a son; he can't want you to go."

"It sounded like that to me", answered George, coldly.

"But it wasn't your fault", she insisted.

"No, it was yours", he replied. "It's your fault that I had to duel, and it's your fault that I'm banished. If you hadn't have gone crying to daddy when things turned nasty, Justus wouldn't have known anything about it! What did you expect to happen? Did you think that two fierce rivals, swinging heavy sharp objects at each other, would be civilised?"

With that, George turned on his heel and marched toward the gate, feeling oddly triumphant at having silenced his friends with his irrefutable arguments. These smug feelings quickly evaporated, however, giving way to a strong desire to go back, apologise to everyone, and beg Justus not to send him away.

But I can't turn back now, he stubbornly told himself as he passed beneath the boughs of the four olive trees, laden with oval green fruit. He could smell the pleasant aroma of mint, growing in the herb garden, hear the busy clucking of the hens in the coop, the snorting of horses in the stables. This had been his home for five years, but no longer.

A bitter tear ran down George's cheek as he opened the iron gate, which squealed on its rusty hinges. The manner of his departure brought back painful memories of the night he'd fled from his village: he had left without saying goodbye then too. Had his mother got over the loss of her only son? Had Catherine long since forgotten him? Would life now, in Justus's household, continue happily without him?

George closed the gate behind him with a clang, looking up at the cloudless sky. "Where now?" he whispered forlornly. "Or have you given up on me too?"

Chapter 20 – Ambushed!

George sat bolt upright in the darkness; he could feel beads of cold sweat on his brow. It took him a few moments to work out where he was, and then he remembered: the Bacchus Tavern, in Cyrene. He slumped back down onto his bedding. It had only been a dream – a nightmare, but the experience had been so vivid; it had seemed so real! He remembered a woman screaming and a creature with huge fangs and… It was slipping away. George closed his eyes and tried desperately to focus on the pictures that had so recently filled his mind. *The woman: who was she?* It had been someone familiar, someone he cared about. *Cassie?* It had gone.

Yawning loudly, George rolled out of the tangled mass of blankets and got to his feet. It was just beginning to get light outside and he needed to hurry if he was going to be assured of employment.

After a quick breakfast of bread and honey, George exited the inn and headed for the market square, walking along one of the many mosaic covered paths that crisscrossed the town. He had no time to marvel at the skill of the craftsmen who had created these walkways, though; he had another hard day of harvesting ahead of him.

Arriving at the market square, George joined the group of potential workers waiting patiently for inspection. Each day was the same: the workers would gather in the marketplace and the hirers would arrive, pick those that looked healthy and strong, and set them to work harvesting their crops alongside their own servants and slaves.

It was now three weeks since he had left Silene, and not a day had gone by without his having a strong urge to return. But his pride would not allow him to go back; he was the one owed an apology, not Justus. So far, though, no apology had been forthcoming; in fact, he hadn't seen anyone from Justus's household since he'd left.

"George!"

He looked up, recognising the voice at once: it was Publius, and he was leading two horses: his own short dumpy coal black one, and a chestnut stallion: Gideon.

"Thank the gods!" exclaimed the little Roman, panting heavily. "I've found you."

"Why, what's the matter?" enquired George, hopes of imminent reinstatement blossoming.

"I've just received word that master Justus has been shipwrecked!"

"What?" George gasped in horror.

"He's all right", reassured Publius, still panting heavily from his recent exertions. "The ship had almost made it back from Alexandria when it got into difficulty and ran aground near Darnis.[1]"

"Darnis? That's just down the coast from Apollonia isn't it?"

"Yes", replied the head servant. "It's about fifty miles east of here. According to the letter that has just been delivered", Publius continued, waving a piece of parchment under George's nose, "Brennos and Hector were injured in the accident, but the cargo remains undamaged."

"How badly injured?" asked George, concerned for his friends.

"He doesn't say", replied Publius dismissively. "But he was most insistent that I find you and send you to meet them in Darnis, so that you can help escort them home from there."

There was no time to lose; George leapt into Gideon's saddle and grabbed the reins.

"Follow the coastal road east from Apollonia; if you ride hard you should reach Darnis before nightfall", called the portly Roman, as George rode out of the market square, "And may the gods be with you."

"May God be with me", echoed George, in a whisper, as he set off on his latest adventure, "And with my friends."

Passing the guard at the north gate, George urged Gideon down the steep track that led to the little port of Apollonia. The road ahead was empty of travellers, the breeze coming in off the sea, far below, was cold and fresh, and as he rode along, hair blowing in the wind, George felt invigorated.

Since leaving Silene, life had been miserable, he mused. He had hoped that Cassia would have sought him out by now, but each day he had been disappointed. The days had been long, hard and lonely, and the little money he'd earned had gone to pay for his food and lodgings. *But this is my chance. Do this right and I'm back with my family!*

---

[1] Derna

It was about the third hour when George arrived at Apollonia, and he wasted no time in the bustling little town, instead heading east along a tree-lined avenue that he knew led to the coastal road. He had had a good breakfast and would do without further sustenance until he had reached his final destination.

A short while later, George found himself passing beyond the last of the port's hillside dwellings. The deep blue waters of the Mare Internum[1] pounded the base of the cliff on his left hand, the Green mountains rose up majestically on his right and, up ahead, the road wound its way snake-like between the two. Along this precarious path, George galloped, his horse, Gideon, in full flight, mane and tail streaming out behind him.

Some distance along the road, George spied a trio of horsemen, the first travellers he had encountered that morning. On seeing him, they spurred their horses into a gallop. George slowed Gideon's pace; he was uneasy about these riders. There was no way off the road, no way to avoid them. Should he run? Looking over his shoulder, George was alarmed to see three more appear from behind a rocky outcrop a short distance away.

George's early morning ride had turned into a nightmare. There was no doubt about it: he was being ambushed! George froze, unable to think. What could he do? The road was blocked in both directions and he had steep rock on one side and pounding surf on the other! He watched in a daze as the sinister horsemen closed, relentlessly, on his position.

George's heart was beating like a drum, his hands hung limply over the reins. Suddenly, as if sensing his master's fear and indecision, Gideon lurched forward. George gripped the reins to stop himself from falling backwards, as his mount accelerated into a gallop.

As the gap between them rapidly diminished, the onrushing riders drew their weapons; two had swords, and the one on the left had a spear. George leaned low over Gideon's neck and drew his own sword. He gritted his teeth; the inevitable collision was only moments away.

Just before impact, George pulled sharply on the reins, steering Gideon to the right; he was going to risk the swords rather than the long-reaching spear. The central horseman swung, George

---

[1] Mediterranean Sea

ducked, thrusting his sword right as he did so. There was a cry as his blade made contact with something and was nearly ripped from his grasp. Slipping sideways in the saddle, the Briton made a desperate grab at Gideon's mane to keep from falling. Tugging on the thick black hair, he managed to right himself; he had survived!

Looking back, George watched the two groups of riders converging. One of the six horses had an empty saddle, its rider lying motionless on the ground. Wasting no time on their fallen comrade, the remaining five horsemen regrouped and started after him.

George bent low in the saddle, adrenalin pumping through his veins; he was still alive, but if he was to remain so he needed to stay ahead of his pursuers.

Was it his imagination or were they slowing down? Anxiously, George glanced over his shoulder: he was being caught.

"Come on, Gideon!" he urged, cracking the horse on its flank, and almost losing the reins in the process, as panic threatened to overwhelm him.

Gideon gave a loud whinny as if to say that he was trying his best. George, still with his sword out, attempted to wipe the sweat from his forehead with the back of his left hand. As he did so, out of the corner of his eye, he noticed a crimson trail running across his fingers: blood!

Where was it coming from? Had he been cut? *Surely I would have felt it.* George glanced anxiously down at his tunic, but could find no trace of blood, except for a small patch at the end of his left sleeve.

Holding his hand up to his face, whilst gripping the reins tightly, George still could not discover the source of the bleeding; there were no cuts on his left hand or his wrist.

Behind him, the sounds of pursuit were growing steadily louder. Anxiety increasing by the moment, George, once more, turned to look over his shoulder. The distance between him and his pursuers had been halved. And then he saw it: a great crimson gash running along Gideon's left flank! The swinging sword, which he had ducked earlier, had struck his horse. Gideon was losing blood, and George was losing speed; it was only a matter of time before he was overtaken!

George swung around, his sharp eyes scanning the road ahead, desperately seeking some way of escape. On one side, the almost sheer drop onto jagged rocks, endlessly battered by foaming waves, offered little prospect. On the other, the Green Mountains loomed large, their steep sides dotted here and there with wild bushes and shrubs. Gideon couldn't go on; there was no way down. Up was the only possible way out.

Yanking hard on the reins, George rolled off Gideon's back, staggered slightly, regained his balance, and charged up the steep slope to his right. His momentum took him as far as a line of prickly bushes, but above these the climb became steeper, and George realised that he was going to have to use hands as well as feet if he was going to get any higher.

Sheathing his sword, the Briton looked back down the way he had come. From his vantage point, he could see four men making the steep ascent after him; a fifth had stayed at the roadside to guard the horses. *Four to one! How am I going to get out of this one?*

As he scrambled his way between a large jagged rock and a particularly aggressive shrub, George tried desperately to focus his mind on a plan. There was no way he could take on four armed men and win; his only hope lay in avoiding them. But then what? Could he double back, sneak up on the remaining man and take one of their horses. It seemed highly unlikely, but what alternatives were there? The far side of the Green Mountains was desert, a vast barren wilderness of sand, where nothing grew, and only the Berber peoples dared to tread. He would have to return to the road at some point, there was no way around it, and if he chose to continue east on foot, he was still many miles from Darnis, and he had no food or water.

Now that George had climbed out of the shadow cast by the rocky slopes, the sun began to beat down upon him mercilessly. His throat was parched, salty sweat was dripping into his eyes, and the intense heat was rapidly sapping his strength. His legs ached from the steep climb, his head ached from the glare of the sun, and the ridge he was aiming for didn't seem to be getting any nearer.

George glanced back over his shoulder; his pursuers showed no sign of giving up the chase. *What do they want with me?* George was starting to panic and he knew it. Turning away from his mysterious foes, he stared hard at the ridge; reaching it was to be his focus, his goal. *If I can get there with a good lead, I've got a chance.*

George hauled his tired frame over the ridge; the ground was almost flat here and covered with vegetation. Directly in front of him, a wall of rock, sheer and smooth, blocked his path; he would not be able to climb that. But to either side of this rock face, the narrow green shelf, on which he now stood, held out some hope.

Unable to see whether this shelf carried on much beyond the corner of the rock, George uttered a quick prayer and picked a direction at random. Moving to his left, he wound his way around several bushes to the edge of the face. The ledge was very narrow here, and there was a steep drop of at least a hundred feet to the rocky slopes below; George inched his way along, pressing his back to the stone, trying not to look down.

Reaching the end of the rock face, George was mightily relieved to find that the ledge widened out considerably around the corner. The ground rose slightly ahead and, beyond the rise, something resembling a path zigzagged its way up to a farther ridge. This was his chance to put some distance between himself and his pursuers.

George swiftly gained the rise, but then came to an abrupt halt. Between him and the dusty path lay a gap of about fifteen feet. George stepped back hurriedly; the drop was almost vertical. If the distance had been nearer ten feet, he might have attempted the jump but, as it was, he would have to stick to the shelf he was on and hope that it led to somewhere other than a nasty fall.

The wide open shelf continued to run parallel with the outcrop on which the path lay, for a few feet, and then began to narrow as it rounded another sharp corner of rock; this way was beginning to look very unpromising. Gritting his teeth, George rounded the bend. It was as he had feared: the shelf tapered to a narrow ledge and fell away, growing steeper and steeper until it became almost vertical. He was at a dead end!

George turned back, heart in his mouth. He had to retrace his steps and quickly; his pursuers would reach the ledge at any moment.

"THERE!"

George's blood turned to ice in his veins; he was too late. One of his mysterious assailants had reached the wide shelf that he had just crossed; the others would soon follow. There was no way back, no hope except…

George swiftly drew his sword and charged towards the bronze-skinned man, hoping to catch his opponent off-guard. His adversary, who for some reason seemed vaguely familiar, unsheathed his own sword and prepared to swing. Sprinting forwards, George caught the slashing stroke on his outstretched blade, slipped slightly under the weight of the blow, recovered his footing, and hurtled onwards toward the edge of the precipice.

At the last moment, George flung his sword skyward and, with a wild cry, leapt into the void. His stomach lurched violently as he reached the apex of the jump and began his rapid descent towards the far side of the crevasse. *I'm not going to make it!* he realised, with horror, as he plunged downwards, just short of his intended target!

George's gut hit the lip of the outcrop and his knees buckled below him. Slipping backwards, the Briton grabbed at a nearby bush, desperately gripping onto the sharp spines that tore into the flesh of his hands. A mangled clump pulled away from the main body of the savage shrub; George teetered on the brink. Then, mercifully, his left foot found a narrow ledge and he was able to steady himself.

"Pin him!"

That voice was all too familiar: *Primus!*

George turned his head. On the side of the rocky plateau that he had just leapt from, stood the unmistakable figure of his nemesis. And with him were three of his lackeys, two of whom held spears in their fists.

Scrambling frantically, George hauled his frame up and over the edge of the outcrop, before diving for cover behind the coarse bush. There was a sharp clang as metal struck stone; the spear that had been intended for him lay just to his left, the shaft broken on impact with the rock.

Suddenly, a harsh croaking cry echoed around the mountainside. Rising out of the ravine on vast leathery wings, was a creature that George could never have imagined, even in his worst nightmares: It was black as night, with a huge horned beak and a long bony crest projecting back behind its piercing eyes. Along the edges of its wings, and protruding from its two stumpy legs, were murderous looking talons.

With one flap of its mighty wings, the creature soared effortlessly upwards and away. George staggered backwards, drawing breath once more; it seemed the monstrous thing wasn't going to attack him, at least not yet.

Keeping a watchful eye on the sky above, George retrieved his sword, which had landed a few feet further back from the edge, and hurried to ascend the steep path. Behind him, his pursuers could only stand and curse; no one was going to risk that leap.

How did Primus know where to attack me? That thought troubled him; surely Primus and his henchmen hadn't been waiting in the mountains for the last three weeks on the off-chance that he would take the road to Darnis? *Publius!* He had to have tipped them off. *But when? Why?* Those questions remained unanswered.

As George pondered these new mysteries, another thought struck him: *If Publius set up the ambush, then there's no shipwreck; Justus isn't in Darnis at all!*

George made fairly rapid progress up to the first ridge and continued to follow the path, if that was what it was, to the next. He wasn't at all sure what he was trying to achieve, other than to put as much distance between him and Primus as he could. At some point he needed to get back to the road, but if he was heading back west to Cyrene instead of east to Darnis, he could make the trip on foot.

As he considered this, George gained the second ridge. Beyond it, the path narrowed and levelled out, while the ground fell away to his left and a vertical rock wall rose up to his right. The slender walkway wound its way around the sheer face and then opened out onto another small plateau. This sheltered piece of level ground was enclosed on all sides by steep rock faces, containing several dark openings, reminding him forcibly of the Necropolis below Cyrene.

Disappointed, George turned and slowly began to retrace his steps; he was starting to feel tired and hungry as well as being very conscious of his parched throat. Reaching the place where the path widened and began to slope downhill, George heard a distant cry. At first he looked up fearing that the winged terror had returned, but the sky was clear. Then, looking down, he caught sight of four figures making their way up the path below. They had found him! Somehow they had negotiated their way around the crevasse and now they were closing in.

George turned back, all heaviness gone from his limbs. His only hope was to climb up to one of the caves and hide from Primus and his men. Perhaps he could find an underground stream to keep himself alive until the Roman gave up the hunt.

Back at the walled plateau, George quickly surveyed his options. The easiest opening to reach was directly in front of him, about twenty feet up, but that would be visible from further down the path. *Whatever happens, I can't let them see which cave I enter!* The openings on his left seemed the next best option, although the way up to them was an almost vertical climb of at least thirty feet.

George placed one foot on the rock, felt above his head for a decent handhold, and began the ascent. It was slow going; the stone was smooth with only a few small cracks and some tiny ledges. About ten feet up, even these seemed to disappear and George came to a complete halt. *I haven't got time for this!* Stretching to his right, he made a grab for a protruding chunk of rock that was frustratingly out of his reach. Next moment, his right foot lost its grip and George found himself sliding helplessly down the wall.

Nursing a scraped knee and a cut finger, he decided to abandon the attempt and try the easier climb instead. *I'll have to be quick though, or they'll see me!* Scrambling up towards the lowest cave entrance, George made far more rapid progress this time. Once again, however, he reached a point where all the handholds seem to vanish. Balancing precariously with all his weight on his right foot, George stretched his left hand upwards, feeling for any cracks that he could get his fingers into.

There was a harsh cry from somewhere overhead. Startled, George lost his grip and tumbled backwards, landing with a crunch on the hard earth below. Groaning, he looked upwards as a huge shadow passed over him; the nightmare fiend was back!

Another cry rang out, this time from behind. George scrambled to his feet, whirling around as he did so. The first of his pursuers had appeared over the ridge; he was too late. Drawing his sword, George rushed towards the foe, reaching the narrow path just in time to prevent his opponents from outflanking him; they would have to attack one at a time.

Parrying the first sword thrust, George lunged, forcing his opponent back.

"Let me through!" insisted a gruff voice, and the first man gave way for his spear-wielding comrade: a huge hulk of a man, whom George instantly recognised as the brute who had knocked him off his horse during the hunting match.

George steadied himself as the colossus thrust his spear at him, turning aside the gleaming point with the flat of his blade. The next attack was swifter, forcing George to give ground. This was followed by a fierce lunge, which caused him to retreat still further.

Anger and frustration replaced fear, as George found himself pushed relentlessly backward by the long reach of his opponent's weapon, with seemingly nothing he could do about it. Desperate to hold his remaining ground, the Briton attempted to turn the latest spear thrust aside with his sword.

A cry of pain escaped his lips and his weapon dropped to the ground with a clang; the razor-sharp point of his enemy's spear had cut into his forearm.

With a triumphant yell, the hulking Roman charged forward, forcing George to jump backwards and flatten himself against the rock to avoid being skewered. As his gloating foe reached George's position, the furious Briton leapt at him. Taken by surprise, the huge Roman swung his spear, but he was too slow: George struck him in the chest with the full weight of his body. The spear-wielding Roman teetered on the edge and then, with a terrified scream, toppled backwards onto the rocks below.

Darting back for his sword, George was forced to leap backwards yet again, this time to avoid Primus's lunge.

"You'll pay for that!" spat the incensed Roman.

George backed away from his enemy, pulling out his dagger as he did so, refusing to accept defeat even now.

"He's mine", commanded Primus, and his two remaining servants stepped back, leaving this battle to their leader.

Primus swung his sword lazily as he walked towards the Briton; he seemed in no hurry to finish this one-sided contest. Sensing his foe's overconfidence, George darted forward, lunging with his short blade. But Primus was ready and, with a deft flick of his sword, he scraped George's outstretched right leg, drawing blood.

"That's right, Briton", smiled Primus, as George reeled back clutching his wound. "I'm going to kill you slowly."

Angrily, George lunged at his opponent once more. This time he received a cut on the arm for his trouble. George staggered backwards; this wasn't a contest, it was a cruel game, a game that Primus could end any time he wanted to.

Well, I'm not playing by his rules any more!

Lifting the dagger high in the air, George whipped his right arm back. Primus's eyes widened in fear as he realised what his enemy was about to do; he lunged at him, but he was too late. George's right arm shot forward, sending the blade flying through the air.

The Roman let out a cry of pain as the knife sank into the flesh of his thigh. With no time to lament his lack of accuracy, George surged at Primus, knocking him to the ground and grabbing his sword arm. This sudden move caught his stricken foe off-guard, and George succeeded in wrestling the shortsword from his weakened grip.

Scrambling to his feet, George sensed movement to his left and reacted instinctively, swinging his stolen weapon upwards to block the attack of Primus's henchman. There was a clash of steel and George lurched right, fighting to keep his balance as he sprinted for freedom. A shadow loomed: the other henchman; George swung his sword.

His opponent's blade bit deep into George's side; with an anguished howl, he fell, hitting the stony ground hard, sword slipping from his outstretched hand. The pain was excruciating. It was over; he had so nearly escaped, but now he lay face-down, bleeding to death in the wilderness with only his murderers for company!

Chapter 21 – Trolls & Tunnels

Give me a quick death. George shut his eyes tight, biting his lip to keep from crying out with the pain. He was going to show Primus how a Christian could die, with dignity and without fear.

Next moment, a loud yell escaped his lips as George was rolled roughly onto his back. He opened his eyes, squinting up through the glare of the midday sun overhead. Primus stood triumphantly over him, his thigh heavily strapped with a piece of cloth.

"That's right, Briton", he crowed. "Look up at your conqueror, the one who is about to dispatch your soul to the dark halls of Hades."

"You may kill my body", replied George defiantly, grimacing as each word caused him further pain. "But my soul is safe in God's hands."

Primus started to reply, but whatever he said was drowned out by a harsh cry from above. A huge shadow passed across George's fallen body, for a fleeting moment blotting out the glaring rays of the sun.

"Maybe I'll leave you to the thunder drake", mused Primus, a cruel smile crossing his face. "They prey on wounded animals, and I'm told they like their food to be alive for as long as possible – must improve the flavour. Let's see how much of you it can eat before you die!"

Primus's evil laughter was cut short by another cry, human this time: one of his companions.

"TROLLS!"

"What?" Primus turned his head, alarmed.

"FROM THE CAVE ABOVE!" continued his companion, yelling wildly.

George twisted his head, trying to locate the source of the commotion. Behind and above him, emerging from the opening that he had earlier been trying to reach, were several enormous figures armed with clubs and spears.

"Leave him to the trolls!" called Primus, limping back towards the narrow section of path.

His two lackeys followed swiftly behind, almost falling over themselves in their haste to escape.

George tried desperately to rise, but the pain along his ribs was too great, and he fell back to the dusty ground, groaning. Moments later, he was staring up into the hooded faces of half a dozen savage looking giants.

George had seen plenty of tall men in his travels: Primus was a head taller than he, but these trolls were true giants. They seemed to be built on an entirely different scale to ordinary mortals: the shortest of them must have been well over seven feet tall, but they were all correspondingly broad and well muscled, not thin and gangly as you would expect men who approached that height to be. The next thing George noticed about these trolls, after their size, was that they all stooped, none of them stood fully upright, and they were bow-legged too. Also the skin of their bare arms (he couldn't properly see their faces) was pale, almost untouched by the sun, as though they rarely ventured out beneath its rays.

The trolls spoke in deep guttural voices, in a language that George had never heard, gesturing at him and pointing after the fleeing men, while shielding their eyes from the sun's glare with huge hands.

George couldn't stand it: the pain, the thirst, the blinding light, the anticipation of death.

"Just kill me and get it over", he moaned, weakly.

He was certain that no one understood what he had just said, but his feeble words provoked a reaction, though not the one George wanted. With a mighty heave, he was lifted off the ground and swiftly carried into the darkness.

George opened one eye. At first he could make out nothing then, as his eyes adjusted to the blackness, he discerned a faint orange glow some way off to his left: *a fire, perhaps.* He was still alive, that much was clear, and being held in an underground cavern. He was lying on some kind of grassy mat, and he seemed to be alone although he could make out several distant voices. George moved his right hand cautiously to his injured side; someone had wound a piece of cloth around his ribs. He tried to rise but, once more, fell back with a moan.

Footsteps. Someone's coming.

George closed his eyes, praying that the owner of the footsteps would leave him alone. But they didn't; he was shaken roughly by the elbow and then lifted into a sitting position. A wooden cup was put to his lips, and a thick foul-smelling potion was tipped down his throat. George swallowed some and gagged, coughing uncontrollably as the hot liquid stung his throat.

Were they trying to poison him? He shut his mouth, trying to prevent anything further from passing his lips. The troll who was supplying this vile concoction didn't seem to like this reaction. He growled something in the harsh throaty language of his kind, and his companion, who was propping George up, placed his huge cold hand on George's face. Next thing, his jaws were being forced apart and the vile stuff was running down his throat again.

When the trolls had carried out this strange form of torture, they left him alone for a while. As he lay there, helpless, George fought against a drowsiness that threatened to overcome him. *They have poisoned me, they must have, they...*

George slowly opened his eyes. He was still in darkness; this didn't look like the afterlife, or at least not how he'd imagined it to be. He attempted to sit up and felt a shooting pain in his side; he was definitely still alive. *But why?*

George ran his hand absent-mindedly over the cloth wrapped around his injured side. The trolls had bandaged his wound; maybe that foul-tasting concoction had been some sort of medicine. George turned over onto his hands and knees; the pain in his side did seem to have subsided a little. He crouched in the dark, pondering this surprising turn of events. All the stories that he had heard about trolls made them out to be savage man-eating monsters, but these ones seemed to be helping him. Suddenly it struck him: *They're only keeping me alive to eat me!*

It made sense: the trolls wouldn't want to eat a wounded man any more than he would want to eat a sheep torn by wolves. He had to get out of here! George hesitantly put his weight onto his left leg and got to his feet, grimacing as a sharp pain ran down his right side. All was quiet; it felt like the middle of the night, but George had no way of telling what time of day or night it was. *I could have been lying here for hours.*

The trolls weren't guarding him closely, believing him to be incapacitated; now was his only chance. George moved carefully to his left, the only direction that offered any illumination. As he approached the orange glow, he could see that it was indeed a fire, and it was burning low. By its fading light, he could make out several enormous prone forms wrapped in furs. From the general snuffling and snorting noises, George guessed that all the inhabitants of this cave were currently asleep.

Tiptoeing between the slumbering giants, George made his way to a narrow opening in the rock that was illuminated by the firelight. Stepping through this, he found himself in a dimly lit passage. The faint radiance was coming from torches wedged into the rock wall at various intervals.

There was no indication as to which direction led to the exit so, picking one at random, George headed right, walking slowly, careful not to snag his feet on the uneven floor. Presently, he came to another opening on his right and, peering through it, saw a second small fire with several more fur-covered figures lying beside it. One of the bundles stirred, and George quickly turned away and moved on down the passage.

After a while, George stopped; the tunnel seemed to be heading downhill. He was pretty sure that when the trolls had captured him they had carried him down into their lair, not up, so the way out must lie somewhere above. George turned around, preparing to head in the opposite direction, and then stopped dead in his tracks; something had just moved in the shadows. His heart skipped a beat; he was being followed.

George turned, heading downhill once more, and started to quicken his pace. As he made his way deeper into the mountain, he strained his ears, listening for any sounds of pursuit. *There, footsteps.* He was sure of it. *But why don't they call out and alert the other trolls?*

The tunnel led ever deeper. They passed another dimly lit cavern containing yet more sleeping trolls, but still his mysterious pursuer didn't call out. As he sneaked past the entrance to this latest dwelling, George had a chilling thought: *Maybe they want to get me in a quiet cave, away from the other trolls, and then eat me all to themselves!*

Rounding a bend in the passage, George discovered a sizeable side passage leading off the main way. This was his chance; he quickly slipped into the darkness, hands out in front of him to prevent himself from bumping into a rock wall.

He had not gone far when his fingers did indeed make contact with solid rock. Stretching his arms out to either side, George soon discovered, to his dismay that he had arrived at a dead end; what he had thought to be a new tunnel was, in fact, merely a deep alcove. He turned to face the torch-lit passage that he had just left. *I'm not far enough into the dark; the troll's going to see me.*

George pressed himself into the recess, as the footsteps of his pursuer grew steadily louder. If he was seen now it was over; George knew that he had no hope of defending himself against a troll. He would have been hard pressed even if he was armed and healthy, but in his current condition he couldn't fight off a desert fox!

A bead of cold sweat dripped onto his nose. George moved to wipe it and then froze; a shadow had appeared in the torchlight. He stood like a statue as a dark figure walked into his field of view.

George was surprised by what he saw. He had been expecting a huge hulking troll, stooping to avoid banging his head on the tunnel roof, but instead the weak light briefly silhouetted a smaller upright shape as it passed across the alcove.

Having avoided detection, a relieved George waited a few moments for the footsteps to die away, and then doubled back on himself, heading uphill and, hopefully, towards the outside world.

George's eyes were fully adjusted to this shadowy realm by now, and he made rapid progress, passing the two inhabited caverns, he had seen earlier, without mishap, and pressing on past the cave where he had recently been held. So far he had seen no further signs of prowling trolls, but he wasn't foolish enough to think that they would all be asleep; there would surely be watchmen.

George plodded on; this tunnel seemed to go on for miles. He was starting to feel very weary; he had lost a lot of blood, and it was beginning to take its toll. Telling himself that the exit couldn't be much further, George continued doggedly, passing a number of unlit side passages that led to who knows where. A short distance further on, the main way that he had been following began to widen out into a fair-sized cave. Along the walls were a number of niches, one of which contained several joints of meat, suspended from hooks embedded in the rock. He didn't spot anything that looked like it might have come from a human, but it crossed his mind that there was probably a hook in there with his name on it!

Making a hasty exit from this storage cave, George followed the passage as it climbed steeply uphill. His wound was aching badly now, but this rapid ascent was encouraging; he must be nearing the exit. Sure enough, after a few more painful steps,

George could see light up ahead: not the flickering orange glow of torchlight, but the bright yellow rays of sunlight. His pace quickened; he was nearly there.

Then he saw the guards: two giant figures blocking the way. George slowly retreated; they hadn't seen him. The trolls continued to keep watch on the outside world as George crouched in the shadows, unsure of what to do next. *Is that the only exit?*

George looked around desperately for another option. The passage was narrow at this point, only about three feet wide, but the roof was almost lofty enough to be out of sight of the subdued lighting. He craned his neck backwards, staring up at a patch of light somewhere high above him. *That can't be torchlight. No one would put a torch all the way up there; it has to be another way out!*

There was a ledge about fifteen feet up on his right hand side, which seemed to climb up towards the distant light. George placed his hands on the rock above his head, thinking that he might be able to climb up to it but, even as he did so, a spasm of pain shot up his right side. He dropped his hands in dismay; there was no way he was climbing anywhere in this condition.

Even as he stared up at the path to freedom that was so tantalisingly out of his reach, a new problem emerged: footsteps. He was trapped between the guards and this new arrival!

As the sound of feet echoing on rock grew steadily louder, George's mind was racing. There was still one chance. George put his back to the right side of the tunnel, his left foot on the rock wall opposite, and, wedging himself in the narrow gap, began to lever himself upward.

It was a slow and painful process, and George was sure that he would be seen before he gained the ledge. Sure enough, as he stared back along the passage from his elevated position, George spotted a shadowy figure approaching from further down the tunnel.

George stopped rigid, frozen with one foot on each of the parallel rock faces, forming a kind of bridge under which the troll would pass. He held his breath as the figure moved closer. It was smaller than the trolls he had seen so far, and walked with only a slight stoop: *It's the one that was following me earlier.* It suddenly dawned on George that trolls must have good eyes for seeing in the dark, as they spent so much of their time underground; surely he would be seen this time! But no, the troll, not expecting anyone to be hovering above it, walked under him and continued straight ahead without glancing upward. George, breathing a very quiet sigh of relief, worked his way up between the walls and, after a bit of shuffling, heaved his backside up onto the ledge.

Attempting to move from a sitting position to standing on the narrow shelf proved tricky, and George dislodged some loose rocks as he did so. The crumbling pieces dropped to the floor of the tunnel, making a clattering sound that echoed alarmingly loudly. *Someone must have heard that!*

Someone had heard that. The midget troll was back, and this time he looked up, straight at George! George scrambled along the ledge; it was a race for freedom, and he needed all the start he could get. Below, the troll had already begun to scale the wall, making rapid progress as he hauled his agile frame over the rock.

George staggered onward towards the light. The ledge widened and began to rise, before dipping unexpectedly. George slid on the smooth rock as he attempted to slow his momentum. Ahead, a dark chasm loomed like a hungry mouth, open to receive unwary climbers. He tried desperately to stop, but it was no good, he was going to plunge into the crevasse!

Unable to halt his downward slide, George leapt into the darkness, shouting wildly in his panic. His flight ended abruptly, feet landing on solid rock at the other side of the crack, which turned out to be less than three feet wide.

Wincing with the pain of the impact, George struggled back to his feet. There was a cry from behind, and he whirled around in time to see his pursuer sliding down the slippery slope that he'd just negotiated. With a scream, the troll plunged headlong into the void. George could only stare as the yawning mouth swallowed up the troll; the scream had told him something about his pursuer: he was only a child!

As the Briton stood motionless, staring into the blackness, another cry rang out. The troll child was still alive, clinging to the lip of the crevasse by his pale thin fingers. There was a shout from somewhere below; the guards must have heard all the commotion and were coming to investigate.

George turned back towards the light; freedom beckoned. This was his only chance; if they caught him a second time he would not be allowed to escape again. The troll cried out once more, sounding desperate. George wondered how old he was: *twelve? Maybe only ten? The guards are getting nearer; they'll rescue him.*

George's mind flitted back to another cave a long way away and what seemed a lifetime ago.

A desperate voice was calling his name; it was Tristan. His friend was pleading with him to help, but George didn't turn back, he didn't even slow down; he just raced towards the light. He had no thought for the boy who had once saved his life; at that moment George's only concern was for his own survival. Behind him, Tristan's scream echoed in the dark, and then he was gone, snatched from this life into the next, his plea for aid forever unanswered.

George swallowed hard, tears welling up in his eyes. Another boy was pleading with him in the dark, and this time he was going to answer, whatever the cost.

His mind made up, George raced back to the edge of the chasm and dropped to the ground, reaching for the child's arm. His hand closing around flesh, George yanked with all his might, yelling with the pain his efforts were causing to his wounded side.

Panicking, the young troll grabbed George's leg, desperate to cling onto anything that would save him from falling to his death. With a gargantuan effort, George hauled the troll up and over the edge, and the pair collapsed exhausted.

George had nothing left, the pain in his side was unbearable; he just wanted to lie there and die. But there was still some part of him that hadn't given up, that wanted to fight on, and that voice was growing louder. Forcing his eyes open, George hauled his battered body off the ground. The young troll stared at him, wide-eyed, but did nothing to try to prevent George from reaching the exit.

As he staggered towards freedom, the light grew brighter and brighter, and then suddenly it was gone. Something was blocking it; a huge figure had entered the cave and was now barring the way. George stopped dead in his tracks; he had been so close, but now his act of kindness was going to cost him.

He turned to run, but another troll had appeared at the far side of the crevasse; he was trapped! Two huge arms encircled his waist and George was lifted bodily off the ground. Crying out in pain, he struggled to break free, but it was no good, the troll's grip was like iron.

"I saved his life!" George cried, pointing at the boy who was now being helped to his feet by the other troll, appalled at the injustice of what was happening.

The trolls exchanged words in their strange language and then, to George's surprise, he was carried out into the sunlight. After all this time in the dark of the caves, he had to shield his eyes from its glare, even though outside it was evening and the sun would soon be setting.

His eyes having adjusted to the increased lighting, George started to take in his surroundings. From up there, slung over the troll's right shoulder, he could make out the walled plateau where he had recently fought for his life against Primus and his men. They were about forty feet up and George felt very precariously perched as the troll began his near vertical descent.

Even in his discomfort, George could only marvel at this giant's strength and dexterity: he climbed down the sheer rock as if it had been a staircase, balancing George over his shoulder like a sack of flour.

Halfway down the climb, this admiration turned to dismay as his captor reached a rock ledge and then approached a large familiar opening in the mountainside: the cave that he'd been attempting to reach when Primus's men had caught up with him, and the entrance to the trolls' lair!

George screamed in frustration and pounded his fists on the troll's broad back, but he might as well have attacked the mountain itself for all the reaction he got. He was a prisoner once again, and this time, he knew there would be no escape!

Chapter 22 – The Fallen

Deeper and deeper into the heart of the mountain they descended. Here, no ray of sunshine ever pierced, no breath of wind ever disturbed, no drop of rain ever refreshed. Here there was no night, no day, it was always cold, always gloomy, and here George's hope had died. His struggles had ceased long ago; he was powerless to prevent whatever awful fate awaited him. The silent colossus, in whose grip he languished, bore him onward, downward, into the very bowels of the underworld. Was this the way to the gates of Hades?

The tunnel they were following opened out into a small fire-lit cave. Beyond the flames, George could make out a hunched misshapen figure, standing, warming himself. The troll, if that's what it was, was no taller than George, and even in this subdued light, he could tell that it was an aged creature.

George found himself being lowered to the ground. His captor spoke slowly and respectfully to the one by the fire. Even though the words meant nothing to George, he could tell that much; though still deep and throaty there was a slight softening of the tone.

He shuddered involuntarily; there was something eerie about this stooped wizened white-haired thing. Its head seemed far too big for the body; its arms appeared to reach almost to the ground. George gasped; the figure was slowly levitating upward! And then he realised that it hadn't been standing by the fire, it had been sitting down! The aged giant moved away from the thing it had been squatting on, what appeared to be a pillar of rock rising up from the floor of the cave, and moved around the fire towards him.

The giant's steps were slow and purposeful. A great dread fell on George; he felt as though he was in the presence of some ancient evil. There was something inhuman about the being standing before him, even more so than the other trolls he had encountered. This giant was by far the tallest he had seen, standing almost nine feet in height, despite being severely bow-legged and badly stooped!

He stared up into the huge creature's pale face. The giant returned his gaze steadily and began speaking, not in the harsh guttural tongue of his kind, but in words that seemed strangely familiar. George was almost certain that he had just been addressed in the 'old language'.

The 'old language' was Greek. From what George had learned, the Greeks had once ruled a large part of the civilised world and much of their culture had been preserved in the Roman Empire. Justus spoke Greek fluently, as did Hector, but George's grasp of it was extremely limited; it had taken him long enough to reach a decent standard in Latin, and he had had no wish to attempt yet another foreign tongue.

"My... name... is... George", he began haltingly in Greek, trying to call to mind the little of the 'old language' he had picked up.

The white-haired troll replied, but George could decipher none of it.

"I'm sorry, I didn't..." George began in Latin, and then stopped, realising he needed to translate into Greek. Before he could summon up the Greek for 'I don't understand', the troll spoke again, this time, to George's astonishment, in Latin.

"My name is Crius", he began, his voice very croaky and thickly accented, "And this is Coeus, one of my sons sons", he added, indicating the troll standing beside George.

George opened his mouth to speak, but nothing came out. 'Nice to meet you' didn't really seem appropriate! Instead, he managed a weak nod.

"I am sorry my Latin is a little... rusted", the troll continued, obviously struggling to recall words he hadn't used for some time.

George stared at him; this was bizarre! *Here I am, having a polite conversation with a cannibalistic giant!*

"It is long since I spoke with a maatag. Forgive me: a mortal", he corrected.

But you are mortal, thought George, although he didn't dare say it out loud. He had no wish to anger this giant. He had expected to have been put in a huge cooking pot or attached to a great roasting spit by now, and the fact that he was here conversing with, what appeared to be, the leader of the trolls, had rekindled an ember of hope within him.

"What name do mortals call us in these days?" asked the ancient troll. "Titans? Giants?"

"Trolls", answered George.

"Trolls?" grimaced the white-haired giant, obviously less than impressed. "There was a time when my people were treated like gods."

George looked nervously up into the huge wrinkled face; had he angered the giant? The troll's eyes seemed far away, as if recalling the distant past. He didn't look angry, just a little wistful.

"Now we hide away in holes in the ground, like beasts... who run from the hunter's spear!"

"But why?" questioned George, before he could help himself.

"What do maatags do to those that be strange, that be different?" countered the troll, a trace of anger creeping into his croaky voice.

George hesitated, unsure of how to reply.

"They put them in cages", he continued, answering his own question. "They lead them in chains. They show them to all the world, and when they be... tired of them..." He paused, searching for the right words. "...they kill them!" he finished, his grey eyes flashing dangerously.

Somewhere in George's mind, the image of a caged wagon containing a large golden-maned lion appeared. The old giant was right; if the might of Rome ever conquered his people, they would surely be led into the many amphitheatres, dotted around the empire, to fight and die for the amusement of the crowds.

"I have lived long", the aged troll continued, staring down at George with sadness in his face. "I have seen my sons grow old, my sons sons grow strong; their children bear children of their own, and in all that... time..." He coughed, turning his great head away. "...I do not see the sun. Only when he sets and when he... rises."

For the first time, George felt a tinge of pity for his captors. To live out your life in darkness and seclusion was a fate almost worse than death. He stared up into the troll's deep grey eyes. Was this how they justified killing and eating people: as a sort of revenge against the society that had condemned them to their miserable existence?

"It is our curse", continued the troll, interrupting George's worrying thoughts. "The curse of the Nephilim."

"The who?" asked George, interested in spite of his predicament.

"We are Nephilim", repeated the troll. "The Fallen", he translated, looking at George as if he expected him to see some great significance in these words.

"You do not know of the Fallen?"

George shook his head.

The giant stared down at him, shaking his own huge head in disbelief, coughed once more, and began his tale.

"Long time past, when the earth was not, the great God made saraf... How would you say it? Angels?"

George nodded, wondering where this was going.

"The angels be great... powers, and one, Lucifer, wanted to be as God. Lucifer and his army fought against the angels of God, but lost. They be fallen to earth. Some took... mortal woman and had children. Their children be tall and strong – the Fallen."

George gaped in horror at the creature standing before him; he now understood why he felt the strong presence of evil. The white-haired, wizened giant before him had been spawned by a demon!

Someone was calling his name, a woman, someone that meant a great deal to him. "George... George!" It was dark, pitch black; he couldn't see her. She gave a scream. George tried to run towards the sound, but he couldn't get to her, something was blocking him, hemming him in. A dim reddish glow was rising from somewhere down below. By its faint light, George could make out his surroundings: he was in a huge pot, suspended on a thick rope. Startled, George moved towards the side; the cauldron swayed suddenly and he was forced to grip onto the metal lip. Staring down, he could see the source of the red glow: a lake of fire, endlessly burning, throwing gouts of orange and yellow flames upwards! The bottom seemed to drop out of his stomach; he was being lowered down towards the inferno! George cried out, looking up into the darkness. Huge pale faces leered at him from above, laughing deep croaky laughs as he plummeted into the fiery abyss...

"George."

A deep throaty voice was calling his name. George slowly opened his eyes, and then gasped; a huge pale face was staring down at him. Then he remembered: he was still in the trolls' lair. Wincing only slightly, George sat up, threw off his cloak, and looked about him. The cave was packed with pale-skinned giants: men, women and children, all staring at him. George looked into their faces and saw expressions of curiosity, some of suspicion, and even a few smiles. He winked at a little girl who goggled at him; she was barely five feet tall and was clutching her mother's hand tightly. Her mother, who stood more than a head taller than George, smiled down at him.

It was incredible to think that last night he had thought himself fleeing from flesh-eating monsters! He smiled as he recalled old Crius's response to the question of whether he was going to eat him: *"I could not eat Maatag; all bone and no meat, and too tough and stringy."*

The troll who had awoken George, bent down and offered his huge white hand. Taking it, George was gently pulled to his feet. In a neat pile by the wall, lay his possessions: his moneybag, his belt, his dagger and his sword. A large troll, George recognised as Coeus, handed him the belt and bag and, after a moment's hesitation, the weapons too. It seemed that he had gained their complete trust. They, in turn, had his trust: they had rescued him from Primus's clutches, they had washed and bound his wounds, they had nursed him back to health, and now they were going to escort him to the boundary of their land.

Coeus led the way up the long torch-lit tunnel that climbed to the surface. Reaching the exit, George turned to his saviours. A boy stepped out of the small party of well-wishers that had followed them: the inquisitive troll that had followed George while everyone else slept. One of the adult males, standing beside George, beckoned him forward. The youngster shyly moved towards George, holding out his right hand in a gesture of friendship. The Briton held out his own hand and the young troll clasped his arm, unspoken words of gratitude clearly showing in his smiling eyes. The adult troll embraced the boy and then clasped George's arm.

"Marku", he said, an expression of thankfulness on his pale face.

George looked at the pair of them, standing side-by-side, father and son it seemed, and felt warm inside. Then, turning to the crowd that had gathered to see him off, he mimicked the father's word: "Marku."

George felt very safe, flanked as he was by four giant spear-wielding bodyguards. It was a cold cloudless night, and the light of the silvery moon guided them down the rocky mountain path.

When Crius had suggested that his people lead him safely to the borders of their land, George had been forced to make a decision as to whether to head east, to Darnis, or west, back to Cyrene. Praying that his instincts would not be wrong, he had chosen to return the way he had come, travel on to Silene and confront Publius about the ambush.

His giant guides led him along a winding ledge that overlooked the road on which he had been ambushed two, or perhaps three, days ago. Instead of descending to the road, the trolls climbed up a steep path that led to a narrow ridge with a sheer drop on either side. George had never suffered from a fear of heights, but staring straight down at the road hundreds of feet below, and then out to sea, perhaps another hundred feet below that, made him feel a little queasy.

After a nervy scramble across needle-sharp rocks, Coeus led them along a winding mountain path which was somewhat easier to navigate. Even so, George was grateful for the bright moonlight as he followed his giant guide, picking his way through dense bushes and around craggy boulders.

Eventually, after a gruelling march up a narrow steep-sided gorge, one exhausted Briton and four seemingly fresh giants emerged on level ground: they had reached the grassy plateau on which Cyrene was built.

Their destination was in sight now; George could make out the east wall of the town by the light of the moon. It was still the second watch of the night, however, and the gates would be tight shut; there would be no way of getting in. George wondered to himself why his guides had not realised this, but it was clear that they knew little of men's ways. To them, this was mid-morning and it wouldn't have occurred to them that the inhabitants of Cyrene would not be stirring for several hours.

Presently, Coeus halted. He looked edgy; they were standing overlooking a road built by mortals, next to a town inhabited by tens of thousands of them. George supposed that this was the nearest to civilisation any of the trolls had ventured. It was time for his bodyguards to return home. George looked up into their hooded faces, towering above his own, and wished that he could say what

213

was in his heart. They would leave him now and return to their cursed lives: a hated people, treated like monsters, dwelling always in darkness, prisoners in the land of a prejudiced and greedy self-seeking culture.

"Marku, Nephilim. Marku."

George turned away, a lump in his throat, and headed towards the town.

As there was no way of passing through Cyrene at this hour of the night, he was going to have to skirt the town. This was easier said than done, as the walls extended to the edge of the plateau on which the town was built. It didn't take him long to find a way down, though, and after scrabbling through some thick bushes that bordered the edge, George followed a stony path leading to the steep slopes below Cyrene.

Following this narrow way, George was a little surprised to see a small fire burning some distance ahead. Wondering who would be sleeping out in the open when the shelter of the town was so close, he approached cautiously.

As he neared the inviting glow, George heard drunken singing. He stopped, wondering whether to turn around and find another path down. As he hesitated, a feeling of shame came over him: *Here you are, the conquering hero, returning from battle, and you're afraid of a few drunks?*

George fingered the hilt of his sword and walked on, trying to convince himself that his misgivings were foolish, that he had nothing to fear.

"Hey, you! Where do yer think yer going?" called a slightly slurred voice, as George approached.

"Come and join us forra drink", added another, belching loudly.

"No thanks", replied George, without slowing his pace.

As he walked past the fire, another man moved to block his path. "I don't like yer tone", he said, menacingly.

Behind him, the rasping sound of a sword being unsheathed filled the night air. As George whirled around to face this new foe, his arms were grabbed from behind.

"Give us yer money!"

Something hit George on the temple and he stumbled sideways. Before he could react, a great weight bore him to the ground and eager hands rummaged for his possessions.

"Look ar'all this silver!" cried a triumphant voice.

George forced his head up, spitting soil from his mouth. He was scared; he just wanted to get home. Why was this happening after all he'd been through?

"A sword an' a knife! Looks like ee thinks ee's an 'ero!"

"Come on then, let's 'ave a fight", called another voice, and George was dragged to his feet.

Two men held George's arms as a third punched him in the gut. George buckled, falling forwards, winded. Another blow struck him to the back of the head and he fell on his face, blood trickling down his cheek.

He was hauled to his feet once more; steel flashed in the firelight. They were going to kill him! George swung sideways, breaking free of the man holding him, and aimed a kick at an assailant's knee. There was a loud curse and someone struck him hard on the jaw. Reeling from the blow, George staggered backwards.

The man with the drawn sword stepped out of the darkness, blade pointing at George's chest. He moved closer, raised the weapon and… giving a sudden gasp, pitched forward into the dirt, a long spear protruding from his back!

There was a cry of alarm and, before George could work out what was going on, one of his assailants was flying through the air, landing, with a crunch, in the lower branches of a nearby mastic tree. There was another yelp, a snapping sound, and a heavy thud as the man dropped the remaining distance to the ground.

Wild cries of terror were now erupting on every side, and moments later another of the brigands came hurtling through the air, narrowly missing George, as he crashed to the ground amid the hot ashes of the fire. With a howl, the bandit leapt to his feet, clutching his scalded buttocks, and sped away into the darkness.

A huge dark figure sprang out from behind a bush on the other side of the path, at which point the remainder of the thieves scattered in all directions, shrieking with fear. In the confusion, one of the men charged past George, who promptly stuck his leg out, tripping the unfortunate fellow and causing him to fall flat on his face. Bending down, George retrieved his moneybag from the prone thief and then, as the man struggled to get to his feet, hit him on the back of the head with it. There was a satisfying clunk, a groan, and the man slumped back down, unconscious.

George looked up at the four huge trolls emerging from the undergrowth. Coeus stared down at him and gave him a look that, even in the moonlight, George could read like a book (a lot better than a book, in fact!) It said: *You need a lot of looking after!*

Smiling sheepishly back at him, George took his dagger and sword once more from the troll's huge hand, and watched as the giant forms slipped silently away into the night.

George felt ready to drop: he was hurting all over, his face was covered with both blood and mud, and he was sorely tempted to just curl up by the thieves' fire and go to sleep. But he had to resist the temptation and keep going; it would not do to wake up later, surrounded by a gang of murderous brigands nursing sore heads.

By the light of the gibbous moon, George picked his way around the walls of Cyrene and found a steep rocky path that led back onto the plateau. Now, he had only a three-mile journey, along a well maintained road, to reach the little village of Silene.

As he walked along, George couldn't help wondering to himself what he would discover when he reached Justus's villa. Would he find his friends safe and well? Or would he meet an anxious Julia, waiting in vain for the safe return of her husband and family?

It was still dark when he entered Silene. As George approached his former home, he wondered whether he should wait until first light before disturbing the household. He felt awkward about waking everyone at this hour, especially after the manner of his departure. He had not forgotten the harsh words he had spoken to his friends; they had seemed necessary at the time, well chosen, even clever. Now everything he had said and done after the duel seemed childish. He had acted like a spoiled brat who hits out at everyone and everything when it finds that it can't get its own way.

It wasn't that cold; maybe he should sleep outside in his travelling cloak until the sun came up. But no, this was an emergency: either his friends were stranded in Darnis in various states of discomfort, or Publius was a traitor who had tried to get him killed, and needed to be brought to justice.

Feelings of righteous anger welling up inside him, George walked up to the gates and called out. At first he wondered if he would be heard, but presently a figure could be seen, carrying an oil lamp, and making its way through the olive grove. George strained to see who it was: *Brennos - so Publius is a traitor!*

"Who is it?" called his mentor in the calm assured voice that George knew so well.

"It's me, George."

There was the sound of a key turning in a lock, and the gates swung open with their characteristic squeal.

"George, what are you…?" began Brennos, and then, noticing his friend's dishevelled appearance, stopped and began again. "What happened to you?"

"It's a long story", replied George impatiently, entering the grounds of the villa. "Have you been to Alexandria?"

"Yes", replied his friend, "We just got back last night."

"Were you shipwrecked?"

"No. Why do you…?"

But Brennos was interrupted again, this time by a squeaky Roman voice: "What's going on? Who is it at this hour?"

A short podgy figure emerged from the trees, clad in a plain robe and carrying a lamp. By its light, the new arrival's face could be clearly seen. Publius's mouth fell open, and his eyes widened in disbelief at the sight of the ragged figure standing before him. Then, taking a step forward, George landed a left hook right on the astonished Roman's jaw!

Chapter 23 – Conspiracies

The hooded figure moved silently down the road, his long cloak almost brushing the ground behind him. Approaching the end of the street, he glanced over his shoulder, as if fearing pursuit, before crossing to the far side. It was a cold evening and the relentless driving rain made it feel even more so. Wrapping the woollen cloak more tightly around his stout frame, the man leant into the wind as he battled his way along the exposed path that led down to the docks.

The roar of the sea was stronger here, and the sound of huge waves breaking on the rocky shore drowned out the steady beating of the rain. Quickening his pace, the hooded man made his way toward the large stone building at the corner of the jetty: his destination.

Reaching inside his cloak for the package he was carrying, the windswept, bedraggled figure, stretched out his right hand to knock on the large wooden door and…

"Stop right there!"

George stepped out from the shadows across the street, satisfied that he had caught his quarry in the act. Hector followed more reluctantly, shivering as water streamed through his long auburn hair, running into his eyes and down the back of his neck.

The hooded figure turned in alarm then, seeing whom it was, tried to regain his composure.

"Why are you following me?" Publius demanded to know, his voice indignant, though George thought he detected a hint of uncertainty, even fear, in those normally arrogant tones.

"What have you got there?" pressed George, ignoring the Roman's question.

"That doesn't concern you", replied Publius, stiffly.

"Oh, I think it does", countered George. "I think that you've been sending letters to your real master: Primus."

"What?" exclaimed the Roman incredulously. "I hardly know Primus, I've met him a handful of times, and I've no idea where he is at the moment. My master, Justus", continued Publius, emphasising Justus's name and waving his arms in an animated manner, "Said he'd heard that Primus had left the country. So how am I supposed to send him letters? Why would I even want to?"

"You've been getting letters from him", asserted George, unconvinced by the Roman's theatrics. "One arrived two days ago."

Publius paused, either attempting to recall the letter in question, or to think of a good cover story, or just to wipe rainwater from his eyes.

"Hector saw the messenger arrive", added George, glancing at his silent companion for support.

"I did", confirmed the Gaul, before sneezing violently.

"Is everyone in the household spying on me or is it just you two?" blurted Publius, angrily.

"Answer the question", insisted George, his tone threatening.

"Or what? You'll hit me again?" retorted Publius. "I thought you Christians were against violence."

A wave of guilt washed over George; he regretted striking the Roman. He had never attacked someone like that before. Even since joining Justus, as a bodyguard, he had only fought in self-defence. *But he tried to get me killed!* The angry voice in George's head did nothing to lessen the pangs of guilt.

"The letter I received, two days ago, was from an Egyptian merchant", stated Publius, his tone now calm and deliberate. "It was regarding the items of pottery that you will be picking up in Alexandria next week."

The Roman paused as a particularly large breaker boomed onto the jetty, and then resumed his explanations. "The letter I have here", continued Publius, indicating the scroll that he'd been carrying, "Is a message to Flavius, a good friend of my master, Justus." Once more, Publius emphasised Justus's name, overstating his point. "Justus intends to visit Flavius, who lives in Ostia, during this year's trading voyage."

There was a pause as George inwardly digested this information, during which another huge wave crashed over the wooden boards, sending up spray that almost reached them. It all seemed quite plausible: George had met Flavius, the merchant specialising in medicines and strange potions, when first travelling with Justus; he'd even been to his villa, in Ostia, last year. But was Publius telling the truth?

"Now, if there's nothing more", continued the Roman, a hint of sarcasm in his squeaky voice, "I will deliver this letter to the postmaster."

There was nothing more. George watched as Publius gained entry to the postmaster's house, and then turned to leave.

"He's up to something", the Briton concluded, shaking his head at Hector.

"Perhaps he's telling the truth", sniffed Hector, apparently less convinced of the Roman's guilt.

"He almost sent me to my death!" exclaimed George, disappointed by the Gaul's seeming lack of loyalty to his cause.

"I don't know", mumbled Hector, unwilling to commit himself either way. "Maybe he really thought Justus had sent that letter about the shipwreck. Even Justus admitted that the writing was not dissimilar to his own hand."

"But why didn't he mention the letter to anyone else then?"

The Gaul shrugged his shoulders. "He said he hadn't wanted Julia to know about the accident; he didn't want to worry her."

"And why didn't he ask about the shipwreck when you arrived back without me?"

"I don't know", replied Hector, shifting from foot to foot as the rain continued to lash down, obviously eager to return to Silene. "He didn't want to bother Justus with it after a hard day?"

"You believe that?" Now it was George's turn to be incredulous.

It was no use; they had been over all these arguments before. George seemed to be the only one convinced of Publius's guilt. For some reason, inexplicable to him, no one else could see it.

As they trudged back up the steep slope from Apollonia to Cyrene, the downpour became a drizzle and then stopped completely. Soon, the sun began to emerge from behind grey clouds, and a rainbow appeared. The sky, which had been dark and miserable, was now bathed in a multitude of beautiful bright colours.

George stared up at this awesome work of God, the master painter, whose canvas is the skies, and his heart filled with thankfulness; it was impossible to see a rainbow and not be lifted by its beauty. His thoughts mirrored the sky, turning from the dark and miserable to the bright and positive.

Despite his frustrations with Publius, George had to admit that life was a lot better now than it had been six months ago, when through his own stubbornness, he had been banished from Justus's household and left to fend for himself. Fortunately for him, while visiting Alexandria, Cassia had admitted her part in what led to the duel, and so, despite his attack on Publius, Justus had accepted George back into his family.

It had not been easy; there had been a lot of apologies to make, but the strong ties of friendship had overcome all grievances. The story of his encounter with the trolls had done no harm either; he had held the whole household spellbound with this exciting tale, and soon his exploits were known throughout the village. He had become something of a celebrity; people had even stopped him in the street in Cyrene, eager to hear of his adventures. And, even more importantly to George, Cassia now treated him with a new respect; the rift between them, that the duel had left, had all but vanished; they were friends once more.

George stood on the Alexandrian docks and stared out at the magnificent Pharos lighthouse, one of the architectural wonders of the world. George had seen it before, having made several visits to Alexandria since joining Justus, but he still marvelled that man could build a structure more than fifty times as tall as himself!

The lighthouse stood on a small island connected to the mainland by a narrow walkway. Its huge square base was topped with a smaller octagonal tower, at the top of which was the circular housing for the beacon itself. This colossal structure had stood there, overlooking the harbour, for centuries, a shining light to guide the many ships that visited this port.

George's gaze travelled from the top of the lighthouse down to the clear blue waters of the harbour and back to their ship. They had spent a good proportion of the day loading Justus's newly acquired Egyptian pottery on board, and soon it would be time to leave these shores for their next destination. But before they did, there was something that George wanted Cassia to see, something that he had seen the dockhands winching into the hold earlier that day.

It was the first time that Cassia had travelled on a full merchant voyage with them. She had begged her father for ages to be allowed and finally, this year, he had consented.

George turned his attention from the handsome sailing vessel moored at the dockside, to the busy entrance of the port. Soon, he had spotted Justus and there, walking beside him, dressed in a beautiful azure tunic, was Cassia. She had been clothes shopping again. George couldn't understand the concept of buying new clothes before your old ones had even worn thin, but he had to admit that the colour suited her.

"Cassie", he called, "There's something you've got to see."

George led an inquisitive Cassia up the gangplank and onto their ship. Descending the wooden steps into the hold, he ushered her past a row of amphorae and several sacks of grain to where a large cage stood, thick iron bars preventing its cargo from escaping.

Cassia peered in and then jumped back as the creature within rushed forward with a savage hissing sound.

"It's all right", calmed George, offering her his hand, "It can't get out."

Cassia placed her hand in his and hesitantly moved towards the cage; George felt his heart begin to beat a little faster. Within the dark interior of the little prison, something large moved. The creature had a scaly hide that was grey-green in colour, with a number of yellow bands running across its back and right down to the end of its long powerful tail. Four stumpy legs splayed out at right angles to its low body, each one armed with five cruel claws. From its flat head, a forked tongue protruded, and its mouth looked to contain a large number of razor-sharp teeth.

"What is it?" asked Cassia, fascinated by this strange beast.

"A dragon", proclaimed Juba, appearing at the top of the steps.

Both Cassia and George jumped, the Briton letting go of Cassia's hand as if it were a burning coal plucked from the fire.

"Dragon? Where?" enquired a voice with a Gallic accent.

Juba and Hector descended the stairs into the hold to get a better view of the creature, as George inwardly seethed. *The first time on this voyage I get chance to be alone with Cassie, and these two jokers ruin it!*

The Gaul chuckled. "Brennos has got to see this."

"Brennos has got to see what?" enquired the big Briton, appearing above them.

George closed his eyes in disbelief. *Are they all spying on me?*

"I seem to remember you saying once that you would eat your own loincloth if you ever saw a dragon", smiled Juba, as Brennos arrived at the cage.

"Would you prefer your loincloth stewed or roasted?" laughed Hector.

Brennos peered into the cage at the strange creature, and then snorted in derision. "I seem to remember you saying once that a dragon was twice as tall as a man and as long as three camels!"

"So my grandfather told me", replied Juba, defensively.

"Well it's nearly as long as one camel", laughed Brennos. "Maybe your grandfather wasn't good with numbers."

"Dragons come in all shapes and sizes", insisted the Berber, determined not to back down.

There was a loud hiss and a crack as the dragon whipped his tail into the bars of the cage, clearly unhappy at his audience.

"He's a bit savage isn't he?" Cassia exclaimed.

"Not really", snorted Brennos. "When you've fought the Bulls of Hades, anything else seems a bit small."

"Oh, go and boil your undergarments!" suggested Hector.

"When I see a 'three camel' dragon", countered the Briton. "Until then, my undergarments are off the menu."

As they all trooped back onto the deck of the ship, Brennos put a hand on George's shoulder, steering him away from the others.

"Be careful, George", he warned, a serious look on his face.

"Of what?"

"Cassia", answered his mentor, knowingly. "Women are like fires: without them life is cold; as you draw closer everything becomes warm and cosy, but get too close and you'll be burned!"

George wasn't too sure how to take this advice. He was pretty sure that his friend was still smarting from a fall out he'd had with Antonia, a girl from the village, and this was causing him to have bitter thoughts about women in general.

"Err... right", he replied uncertainly, patting Brennos on the arm.

As George moved off after Cassia, another friend ambushed him with advice: Juba.

"Can I ask a personal question?"

"As long as it's not about women and fires", replied George, slightly annoyed at these intrusions.

"It is about women", confirmed Juba, his brow creased in an expression of uncertainty.

"Go on then", submitted George, resignedly.

Juba hesitated, apparently unsure of how to begin; George braced himself.

"Can you 'be' with Cassia?"

"Eh?"

Juba tried again: "Do you have to 'do' when you are with her or can you just 'be'? Do you have to impress Cassia or can you be yourself?"

It was George's turn to hesitate.

"Do you have to be George the Bull slayer or George, the friend of trolls, or George, the champion dueller, or can you just be George?"

"Uh… I don't know", fumbled George, feeling awkward. "I'll… err… have to think about it."

George had thought about it; he had thought of little else since leaving Alexandria, and that had been over four weeks ago! Since then, they had travelled to the port of Gaza, in Judea, visited the islands of Cyprus, Rhodes and Crete, traded in Ephesus, the Roman capital of Asia, moved along the coast to the bustling Greek port of Corinth, and from there, sailed to Silicia[1]. This was now the sixth week of their two month voyage, and he had still had no chance to talk to Cassia alone. Every time he plucked up the courage to approach her, someone else got in the way. He was beginning to think that there must be some kind of conspiracy among his friends to keep them apart.

Having just departed from Neapolis[2], the merchant vessel was currently sailing up the west cost of Italy, making for Ostia, the port of Rome, capital of the empire. They were scheduled to stay overnight in Ostia and then spend a further two days in Rome, and George was determined to grab some time alone with Cassia. *But how? And what to do?* He needed help. It was no use asking Brennos; he would warn George not to get too close. *And I seem to be able to manage that on my own!* Juba would advise him to just 'be'. *I've been just 'being' for the last month, and Cassia has hardly noticed me!* He was certainly not going to ask Justus's advice on dating his daughter, so that left Hector.

"So you have come to the love doctor, eh?" smiled Hector, when George approached him. "You will not regret it. When I have finished with you, Venus, herself, would be unable to resist your charms!"

---

[1] Sicily
[2] Naples

"The first step is to prepare for the opening performance", explained the Gaul. "You must sweep her off her feet, and then she will be eager for more. I think that Ostia will make the perfect stage: wine and dine her, take her to the theatre, a moonlit stroll on the beach, and voila!"

It was midday at the 'nones' of April (5th April) when their ship arrived at Ostia and joined the queue of vessels, of all shapes and sizes, waiting to enter the port. Fortunately, many of them, including three huge slow-moving grain ships, also arriving from North Africa, were heading for the larger docks of Portus, situated just north of Ostia.

After a lengthy wait, they reached the mouth of the river Tiber, and the sailors were able to moor the ship to the quay, with much shouting and throwing of ropes. Then it was time to unload the cargo; Justus's goods would be stored in one of the horrea (storehouses) overnight before being shipped up the Tiber to Rome, on the following day.

The Ostian docks were as busy as any that George had experienced. More ships were arriving all the time, and all haste was made in unloading the cargoes. As soon as one vessel had been dealt with, it was cast off and another took its place. The quayside was awash with crates, cages, barrels and amphorae, many of which were being taken off sailing ships and transferred onto flat-bottomed barges that were to be towed up the river to Rome by pairs of oxen.

The docks were crowded with people from all over the empire: Romans, Greeks, Gauls, Spaniards, Africans, even Britons: *Well, at least two.* There were merchants wearing richly ornamented robes, some with turbans on their heads; bare-chested slaves, toga-clad officials clutching wax tablets and styluses, and a small contingent of heavily armed legionaries, keeping a close eye on proceedings.

Someone else seemed to be watching activities at the quayside with a great deal of interest: a dark-haired man with a hooked nose and a scar on his left cheek. He was wearing the simple tunic and belt of a servant, but seemed to be engaged in no task other than spying on visitors to Ostia.

George watched this suspicious looking fellow for a few moments; he appeared to be staring at something to George's left. Following the man's gaze, George's eyes alighted on Cassia and

Hector, who were deep in conversation, standing a few feet away from the ship's gangplank George glanced back over at the hook-nosed man, beginning to feel uncomfortable.

A hand tapped George lightly on the shoulder and he whirled around.

"Oh. Cassie."

"Hector said you had something to ask me", said Cassia, her big brown eyes fixed enquiringly on him.

"He did? I did?" stammered George, "Err… I mean… I did", he confirmed, regaining his train of thought. "I would like to take you on a tour of Ostia this evening."

"What does your tour include?" asked Cassia, a mischievous twinkle in her eye.

"Good food, fine wine, a visit to the theatre, a moonlit stroll on the beach, and voila!"

"Voila?" enquired Cassia, smiling.

"That's Gallic for err… 'Just say yes, you'll enjoy it'", replied George, improvising.

"How can I refuse?" laughed Cassia.

George wandered around in a daze; he absent-mindedly walked back onto the ship with a stack of patterned bowls he'd just unloaded, and then proceeded to take a large quantity of two-handled jugs to the wrong horreum, but it didn't really matter; nothing could overly bother him today.

It was only after everything was safely stored away that George remembered the mysterious hook-nosed spy who had so disturbed him earlier, but the man was nowhere to be seen. Everything was right with the world.

Chapter 24 – The Ostian Performance

"Not bad, George", commented Cassia, admiring the new midnight blue tunic that he'd bought from the market in Ostia, on Hector's advice.

George stared back at her. Cassia was wearing a rather flimsy looking scarlet silk tunic with matching sandals; her face was heavily made up: cherry red lips, rosy cheeks and the rest whitened with some kind of powder, and she was sporting a gold half-moon necklace and earrings. The overall effect was certainly pleasing on the eye, but George couldn't help thinking that she was showing a little more leg than her father would have liked.

What he said though was: "Wow, you look great!"

"So, where does the tour begin?" she asked, slipping her hand into his.

"Apicius's", replied George, confidently.

Apicius's was the place to eat in Ostia, or at least that was George's assumption based on the fact that he charged almost double what everyone else was asking! But Hector had told him that women gauge a man's feelings toward them by the amount of money he is willing to spend, so George had taken a deep breath and plunged in.

It was certainly set in an upmarket part of the city, standing at the corner of the Decumanus Maximus (the main street) and overlooking beautiful well-tended gardens, obviously belonging to some of the richer patrons of Ostia. On arrival, Cassia and George were shown to their table by a short, almost spherical Roman with white hair, smiling blue eyes and innumerable chins: Apicius himself.

The stone benches, to which they were directed, were festooned with soft cushions, and their table was topped with beautifully patterned coloured marble. George sank down into the cushions, making himself comfortable, and cast his eyes around this luxurious eating-place.

There were about a dozen tables in all, surrounding a central hearth where a plump pig was turning slowly on a metal spit. Adjoining the hearth was a long stone counter, built into which were a number of large pots containing the many sauces used in Roman cuisine. Apicius's was lavishly decorated with bronze statues, colourful mosaics and ornate vases. It was open on two sides, the pillared arches offering an excellent view of both the main street and the gardens.

A group of towel-carrying men were walking past, returning from an afternoon's bathing session at one of the city's many public baths. Across the road, two women were shouting at each other, while a large retinue of servants looked on bewildered. It seemed that they had both arrived for a dinner party dressed in identical purple stolas – a disaster unparalleled from the foundation of Rome to this day! Standing slightly apart from this noisy scene was a dark haired, hook-nosed man dressed in a brown tunic.

"George, what are you going to order?" interrupted Cassia, bringing his wandering gaze back to the task in hand.

"Eh? Oh. Err… hot sausage please", he replied, distractedly.

"You can get that at any common thermopolium", chided Cassia. "Be a little adventurous will you?"

A thermopolium was a small shop that sold wines and simple food that could be quickly prepared, and the sausage that they served happened to be one of George's favourite dishes, but it seemed that wasn't going to be good enough for tonight's performance. "I'll have whatever you're having then", he conceded, staring out into the street once more. The man with the hooked nose had disappeared.

'Whatever Cassia was having' turned out to be oysters. George had never seen these before, and the plate of grey-green shells that arrived at their table took him by surprise. He eyed them suspiciously as Cassia looked on with an amused smile, waiting for him to take the first bite.

Resigned to his fate, George lifted one of the shells to his lips and…

"Wait!" cautioned Cassia. "You don't eat the shell; you need to open it up with a knife."

She handed him a small silver knife with which to perform the operation, and after several failed attempts, including an embarrassing incident involving an airborne oyster and a jug of mulled wine, George succeeded in exposing the slimy white innards of his first morsel.

Reluctantly, the Briton slurped as much of the contents of the shell as he could stomach. The taste was difficult to describe; the closest he had been to it was when he had got a mouthful of the Mare Internum during a violent storm!

Ignoring the warnings that both his taste buds and stomach were giving him, George pressed on, determined not to spoil 'the performance'. In stark contrast, Cassia downed her seafood with great relish, savouring each mouthful and licking her cherry lips.

By the time the plate was empty of oysters, George was feeling distinctly nauseous despite having only eaten half a dozen or so (he had managed to secrete the rest in a nearby vase when Cassia had been distracted.)

"And now for the main event", announced an enthusiastic Apicius, treating all the diners as if they were his own personal audience. "If anyone leaves here tonight without having tasted my exquisite Trojan Pig, they will be destined for eternal regret!"

With a dramatic flourish, the rotund Roman whisked the plump roasted pig from the hearth and slid it onto a huge silver platter. He then produced a skewer and a large carving knife and proceeded to cut into the meat. There was a splattering sound as something like intestines spilled out onto the plate. George turned away, his nausea threatening to overcome him.

"They're just sausages", whispered Cassia, noticing his reaction. "You wanted sausage, didn't you?"

George was still feeling slightly queasy as they made their way briskly down the Decumanus Maximus to the eastern end of the city. The Trojan Pig had actually tasted pretty good, filled as it was with a mixture of fruit as well as a large quantity of sausages. On another day George would have probably enjoyed it, but his stomach had still been protesting over the oysters, and the fine pork had been wasted on him. He wasn't sure he was going to like the theatre much either. From what Cassia had told him of plays she had watched, he expected it to be rather dull.

As they neared the huge circular building, the pair were met with a surprising amount of noise; the crowd inside certainly seemed to be enjoying the show. *Perhaps I'll like this after all*, mused George, as they walked through one of the high arched entrances.

A flight of stone steps led up from the dingy interior of this immense building to a point high above them, where the golden rays of the late afternoon sun shone through the gloom, beckoning them to their seats. The thunderous noise seemed to grow in a crescendo as they climbed towards the open sky, and then they were out, shielding their eyes from the sudden brightness.

George led Cassia through the wildly chanting crowd to a place where they could get a good view of events transpiring below. The actors seemed to be portraying some sort of battle scene; they weren't on a stage, as he had expected, but were dotted about in the open area at the centre of the great bowl-shaped structure.

There were around a dozen participants in the battle, fighting in pairs, although some actors were lying on the ground, covered with what looked like blood, obviously playing dead. One side were heavily armed, each with a shortsword and curved rectangular shield, their faces masked by large round helmets with only two small holes for eyes. The other side had only scant armour and wielded tridents and, what looked to be, weighted nets. They appeared to be re-enacting a skirmish between the Roman army and some barbarian tribe.

Something was wrong; George could feel it. The frenzy of the crowd, the desperate lunges of the combatants down below; it all seemed a bit too intense. He focused in on the nearest pairing: the barbarian had just made an unsuccessful attempt to slip his net over his opponent's helmet, and was now lunging at him with his trident. The Roman soldier turned the three-pronged spear aside with his shield and, with a lightning strike, brought his shortsword down on the man's arm. With a shriek of agony that sounded very real, the barbarian fell to the ground. The helmeted actor stepped away, looking up to the crowd for affirmation of his heroic victory.

George stared down at the fallen man; his arm was covered in something red. *Some sort of dye? And what's that thing lying beside the trident?* George's eyes widened in horror and disbelief: the thing was a severed hand!

George could taste bile, he felt faint, the fanatical cheering of the crowd, lost in their bloodlust, sickened him to the core. It pressed in on him, making it difficult to breathe. Grabbing Cassia by the hand, he started dragging her towards the exit. At first she resisted and then, resignedly, she let herself be pulled along. George didn't slow his pace for an instant until they were both back outside the imposing building.

"I'm sorry", he gulped, taking in a deep lungful of fresh air and leaning against the stone arch that they had entered through.

"I'm not a child any more, you know", she replied curtly.

George looked up at her, surprised by this reaction. "I didn't know it was…" His voice trailed off; there was a lump in his throat. "I thought…"

She patted him on the arm, her flashing eyes calm once more. "Don't worry your head about it."

George let out a deep sigh, straightened up and took Cassia's hand once more. "Let's find that beach", he said.

As they walked back up the main street, George mulled over the evening's events so far: it certainly wasn't working out the way he had planned. *What else can go wrong?*

Cassia tugged on his arm. "Why don't we try this place?"

George looked up, surprised. This certainly wasn't the beach; it was a rather grubby looking tavern on the ground floor of a four-storey insula (apartment block). His spirits sank; the sounds of raucous merriment coming from within were not appealing. The last thing he wanted to do right now was spend time in the company of strangers, especially those in various stages of inebriation. Trying to conceal his disappointment, George allowed himself to be led into the dubious establishment.

Inside, Cassia ordered a couple of mugs of conditum, a drink containing wine mixed with honey and spices, and after George had paid for them, she led him upstairs to escape from the pressing throng. The stone steps led to another noisy crowded room, but unlike the ground floor, this was furnished with several round wooden tables.

"They're playing dice; you'll like this, George", insisted Cassia, beckoning him forward with her free hand.

Walking slowly, so as not to spill his wine, George followed her as she wove her way through the muddle of tables and dice players, to the far corner of the room where there stood three empty stools.

As he and Cassia approached the vacant places, George noticed a wooden 'Circus' board in the middle of the table. Three scruffily dressed, greasy-haired Romans, sat across from them: two fat men in shapeless brown tunics, slurping wine from large mugs, and a sharp-eyed, pointy-nosed individual in a green tunic, who was talking in a low voice to the other two. As Cassia sat down, they looked up.

"Good evening, my lady", said the pointy-nosed one, staring at Cassia in a way that George didn't like. "I'm Felix; would you care for a game?"

"Oh no", she replied, "But George will play". She patted his arm. "He's good at dice."

The three men immediately turned their attention to George. "Five denarii for the first race?" asked Felix, gesturing to the board.

"Count me in", declared a voice from across the room.

George turned to see a young man, sporting a white linen tunic with a purple stripe, showing his status in the upper echelons of Roman society. "Antonius will teach you plebeians how to play dice!"

A plebeian was a less than polite term used to describe the lowest caste of Roman society, but none of the three Romans sitting opposite George seemed at all bothered by the insult.

While the others were distracted by this new arrival, George took advantage of the situation to whisper in Cassia's ear: "This is gambling; what would your father say?"

"Don't think of it as gambling", replied Cassia in an undertone, "Think of it as paying to enter a competition, challenging for the winning prize."

George thought about it; put that way it didn't seem so bad. It was only five denarii after all; he'd spent way more than that to feel sick at Apicius's!

"Count me in too", he said, placing his silver on the table.

"Good", replied Felix. "Let's play."

For the first time that evening, George was beginning to enjoy himself. The game was going well; he was ahead on the last lap and only Antonius, who turned out to be the son of a senator (a Roman politician), had any chance of catching him. The other three seemed to have no idea of the strategy of the game: they threw only one die when two would have been safe, and cast all three when the risk was too great. As a result, two of them had already crashed out and the third was still on his second lap!

George was approaching the final turn; he picked up two of the bone dice, placed them in a small wooden cup, and cast them across the table.

"Nine", called Felix who, since he had crashed out, seemed content to referee the game. "That's five stones."

Having five penalty stones meant that you could roll only one die on your turn, but George wasn't worried: he was only five spaces away from winning the race.

"Eight."

The young Roman was now five spaces behind George but, crucially, had only four stones and so could still roll two dice; it was going to be close.

After the trailing plebeian had taken his turn, George picked up the one die he was allowed and rolled it.

"Four. One away from victory."

George held his breath; the senator's son needed ten to win, or an eight or nine to ram him, which could result in his crashing out of the race. The dice tumbled across the table.

"Seven."

George had won. A terrific sense of elation welled up inside him. He had never experienced anything like this when beating Brennos or Hector. He pulled the pile of silver towards him; it was clear that playing for a prize added greatly to the excitement of the game.

"Well played", congratulated one of the scruffy Romans. "That's one-nil to the plebeians."

"I'm just warming up", responded Antonius.

"Are you up for a man's race then?" asked Felix, eyeing the pile of silver greedily.

"Twenty denarii?" enquired one of his slovenly colleagues.

"Fifty", countered Felix.

"Fifty denarii?" gasped George before he could stop himself.

"I'm in", stated Antonius, forcibly. "This race is mine."

"Go on, George", whispered Cassia, smiling at him. "Two porky plebs and an arrogant son of a senator: you can beat them."

Smiling at her descriptions, George's confidence soared.

"Watch out for Felix though", she cautioned in an undertone. "His name means 'lucky'."

"Well, George means 'dace miester'."

"Do you mean 'dice master'?" she giggled. "You'd better take it easy on the conditum until after the game."

"All right", nodded George, his heart beating faster, "Let's play."

He was being hustled. George could see what they were doing: the three greasy-haired Romans had drawn him in by deliberately losing the first race, and now they were playing as a team to stop him and the senator's son from winning; doubtless they would share the profits later.

He should have walked away. George had spotted what they were up to several races ago, but he had been too proud, too stubborn, to simply admit defeat and leave. He wanted to beat them at their own game, to pay them back for their trickery. And so now he sat there, adrenalin coursing through his veins, with all the money he owned in the world sitting on a big pile in the middle of the table, and a cup with three dice in his hand.

"Eight."

No stones but he was too close to the turn for comfort, an ideal target for being rammed. One of the hustlers had crashed out early but the others were in good positions: one was right behind George, and Felix had just succeeded in ramming the young Roman.

"All three", said the sharp-eyed trickster, with a grin.

The senator's son picked up the dice, placed them in the cup and, after a quick appeal to any gods that might be watching, cast them onto the table.

"Fifteen! You're out."

With a curse, the young Roman got to his feet, turned on his heel and stomped away, muttering that all plebs ought to be fed to the lions.

George waited tensely to see if he would share the same fate. The hustler in position behind him needed a ten, eleven or twelve with three dice.

He rolled a three, a four and a... six. George breathed a sigh of relief; his opponent had overshot him. Felix rolled seven, picked up his fourth penalty stone, and moved his chariot to the beginning of the back straight.

George stared at the board; he had a choice to make. Should he take two dice and try to keep up with the lead chariot or should he take one and attempt to ram the other man? George wiped his forehead with the back of his hand, mopping away beads of sweat that had nothing to do with the temperature of the room. He stared at the huge stack of silver coins in front of him; this choice could well prove very costly.

George picked up one of the bone dice; currently he was playing two against one – it was time to even those odds.

"Three."

Yes! George moved his chariot one space in front of his opponent's. He was halfway there; now he needed the pleb to get more than ten.

"All three", announced George, his voice strained with tension.

This was almost too much to bear; George hardly dared to look as the dice tumbled across the table... *Three fours!* George whooped with delight, causing those around the room to stare across at him.

"He won't catch you, Felix", stated the ousted hustler confidently.

Felix calmly rolled his two dice and moved his wooden chariot piece to the middle of the back straight. It seemed unlikely that George would catch him with less than half a lap to go.

There was no time left for half measures; George rolled all three dice, picked up his third penalty stone, and moved his chariot to within six spaces of his opponent. Felix's next turn brought him his fifth penalty stone: he had reached the final bend, only ten spaces from victory, but he was going to have to complete the race with one die.

George and Felix had quite an audience now; all the gamblers at the nearby tables had turned to view these tense final stages. *Cassia's not watching, though,* he thought bitterly, as he moved his game piece to the start of the final bend, three behind his last remaining opponent. She had become bored with the game some time ago, and had gone downstairs for another drink, but had never reappeared. This wasn't the first time she had led him into a difficult position and then disappeared - George was spotting a pattern.

George held his breath as Felix's die tumbled through the air. *One, please, one!*

"Five."

George's stomach tightened. This was it: if he couldn't roll ten with two dice, Felix would need only two to win. He picked up the dice, placed them in the cup, shook them vigorously, closed his eyes and rolled... a five and a one.

There was a sharp intake of breath from the audience, and George slumped, his head dropping into his hands. It was surely over; all Felix had to do was avoid rolling one and all the money was his. The Roman took the cup, dropped a single die into it and cast the cube across the table.

The tense silence was broken by a jubilant shout, followed by the muttering and murmuring of the spectators. George said nothing, just staring numbly at the six spots on the upturned face of the bone die in front of him. He had lost everything; all the silver he had earned over the course of almost five years!

George got slowly to his feet. Felix was already pulling the pile of coins towards him; all around, the conversation returned to previous levels. Money was staked, dice were rolled and life went on. No one cared about the forlorn figure who meandered through their midst, making for the door.

Downstairs, George located Cassia in a small mixed group by the stone bar, laughing and joking. When he had finally got her attention and managed to prise her away from her newfound friends, he told her what had happened.

"You've lost all your money?" she repeated incredulously.

"You wanted me to gamble", replied George, putting the blame firmly where he felt it belonged.

"I didn't tell you to gamble everything", countered Cassia. "You're a grown man; surely you can think for yourself!"

George wanted to yell, to hit back at her for being so unfair, but he realised it would only make a bad situation worse. He closed his eyes, attempting to calm down.

"I need to get out of here", he said.

"Well I'm enjoying myself", replied Cassia curtly, "Or I was. You just think about yourself, about your needs, about what you want to do."

"Well I'm leaving", stated George flatly, unwilling to argue.

He felt tired and upset; he hated this place, hated the coarse laughter and loud voices that seemed to mock his pain.

"Go then", answered Cassia stubbornly, turning back towards the crowd at the bar.

George walked out into the street. The sun had now set, but the flickering yellow light of oil lamps, shining out from the many inns and taverns along the main street of Ostia, provided him with adequate illumination.

What an evening! George walked quickly over the cobbles, muttering dark words into the night air. How could it all have gone so horribly wrong? Everything had been against him: the oysters, the theatre, the dice, and most of all Cassia. If it hadn't been for her he would still have all those silver coins...

George's angry thoughts trailed off; in his mind he was back in his childhood home. Outside, the storm raged, the lightning flashes clearly visible through the slats in the wooden door. Inside, he had found what he was looking for: a leather bag with a drawstring. The bag clinked against his leg as he got to his feet; it was heavy with silver coins. He reached to put it in his backpack, and a wave of guilt flooded over him. *I will pay it back someday.*

A bitter tear trickled down George's cheek. How could he pay his debt now? For the last five years he had had little or no thought for the woman who had raised him, clothed and fed him, given him the best years of her life. And what had he given her in return? Nothing but heartache and misery!

Consumed with self-pity, George had not really been paying attention to his surroundings. Now, looking up, he found that he had wandered into an unlit side-street. Something moved in the darkness up ahead. George took a step back and reached for his sword hilt. What had he been thinking? Retreating slowly, his ears straining for sounds of movement, he moved back into the comparatively well-lit main road.

George turned and jogged back in the direction of the tavern he'd left. He couldn't leave Cassia alone in this dangerous town, even if she had been a complete pain; he would never forgive himself if she came to any harm. Reaching the scruffy four-storey building, he pushed his way back inside.

Cassia was no longer standing by the bar; nor did she seem to be among those sitting at the handful of tables in the centre. Jostling his way through the merrymakers, George glanced left and right, painstakingly searching the packed room for any sign of his erstwhile companion. Eventually, he was forced to conclude that she wasn't anywhere downstairs.

Anxiously, he climbed the creaking staircase to check the rest of the establishment, but Cassia wasn't in any of the upstairs rooms either. He was starting to panic. Returning to the crowded bar once more, George approached several revellers, frantically asking if anyone had seen what had become of "the black-haired girl in the red silk tunic", but no one knew. Finally, George spied Felix in a dark corner of the tavern and asked him the same question.

"I may know something", he replied casually, "But why should I tell you?"

Angrily, George seized the front of his tunic and pushed him back against the wall. "You'll tell me what you know or I'll…"

He broke off as something sharp pressed against his ribs.

"Let him go or I'll gut you right here", threatened the owner of the knife.

George's heart was pounding. Slowly, he relaxed his grip on Felix and backed away.

"That's better", smoothed the Roman, straightening his grubby tunic as if it were some expensive garment. "If you can be civilised for a moment, you might get your woman back."

"What have you done with her?" snarled George through gritted teeth, the knife still resting against his ribcage.

"I have done nothing to your little friend", replied Felix calmly, "But I saw who did, and in which direction they went. Memory is a funny thing though: one moment it's clear, the next it goes all hazy. I find that gold helps me focus."

"You've already taken all my money!" shouted George, incensed by this unjust demand.

"You have a master." It was a statement not a question. "My price is one aureus. And I suggest you hurry or there may not be much left of the lady to save."

Chapter 25 – Pursuit

George stumbled over the threshold of Flavius's villa. He had a painful stitch in his side; he was hot and sweaty, out of breath, and desperate to find Justus.

"He's not here", was the unwelcome reply from Marius, the first member of Flavius's household that he encountered.

"What's the matter?" asked a concerned Juba, hurrying into the atrium.

"I've lost Cassia", was all that George could manage, still trying to restore air to his lungs.

"That's careless of you", chimed a familiar voice from the room beyond.

A moment later, Brennos entered the atrium with Hector at his heels. George wasted no time in explaining his predicament to them, pausing only to gulp more air at regular intervals.

"Master Justus has gone with Flavius to the house of a friend of his", explained Juba, in worried tones, when George had finished his tale of woe. "There's no knowing when he will be back."

"So it's up to us", interjected Brennos, taking command. "First we're going to need money."

"But I told Felix that my master would pay him", wailed George, anxiety getting the better of him.

"Calm down", instructed Brennos. "This Felix won't care if Caesar's grandmother turns up, as long as he gets his money!"

"I've got about 150 denarii", declared Juba. "What about you two?"

"Three or four, I think", replied the Gaul, hesitantly.

"Hundred?"

"No, three or four denarii", clarified Hector, looking sheepish.

"By Juno!" exclaimed Brennos. "What have you been spending it all on?"

"The usual: wine, women… more wine. Anyway, what about you?"

"Around forty", admitted the Briton. "Sadly the rest only went on wine."

"But that gives us less than half what we need!" pointed out George, panic beginning to engulf him again.

"We'll have to bluff our way through", conceded Brennos. "Have a little faith. You're a Christian; shouldn't you be praying or something?"

His mentor was right; George felt ashamed that he had not thought to do this already. Closing his eyes, he uttered a simple request: *Great Father in heaven, please go with us to rescue Cassie.*

Opening his eyes, George saw that Juba was on his knees, deep in prayer for the miracle they so badly needed.

"Let's go, Juba", called the ever-practical Brennos. "I'm sure God knows the details."

The flicker of a smile appeared on George's face. He was surprised at himself; mysteriously, a glimmer of hope seemed to have appeared on the bleak horizon. Although generally a bit of a joker, Brennos was certainly one for a crisis.

Brennos quickly persuaded Marius to open up the stable for them, and soon the companions were galloping through the streets of Ostia on borrowed horses. It was a balmy night with just the ghost of a breeze; overhead the clouds had parted to reveal an almost full moon, which now favoured them with its silvery light. As the foursome passed the theatre on their right, George called them to a halt.

"THIS IS IT", he yelled over the thunder of the hooves on the cobbled streets.

The group reined in their steeds and dismounted, Brennos, once more, taking charge.

"George: you're with me. Hector and Juba: wait here with the horses; give us a 500 count and then draw your swords and come and get us."

There were no arguments, no comments; Brennos led the way into the scruffy tavern and George followed, feeling as though a lead weight had just dropped into the pit of his stomach.

The room was still pretty full, given the lateness of the hour, and it took George some time before he spotted Felix in the far corner, surrounded by a group of his shifty looking accomplices.

"That's him over there, the one in the green tunic."

Brennos immediately headed over in the direction that his companion was indicating; George followed somewhat more reluctantly.

"I believe you have some information for me", announced the big Briton boldly, interrupting Felix in the middle of a conversation.

"And who are you?" enquired the Roman, annoyed at this intrusion. His expression soon changed to one of shrewdness and cunning, however, as he spotted George in the big man's wake. "You are not George's master."

"I am head servant to the house of Justus", stated Brennos, giving himself an instant promotion. "I have been authorised to deal with you on behalf of our master."

"The promised price?"

The blond Briton reached into his cloak and slowly drew out the bag containing the money they had pooled.

"This is much less than we agreed", sniped Felix, as he weighed the bag expertly in his right hand.

George looked on anxiously, wondering how his friend was going to get them out of this one.

"It's half", exaggerated Brennos. "You'll get the other half if the information merits it."

"You are not in a good position to barter", stated the Roman shrewdly. "I have the information you need, time is on my side: I have all evening, whereas every moment you waste lessens the chances of you finding your friend alive. And also..." he concluded, "We outnumber you seven to two."

George was suddenly conscious of the circle of Felix's friends closing ranks behind them; they were trapped!

"I hold all the dice", reinforced Felix, smugness written all over his pointed face.

"Not quite", replied Brennos calmly. "Outside stand a dozen heavily armed men from the households of Justus Liberius and Flavius Marcellus."

In his mind's eye, George pictured his two lightly armed friends, stamping their feet nervously against the evening's chill, clinging on to the horses' reins, and slowly counting to 500, doubtless hoping that they wouldn't reach that total before he and Brennos reappeared; the mental image was not reassuring.

"As we speak, my master is rounding up a dozen or so more from the households of Jubelus, Hectorus and Cassius", continued Brennos, in full flow, plucking names out of the air. "If he returns and we're not there to meet him with news of his daughter, they will tear this place apart."

George watched Felix anxiously; would the hustler believe this utter fabrication? The Roman's expression was unreadable; here was a man who was well used to bluff and deception.

"Your master wouldn't dare assault a public building", replied Felix, after a short pause. "He would be arrested."

There was a note of uncertainty in the hustler's tone; he had either believed the story, or wasn't sure that he dared risk the possibility of its being true.

"My master has lost his only daughter", stated Brennos, pressing his advantage. "There's nothing he won't do."

The force of these words seemed to hit home. Felix looked uncomfortable; he was no longer in control.

"Soon after George left the tavern", the hustler began slowly, "A tall dark-haired Roman entered with a man I know – Septimus: shorter, dark, with a hooked nose and a scar on his left cheek."

"I've seen that man!" interrupted George excitedly.

Brennos held up a hand to quieten him.

"The tall man went up to your master's daughter", continued Felix, "And, after a brief exchange, appeared to ask her to accompany him. She refused and the two men dragged her out."

"Did no one try to stop them?" cried George incredulously.

Felix ignored him; something had caught his eye. George wanted to turn and see what the Roman was looking at, but found his arms caught in a vice-like grip.

"There's no army outside", someone said. "I just had a look."

George felt cold steel against the back of his neck. His heart was in his mouth; their story was blown!

"They're not just standing in the street", insisted Brennos hurriedly, "But they're watching this place, believe me."

"I don't", replied Felix, his tone arrogant once more, control back in his grasp. "I think you're bluffing."

Suddenly, the level of background noise in the room rose tenfold. George craned his neck to see what was causing the commotion, his arms still pinned behind his back. There was a rush to get away from the front door; people were pushing and shoving and several loud oaths rang out. Through the melee, George could make out a red-haired man, with a moustache, brandishing a drawn sword: Hector. Behind him, the slight figure of Juba stood in the doorway, his blade flashing in the lamplight.

"WAIT!" yelled Brennos, in a voice so commanding that a hush fell over the whole tavern. Hector stopped in his tracks, and George, like everyone else in the room, turned their eyes on the Briton.

"This is your last chance, Felix", warned Brennos imperiously. "Tell me what I need to know or you'll be using that money to book passage over the River Styx, on your way to Hades!"

All of the colour had drained from the hustler's face. "They b… bundled her onto a horse and rode off", he stammered, words tumbling out at high speed.

"Which road?" demanded Brennos.

"The Via Ostiensis", was the instant reply.

"Let's go then", insisted the Briton, motioning George towards the door.

Felix's henchmen melted away as the two men made their way through the crowd, over to where Hector stood, sword drawn, with a puzzled look on his face.

"Nice timing, boys", commented Brennos, in an undertone, as he reached the Gaul.

"Dramatic performance", acknowledged Hector in a whisper, as they exited. "The river of the damned? The underworld?"

"That's your fault", chuckled Brennos. "I've spent too long listening to your crazy stories!"

Back in the moonlit street, George turned to his mentor with a look of admiration. "I can't believe you pulled that off!"

"That was the easy part", Brennos replied. "Now, where are those horses? We need to get out of here before someone calls out the guard!"

The Via Ostiensis was the principal route from the port of Ostia to the capital city of Rome. It led out of the east gate of the port city and headed northeast along the eastern bank of the River Tiber. Presently, the river snaked off northward, but the road continued straight and true, as George had come to expect from Roman engineering.

The gibbous moon shone brightly, illuminating the marshy lowlands on either side of the road and the wooded area that they were fast approaching. Up ahead, by the side of the road, stood a five-foot high pillar: a Roman milestone.

"HALT", called Brennos in his commanding voice.

George reined in his horse, with the others, as his mentor dismounted and examined the road. Fortunately, the big Briton had thought to bring a lantern. The flickering yellow light showed a large dark patch of dried mud covering the smooth stones.

"I think we're in trouble", he muttered, as he surveyed the ground. "Juba, get down here and put those Berber tracking skills to work."

Juba dismounted and examined the mud. Peering down to see what had so interested his friends, George noticed several hoof marks in the dirt.

"There's more than two of them aren't there?"

"At least a dozen", agreed Juba with worried tones.

"A dozen?" exclaimed George, horrified. "But Felix said there were two?"

"Plus another ten, or so, waiting outside, that he neglected to mention", added Brennos darkly. "Remind me not to pay him the rest of the money."

"We had better go back for reinforcements", suggested Hector, frowning.

"What reinforcements?" questioned the Briton, shaking his head. "Even with Flavius's men, they still outnumber us. Our only chance is a surprise attack, and extra bodies won't help that."

As they set off again, at a canter, George's stomach began to tighten. They were pursuing a group they could not hope to overpower and who had a massive head start on them. According to the writing engraved on the stone pillar, they were sixteen miles from Rome. George had been to Rome before: a city of vast proportions where the buildings just seemed to go on and on, getting larger and more impressive the farther you looked. If Cassia had been taken there, how would they ever find her? *Please God, don't let them reach Rome.*

"LOOK OVER THERE!" called Juba in an uncharacteristically loud voice.

George stared in the direction the Berber was pointing. At first he could see nothing and then, through the trees, he caught sight of an orange glow: a fire!

George moved cautiously through the woods, stepping lightly to avoid breaking fallen branches underfoot. A cloud crossed in front of the moon, plunging the land into deep darkness; at least he had the orange glow of the fire to aim for. *But how am I going to find my way back to the road if the moon stays hidden?* No, he wasn't going to think about that; he had to free Cassie first. *One problem at a time!*

Under cover of the darkness, George reached the edge of the firelight without being detected. The mysterious kidnappers had set up camp in a little hollow. A few feet away, two watchmen sat on logs, staring into the leaping flames; to his left, but still within the circle of light, lay a number of dark figures, bundled in cloaks and sleeping soundly.

A low moan came from somewhere beyond the fire. George stared intently at the cluster of trees opposite, which stood at the foot of a steep bank.

"Be quiet or I'll give you something to cry about!" threatened the man nearest to George.

The moaning stopped. A sliver of moonlight shone out from behind the dark clouds and, with its aid, George could just about trace the outline of a slender figure tied to one of the trees: *Cassie!*

A raging anger burned within George. How dare these evil men treat his friend like this? His hand moved instinctively to the hilt of his sword; he longed to charge out at them, to cut them down with its blade, to wreak his righteous revenge on them for trussing her up like an animal. But that was not the plan; he had to wait.

George strained his eyes, looking left, beyond the firelight, to the place where he imagined the kidnappers' horses to be. He would not have to wait long; his friends would be in position by now.

A horse's whinny broke the silence, followed by much snorting and stamping and a considerable amount of neighing and braying.

"What's going on?" exclaimed one of the watchmen, jumping to his feet.

"Someone's stealing the horses, by Saturn!" swore his companion, tripping over one of his sleeping companions in his haste to investigate.

"WAKE UP, YOU FOOLS!" yelled the first man, kicking the nearest bundle.

With much cursing, the groggy sleepers emerged from under their cloaks and blankets, and stumbled towards the source of the commotion. Those that were more alert stopped to grab burning brands from the fire; a tall man, obviously the leader, tried to restore some sense of discipline to the chaos, but his shouts went unheeded as the whole crowd charged off into the woods.

His friends had done their job, now it was his turn. George stepped out from the shadows, skirted the fire and hurried towards the trees at the edge of the hollow.

"It's me, George", he whispered, as he approached the bound figure at the base of the trunk.

He received only a moan in reply. Cassia was in a bad way; she had been bound to the tree by several coils of thick rope. Her face, from what he could make out in the poor light, was bruised and swollen, and there was dried blood at the corner of her mouth. She was barefoot and her silk tunic had been torn in a number of places.

Trying hard not to think of the ordeal she must have been through, George drew his knife and started cutting at her bonds. Before he was through the first coil, he was startled by a shout from the far side of the clearing. Whirling round, George was horrified to see that one of the kidnappers had returned.

The man yelled wildly and charged towards him, waving a sword in one hand and brandishing a flaming torch in the other. George switched the dagger from his right hand to his left and swiftly drew his sword, stepping out between Cassia and his assailant.

George parried the first wild blow but, before he could counter, he was forced to jump backwards to avoid the burning branch that was swung at him. The clash of steel on steel rang out again as he blocked his opponent's thrust, but once more he had to give ground as the flaming bough flailed through the night air.

He was only a few feet from Cassia now. Fighting down the sense of panic, George focused on his opponent. Blocking the sideswipe aimed at his ribs, he brought his left arm up as the man swung the burning brand down at his head. There was a cry of pain as his knife sliced into the man's left hand, and then George was forced to duck as the torch spun through the air, a wall of heat passing inches above him. Parrying another slashing stroke from his stricken foe, George ran him through with a thrust of his blade.

Even as his enemy slumped to the ground, a frightened scream filled the night air. George whirled around; flames, from the dropped torch, were licking at the dry leaves and twigs at the foot of Cassia's tree! Rushing to her aid, he attempted to stamp out the blaze before it could get out of control, but his desperate attempts merely fanned the flames.

George cried out in pain, hopping backwards as the heat from the rapidly spreading fire penetrated his leather boot. He had to get Cassia out of there before she burned to death! Dropping his sword, he charged past the flames and began frantically cutting at the rope with his bloodstained knife.

Chapter 26 – Fire and Vengeance

The flames leapt higher and the blaze swept closer, fuelled by the abundance of dry kindling on the woodland floor. George cut vigorously at the thick rope that bound Cassia to the tree, but before he could make significant progress, he was interrupted by another angry shout. Despairingly, he continued to saw away at the ropes for a moment longer, yanking at them out of sheer frustration, before turning to face this new foe. Even as he did so, another terrified scream escaped Cassia's lips; the fire had now spread to the tree!

George hesitated, momentarily paralysed by fear and uncertainty. Then, shaking himself free of indecision, he spun around the leaping flames. But he wasn't going to make it; he had delayed too long. His sword lay, on the ground, several feet away, and his opponent was almost upon him, charging madly, torch held high. With no time to think, George used the only weapon he had, the dagger, hurling it at his onrushing foe.

The battle-cry changed to a howl of pain as the blade buried itself deep into the man's shoulder. Staggering backwards, he dropped his lighted branch to the ground. Another scream from Cassia brought George pelting back; then he pulled up short. *My knife!*

Turning once more, he scanned the hollow; there was no sign of the man he had just incapacitated. Had he fallen, or just staggered out of sight? Cassia screamed again. There was no time; George grabbed his discarded sword and ran back past the raging wall of flame that was threatening to engulf his master's daughter.

He could feel the heat of the blaze on the back of his legs now, as he hacked wildly at the tightly knotted coils that bound Cassia to the burning tree. George began to cough as the smoke got into his lungs. He swung his blade ferociously at the ropes once more; it was no good: swords just weren't made for this kind of thing; he needed a knife.

"Having a spot of bother, are we?" called a voice that George had hoped never to hear again.

"Primus!"

"That's right, Briton", crowed his archenemy. "And it looks like I'm just in time to watch you die." He laughed mirthlessly. "What kind of fool tries to rescue his true love by setting fire to the tree she's tied to? Granted she's fickle and, I must say, I've tired of her, but to burn her alive? That's a little extreme, don't you think?"

"I'll see you burn in Hades for this!" cursed George, coughing once more, as he swung his sword at the ropes and then yanked at them with all his might. They didn't budge.

"I think not", sniggered the Roman. "You see, I've brought you here for my revenge, not yours."

Primus seemed content to gloat, for the moment, and the two lackeys who flanked him, one of whom George recognised as the hook-nosed spy, were not making any moves to attack. George swung again.

"When Publius wrote me a letter stating that you and lady Cassia would be in the neighbourhood, I couldn't resist the opportunity", Primus continued conversationally, seemingly unconcerned at Cassia's fate.

George hacked at the ropes again, screaming with frustration, as he tried to block out the Roman's callous words.

"Publius doesn't like you very much", sneered Primus. "I invited him to my home for a few drinks, shortly after I first met Cassia, and he told me all about you all."

George yanked at Cassia's bonds, but it was no good, they still wouldn't move. It was maddening; no one had believed his suspicions about Publius, and now Cassia was going to die!

"Tedious business", continued the Roman, watching George's increasingly frantic efforts with morbid amusement, "But worthwhile. When it came to it, he was only too happy to betray you; I didn't even have to offer him any money. I think he's hoping I'll give him a better job."

The tree was ablaze now, the leaping flames moving inexorably towards their victim. Cassia's desperate screams choked off into uncontrollable coughing; George was now forced to move sideways to avoid being caught in the fire himself. There was nothing more he could do; tears streamed down his face. *Please God, no...*

As he watched Cassia succumb to the smoke, her head dropping forward as she lost consciousness, George heard a familiar voice call his name, and instinctively turned his head. Before he could work out where the sound had originated, something hit him on the shoulder, and a heavy weight bore down on him. The prone form of Cassia had just collapsed into his arms! *But how?*

George stared at the frayed ropes in astonishment; they had burned through!

"George!"

The voice belonged to Brennos, and it was coming from somewhere behind and above. Hoisting Cassia over his left shoulder, he turned and started to climb up the banking, away from the spreading flames.

"KILL THEM!" screamed Primus.

George hastily traversed the steep bank. The slope was covered with trees whose exposed roots seemed intent on tripping him. Ahead, he could see the figure of his friend sitting astride a stolen horse, silhouetted against the moon. Behind him the sounds of pursuit grew closer; they had rounded the fire and were racing up the hill after him.

George stumbled, slipping onto one knee; any moment now he was going to be overhauled. Fear lending him strength, he righted himself and staggered on upwards. The panting and blowing of his pursuers grew steadily louder; they were almost upon him.

Suddenly, something hurtled through the air, whistling past George's right ear. There was a groan from behind, followed by a thud, as a body dropped to the ground.

Brennos already had another dagger in his hand as George reached him, but Primus's remaining servant was hanging back, unwilling to become the target of another of the Briton's knives.

Between them, the two fellow countrymen managed to heave the unconscious Cassia onto the horse and then, holding the reins with one hand and supporting her with the other, Brennos urged his mount forward.

George followed at a jog, his sword still drawn, peering anxiously through the darkness, all of his senses on heightened alert. The woods rang with the shouts and clamour of a dozen bewildered men, chasing shadows. George caught a glimpse of a torch some distance away to his right, but then it was gone. They were moving steadily downhill and, if his friend's sense of direction had not abandoned him, should be nearing the road.

George cocked his head to one side; he was almost sure he'd just heard the sound of footfalls and heavy breathing. There was no sign of a torch; whoever it was must be navigating his way through the trees using the faint moonlight.

There it was again; someone was definitely out there, and they were getting nearer! George stopped running and turned, his sword raised, as he anxiously awaited his next opponent.

"George?"

"Juba."

George exhaled deeply, feeling mightily relieved. "Where's Hector?" he asked.

"We were separated. I think he… Look out!"

The Berber's warning came only just in time, as a man bearing a flaming torch appeared from behind a nearby tree and lunged at George. Sidestepping the man's wild swipe, the Briton thrust the point of his blade into his assailant's arm, causing the man to drop his sword and stagger backwards, howling with pain.

Before he could press his advantage, George was startled by another cry, to his right, and the clash of metal on metal; Juba was under attack too! Momentarily distracted, George was caught by surprise as the wounded opponent hurled his fiery brand at him. The burning branch arced through the air, a ball of fire spinning through the darkness. With no time to dodge, and acting purely on instinct, George swung his sword across the flight of the torch. His steel blade collided with the burning wood and sent it flying through the air, landing some distance to his left.

Thwarted, the disarmed man gave a loud curse and disappeared into the trees. George quickly moved to his left and stamped out the flames before they could take hold; he had caused enough fires for one night! Then he remembered Juba; in all the excitement he had lost track of his friend. The sound of clashing steel had ceased and there was no sign of his opponent's torch, so that was good news.

"Juba", he called softly, and then, "Juba", a little more loudly.

There was no response. *But why wouldn't he reply unless…?* And then a terrible thought entered his mind: *Unless he's dead!*

George backed up slowly, his sword held vertically in front of him. There was someone here, he could sense it, and by calling out to his friend he had just told this silent assassin exactly where to find him! His eyes were useless in this situation, he couldn't even see the blade of his own weapon, a foot from his face; all he had now to rely on were his ears.

George crept silently through the darkness. He had completely lost his bearings and had no idea in which direction the road lay, nor did he have any clue as to where his soundless foe waited, ready to strike. All the hairs stood up on the back of his neck; was that the faint sound of breathing that he had just heard? Moving to his left, George drew his blade back, preparing to swing.

Halfway through a stride, his foot snagged on an invisible obstacle and he tumbled forward, throwing his left arm out to break his fall. To George's surprise, the thing he had just tripped over let out a groan. *Juba!*

Before he could get to his feet, there was a whooshing sound and something passed through the air just above George's head. Still down on one knee, he swung his sword at the unseen enemy, but his blind strike didn't make contact with anything.

Stooping low and holding his sword out in front of him, George moved away from Juba's body. If only the moon would emerge from behind the clouds and show him his foe. He would take his chances with an enemy he could see over this deadly game of hide and seek any day!

Bent almost double, George used his free hand to check for fallen twigs and tree roots lying in his path, knowing that one false step: another trip, or a cracking branch underfoot, could prove fatal. Before he had moved more than a few feet, in this manner, his fingers made contact with a sizeable stick that would have undoubtedly made a loud noise if he had stepped on it. A sudden thought came to him, and gripping the piece of wood tightly in his left hand, he tossed it in front of him.

The branch landed with a dull thump, and immediately there was the sound of scurrying feet and a whoosh of a weapon being swung somewhere in front of him. Lurching forwards, George took a wild swipe with his sword. This time it struck something, there was a choking cry followed by a heavy thud and then everything was still.

A great feeling of relief flooded over George, but it was soon tempered; he wasn't out of the woods yet. He had lost Brennos and Cassia, nobody knew where Hector was or even if he was still alive, and Juba was injured, perhaps badly.

George attempted to retrace his steps to relocate his friend.

"Juba", he whispered.

There was no reply. He tried again, a bit louder this time and, after a pause, received a low groan in response. Following this sound, George moved to his right. He could just about make out the dark shape of Juba's prone form lying on the ground; the clouds were thinning.

"Come on, Juba", exhorted George, struggling to lift his friend into a sitting position.

Juba let out a moan. The moon had emerged once more and now George could get a good look at the Berber. What he saw was not encouraging: his friend's face was almost completely covered in blood!

"Where does it hurt?"

Juba's replying groan was less than helpful so George ran his fingers around the Berber's bloodstained head looking for deep wounds.

His friend's muffled groaning gave way to a pained yelp. He had found it: a deep gash across the top of the scalp. Tearing off the sleeve of his brand new tunic, George attempted to bandage the wound and staunch the flow of blood. His first attempt was a disaster: the whole thing unravelled and, as he grabbed for the end of the bandage, he let go of Juba and the barely conscious Berber fell backwards, hitting his head on the hard ground, and letting out another cry of pain. His second attempt was far more successful, however, resulting in what looked like a makeshift turban.

Having dealt with his friend's medical needs, as best as he could manage, George turned his attention to the next problem: finding their way back to the road. He looked around anxiously; the rows of trunks seemed to extend unbroken in every direction.

As he hesitated, unsure of the right way, his gaze fell on the fallen body of his recent foe. There was a crimson slash across the man's throat, where George's sword had caught him, and a look of horror on his face, a face that he knew well. *Primus!*

George stared into the unseeing eyes of his nemesis. He had avenged himself on his great enemy, but there were no feelings of triumph, just numbness. He was looking at an empty shell; the real Primus, his soul, had been catapulted into the afterlife. The horrified expression on his lifeless face told its own story; it was almost as if, in the very instant of death, he'd seen what was coming: unimaginable torment that would go on and on forever!

George wrenched his gaze away; he didn't want to think about it. Somewhere in the distance an orange glow appeared, twinkling between the trees. It vanished as suddenly as it had appeared, but then another came into view and another. He could hear low voices now too.

The approach of Primus's men made George's mind up for him; he didn't know in which direction the road lay, but any direction away from the advancing mob would do for now. Hoisting a protesting Juba onto his feet, George half dragged, half carried, his friend through the trees.

George's anxiety levels were increasing. They were making agonisingly slow progress, he still had no idea whether they were even heading in the right direction and, to make matters worse, the torches were growing ever closer. It was no good, he was going to have to speed things along or they were both dead.

With considerable exertion, George hefted Juba over his shoulder, staggering slightly under the load, and moved off at as quick a pace as he could manage. The Berber had a slender frame but he was still a dead weight and considerably heavier than Cassia had been. A shout went up from somewhere behind: he had been seen!

George increased his strides, beads of sweat breaking out on his brow. Ahead of him, the trees began to thin out and beyond them he caught a glimpse of... *The road!*

Passing the last trunk, George broke into a staggering run. As he neared the drainage ditch at the side of the Roman highway, he stumbled, collapsing under the weight of his semi-conscious burden. Juba let out a loud groan as he rolled off his friend's back onto the hard earth; George pulled himself to his feet and looked around. To his dismay, the road was empty; there was no sign either of Brennos or of Flavius's horses.

As he looked about him, helplessly, a group of flickering orange lights emerged from the trees to his right. Moments later, more torches appeared, this time from a little way off to his left; they were surrounded!

George drew his sword. Both of the groups consisted of at least four men; he didn't have a chance. Should he run? He would be leaving Juba to certain death, but what was the alternative? *To die with him?*

Hearing a sudden snorting noise, George whirled around.

"Put that sword away before you hurt yourself", called Brennos, as he directed his horse, which still bore himself and Cassia, onto the stone pathway.

"What happened to Juba?" asked a concerned voice with a thick Gallic accent.

"Head wound", replied George, relieved beyond words as he watched Hector, who was riding one horse and leading another two by the reins, join the group.

"Quick, let's get him onto a horse!" called the Gaul, dismounting to help.

Between the two of them, they managed to bundle Juba onto Hector's mount. Angry shouts from both directions, followed by the sound of pounding feet, told them that time was short. Flinging himself onto the nearest horse, George dug his knees into its flanks, urging the beast forward. Ahead of him, Hector was attempting to draw his sword while holding the reins and propping up a very droopy Juba.

"GO!" shouted Brennos, cantering forward.

George bent low over his horse's mane and drew his own sword. Wheeling around, he swung it wildly at the men who had reached him, keeping them at bay, using the height advantage that his mounted position gave him. Then, with a clatter of hooves, he was gone, leaving his pursuers far behind.

Up ahead, there was a clash of steel and wild cries as Brennos carved a path through the group attempting to block the road. Hector followed in his wake and then it was George's turn to scatter the torches as he galloped into the night.

Chapter 27 - The Evil Grows

Catalina stared down at the lake below and shuddered involuntarily. Though it was less than three miles from the place she called home, she had not looked upon its dark waters for more than two years. As the wind whipped at her long blonde hair, unwanted memories came flooding back.

Fighting the tears, she gazed steadily down at the place that had haunted her dreams for so many nights. Her resolve strengthened as she thought of her friend who, as much as she wanted to see her father's death avenged, could never return to this place. She was doing this for Drusilla, and all the other poor folk who had lost loved ones to the beast by the lake. But she was also doing this for herself; there were deeper reasons for what she did today, a desire for personal vengeance of which she had never spoken.

"Are you all right?" asked Julius, his normally gruff voice touched with concern.

"Yes", she replied, without thinking, her voice far away.

"Where was it that you found Vitus's body?"

"Err... what?" She shook her head, as if to clear it, and focused on the battle-scarred veteran.

"Drusilla's father, his body; where did you find it?"

"On the far side of the lake, not far from the woods."

Julius turned to his well-armed companions. "Right, men", he bellowed, instantly silencing the chatter in the ranks. "Follow me."

The men obediently fell into step behind their self-appointed leader, his formidable presence commanding respect just as effectively as it had when he'd been a centurion in the Roman army. Catalina joined him at the head of the troop.

"Not you", he insisted, looking down at Catalina reproachfully. "This will be dangerous; I don't want you getting hurt."

"But I know what we're looking for", she argued, unwilling to be left behind.

"You told me that it was dark when you encountered the beast and that you never saw it", countered Julius.

"I saw a footprint", replied Catalina. "I'll be able to help you track it. And anyway", she continued, seeing the stocky Roman about to argue the point, "The beast might be roaming the hills. It would be dangerous for you to leave me all alone at its mercy."

Julius reluctantly conceded this with a grunt. "All right, but you must promise to stay close to me, and when I give you an order, I expect you to follow it immediately without question. Is that clear?"

"Yes, sir", she affirmed meekly.

"Right, men", he barked out once more, "Let's march."

A dozen sturdy, broad-shouldered, dark-haired men, and one slender fair-haired woman, marched down to the water's edge. They passed the boat, still lying on the near shore, where the women had landed it after crossing the lake on that dreadful night. It cast a very forlorn image: the vessel that had saved their lives abandoned to the elements and succumbing to the silent green assassin - lichen.

Moving on to the eastern end of the lake, the troop followed the slippery stone pathway between the sheer rock face and the foaming water, crossing in single file. As they reached the farther shore, Catalina glanced at the bushes by the water's edge, remembering the strange bundle of skin that she had seen here on her last visit. There was nothing there now though, the skin had long since rotted away, and there was no sign of footprints either.

Catalina shook her head, muttering to herself; it had all taken too long. The morning after she and Drusilla had fled from the lake, barely escaping with their lives, she had gone to the basilica to inform the town governor that a man-eating beast had taken up residence by the lake. When she had finally been granted an audience with him, about a month later, on her six or seventh visit, she had urged him to send a detachment of soldiers to hunt down the creature. After that, she had waited in vain for several months for something to be done, not realising that when the governor had said that he would "look into it", he had actually meant that he would wait and see if another ten people complained and, if they didn't, he would do precisely nothing. It seemed that as long as the prices of meat and wine didn't go up, the amount of tax collected didn't go down, and he was able to leave work and visit the baths by the eighth hour every day, the governor was content with inaction. Catalina had tried everything, from introducing him to a tearful Drusilla to ambushing him outside the baths! But nothing had worked; it seemed that he would still be 'looking into it' when 'the River Styx ran dry!'

"Is this where you found Vitus?"

Julius's question roused Catalina from her thoughts; she looked around, taking in her surroundings. There was no evidence of a body; she scanned the nearby shoreline: nothing.

"It was somewhere around here", she confirmed, vaguely, "But it was dark… It's difficult to tell."

If the governor had acted, the evidence would still have been here, she thought grimly. But he hadn't acted, even when she had spent months investigating other disappearances, questioning locals and preparing a dossier of evidence of the sinister goings on in the vicinity of the lake. She had shown him the roll of parchment containing carefully written accounts of more than a dozen separate incidents, but he had dismissed them as inconclusive. Catalina recalled exploding at that point, insisting that the governor get off his fat rear end and take a midnight fishing trip with her, and then he would see for himself! Shortly after that, she had been ejected from the basilica.

"What about that cave?" shouted one of the men. "Worth a look?"

Catalina turned to see what the man was referring to, and saw a dark opening cut into the hillside a short distance away from the stony shoreline. She walked towards it, scanning the ground for any trace of a three-toed footprint that would prove that the creature still inhabited these parts.

Was it still here? Or had she spent all this time and effort for nothing? The men were getting restless, she could tell. It had been Drusilla's idea to involve her father's army pals; Julius had been a good friend of her father's, and many of the others had served with him. Between them, the two women had persuaded a dozen men to help; most had been sceptical of the account of the lakeside monster. How long would they continue the search without firm evidence that their quarry even existed?

"There's nothing in there", called one of the men. "It only goes back a dozen paces."

But Catalina wasn't listening; her attention was focused on a large patch of bare earth between her and the wood. She had found what she was looking for.

"Julius!" she called out, her voice high-pitched with excitement as she walked purposefully towards the trees.

"What is it?"

"The beast; it's in the wood!"

The tracks she had discovered consisted of about a dozen prints, most of which were very clearly defined in the soft earth. Each one had a round heal and three toes, sticking out at angles to each other, almost like the front of a bird's foot, but this was no bird! They were identical to the footprint she had seen on that awful night, except... Catalina placed her slender sandaled foot into the left toe of the nearest imprint. It fit snugly; the creature had grown!

"What are you...?" began Julius in his gruff voice, and then fell silent, his mouth agape.

"Apollos!" he called hoarsely, when he had recovered the power of speech. "Over here!"

Apollos, a tall man with an untidy mop of jet black hair and a weather-beaten face, jogged over to them and then, seeing what they were both staring at, froze, his dark eyes growing wide at the sight of the monstrous footprints.

"What do you make of those?" barked Julius.

Apollos didn't speak, he just stared at the tracks as though mesmerised.

"Well?"

"It's something huge!" Apollos ventured at last.

"I got that far on my own", muttered Julius, impatiently. "What, in Jupiter's name, is it?"

The rest of the soldiers began to gather round, curious to see what they were looking at.

"It's a biped", commented Apollos at last, crouching by the nearest print. "It walks on two legs."

"I know what a biped is", blustered Julius.

"You can tell from the identical nature of the prints", continued the crouching Roman, unperturbed. "Four-legged creatures have distinct differences between their front and hind feet."

"Is it a bear?" asked one of the men, staring wide-eyed at the colossal footprints, "They can walk on two legs."

"No", replied Apollos, looking puzzled, "Bears have short toes, not long like this"; he indicated the three substantial indents in the nearest prints. "And they have five toes, not three."

"What about an ape?" suggested another man.

Apollos shook his head. "They have five too." He paused, scratching his chin thoughtfully, "And I've never heard of an ape eating a human. These prints don't match any carnivore that I've ever encountered; in fact they more closely resemble those of a turkey."

Julius exploded. "Are you telling me that Vitus was eaten by a giant turkey?"

Nothing stirred in the wood; all was quiet. But it was not a peaceful quietness; the silence was eerie. The warm summer sun could do little to penetrate the thick tangle of boughs overhead, but what light there was revealed no scurrying squirrels, no fluttering birds; no wildlife at all. The only sounds Catalina could hear were the steady breathing of her companions and the rhythmical tread of their boots on the hard earth.

The footprints they had been tracking on the edge of the wood had quickly vanished as the ground within became harder and drier, and the soldiers had split into three groups in order to search the woods more efficiently. This decision had made Catalina uneasy; she had felt secure in the big group, but now in the eerie half-light of the strangely silent wood, she felt vulnerable, exposed. She hadn't dared to argue with Julius over his choice; after all, he was an experienced campaigner, well used to seeking out the enemy and bringing them to battle, and she was just a seamstress. But there was something in here that had killed at least a dozen people...

A gut-wrenching scream shattered the silence. The whole group turned, as one, to stare wide-eyed in the direction of the awful sound.

Julius recovered his composure first. "Follow me!" he ordered, drawing his sword from its sheath and dashing off into the undergrowth.

The others raced after their leader, and Catalina soon found herself at the rear of the group, struggling to keep up. Another hideous cry echoed through the forest, momentarily turning her blood to ice. Fear lent her speed; whatever happened she mustn't lose touch with her guardians.

Ducking to avoid a low branch, Catalina almost ran headlong into the man whom she had been trailing. Pulling up short, she stared around, panting heavily as she took in the scene. They were in a small clearing, at one side of which an ancient gnarled trunk rested on the forest floor. Slumped with his back to this fallen tree was one of their dark-haired companions, his eyes shut and his face set in a grimace of pain. The far side of the open space was covered with a beautiful thick carpet of bluebells. Catalina let out an involuntary gasp as she spied the broken body of another soldier, lying face-down in their midst, his dark blood staining the delicate mauve flowers.

The man she had nearly collided with let out a cry and pointed upwards. The others followed his finger, staring into the branches above, where a third body was draped unnaturally over one of the thicker boughs some ten feet off the ground!

There was a groan from across the clearing; the man slumped against the fallen trunk was stirring.

"Gracus!" called Julius, moving across to his wounded comrade.

Gracus opened one eye and attempted to straighten up; he let out another groan.

"Don't try to move", instructed his commander, his voice taking on an unfamiliar tender tone. "What attacked you?"

"D…dr…ag…" Gracus coughed, blood trickling from his mouth.

"Drag?" repeated one of the men, puzzled.

"Dragon?" guessed Julius.

Gracus nodded weakly.

"What's a dragon?" asked Catalina, trying to keep her voice steady, though she was shaking like a leaf.

"They're mythical monsters", replied the nearest soldier.

"Myths don't do that!" countered Julius sharply, indicating the corpse hanging from the tree above their heads.

Catalina spun round; something large was approaching. She could hear the sound of heavy breathing, the breaking of branches underfoot. The thing was emerging from the undergrowth behind her…

"By Pluto!" somebody yelled.

"Not Pluto, just us", replied a familiar voice.

The scream died on her lips; it was Apollos, leading his detachment of three soldiers.

There were sharp intakes of breath from the newcomers as they surveyed the scene of carnage. Then someone said, "Where's Marcus?"

"He was with Gracus."

"Gracus, did you see what happened to Marcus?"

Gracus looked around slowly, but before he could attempt to reply, a terrible roar filled the air, draining his face of colour. The awful noise was followed by an equally dreadful sound: a man's shout of blind terror.

"Antonius, watch Gracus", commanded Julius, his face pale but his voice steady. "The rest of you, follow me, and stay close."

With this, Julius charged off in the direction of the shouts, sword in hand. With a clatter of swords and spears, six men chased after him. Catalina hesitated, a sense of foreboding hanging over her like a storm cloud, and then turned and headed back into the trees.

Catalina forced her way through the dense undergrowth, her eyes trained on the running figures ahead. A terrible anguished cry reverberated through the wood; it sounded uncomfortably close. Her heart was pounding; her hands shook. *I can't do this!* She stumbled over an exposed root, almost losing her footing.

This wasn't what she had meant to happen; people were dying and it was her fault! *If I hadn't been so hungry for revenge...*

She looked up, and then frantically turned her head left and right; there was no sign of the soldiers. Which way had they been heading? She had lost her bearings. Wringing her hands in desperation, she let out a sob. The noise was magnified in the eerie silence and she stopped immediately. *Don't be a fool!*

Catalina stumbled on, her eyes half blinded by tears. Endless rows of trees spread out before her in every direction, offering no clue as to which way her friends had gone.

"Catalina!"

She looked round and gasped with relief: it was Julius.

"I thought I told you to stay close", he scolded.

"I couldn't keep up", she replied, a lump in her throat.

She clasped his muscular arm and he led her through the trees to a small clearing where the others had gathered. Apollos was on his hands and knees, doubtless examining new tracks. The others were all standing at the far side of the open space, staring up into the branches of a large oak tree. Catalina followed their gaze and let out a gasp of horror: another body - that of Marcus, hung suspended over one of the lower branches, staining the grey bark a deep brown with recently shed blood.

"Why is it doing that?" asked one of the men, his voice betraying a trace of fear.

Apollos straightened up and spoke, his tone no longer that of an interested spectator. "It's storing meat", he replied, his voice grim. "It's coming back."

Everyone was looking at him open-mouthed now, even Julius. His words had an almost prophetic quality. "We are not the hunters, we are the prey!"

For a moment everyone hung on the tracker's words, spellbound; then there came a series of crashing and crunching noises from somewhere to his right and the spell was broken.

There was a splintering sound and the bushes to Catalina's left burst open as, exploding into the clearing, the dragon leapt upon its prey. The hapless soldier never knew what hit him as the beast's huge clawed feet crashed down, crushing him to the ground. Its next victim had barely opened his mouth to scream when the powerful neck arched forwards and the huge jaws snapped shut with a bone-shattering crunch.

Catalina felt an arm grab her shoulder and next moment she was dragged to the ground just as the dragon's thick tail whipped through the air, narrowly missing her head. There was a horrible cracking sound, followed by a choking cry, as it caught one of the men square in the chest and flung him right across the clearing!

Staring up from her prone position on the forest floor, she saw Apollos bravely lunge at the fearsome creature, striking the dragon in the midriff. But the blade failed to bite, merely scraping across the monster's green scaly hide. Catalina bit her lip as the Roman ducked, just managing to avoid the creature's stumpy foreleg, as it slashed at him with cruel curved claws.

There was a grunt from somewhere close by, and a spear was launched through the air, striking the dragon between the shoulder blades. It wheeled around, arched its neck back and roared as the weapon fell back to earth, its shaft snapped at the point.

"GET BEHIND ME!" yelled Julius, pulling Catalina to her feet and stepping between her and the charging monster.

The beast moved with incredible speed for something so huge; it crossed the clearing in three strides, its head held low, level with its broad hips and tail, about six feet off the ground. It opened its gigantic mouth wide, exposing a great red tongue and teeth like rows of daggers.

Before the dragon reached them, a blade swung down on the outstretched neck. It turned at once, stopping to give another deafening roar. The sword flashed down again, striking the beast on the snout but, as the soldier lifted his arm for another blow, the great head darted forwards and he was engulfed in the terrible jaws.

"NO!" yelled Julius, enraged at the sight of yet another of his men succumbing to this merciless killer.

He leapt forward, swinging his sword at the beast's yellow eye. The dragon was too quick, though, and reared up to its full height, drawing its head well out of reach, the spines on the back of its skull rising up in a terrifying display.

"RUN, JULIUS; ITS HIDE IS TOO THICK!" yelled Apollos, racing across the clearing, the one other surviving soldier close on his heels.

The dragon turned, distracted by the shouting, and swung its mighty tail. The tracker dived forward, ducking below the savage blow, but the other man was not as quick. The pointed end of the tail hit him in the gut and he was flung into the air, landing with a thud at the far side of the clearing, his broken body limp and lifeless.

"RETREAT!" shouted Julius, reluctantly, and grabbed Catalina by the hand, pulling her towards the trees.

The three survivors ran for their lives, the dragon's bloodcurdling roars echoing in their ears. Branches whipped at their faces, thorn bushes tugged at their clothes, but terror drove them on as the great beast crashed through the forest in hot pursuit.

It was nearly on them now; the noises were growing louder with every stride they took. Catalina turned her head as she ran.

"NO!" yelled Julius, "Don't look back!"

Startled, she snapped her terrified gaze away and stared straight ahead. A fallen tree appeared out of the shadows, blocking their path. The two men grabbed Catalina by the arms and jumped, hoisting her up onto it. The noise of pursuit had died away; something was wrong.

Without warning, a set of enormous jaws plunged out from the undergrowth to their left and snatched Apollos from the log.

Catalina jumped with fright, lost her footing on the slippery wood, and tumbled sideways. A strong arm caught her as she fell, and pulled her back to her feet.

"Keep going!"

Julius tugged her arm, dragging her away from this awful scene, forcing her to keep moving. She stumbled, her tired legs giving way beneath her, but his vice-like grip on her arm held her up. Behind them, Apollos's anguished cries choked off.

There was a stitch in her side, her thighs ached, and her breath came in ragged gasps. All Catalina wanted to do was flop on the ground, but she couldn't; Julius's iron grip kept her upright, kept her moving forwards. At last, when she felt she couldn't go another step even to save her life, the trees began to thin out and beams of sunlight could be glimpsed through their tangled branches.

They burst forth into the light, which seemed too bright after the subdued green of the wood, and Catalina slumped to her knees, panting heavily.

"No… time…" breathed Julius, hauling her roughly back onto her feet.

At the sound of splintering wood, both soldier and seamstress whirled around; the dragon was emerging from the trees.

"Get to the cave!" commanded Julius, shoving Catalina in the direction of the dark opening.

She hesitated, still exhaling painfully.

"GO!"

Catalina stumbled up the slope as fast as her weak knees would carry her; behind her the dragon let out another heart-stopping roar. Halfway to the cave, she turned her head to see if the beast was pursuing; Julius would have told her to keep going and not look back, but she couldn't help herself.

The Roman commander had not followed her; he was standing his ground, sword held aloft. Only a couple of paces from him, the dragon crouched, perfectly balanced on its muscular hind legs, tail held out horizontally behind it, its viciously clawed forelegs and savage jaws poised to strike.

The monster struck, its neck shooting forward, the terrible jaws opening to receive its latest victim. At the same instant, Julius swung his sword; there was a dull clang as the steel blade connected with the dragon's jaw.

The beast howled in anger and reared up on its hind legs, the spines at the back of its head suddenly jutting out like horns. Seizing his opportunity, Julius lunged forward, thrusting his sword point downwards into the monstrous foot.

The dragon let out a grunt of pain and kicked out with its powerful leg. Catalina screamed as the Roman commander tumbled backwards, his sword spinning through the air. The beast turned its head and the terrible yellow eyes gazed into hers.

For a few moments it remained motionless, staring at her as if sizing up new prey. From the corner of her eye, she could see her protector struggle to his feet; he was cradling his right arm, obviously injured. He staggered up the slope towards the cave.

"Get back!" Julius cried weakly, as he headed towards her, stumbling on the stony ground.

Catalina looked on in horror as the merciless beast turned its attention to the fleeing man.

"LOOK OUT!"

She was too late; the dragon pounced, pinning the helpless Roman beneath its mighty foot and, in a heartbeat, his life was over.

"NO!"

The ruthless predator looked up from this latest kill, its jaws dripping with blood. Standing a short distance away, on open ground, was another potential meal. It swung around and lurched forward, covering a quarter of the distance in two giant strides. Catalina stumbled backwards, suddenly aware of her danger, and ran for the cave.

She could almost feel the great beast's snorting breaths on her exposed back as she sprinted towards the opening in the hillside with every last ounce of strength. The monster was almost upon her as she stumbled, half falling through the narrow opening in the rock, and collapsed on the cold hard floor of the cave.

A harsh snorting sound echoed around the walls. Frantically, Catalina scrambled forwards on hands and knees, and then flopped down against the opposite wall. Turning, she let out a shriek of fear as a huge snout poked in through the narrow entrance, blocking out most of the light. The gigantic jaws opened and then snapped shut as Catalina scrabbled to get as far away from them as possible.

"God, help me", she pleaded in the darkness. "God, help us all!"

Chapter 28 – Destiny

The tunnel stretched onwards, leading down, down, down into the bowels of the earth. How long he had been walking for, George couldn't say; it seemed like forever. But he had to keep going; he must reach his destination soon or…

A woman screamed. George began to run, his torch held out in front of him, its flickering light casting monstrous shadows on the walls. A yawning cavern opened up before him, its vaulted ceiling hidden in darkness too thick for the flame to penetrate. The screams were growing louder now, echoing off the rock, and mocking his attempts to save her.

A huge mouth loomed out of the dark, its razor-sharp fangs dripping with blood. The monster gave a thunderous roar, and the torch sputtered and died, leaving him in total blackness. Feelings of dread overwhelming him, George turned to run, but a wall of rock blocked his path. Where was the tunnel entrance? Desperately, George ran his hands over the jagged stone, searching for a way out.

Something dropped from the roof above; there was a thud followed by a metallic clinking. George whirled around and, as he did so, a light shone through the pitch darkness. His eyes scanned the cave frantically; where was it coming from? It seemed to be shining up at him from the floor of the cavern. Peering down to discover the source of the illumination, he was taken aback to see a large number of tiny silver discs, scattered across the rocky ground, glittering with an eerie glow.

"Help me, George!"

George looked up, startled by the woman's pleading cry. He caught a glimpse of long golden hair and then she was gone, swallowed up by the blackness.

"George, George."

The call was faint, distant, as if travelling to his ear from a long way away. He was moving towards it, leaving the golden-haired woman behind. He didn't want to, but the call was irresistible.

"George, wake up."

George opened one eye and peered up at the dark face above him – Juba.

"I knew you were in there somewhere", grinned his friend, showing sparkling white teeth. "You don't want to be sleeping on a day like today."

George rubbed his eyes blearily and reached for the pile of clothes that lay somewhere by his head. "On a day like what?" he muttered, but the Berber had already gone.

As he dressed, George tried to recall his dream; he was almost certain that he'd had it before. He had been walking down a dark tunnel and… but it was slipping away, like fine sand through his fingers. He pressed his clenched fists to his temple, as if he could hold the dream in his head by force.

"Silver coins!" he exclaimed out loud, and then fell silent. Those coins reminded him of one thing: his mother. He had made a promise to himself when he had taken the money from under his mother's bed; he had vowed to repay the debt one day.

George knelt down and retrieved the worn leather bag that he had kept with him ever since that fateful stormy night. It was almost two years since he had emptied it of silver in an Ostian gambling den, and from that day until this he had worked hard to atone for his foolishness. He had saved what he earned, spending as little as necessary, as his faded blue tunic and worn leather boots testified. And now, the bag was, once again, heavy with silver. But as to fulfilling his vow, he was a world away, with no guarantee that Britannia was even still under Roman rule!

"FIRE!"

George jumped to his feet, startled by the cry; it sounded like Cassia. He charged through the atrium, almost slipping into the pool in his haste to reach the kitchen, where the scream had originated.

Arriving at the doorway, he was just in time to see Justus struggling to remove a tray of smouldering bread from the stone oven.

"There's no need to panic", the Roman reassured his daughter. "I think I can save the top half."

"What's going on?" George enquired.

"Sol Invictus!" called Hector, enthusiastically, popping his head around the corner.

"The unconquered Sun", agreed Brennos, joining him.

"Not in this household", reproved Justus, sounding flustered, as he attempted to salvage something edible from the smoking tray.

"We are celebrating the birthday of Jesus, the true unconquered son."

"This Christian notion of hijacking a pagan festival to celebrate the birth of Christ, on the twenty-fifth day of December, will never catch on, you know", replied Brennos, shaking his head.

"Can we have all non-servants away from the kitchen area, please", called Justus, keeping his temper with difficulty.

George now realised why his master was in the unlikely position of cooking breakfast. The Roman festival of 'Sol Invictus' was a new institution, popularised by Aurelian, the emperor who had recently come to power, but it borrowed many old traditions from the earlier festival of 'Saturnalia', one of which demanded that the master of the house swap places with his servants for the day.

George followed the others into the dinning room, where Juba and Cahina were chatting quietly, away from the commotion in the kitchen. Sitting beside them was Amon, the Egyptian Christian whom Justus had hired to replace Publius. Amon was an efficient household manager, but in every other respect he was the exact opposite of the man he had succeeded: tall and thin, with a quiet, respectful disposition.

As he took his place on the couch, George briefly wondered what had become of the Roman traitor. He could still remember, as if it were yesterday, the shocked look Publius had given him when he had stepped off the boat at the Apollonia docks. Of course, the slimy little coward had denied everything and, since it was his word against George's, the authorities had been unable to convict him. Justus had had no hesitation in dismissing him, though, and then, feeling that justice had not been properly served, Brennos and Hector had followed the podgy Roman and, on overtaking him, the big Briton had given him a sound beating with his wooden training sword, whilst the Gaul had force-fed him a whole raw onion! Needless to say, Publius had not been seen since.

"How are things going in the kitchen?" asked Amon, bringing George back to the present.

Brennos shook his head meaningfully. "Not good."

"Perhaps the master would appreciate some help?"

"We have been banished", replied Hector, with a shrug of his shoulders.

"I hope that master Justus will accept some help with the evening meal", continued Amon, looking concerned. "There are going to be a number of guests."

"What are we having?" George wanted to know.

"Roasted dormice", supplied Juba, a broad grin on his dark face.

"You're joking!" exclaimed the horrified Briton.

"No he's not", assured Cahina. "They're in the third outhouse; I've been feeding them on nuts."

"It improves their flavour", nodded Juba, still beaming.

George looked across at Brennos, who grimaced.

Hector laughed. "By Mercury, you Britons have the pallets of children!"

"Some things are just not meant to be eaten", replied Brennos, with feeling.

"Breakfast is served", called Justus, enthusiastically, entering the room with a large platter of what looked, at first glance, to be charcoal. "If you spread plenty of honey on them, I doubt you'll even be able to taste the burnt bits."

Some time later, after much crunching and cracking, an empty honey pot stood on the table, and even Justus had admitted defeat.

"So what are you going to do with your day of freedom?" he asked.

"Some of us are going into Cyrene", volunteered Hector, without hesitation.

"You're not going to the baths are you?" asked George, who had never managed to come to terms with this popular Roman pastime.

"Certainly not", replied Brennos, looking indignant. "Freedom is too precious to waste on bathing; there's a full day's program at the circus."

"And what are you doing, Cassie?" George enquired, hoping that she might join them.

Cassia sniffed dismissively and looked away. "Nothing that would interest you smelly boys."

George's heart ached; the incident in Ostia had broken something between them, and even time seemed incapable of healing the wound. He had tried to understand, tried to fathom why communication between them, which had once flowed so freely and easily, had dried up like a stream in the desert. Was she still angry with him for deserting her in Ostia? She said not, but if she had forgiven him completely, as she claimed, and if she was happy to be 'just friends', why hadn't things gone back to the way they had been?

"Before you go out and enjoy yourselves, I have something to say", announced Justus, interrupting George's thoughts of self-pity.

The room fell silent, every ear intent on the master's words. "I received a letter from my good friend, Flavius, yesterday. He informs me that Emperor Aurelian has defeated Tetricus on Gallic soil."

"Who's Tetricus?" asked George, unsure what relevance this announcement had to real life.

Cassia tutted loudly, making it abundantly clear what she thought of this gap in his political knowledge.

"No one of consequence", sighed Hector, rolling his eyes; "Only the ruler of the Gallic empire."

"That's Gaul, Spain and Britannia", supplied Juba, helpfully.

"And that means", continued Justus, "That the empire has been reunited. And furthermore", he went on, "Flavius reports that the northern barbarians have been pushed back beyond the borders of Gaul, and the trade routes are open once more."

"Does that mean that we'll be travelling to Gaul this year?" asked Hector, voicing George's question.

There was a murmur of interest; it seemed that everyone in the room had been thinking the same thing.

Justus held up his hand, motioning for silence. "I discussed that with Julia last night", he began, smiling, "And she was happy with the idea. I think, with all this time I've been spending at home, that I've been getting under her feet." The merchant chuckled to himself. "So, in and among all the other tasks that I'll be performing today, I'll write a letter to Flavius, telling him that we'll meet him in Ostia before the ides of April[1]."

A murmur of excited chatter once again filled the room on Justus's conclusion.

---

[1] April 13th

"So, are you up for a day of racing?" asked Brennos, approaching with Hector in tow.

George nodded, getting to his feet, but then stopped in his tracks; there was something he had to do first.

"I'll catch you up", he said, and then turned to Justus. "Can I have a word with you?"

"I am at your service", replied the silver-haired Roman, smiling and giving an elaborate bow.

"Do you believe that God speaks through dreams?" George's words sounded foolish even to his own ears. He was standing in the tablinum, the little office between the atrium and the peristylium; the curtains had been drawn for privacy and Justus was sitting at the desk, facing him, a thoughtful look on his face.

"When God wants to speak to us, he always finds a way", affirmed the merchant, "But tell me about this dream."

George looked into the Roman's steady grey eyes; everything about Justus engendered trust. He had trusted the merchant the same hour he had met him and he had never been let down from that day to this.

"In the dream", he began, "I'm walking down a dark tunnel. I can hear a woman screaming; I think she's being attacked by some kind of monster." George scratched his head, trying to put the hazy details into some semblance of order. "She calls out to me for help and then I see this pile of silver coins..." George's voice trailed off.

"And then what?"

"That's all", replied George.

"And what do you think this all means?" asked Justus, looking puzzled.

"I know what the silver coins mean", stated George, looking down at his feet, guiltily. "When I left home, I took a bag of silver from under my mother's bed. At the time, I vowed, one day, to return it. And now..." He paused, glancing up to see the Roman's expression, waiting for his reaction to what was coming next. "...I believe it is time to repay that debt."

Justus didn't reply at once, but instead reached across the desk for a scroll. Silently, he unfurled it, tracing his finger over the words until he located the portion of text he was seeking, and then he began to read: "Let no debt remain outstanding, except the continuing debt to love one another."

Rolling the parchment up, the merchant stared solemnly at George. "Those words were written by Paul to the early Roman church", he explained. "I happened to read them last night."

Justus bowed his head, as though in prayer, and sighed deeply before continuing. "You have been like a son to me for these past six years; I owe you my life and the life of my daughter."

The merchant looked straight at George, and the Briton could see tears in his master's eyes. "It breaks my heart to say this", he said, swallowing hard, "But I'm certain you're right; God is calling you home."

George stood in the bows of the little sailing ship and waved farewell, tears welling up in the corners of his eyes, and a lump in his throat. Down below, at the dockside, Julia, Cahina and Amon waved back, enthusiastically. Julia, resplendent in a beautiful long flowing silk stola, dabbed at her own eyes with a small white handkerchief, while Cahina clasped her mistress's arm, looking up at him with a watery smile.

George felt a sudden pang of uncertainty. *Am I doing the right thing?* This was his family, and he was leaving them behind. He was never going to see them again; there was a horrid finality in that thought. Standing on either side of him, were the remaining members of that family: Brennos, Hector, Juba, Justus and Cassia. As the boat glided away from the docks, pulled by two smaller oared vessels, Cahina blew Juba a kiss; she would not see him again for more than eight months. *But at least she will see him again*, thought George, choking back his tears. He knew that the couple planned to be married before the end of the year; it would be a joyous occasion. *But I won't be there.*

As the boat sailed out of the harbour, George looked back at the spectacular view for the last time. The rocky shoreline, the many olive groves decorating the pleasant port of Apollonia, bathed in the early morning sunshine; the winding road, dotted here and there with junipers and mastic trees, leading up past the dark caves of the Necropolis to the walled town of Cyrene, with its many temples. And, to either side: the lush slopes of the Green Mountains rising up to the horizon.

George had an uncomfortable feeling in the pit of his stomach that had nothing to do with the gentle rocking of the boat. He, like his master, had fallen in love with Cyrenaica. *I'm leaving my home as well as my family.* And what awaited him? Had the villagers accepted that a savage bear was to blame for the deaths of both Tristan and the druid, or did they still hold him somehow responsible? How would his mother react to his appearing out of the blue after an absence of seven years? And would Catherine have forgiven him for his misadventure that had led her brother to his death? He was leaving a situation in which he was loved, cared for and secure, for one that was doubtful, at the least, and potentially dangerous.

Try as he might, George could not enjoy this final voyage with his friends. By day, his head was full of the insurmountable problems that faced him; he was withdrawn and moody, and spent much of his time staring silently out across the clear blue waters. At night, he was repeatedly visited by the same nightmare. Two questions plagued him: who was the blonde-haired woman that called to him for help? And what did the shadowy monster represent? Was he going to return home only to find that it had been ravaged by a barbarian horde?

As they sailed west from Cyprus, the weather began to mirror George's mood: fluffy white clouds were replaced with heavy grey ones, the pleasant breeze became a chill wind, and the bright sunshine turned into squally showers. On leaving Rhodes, things deteriorated still further: grey skies became black, the rain beat down upon them and the wind whipped at the sails. The weather became so bad that when they reached Crete, the captain decided to delay their voyage until the storm had passed.

Whilst on Crete, the companions visited the city of Knossos, site of the palace of the legendary King Minos. Hector regaled them with tales of the Greek hero, Theseus, who had entered the labyrinth beneath Minos's palace and slain the minotaur, a terrifying beast with a man's body and the head of a bull, and thus saved those Athenians who were due to be sacrificed to it.

Even these heroic stories did little to lift George's sombre mood, however. He felt like one of the condemned Athenian prisoners, sitting in silence, as the boat sailed ever nearer to the island upon which his doom would be sealed.

Once the storm had passed, they sailed on from Crete and made good headway, finally arriving at the port of Ostia on the twelfth day of April, the day before the 'ides'. Here, there was a joyous reunion with the household of Flavius: tales were told, songs were sung, a sizeable joint of roast beef was consumed, along with a wonderful variety of vegetables, each in its own sweet or spicy sauce, and honey-sweetened wine flowed freely. Several games of 'Circus' were played in honour of George, whose escapades in the gambling den were by now legendary, thanks to Brennos and Hector. When he finally consented to join in, and won three times in a row, even Cassia found it amusing.

"It's a pity that you weren't on this form two years ago", she laughed.

"The night is young", joked Brennos, turning to George. "Maybe you should go back into Ostia for a rematch with the Plebs."

George, who was feeling more relaxed than he had in ages, looked over at Cassia and smiled. "What do you reckon?"

"It's tempting", she returned his smile, "But being kidnapped by a gang of ruffians and tied to a tree is hardly my idea of a good time."

"Aw, come on; I promise to rescue you", he chuckled, a comfortable warm feeling welling up inside him.

"You may get a little singed in the process, though", warned Brennos.

"THIEF!"

Startled, George looked up; he had been daydreaming again. His mind was whisked away from that happy evening in Ostia, back to his present situation: a warm spring morning in the Gallic town of Lugdunum[1].

It took the Briton a moment to comprehend what Justus was shouting about; a small ragged looking boy, with an untidy mop of jet black hair, was racing out of the market square, one of their ornate golden plates clutched to his chest.

Brennos had already set off in pursuit, and George quickly hared after him, chasing his friend through the crowded streets, weaving in and out of its busy inhabitants. The boy was fleet-footed and soon reached the nearest town gate, which unfortunately stood unguarded at this time of day. Passing unchallenged beneath its stone arch, the youth, with his golden cargo, vanished from sight.

---

[1] Lyons

"THERE HE IS!" yelled Brennos, moments later, as they raced through the gate.

George followed his friend's finger and saw the scruffy lad dart off the road that led down the western slope of the Fourviere Heights, on which the town was built. Scrambling downhill, he passed beneath a section of the huge aqueduct, which ran beside the Roman highway, and once again disappeared from view. Leaving the road, the two Britons charged down the incline after him, swerving between the stone pillars that supported the water channel above them.

Emerging from beneath one of the archways, George scanned the surrounding area, looking for any sign of the thief, but their quarry had vanished.

"He can't have got far", Brennos panted, pulling up alongside. The big Briton held up a hand to shield his gaze from the glare of the midday sun. "Over there", he said, gesturing towards a mass of greenery to their right. "I saw something move."

They drew nearer to the thief's suspected hiding place: a dense clump of bushes sprouting forth from the steep hillside. Between the tangled mass of undergrowth, George could now make out an opening in the rock.

"A cave", confirmed Brennos, staring into the darkness. "I'll wager he's hiding in there."

George stepped forward, pushing a protruding branch out of the way.

"You go in; I'll make sure he doesn't double back on us", suggested his mentor.

Obediently, George stepped up to the cave entrance and peered in; he couldn't make out much yet, but his eyes would adjust to the darkness momentarily. He moved cautiously forward.

It was seven years earlier and he was following Tristan into the blackness. The little orphan advanced boldly into the cavernous depths and George had to follow, cowering behind his companion, sword shaking in his trembling fist. A feeling of dread washed over George, a wave of despair; somewhere at the end of this tunnel, death awaited them, and every step they took just brought them closer to its icy clutches.

George's heart was thumping in his chest. His cowardice had saved him on that occasion, but now there was no one to stand between him and the reaper, no one to die in his place. He forced himself to take a deep breath. *There are no bears in here, just you and a frightened boy.* He took another faltering step. Ahead of him, something stirred. *What was that noise?* He halted again, desperately trying to combat the fear that was threatening to overwhelm him. *It's just your imagination.*

Suddenly, the dank air of the cave exploded with a ferocious roar, and George's blood turned to ice!

Chapter 29 – Prepare to die

Yelling wildly, George raced back into the sunlight, charged through the undergrowth, and sprinted past his astonished friend.

"What's the mat…?"

But Brennos never finished his question. Instead, George heard a savage snarl, followed by an oath that quickly turned into a cry of pain.

George whirled around in time to see something large and black knock his friend to the ground. For an instant, he looked on in horror, frozen.

"NO!"

He had left one best friend to die; he would rather die himself than do that again. Drawing his sword, he rushed into the fray.

Screaming at the top of his lungs, George swung at the snarling thing. Alerted to the presence of its attacker, the creature reared up on its hind legs, avoiding George's hasty swing, and let out a roar of its own. It stood a head taller than he, massively built, with wickedly curved claws and covered all over with a thick carpet of dark brown fur. It had a snout like a dog, but its head was much broader and its ears were shorter and more rounded.

For a moment, time seemed to stand still. The cave-dweller stared at the puny creature that had disturbed its slumber, the tiny black eyes in its great round head, viewing him with a malevolent gaze. George stared back, conscious of his heart hammering away in his chest like a beating drum.

Time resumed; the huge animal lunged at George, the speed of its attack taking him by surprise. He barely had time to raise his sword before the colossus was on him, and his attempt to pierce its throat with the blade, as it bore down on him, went awry. Instead, the weapon sliced into the creature's muscular shoulder and was jarred from his grip. He was knocked to the ground, a great weight pressing down on his chest, forcing all the air out of his lungs. Moments later, a pair of ferocious jaws appeared above his head and he felt the beast's hot breath on his face.

Grabbing a handful of fur, George struggled desperately to fend off the snarling maw. The monster gave another thunderous roar and threw its head back, digging its claws painfully into his ribs as it did so. George cried out in pain as his attacker's great weight pushed the sharp talons into his flesh; he was suffocating, he couldn't draw breath. Just at the point where he felt sure his chest must collapse under this tremendous pressure, the brute swung around and the heavy weight had gone.

Coughing painfully, George rolled onto his side. An anguished cry filled the air, followed by a sickening crunching sound. The hairy fiend had moved away to his left, where it was once again attending to Brennos. With a huge effort, George hauled himself back onto his feet and staggered towards the savage animal.

"Get off him!"

His cry was futile; he was powerless to stop the brutal beast as its teeth tore into his friend's head, dyeing the Briton's fair hair crimson with his own blood. George didn't even have his sword; it was lost in the long grass. With no idea of what to do, only that he must end his friend's suffering, he lurched towards the brute. When he had closed to within a couple of strides of it, he noticed a shiny dagger protruding from the hump at the great creature's shoulders. *Brennos must have thrown it; that's why the thing got off me.*

Without pausing to think, George launched himself onto the mountain of thick brown fur, his fingers closing around the hilt of the dagger as he landed on the broad back, pushing the blade deeper into the thick hide. Throwing its huge head backwards in a savage snarl, the beast swung around and George was flung sideways, landing face-down in the long grass, the bloodstained dagger still clasped in his right hand.

As he struggled to rise again, a wave of dizziness came over George and he flopped back onto the turf, defeated. There was a low grunt from somewhere nearby. A few moments passed, during which George expected to feel a sharp claw on his midriff or a jagged tooth on his scalp. When he experienced neither, he opened one eye and turned his head. A few feet to his left, the monster lay slumped in the grass, its brown fur matted with blood.

Brennos? George rolled onto his stomach and got unsteadily to his feet. As he did so, something moved at the edge of his vision. Swinging around, he caught sight of a small ragged figure, clutching a large golden dish, emerging from the bushes beside the cave, where he had been hiding – *The thief!* The look of terror on the boy's face was not improved when George grabbed him by the scruff of the neck and waved a bloodstained dagger in his face.

Confident that the young villain was sufficiently cowed, George turned his attention to his friend. Brennos lay on his back, his face pale. A section of his scalp had been peeled off and the flap of skin hung down, held in place by the sticky mass of blood.

Gritting his teeth, George felt the Briton's neck for a pulse. *He's still alive.*

"Don't even think about it!" he yelled, turning to the scruffy boy, who had started to edge away.

Brennos groaned, opened an eye, and moved his head.

"Lie still", George told him, gently. "I'll go and get Flavius."

"I'm… all right", replied the injured Briton, manoeuvring himself into a sitting position and putting a hand to his bleeding scalp. "Ow! Maybe not."

Brennos withdrew his hand, now stained dark red. "Help me up."

George hauled the big man to his feet and steadied him as he swayed slightly. "Easy, you've lost a lot of blood."

"Looks like I'm doing better than the bear."

"What?" George stared at Brennos, open-mouthed.

"I'm doing better than the bear." He gestured to the animal lying still and silent in the long grass.

"That was a bear?"

George stared down at the creature they had killed. *So, that was a bear.* He shook his head, pondering; something wasn't quite right. A nagging doubt gnawed away at the back of his mind, but there was no time to think about it now. Putting the unformed questions away, for the moment, George began looking for his missing sword. After a brief search, he managed to locate it and then, supporting his stricken friend with one arm and keeping a firm grip on the thief with the other, he led the way up to the road.

As this curious threesome made their way back into Lugdunum, they attracted a great deal of attention from passers by.

"We were attacked by a bear", George felt compelled to explain, every time they passed a new traveller. After the fifth time he was starting to lose patience.

"He tripped over his toga", George called out to a group of boys who were standing by the gate, staring at them and chattering excitedly.

"He slipped on a wet towel."

"His girlfriend hit him with an amphora."

"You should have let the bear eat me", moaned Brennos.

"What happened to you?" asked a concerned Justus when the trio finally reached the marketplace.

"Attacked by a bear…" moaned Brennos, weakly, obviously unwilling to risk George's explanation.

"Here, sit down", gestured the merchant. "I'll fetch Flavius."

While Flavius attended to the wounded Briton, George explained their encounter with the bear more fully.

"Why did you steal from my stall?" Justus enquired of the boy, when George had finished.

The ragged urchin stood there, wide-eyed, uncomprehending.

"Tell him why you stole", demanded George, switching from Latin to his native tongue.

"For my family", the boy replied, staring down at his feet. "We need to eat."

"Well, you should work for your food, shouldn't you", replied George, unsympathetically.

"Take him to his home", instructed Justus, when George had relayed the boy's answer to him. "Tell his parents what he has done, and tell them I would like to see them tonight."

George looked at his master, surprised by his response. "Surely his parents aren't going to care; they probably taught him to steal."

"We shall see", was Justus's only reply.

The journey to the boy's home was a tiring one. The sun beat down from a cloudless sky, with hardly a breath of wind to ease George's discomfort. Exhausted as he was from his earlier tussle with the bear, the last thing the Briton wanted was to wander across open fields and meadows at midday, where there was not even a line of trees to offer shade from the baking heat. *Why am I wasting my time with this urchin? He should be beaten and sent on his way, not escorted to his home like an honoured guest.*

After walking what must have been a couple of miles, but felt considerably further, George spied a collection of thatched brick dwellings ahead: the boy's village. As they drew nearer, he was reminded, forcibly, of his own home, still many hundreds of miles away. There were many similarities between the two settlements:

both were part of the Roman Empire yet still tied to their ancient Celtic heritage; both were in close proximity to large Roman towns, but managed to retain their separate lifestyles and customs.

A low mud brick wall, that looked as if it had been thrown together in a hurry, surrounded the village, testament, to the threat of barbarian invasion that Gaul had lived under for many years. The ragged youth led George through the entrance and past several thatched houses that were dotted here and there, in no particular order. It was strange, after spending so much time in neatly ordered Roman towns, to wander through this random collection of structures.

Even the pace of life was different here: to his left, a donkey traced out an endless circular path around a large well, hoisting a bucket of water up the deep shaft, while a stony-faced woman looked on, stick in hand, in case the beast should cease from its task. To his right, a row of mud bricks lay drying in the midday sun.

As they passed, the woman glared at him and then rapped the donkey on its rump as it slowed, hoping to take advantage of her sudden inattention. Up ahead, a short thickset man, who was chopping wood, eyed George threateningly, his axe hovering above his head in mid swing.

Everywhere George looked, people were watching him; many were just standing there, staring at him from the doorways of their homes, their expressions heavy with mistrust and suspicion. It was obvious that these folk didn't get many visitors. George began to feel distinctly uncomfortable. *What if the boy calls for help? Will they attack me?*

The boy didn't call for help; instead, he led George to the entrance of a dishevelled dwelling with a number of gaps in the crumbling brickwork and loose straw dangling from numerous places on the thatched roof. It reminded the Briton of Catherine and Tristan's house back home.

The door was wide open, and George followed the scruffy youth straight in. Inside, it was just as untidy as the exterior had suggested: at the centre of the house, a middle-aged woman in a stain-covered apron sat, spinning clay on a potter's wheel; in one corner, a young girl, with long dark hair, was entertaining a small red-headed child with a dirty face. In another corner, a balding man with an unkempt beard was pressing red clay into some sort of mould, and over by the far wall, a shabbily dressed woman, of a similar age to George, was stacking several clay pots into a large stone oven. The earth floor was strewn with sacks, bedding and an assortment of clay pots and bowls.

The woman at the potter's wheel looked up from her work as George entered, and called to the girl stacking the oven. "Allicia."

Allicia turned around and, giving a start of surprise on seeing George, dropped the red clay pot she was holding. It fell to the floor with a thud and, immediately, the man rushed across to her, muttering under his breath, and picked up the piece of pottery, cradling it in his arms as if he was comforting a fallen child.

Feeling slightly embarrassed at his intrusion, George hesitated. There was an awkward silence, broken by the little red-haired boy, who started to cry.

"I am returning this boy", began George, uncertainly, not sure of whom he should be addressing. "I caught him stealing from my master's cart."

The older woman turned to the bearded man and said something that George didn't catch. The younger woman looked shocked, although whether this was genuine or merely for his benefit, George couldn't guess.

"My master told me to tell you that he would like to speak to the boy's parents."

George looked around awkwardly, unsure if the boy's parents were, in fact, present; the grey-haired woman and the bald man both looked too old, while Allicia seemed too young. Determined to say his piece and get out of there as quickly as possible, he ploughed on.

"If you care that this boy is a thief, and that he nearly got my friend killed", George added, with feeling, "And if you have any wish to apologise, then you can find my master, tonight, camped by the river, east of Lugdunum; his is the large crimson tent."

His task complete, George turned on his heel and exited the house without further ado, hurrying past the many spectators who had gathered to see the stranger. Enduring their suspicious glances and a good deal of muttering, George made his way back through the village, as rapidly as he could, without giving the impression of running away. He felt like a child walking past a pack of wild dogs, trying not to show fear, knowing that if he did, the dogs would smell it and attack. Despite his foreboding, however, no one challenged him and, feeling relieved, George passed beyond the low wall that encircled the village, and headed back towards the relative safety of Lugdunum.

"Is that another bear I hear?" laughed Juba, as George's stomach rumbled for the umpteenth time that evening.

"I only got a hunk of bread, and a bit of that dodgy soft Gaulish cheese, for dinner", George complained. "I'm starving!"

"It's almost ready", called Hector. "Where are those guests, Justus was expecting?"

"There won't be any guests", predicted George, sceptically.

"That'll be more food for us then", chimed in Brennos, emerging from the large crimson tent.

"Shouldn't you be resting?" George chided his friend, who was sporting a large bandage on his head that resembled a turban.

"I was getting depressed, staring up at dyed animal skin", replied the big Briton, shrugging his shoulders.

"I may be able to cure that too", Flavius interjected, smiling. "I've heard that taking calf's dung, boiled in wine, has a great effect on depression."

"You're joking!"

"No, I'm serious. Some healers swear by it."

"And you?"

"I need to test it on someone before I can form an opinion", replied Flavius, a twinkle in his eye.

"I tell you what would cure my depression", suggested Brennos: "Add some boiled calf dung to Hector's wine and then let me watch how he gets on with the ladies."

George started to laugh and then gasped, swallowed a big gulp of air, and began to hiccough violently.

"I've got several cures for that", chortled Flavius.

"Great", enthused Brennos. "What kind of dung do you need?"

George stared disbelievingly at the five figures approaching their tent; the thief's family had turned up after all. There was the bearded man carrying the small red-haired boy, the young woman – Allicia in her shabby patched dress, the girl with long dark hair, and at the rear of the party, the thief himself.

Justus had also spotted the new arrivals. "Help me, will you, George?" he called over, "You seem to have a knack for understanding their accent."

"Why me? Hector is the native Gaul; why can't he do it?" George was aggrieved that Justus seemed to be intent on forcing him into close proximity with these lowlifes. Hadn't he done enough already?

"Please, George."

Resigned, George wandered slowly across to his master.

"Now, tell them I'm honoured to meet them."

"My master is… honoured to meet you", began George, resisting the temptation to make up his own lines and say something far less complementary to the Gauls.

"I beg your forgiveness for the shameful way that my son treated you", Allicia volunteered, bowing low before Justus.

She gave the elder boy a sharp look, and he mumbled a hasty apology and stared down at the grass.

"Please accept this humble offering", she continued, unwrapping a red clay bowl from her tatty shawl.

Justus accepted the pot with delight, casting his expert eye over the intricate pattern that adorned it. "Gaulish red-slipped ware!" he exclaimed, "And very fine too. Where did you get it?"

"My brother is a potter", Allicia replied, indicating the balding man beside her.

"This is exquisite workmanship", praised the Roman, handling the bowl like a child with a new toy. "You must accept some money for it."

Allicia shook her head solemnly.

"Eat with us", insisted Justus, gesturing over to where Hector was busily turning a joint of venison over a small fire. "I think I may have a business proposal for you."

There was a noise in the darkness, the sound of claws clicking on the stone floor, as something large moved towards him. An ear-splitting roar filled the cavern, and George staggered backwards, horrified. Something touched him on the shoulder.

"George, it's time for your watch."

George stirred and opened his eyes; it was only Hector. Yawning, the Briton got unsteadily to his feet and stumbled out of the tent, plonking himself down beside the low-burning campfire. His was the last watch before dawn.

George stared up at the dark sky overhead. *What was I dreaming about?* He had been reliving the nightmare of Tristan's death, he was sure of it. But there was something wrong, something that he couldn't quite place.

George covered his ears with his hands, blocking out the crackling of the fire, willing his mind to replay the dream.

"I'm not sure that standing guard with your ears covered and your eyes closed is very effective."

George gave a start; it was Brennos. "I thought Flavius had given you some of that poppy milk stuff."

"He did, but I don't think he gave me enough", replied the turban-clad Briton, settling himself by the fire. "It's only knocked me out for half the night."

George sat down alongside his injured companion, and the two Britons stared into the fire, lost in their own thoughts.

Brennos was the first to break the silence. "I don't understand Justus", he declared, shaking his bandaged head. "He's practically agreed to buy that bald pleb's whole stock off him! That thieving wretch steals our stuff, nearly gets us both killed, and Justus rewards his family with a free feast and a lucrative business deal! Where's the justice in that?"

"They said they were sorry."

"And you believed them?"

"Not at first. I've been thinking dark thoughts about them all day; but they didn't have to walk all the way from their village with two small children, did they?" George pointed out. "Justus was showing kindness to those that don't deserve it, just like his master, Jesus."

"What, so because Jesus had a soft spot for thieves and criminals, Justus has to be a soft touch too?" muttered Brennos.

The two men subsided into silence once more, their eyes seemingly mesmerised by the flickering orange flames. After a long pause, Brennos spoke again. "Did you think you were going to die?"

"When the bear had its teeth at my throat?"

"No, when you sampled Hector's food!" laughed Brennos, mirthlessly. "Of course when the bear had you."

George mulled the question over; this was not the sort of issue that his friend usually brought up. "I didn't really have time to think about it."

"Well I did", continued Brennos, "And do you know what?"

George waited, unsure what was coming next. His friend seemed to be in an uncharacteristically melancholy mood.

"It terrified me!"

George stared at his friend, open-mouthed. Was this the same man who had slain one of the Bulls of Hades? Wasn't he the one who had bluffed their way out of the clutches of Felix's gang? Hadn't he saved George and Cassia from certain death at Primus's hands?

"You are the bravest person I've ever met", reassured George, hoping that this complement wouldn't go to his friend's already swollen head. "You must have saved my life three or four times!"

"Five, I think, but who's counting?"

"You can have one for your dagger in the bear's back", chuckled George, "But if you're thinking you saved me from those thieves in Briton, you can forget it."

George was expecting a witty retort, but none came; his friend obviously had something on his mind and was determined to say it.

"I wasn't ready."

"Eh?"

"That's what flashed through my mind as the bear bit into my skull. I'm not ready to die."

"So, what are you going to do about it?"

It was Brennos's turn to be confused. "What do you mean?"

"Well", began George, choosing his words with care, "You're ready for most things. If I needed to pick someone to get me out of a crisis, it would be you. You're good with a sword, a spear or a knife; you're a good hunter, a good rider, and you can talk your way out of anything. How did you get like that?"

"I train", replied Brennos, simply.

"That's right", affirmed George. This was an unusual experience for him; he had rarely had anything to teach his mentor. "In a crisis, you can cope because you've prepared yourself beforehand. So, if you want to be ready for death, you must prepare yourself to meet your maker."

"I know where you're going with this, George. You want me to repent and turn to Jesus, turn from my life of drinking, gambling, womanising, and any other pleasurable activity I can think of. You want me to prepare for death by sacrificing life."

There was silence; George waited.

"It's all right for you." There was a trace of bitterness in Brennos's voice. "You don't curse, you don't lie, you don't mess around with women, and you don't gamble any more; you don't even drink much. God must love you."

"Do you know why I ran away from home to join a merchant caravan?" There was a grim determination in George's tone. "I stole a sword from the village sheriff. I lied to my best friend about how I got it, so that he would come with me on a foolish quest to hunt down a dangerous bear. When we found the bear, in a dark cave, I ran for my life and left my best friend to be eaten."

As George retold the tale he'd vowed never to speak of again, he was glad of the darkness; it hid the tears that ran down his cheeks, and made him feel less vulnerable, even though his unsteady voice betrayed his emotions.

"My only other friend in the village turned her back on me because I'd left her brother to die while I saved my own miserable hide. The village sheriff had some crazy idea that I'd murdered him with the stolen sword. I had no choice but to run away. That's what living for myself did for me." George sniffed loudly and wiped his eyes on the sleeve of his tunic. "That path leads to misery, and it is only by God's mercy that I have escaped from it."

There was another long pause and then, with a loud yawn, Brennos got to his feet. "I'm going to try and get a bit more rest before daybreak."

As his friend ambled back to the tent, George wondered what he had to do to get through to him. How could he be willing to throw away his precious soul for the sake of a few dubious pleasures?

"One day you'll face death again, Brennos", he warned, as his friend pulled back the tent flap. "If you aren't prepared on that day, you will have only yourself to blame."

Chapter 30 – Worse things happen at Sea

"What have you done to Brennos, George?" Hector asked, as he tramped beside their horse-drawn cart, heavily laden with fine Gaulish red-slipped pottery. "He has been acting very strange recently."

"How do you mean?" smiled George, knowingly.

"Let me see", pondered the Gaul, dropping his voice so that Justus, who was driving the cart, wouldn't overhear. "A few days ago, he had the opportunity to sample the delights of Durocortorum[1] with me, but he declined. I thought he must be ill but, when I checked on him later, I caught him reading Justus's scrolls. Then, two or three nights ago, I opened a couple of wineskins and offered one to Brennos while he was on watch - He refused!"

"Was the wine all right?" questioned Cassia, dropping down from her perch beside her father, to join them. "It didn't smell strange at all?"

"Strange?"

"Like err… cows?"

"Cows?" Hector was confused.

"There's a cure for depression that's been doing the rounds", George chuckled. "You mix it with wine."

"This was pure Gaulish wine", stated Hector, indignantly. "The finest in the world."

"So what did you do with the other skin?" Cassia wanted to know.

"I drank them both", admitted the Gaul, with a shrug.

"Was that the night when I tried to wake you for your watch and you just moaned something about a headache, turned over and went back to sleep?" enquired George, his eyebrows raised accusingly.

"I don't remember", muttered Hector. "And another thing", he added, quickly changing the subject, "He's not insulted my nation, my stories, my beliefs or my cooking, for days."

"And that's a bad thing?" queried Cassia, her eyebrows raised now.

---

[1] Rheims

The Gaul shook his head, a puzzled expression on his moustached face. "It's not like him."

"Here he comes", warned Cassia, as the object of their discussion hung back from the cart in front, where he and Juba had been conversing with Flavius.

"Here we are", called Justus, above the clatter of hooves and the rumble of wheels, "Gesoriacum.[1]"

George looked up to see that the sizeable fishing port had indeed appeared below them. Beyond it, the deep blue of the sea stretched to the horizon, and somewhere just over that horizon was his home. George stared out to sea, an uncomfortable sensation in the pit of his stomach; he had managed to put the homecoming mostly out of his mind, but now that they were so close, the feelings of impending doom were returning.

George poked his head into the open. It was a cold, clear morning, with a gentle easterly breeze. He caught a whiff of fried fish on the air; Brennos had risen early to make them all breakfast.

"Come and get it", called the big Briton and, with various yawns and stretches, the others emerged bleary-eyed into the weak sunlight.

"Still not happy with the new Brennos?" Cassia asked Hector, as the Gaul tucked into his fish enthusiastically.

"Mumpth mmm", he replied.

After a hearty breakfast, the companions packed up their tent and set out for the harbour. Gesoriacum was the principal port linking the Roman provinces of Gaul and Britannia, and was also a major centre of the fishing industry. Not surprisingly, the river estuary, upon which the town was built, was busy with a great number and variety of ships. Fishing boats of all shapes and sizes lined both sides of the river, while an enormous Roman galley cruised down the middle, towering majestically over them, its three banks of oars moving in harmony, cutting through the water in time to the beating of a drum.

Moored to the near bank, a short distance ahead, stood the merchant vessel on which they had booked passage, shorter than the galley, but broader and equipped with sails rather than oars. Oars

---

[1] Boulogne

and rowers took up precious cargo space and so were not used on this type of ship.

The stern of the boat was decorated with a huge goose's head, which Hector informed them was a symbol of the Egyptian goddess, Isis. The large square mainsail bore the Roman emblems of the she-wolf suckling the twins, Romulus and Remus, the legendary founders of Rome.

"Roman symbols and an Egyptian goddess? They're hedging their bets aren't they?" laughed Cassia, as the companions began to unload the cart.

"It is wise to take all the divine assistance you can get", stated Hector.

"Ah, but a man who wagers on all the runners in a race can never win", countered Justus.

"Justus?" called a voice from somewhere above them.

They all turned to see a jolly, round-faced man, with streaks of grey in his dark hair, making his way down the gangplank towards them.

"It is you!" he exclaimed as he stepped off. "Justus Liberius - I haven't seen you in years!"

The two men clasped hands warmly. "Festus!" A broad grin spread across Justus's face. "Good to see that you're still in business, my friend."

"Just about", replied Festus, "Though times have been hard recently."

"You have a few more grey hairs than when I saw you last."

"I've not caught up with you yet", laughed Festus.

"This is my daughter, Cassia."

"A pleasure to meet you", the captain bowed.

"And my adopted sons: Brennos, Hector, Juba and George."

"Welcome aboard."

"Flavius Marcellus is here too", Justus informed him.

"Well, things are certainly looking up", Festus nodded, cheerfully. "We must talk. I'll get my men to help yours load up."

Festus turned and shouted to two dark-haired youths, who were lounging against the deck rail. "Claude, Pascal. Give these gentlemen a hand with their goods. You can stack it in the aft hold."

Claude and Pascal assisted George and his friends in loading Justus's merchandise. All his goods had been stored in wooden crates and sealed with a wax seal, stamped with the merchant's signet ring. The hold was already more than three quarters full, piled high with boxes, barrels and amphorae. It did, indeed, look like this was going to be a profitable voyage for Captain Festus.

"I'm just going to entreat Isis for her protection during our voyage", called Hector, when the last of the crates was safely stowed. "Care to join me, Brennos?"

"You go ahead, kiss the goose", sneered Brennos.

"Aha, I knew you were still in there, you sarcastic Briton", chuckled the Gaul, mischievously.

"The only good thing about Isis is she floats", added Brennos. "Why not join me in a prayer to the God who made the sea, instead?"

Hector's jaw nearly hit the deck.

"Do you need a green apple, George?" asked Juba.

"What? Oh... err... no. Not any more." George turned to his Berber friend, who was looking at him, concern written all over his dark face.

"You looked slightly green, that is all."

"No... I'm fine."

This wasn't entirely true. Yes, he wasn't feeling sick, but he now had a clear sight of Britannia's coastline, and the feelings of unease were growing stronger even as the chalky cliffs were becoming sharper and more defined.

"SHIP TO STARBOARD!"

The boat seemed to list slightly as a hundred pairs of feet moved towards that side of the vessel and a hundred pairs of eyes scanned the horizon for what the oarsman had seen.

There it was, soon clearly visible to all: a tiny red sail, but growing larger by the moment.

"SAXON PIRATES!" yelled one of the sailors.

With these words, a state of panic broke over the ship. Oaths were yelled, various gods were invoked, and people began rushing to and fro as if, by a sudden flurry of pointless activity, they thought they could improve the situation.

Over this general hullabaloo, the captain's voice rang out. "THIRTY DEGREES PORT."

The oarsman, standing atop the tower at the stern of the boat, manoeuvred the huge steering oars with all haste and the whole ship tilted, sending up plumes of spray.

The red sail loomed large; the other ship was closing. George could see now that it was powered not only by wind, but a bank of oars, on each flank, dipped rhythmically into the dark water, pulling the boat relentlessly forward.

"WE'VE LOST THE WIND!" someone cried, and as George stared up at the huge square mainsail he saw, along with everyone else, that it hung limply. In steering to avoid the oared vessel, they had lost their only means of propulsion.

"HARD TO STARBOARD", yelled the captain, taking command, hoping to correct his error.

"THAT'S TAKING US TOWARDS THEM!"

It was. They had put themselves in a corner and, as everyone could see, they were swiftly going to be overhauled by the pirates. There was a sudden surge, by the stricken crowd, to reach the port bow.

"STAND AND FIGHT!" yelled a single voice; it was Justus.

"SWORDS OUT!" cried the Captain, taking up the call to arms.

George drew his blade, fighting the fear that was welling up within him. Looking along the deck, he could see that a few others had done the same. Many of the merchants, though, were still cowering away from the starboard side of the ship, unwilling to fight, unable to cope in this moment of crisis.

The pirates' boat was drawing alongside now. It had a high curved prow and a towering stern, but amidships, where the sides were lower, a row of shields was visible and a line of warriors' helmets glinted in the sun.

There was a loud clanging sound. George looked upward and saw a rope, bridging the gap between the two ships. There was a clunk, and a metal hook, attached to another rope, tangled in the rigging of the mainmast. There was a flurry of movement overhead as a dozen more hooks flew through the air. George turned to look at the pirates; they were hauling on the ropes, pulling the boats together. Any moment now they would be close enough to board. George gripped the hilt of his sword tightly; this was it.

There was a blur of movement; more ropes were winging their way between the two craft. A loud war-cry erupted, and a large object hurtled towards George. Before he had time to work out what was going on, something heavy had struck him forcibly in the gut and he was flying backwards. An unstoppable force carried him through the air and threw him to earth, slamming him into the wooden boards of the deck and sending his sword skidding across the flat surface.

Coloured lights burst before his eyes as George struggled to rise. A black-clad figure moved towards him; he had an iron helmet on his head that covered the upper portion of his face. Two dark eyes stared at George malevolently through circular holes in the metal. The Saxon warrior stepped forward, his longsword held high. George reached despairingly for his own sword, but he was too late, his enemy's blade was descending; death was a heartbeat away.

A cry of pain and surprise rent the air, and the pirate stumbled forwards, collapsing on top of George. The Briton fought to push the heavy weight off him, and as he emerged from underneath the Saxon, he saw the hilt of a dagger sticking out of the man's back. George looked up, still slightly dazed and disoriented, to see his saviour.

"How many times do I have to save your life? That's six!"

"Five", insisted George, as he grabbed Brennos's outstretched arm and was pulled to his feet.

Chaos reigned all about them: harsh battle-cries, yelps of fear, grunts of exertion, groans of pain, and the clash of steel on steel. Some distance to his left, George could just make out Juba and Hector, with a couple of sailors, battling a growing band of Saxons. Even as he watched, another pirate landed heavily on the deck and swiftly joined the fray. Up in the rigging of the Saxon ship, more pirates were perched, clinging to ropes, awaiting their chance to swing across the rapidly diminishing gap between the two vessels and join the battle.

Somehow in the midst of all of this, Brennos remained calm and focused, like a sheltered port in a stormy sea. "Courage, George", he said. "If today is our last day on earth, then it will be our first in paradise."

Blue eyes smiling beneath his untidy mop of blond hair, Brennos flicked George's sword off the deck with his left boot, caught it with his right hand and lobbed the weapon, hilt first, in his bemused friend's direction.

"Your sword, George."

George barely had chance to catch it before, with a boom like a clap of thunder, the ships collided and he stumbled on the slippery deck. Regaining his balance, he looked up in time to see a row of pirates, armed with swords, axes and sturdy round shields, pour onto the ship, hacking and slashing at their terrified foes, who fell back under this furious onslaught.

"There's too many!" yelled George, forced backwards by the crush of bodies retreating before the Saxon assault.

"This way", called Brennos, grabbing his left arm.

They were making for the oarsman's tower, which stood at the stern of the boat, and served the dual purposes of a sheltered cabin within and a place to steer the ship from atop the roof.

A fierce Saxon barred their way, an axe held high above his head. There was a clang as Brennos parried his downward blow, followed by a grunt as the big Briton's momentum knocked the pirate off his feet. As the helmeted man crashed to the deck, a swift sword thrust finished him off.

The two Britons charged on, dodging panic-strewn merchants and sailors, before skirting the large wooden trapdoor that covered the aft hold, and reaching the tower just beyond it. At one side of the structure was a sturdy wooden door leading to the interior of the cabin; at the other side, a steep ladder led up onto the roof. Brennos leapt onto this and hauled himself up; George cast a nervous glance over his shoulder, at the advancing pirates, before shinning up after his friend.

At the top of the ladder, a gruesome sight met their eyes: the oarsman lay spread-eagled, a long-shafted spear protruding from his side. Turning his face away, George looked back along the ship, towards the mainmast. From up here, the two friends had a bird's-eye view of the conflict below, and it didn't look good. Helmeted figures swarmed all over the midsection of the ship, forcing their opponents to retreat towards either end. Those at the bow seemed to be putting up stout resistance, as far as George could make out, but the ones that had sought refuge astern were cowering behind the oarsman's tower, most without weapons in their fists. Some were even clinging to the giant carved swan's neck as if they believed that the shaped block of wood could save them.

Startled by a shout to his left, George spun around. One of the pirates had just leapt from the rigging and was swinging down towards them. There was a blur of movement to his right and a knife flew through the air, striking the Saxon in mid flight and sending him crashing to the deck below.

"Watch the ladder!" called Brennos, putting his foot on the chest of the oarsman's corpse and yanking the spear from his side.

Hefting the wooden shaft, the big Briton strode to the starboard side of the roof and took aim at the pirates advancing menacingly towards the little crowd huddled behind the tower. There was a gasp of pain as the metal point struck one of the Saxons squarely between the shoulder blades, followed by a thud as he pitched forward onto the deck.

Several of the pirates turned and stared upwards, wondering where the attack had come from. Spying the two Britons, the leader pointed a finger at them and barked out an order. He may have spoken in a foreign tongue, but his meaning was all too clear: "The two men on the tower – kill them!"

George suddenly remembered that he was supposed to be watching the ladder. He whirled around to find a Saxon helmet emerging from below, and immediately swung his sword at it. There was a ringing clang, a yell, and the helmet disappeared from view.

George turned as a cry of pain erupted from somewhere close by. The blood froze in his veins; this wasn't happening, it couldn't be! As he watched in horror, Brennos, the friend who'd saved his life on so many occasions, reached feebly for the spear that had embedded itself in his back, staggered sideways, and toppled off the roof!

In a daze, George stumbled to the port side of the tower and stared open-mouthed at the motionless figure, sprawled, face-down, on the deck beneath. He was dreaming; he had to be. Any moment now, he was going to wake up and see Brennos's familiar mischievous grin.

As he continued to gape disbelievingly at the body of his friend, George gradually became aware of noises coming from his right and turned slowly, his sword hanging limply from nerveless fingers. Another pirate was climbing the ladder, this one holding a shield out in front of him, so as to avoid his companion's fate.

George felt strangely detached, as if he was watching the unfolding action through somebody else's eyes. Everything seemed distant, surreal; then through the fog, a voice screamed in his brain. Some part of George hadn't given up, hadn't fallen from the tower with his friend. Rousing himself, as if from a deep sleep, he stepped forward and swung his sword. The blade was knocked harmlessly aside as the determined Saxon forced his way onto the roof. George was then forced to dodge as the pirate charged at him shield first.

As he turned to face his opponent, George caught a glint of metal out of the corner of his eye: another pirate was reaching the top of the ladder. Realising that he was about to be surrounded, George lurched towards this new foe. Anticipating his attack, the Saxon clung onto the top rung with one hand and slashed at the onrushing Briton's ankles with his sword.

Instinctively, George jumped the flashing blade and kicked out, his right foot catching the pirate right in his metal-masked face. Both men cried out: George, as pain shot through his big toe, and the Saxon, as he lost his grip on the ladder and fell backwards.

Hopping on his left leg, George twisted to face the pirate who had already gained the roof. The Saxon was charging at him once more; George jumped sideways, but this time he was off-balance and unable to avoid the onrushing warrior. The heavy wood-backed shield hit him square in the chest and he was thrown backwards, plummeting over the edge of the tower!

George's arms flailed wildly as he tumbled through the air, hitting the deck with a sickening crunch. For a moment his whole body was racked with pain, then his stomach lurched again and he was falling, falling into darkness…

Chapter 31 – Alone?

All was silent and dark: not a lonely silence, but a pleasant quiet, and not a terrifying absence of light, but a warm comfortable nothingness. He was dead, of that George was sure. This didn't bother him as much as he thought it would; the anticipation of it had certainly been a lot worse than the actual thing. Now his troubles were over, his struggles ended; now he would meet his maker and all his questions would be answered.

A ray of light shone through the gloom; they were coming for him. The guardian angels would soon bear him aloft, taking him to the great beyond. He was going to see Brennos again, and Tristan. And, presumably, Juba would be joining him soon, assuming the pirates had won, which seemed inevitable. In that case, Justus would be there too. And Cassia? Would she be there? He pondered this for a moment. Had she ever really trusted the God of her parents? As for Hector, he wouldn't be there: Jesus was just one among many to him, not the only way to the Father.

A wave of sadness passed over George; those cursed pirates had condemned his friend to eternal torment! And what of his mother, waiting in vain for her son to come home? Now she would never know what had become of him. All his plans to return and make things right between him and his mother, between him and Catherine, they would never be fulfilled.

A tear welled up in the corner of his eye and ran down his cheek. *Should I still be crying in the afterlife? Those angels are certainly taking their time!* George stared upwards at the shaft of light. *Where am I?* His eyes were adjusting to the darkness now; he turned his head to take in more of the surroundings. As he did so, a spasm of pain shot through him. *I shouldn't still be feeling pain.* He tried moving again, more slowly this time, and, with a great deal of effort, managed to force himself into a sitting position. He had apparently been lying on sacks filled with something soft. *Silk?* All around him were piles of boxes, crates, amphorae and more sacks. *This isn't the afterlife, it's the aft hold!*

George slumped down among the sacks and tried to make sense of what his senses were telling him. The last thing he remembered was falling from the oarsman's tower, so how had he ended up here, in storage, and why hadn't the pirates killed him, or at least tied him up?

He looked up at the sunlight pouring in through the hatch above. *The hatch! I landed on it when I was pushed off the tower.* There had been a splintering sound and his stomach had lurched. *I must have crashed through the trapdoor and landed on these sacks. It's a miracle I'm still alive!*

Grimacing, George sat up again, offering a heartfelt prayer of thanks to the God of miracles. He moved all his limbs experimentally, checking fingers and toes; everything seemed to be in working order. George hauled himself shakily to his feet. He still had several unanswered questions: what had happened to the pirates? What had happened to the rest of his friends and the crew of the ship? And why had no one bothered to look for him?

George moved stiffly across to the wooden steps that led to the deck of the ship; it was time to get some answers. He climbed from slat to slat slowly, bent double like an old man, resting his hands on the steps in front as he went. Both his back and neck ached terribly, not surprisingly considering the fall he'd just had. Approaching the broken hatch above, another question occurred to George: *How long have I been unconscious?*

There were no sounds of battle, no shouts or cries, nothing at all, just the creaking of the ship as it rose and fell gently with the waves. Uncertain of what he was about to see, George cautiously pushed on the section of the hatch that was still intact. Moments later, his head and shoulders emerged above deck. Overhead, the mainsail billowed in the breeze; they were sailing again. Behind him, George could make out a figure standing on the oarsman's tower. Not far to his left, a sailor was busy lashing two frayed pieces of rope together, obviously repairing damage that had been done during the recent skirmish. George's heart gave a sudden leap of relief as he recognised the man.

"Claude."

The dark-haired youth looked up from his work in surprise, staring at George as though he had just arisen from the grave. As the Briton moved forward to step onto the deck of the ship, Claude dropped what he was doing and shook his head vigorously, motioning for George to go back.

George stood there bemused, one foot on the top step, the other on the one below. Claude looked around frantically before crossing to the hatchway.

"Get below, quickly!" he insisted, in his strong Gaulish accent. "The pirates will…"

Claude was suddenly interrupted by a loud bellow. Instinctively, George ducked out of sight, crawling backwards down the steps. As he cowered in the shadows, he heard heavy footsteps overhead, followed by a barrage of words that he didn't recognise.

"I… I don't understand", stammered Claude.

There were more footsteps and another voice spoke, a menacing gravelly voice. "Gaul?"

"Y…yes."

"Work", commanded the new voice, using the Gaulish tongue, "Or die. Understand now?"

"Yes."

George waited, not daring to move or even to draw breath. Sunlight streamed in through the open hatch, robbing him of even the scant protection of shadow. If anyone were to peer into the hold now he would surely be seen. There was movement above; George bit his lip. Next moment, the open trapdoor slammed shut, leaving him in semi-darkness once again.

George lay there on the steps, listening to the sound of retreating footsteps. When he was certain that the pirates were no longer anywhere near the hatch, he crawled backwards down into the depths of the hold and crouched behind a consignment of wooden barrels.

What was he going to do now? The feeling of hope that had briefly sprung to life, on seeing Claude, had been cruelly snatched away. It appeared that the pirates had won the battle after all, and had taken control of the merchant vessel. They had kept some of the crew alive in order to sail the ship, but those who were of no use to them…

He didn't want to think about it; he wished he had died along with his friends. Things had certainly seemed a lot better when he thought he was dead: no more problems, no more pain. It was going to come to the same thing in the end; there was no escape: if he went up on deck, he would be facing dozens of well-armed pirates and, if he stayed skulking around in the hold, the pirates would discover him as soon as they started unloading their plunder.

As George wallowed in self-pity, listening to the gloomy tones of despair, the images of a dark cave and a blonde-haired girl flashed across his mind. It was those dreams that had started him on this foolish quest to return home; was it a message from God or had it just been his own fertile imagination?

Is this what you wanted to happen? Did you plan this all along? "Did you want me to die alone and friendless, like Tristan, just so I'd know what it felt like?"

Unwittingly, George spoke this last question out loud. He stared fearfully up at the damaged hatch, wondering if his muttering had carried up onto the deck. *Not that it will make any difference now*, he thought bitterly. *I've got no more chance of survival than those poor fools who were clasping onto the figure of Isis!*

Another voice spoke inside the Briton's head; this one sounded a lot like Brennos. *"The only good thing about Isis is she floats."*

What if he found something to float on and jumped overboard? George eyed the barrels that he was currently hiding behind; could he make it to land on one of those? He gave the nearest one an experimental push; it didn't budge. He tried another, but it was similarly heavy. *It'll be no good if I jump in with a barrel that sinks!* George looked around for something to prise open the barrel with; if he could lighten the load, this plan might just work. *If the pirates don't see me jump and I'm not too far from land, and the currents aren't too strong, and I don't get bashed to death on some rocks or swept off the barrel by a big wave.*

As George pondered all the things that could go wrong with his plan, there was a loud crash from above. Startled, he retreated back into his hiding place and, staring upwards, saw that the hatch had been reopened. A dark figure was descending the steps, holding an oil lamp. George huddled behind the large collection of barrels, hoping and praying that he wouldn't be discovered.

Peeping through a gap between two kegs, George spotted a second man, following the first down into the hold. As the men drew closer, George could make out their features by the lamp's light. Both had pale skin and long blond hair that was tied back in several braids. They were certainly Saxons; no man in the Roman Empire would wear his hair in such an outlandish fashion!

As the first man neared the bottom step, George caught a glint of something metallic reflecting the light from the pirate's lantern – *My sword.*

The Saxons had reached the foot of the steps; George leaned flat to the wooden container that lay between him and his foes. The lantern light flickered from left to right in the gloom; the man was looking for something *or someone!*

Wooden boards creaked as the pirates moved across the hold towards the place where George was hiding. The Briton tensed; he hadn't heard the Saxons draw their swords yet. He looked up, waiting for a blond head to appear. If he was discovered, George would have mere moments in which to strike before his opponents' weapons were out. Could he get to his sword before they cut him down?

More creaks, then everything went quiet. The tension was unbearable. There was a scraping sound and then, finally, the men spoke. Their language bore no relation to any that George had heard on his travels but, from the tone of their voices, it appeared that the two pirates had found what they were looking for. There were further scraping sounds, grunts of exertion, as if something heavy was being lifted, and then more creaking. George was desperate to see what the Saxons were up to, but he daren't risk being seen and so continued to press up close to the barrel.

Moments later, the noise of creaking boards gave way to a soft thudding; the pirates were climbing back up the steps. George moved cautiously to his left and peered through the gap; the men were now halfway up the staircase, carrying an object between them. It was a large pot, and heavy, judging by the grunting noises they were both making as they climbed. The pot had a pointed base and a rounded section at roughly one third of its length which tapered to a long slender neck, with two handles joining the neck to the main body: an amphora.

Relieved, George flopped down behind the barrels. It didn't take a genius to work out what was going on: the pirates had captured a richly stocked merchant ship and now they were going to celebrate their triumph with the aid of a large quantity of Gaulish wine.

George was alone once again. He crossed the floor of the hold to where he was sure he'd caught a glint of metal in the pirates' lamplight. Sure enough, his sword was lying discarded next to a large crate. Picking it up, George took a practise swing; like its owner it seemed to have survived the drop unscathed. He now had something to prise the barrel open with. *If the pirates are busy drinking, maybe I can jump overboard without being seen.*

George walked back over to the kegs; he was moving more freely now, and the sharp pains he had been experiencing had subsided to dull aches. Suddenly he froze in mid stride; he had had an idea, a crazy idea. The Briton stood upright, swaying with the motion of the ship, his eyes closed in concentration, trying desperately to hang on to that thought. It was like a bubble floating through the recesses of his mind, a delicate thing that could so easily burst.

Opening his eyes, George looked about him; everything was wreathed in shadow once again; the sun must have gone behind a cloud. An enormous jumble of crates, barrels and amphorae lay before him.

I'll never find what I need in all this lot! The bubble was surely bursting. Miraculously, just at that moment, a ray of light shone through the broken hatchway, illuminating his surroundings. Suddenly, George didn't feel alone any more.

Rummaging amongst the crates to his right, he found one with a seal that looked familiar. Peering closely, George could just about make out the imprints of a cross and a pair of weighing scales: Justus's family emblems. *So this one beside it, with the flower symbol, must belong to Flavius.*

George broke the wax seal and lifted the lid. Inside were a number of rough clay pots; they didn't look much compared to the intricately patterned red-slipped pottery that he had packed up earlier that day, but it was what they held that counted.

Removing the top of one of the jars revealed a dark coloured gum within: poppy milk. George's heart was beating faster now; he had what he needed for his desperate plan, now it was time to put it into action.

Retracing the pirates' earlier steps, George crossed the floor of the hold to where three large piles of amphorae stood, separated from each other by towers of crates. The amphorae were stacked tightly, the bases of each successive layer resting snugly on the necks of those below.

Which pile did they pick from? George stared from one stack to the next; there were no obvious gaps, and none of the three top layers were complete. A sense of panic began to rise within him; he had been a fool to think that his crazy plan had any chance of success!

George closed his eyes and took a deep breath; he had to keep it together. Mouthing a silent prayer, he yanked at the nearest jar, sliding it off the top of the stack. The thing was immensely heavy and he quickly dropped it to the floor with a loud boom.

The noise echoed alarmingly around the hold. Steadying the amphora with both hands, George eyed the hatchway, overhead, nervously. He crouched there, stock still, for quite a while before daring to commence his next task: prising off the clay stopper. Neither his long-bladed sword, nor his short brittle fingernails were ideal tools for this job, but after a good deal of tugging, twisting and levering, the bung was out and he could peer into the huge pot.

Ugh! Fish sauce. There was no mistaking that pungent aroma. For some reason, incomprehensible to George, Romans loved the stuff, using it to flavour a great many of their more exotic dishes. *Well the pirates won't be celebrating with this! They might force-feed it to me if I'm discovered*, he mused. *What a horrible way to go!*

Jamming the stopper back in, George hoisted the jar to waist height, then onto his shoulder and, with several grunts and groans, which he subdued as much as possible, manhandled the pot back into its place.

George looked at the remaining two piles, wondering how the pirate had managed to distinguish between them. The amphorae were of slightly different design; perhaps the Saxon had stolen enough of them, by now, to know the difference between those that held wine and those that held fish sauce. Lamenting his lack of knowledge in this area, George opted, at random, for the central stack.

No smell of fish assaulted his nostrils this time but, after tipping the jar slightly, poking a finger into the narrow opening, and tasting the liquid, George knew he'd guessed wrong again. *Olive oil!* He spat. *And that'll be the type that burns better than it tastes!*

Turning to the last pile, George dragged an amphora off the top and, straining with the weight, lowered it to the floor. This time he knew he was right; as soon as the stopper was out, a delicious, fruity aroma emerged.

Now for the next obstacle: *How much should go in?* A pinch of the stuff had been enough to knock him out, but that had been in a cup of wine. How many cups of wine did this amphora hold? *A hundred? Two hundred? More?*

A horrible thought struck him: *There's no way the pirates will get through the amphora they've taken; no one's going to be back for another!*

The feeling of panic was assaulting his stomach once again. George grabbed the jar of poppy milk and started scraping the gummy substance into the amphora. *I'm going to attempt this plan anyway. The rest is up to God.*

Chapter 32 – Recaptured

Bit by bit, George emptied the whole pot of poppy milk into the wine, and then stuck his sword into the amphora and stirred it as best he could. He had no idea whether it had dissolved or not and he wasn't going to think about it. And when the thought entered his head that the pirates might not choose this particular jar of wine, he simply pulled down another and got to work on that. George kept working, not giving himself time to reflect on the flaws in his wild scheme.

He had filled five out of the six amphorae on the top layer, and was just reaching for the last, when a loud bang startled him. Grabbing his sword, George scurried across the floor and ducked behind the barrels.

Looking up, he could see sunlight pouring in through the open trapdoor. Then a shadow crossed the light, and another; two Saxons were heading down into the hold. *Surely they've not drunk all that wine!*

The two men appeared to be grumbling, though about what, George couldn't guess. The wine didn't seem to have affected them greatly, he noted; they were both making their way down the stairs with ease despite the rocking motion of the ship.

George gripped the hilt of his sword tightly, desperately hoping that the pirates were here for another amphora of strong drink and not for him. There was the sound of creaking boards, followed by a familiar scraping. The two pirates exchanged words. Had they noticed that the bungs had been tampered with? George held his breath. There was a loud grunt, more creaking, and the thudding of two pairs of boots on the wooden steps. George risked a quick glance between the barrels, and his heart leapt; they were carrying an amphora of wine.

George stretched his aching leg muscles. How long had it been since they'd taken the drugged wine? One hour? Two? There was no way to tell from down here. He now realised the weak point in his plan: he had no way of knowing when the poppy milk would take effect.

The weak point? George shook his head; his plan had a great many weak points, and now that all he had to do was sit and wait, they all flooded unchecked into his head, each one more depressing than the last. He had been certain that they had taken one of the five drugged jars but, as time went by, the thought that maybe they'd taken the sixth - the one he'd not got around to - grew in his mind. And even if they were all drinking poppy wine, it was highly unlikely that they would all swallow enough to knock them out, before one of them noticed that something was afoot. *And then they'll know someone's down here!*

George could bear it no longer. "If today is my last day on earth, then it will be my first in paradise", he whispered, echoing Brennos's sentiment as he pulled himself to his feet. The words sounded hollow, unreal. Did he really believe them? He thought of his friend's broken body, splayed out on the deck; that wasn't a future he wanted.

George climbed the steps slowly, like a condemned man entering the arena. As he poked his head hesitantly above deck, he heard a shout and ducked back instantly. He had been seen! George waited numbly, unable to move, his chest tight with anxiety.

The yelling continued; it sounded strange, muffled. George had expected war-cries and rapid footsteps, but none came. He stuck his head, once more, out into the open. Turning through a full circle, the only figure he spotted was the oarsman, perched on the flat roof above, and he was pretty sure that the man was one of the captured sailors and not a pirate. The shouting seemed to be coming from inside the cabin itself.

George crouched at the top of the steps, wondering what to do next. Perhaps, while the deck was clear, he should grab a barrel and swim for it. He could clearly see land, less than a mile away, on the starboard side of the boat, and there was still two or three hours of daylight left. He stared out across the dark grey expanse of water; it didn't look very inviting.

George focused once more on the cabin; he was pretty sure that he could only hear one voice. Maybe all the pirates, bar one, were unconscious and the shouter was trying to rouse them. Or perhaps the pirates were being reprimanded, by their captain, for their sloppy behaviour - drinking on the job - and they were all still fairly sober.

George hesitated. Should he risk it? It might be his only chance? On the other hand, he might be about to walk right into the arms of the enemy. George stared back out at the foaming churning waters of the cold dark sea, and finally his mind was made up. He drew his sword from its sheath, uttered a quick prayer, and rushed at the oarsman's tower.

Barging open the heavy wooden door, George charged into the cabin and almost tripped over an unconscious figure lying directly in his path. It took a moment for George to take in the chaotic scene. There were bodies everywhere: some propped up in corners, others lying flat-out on the floor, and several more slumped over the huge rectangular wooden table that was fixed to the right wall; incredibly, his plan had been a success!

But as the door swung shut behind him, his gaze fell on a tall, powerful, and very much awake, Saxon, standing amid a clutter of bodies, his bushy blond moustache bristling with anger. It seemed that at least one of the pirates had not been taking part in the celebrations, and in the time it had taken for the Briton to register this, the big Saxon had drawn his sword.

George lunged forward, hoping to catch the pirate off-guard, but his sober foe reacted swiftly, knocking the blade aside and forcing the Briton back with a sword thrust of his own. There was a clang as the two sharpened metal edges met. George had no idea if any other pirates were still roaming the ship but, if they were, the noise of combat would surely attract them to the cabin; he had to finish this fight quickly.

The big Saxon parried another blow and forced George further back. The man was left-handed, which was something the Briton hadn't encountered before, and he seemed very handy with his sword. George parried a swing at his legs and another at his waist but, as the two blades clashed, he was unprepared for the blow from the pirate's right fist. The punch caught George on the side of his head, sending him reeling.

Off-balance, he tripped over one of the comatose Saxons and collided with the wall. Spinning sideways, he swung wildly at the place he thought his opponent's head might be, but the pirate had not followed up his attack. Instead, he had calmly stooped to pick up a shield from one of his fallen comrades, and now, armed with this extra protection, was advancing purposefully, a confident look in his eye.

With both shield and sword blocking his every thrust, George could find no way through the Saxon's defence. Slowly but surely, he was being backed into a corner. Desperate not to get hemmed in, the Briton lunged forward, striking low, but once again the pirate's blade was there, deflecting his attack, and this time the cunning warrior struck with his shield. The stout wooden weapon hit George in the chest, throwing him backwards into the cabin wall.

Disoriented, his head spinning, George saw a blur of movement as the Saxon's sword point aimed right for his heart. Instinctively, he jumped to his right, sidestepping this deadly attack by inches, but slipping on the wet floor as he did so. As he crashed to the deck, the sound of splintering wood filled his ears; his opponent's blade had lodged in the wall.

George found himself lying next to a broken amphora, in a puddle of liquid, which smelled strongly of wine. With a great effort, he struggled unsteadily to his feet and turned to face his opponent who, with an angry yell, had just yanked his sword free.

Seeing that he was trapped in the corner, George leapt sideways, evading the Saxon's sword thrust, and landed on the table, almost overbalancing as the ship listed slightly.

Seeing his opponent in a precarious position, the big pirate slashed right and left, forcing George to parry twice as he fought to keep his feet on this unsteady perch. Then, as the Saxon swung his shield to bring him down, the Briton launched himself off the far end of the sturdy wooden top, landing awkwardly amid a pile of slumbering bodies. There was a low moan as his knee sank into someone's gut, and another as he inadvertently poked an eye when putting a hand out to steady himself.

Shifting his balance, George grabbed the hilt of a sword that was sticking out invitingly from one of the sleeper's belts, and drew it with his left hand, swinging the blade upwards as his foe rushed around the table. Caught off-guard by this sudden swipe, the Saxon pirate dropped his shield arm to block it, consequently leaving his left side exposed to George's right-hand swing.

The blade cut deep into the big man's shoulder, causing him to let out a howl of pain and stumble backwards. George followed up his advantage, swinging at his opponent with two blades, forcing him to use both shield and sword in a hasty and unbalanced defence.

George moved forwards, slashing left and right, pushing the injured man back towards the cabin door. It was surely only a matter of time, now, before he prevailed; the man was hurt, his defence clumsy. Then, without warning, the crafty Saxon threw his shield arm forward, crunching the knuckles on the Briton's left hand.

George dropped his recently acquired sword, ringing his bloodied hand and yelling with pain as the cunning warrior, a triumphant cry on his lips, stepped forward, sword raised for the killing blow.

Just at that moment, there was a creaking of hinges as the cabin door flew open. Instinctively, the Saxon turned to see the new arrival and then, realising his mistake, whipped his head back around. But he was too late; in the instant that his foe's attention slipped, George had thrust his sword through the man's defences, deep into his chest.

With a choking cry, the pirate fell to his knees, toppling sideways as George withdrew his blade. This battle was over, but what new foes was he about to face? George turned, looking fearfully up at the man who had just entered the cabin.

"Claude!"

George almost sank to his knees in relief. Claude's jaw dropped open as he stared at the bodies strewn all over the cabin. Behind him, another man, Pascal, gasped at the sight of fifteen or so defeated Saxons and one defiant, sword-wielding, Briton.

"Are there… any other… pirates… on board?" asked George, breathing heavily after the exertion of the fight.

"Just two by the fore hold, I think", replied Claude, uncertainly.

Pascal continued to gape at the scene in the cabin. George briefly thought about explaining what had happened. *There's no time; I'll tell them later… maybe.*

"Grab a weapon and come with me", commanded George, with a new air of authority.

The Gauls gave him a surprised look, as if to say: *You've just handled fifteen pirates on your own; what do you need us for?*

"Hurry up!" insisted George.

The two sailors looked around for something they could use as a weapon. Claude added a Saxon sword to the knife he already had, and Pascal grabbed a long pole with a hook on one end, that was lying on the deck. Frowning at this choice of weapon, George led the way toward the bow of the ship.

As the group approached the mainmast, George spotted the two remaining pirates, beside the open trapdoor that led to the forward hold. They were sitting with their backs to him, a small pile of coins between them, and both seemed preoccupied with some kind of gambling game. George motioned to his companions to edge around the port side of the mast, while he approached from the starboard direction.

Moments later, Claude and Pascal jumped out, shouting at the tops of their voices and waving sword and pole wildly from side to side. *There goes the surprise attack!*

Rushing out from behind the mast, George was just in time to see the pirates whirl around, scattering money all over the deck. Claude's knife whistled harmlessly over their heads as the startled pair drew axes from their belts. Charging into the fray, George swung his sword at the nearer man.

The Saxon jumped backwards, almost knocking over his companion, who was now preoccupied with the two Gauls. Seizing his opportunity, George lunged forward. As he did so, Pascal's pole swung through the air, missed its intended target, and crashed down on the Briton's sword, knocking it from his grasp.

George suddenly found himself completely unarmed, facing an axe-wielding opponent. The pirate, equally surprised by this turn of events, took a wild swing at George, attempting to decapitate him. Ducking under the Saxon's hurried stroke, George dived forward, tackling his foe at waist height. This attack took his opponent completely by surprise, and the pirate stumbled backwards before tumbling over. Locked together with his struggling foe, George plunged, with him, through the open hatchway!

For the second time that day, George plummeted into the bowels of the ship. This time, however, his fall was mercifully briefer, broken by his Saxon opponent, who hit the wooden steps first and cushioned the Briton's landing. The two combatants tumbled head-over-heels down the remainder of the steps, coming to rest in an untidy heap at the bottom.

Bruised, battered and winded by yet another fall, George rolled off his opponent and lay there, unable to do anything more than gulp lungfuls of stale air. Fortunately for him, the Saxon seemed unable or unwilling to continue the struggle either, lying where he had landed, unmoving.

"George?"

The Briton jolted upright at once, a shiver running down his spine. The voice came to him from beyond the grave! It must have done, for the man who had spoken was surely dead!

Chapter 33 – Leviathan

A cry echoed from above, a bloodcurdling shriek that grew louder and louder. With a whoosh, something big hurtled past George, missing him by the narrowest of margins, and crashed heavily to the floor, abruptly ending the screams.

There followed the sound of footsteps descending the stairs.

"Are you all right, George?" called a voice with a Gaulish accent.

But George didn't hear him; he had barely even registered the body that had almost collided with him. He had eyes only for the faces that were staring back at him from the darkness: the faces of the dead!

"Justus, Cassie... Juba, Hector..."

"We're all here", replied Justus. "What about Brennos?"

George shook his head sadly. "But how...?"

"You all right?" repeated Claude, arriving, with Pascal in tow.

Tearing his gaze from those he had thought never to see again, George acknowledged the sailor. "I'm still alive", he groaned, getting unsteadily to his feet, "No thanks to you!"

"We got the pirate", insisted Pascal, defensively, pointing at the motionless body nearby.

"After you disarmed me!"

"I think Pascal thought the Saxon needed a chance", chuckled Claude. "It would be too easy for you if you had your sword."

"What about the rest of the pirates?" interrupted another voice, that of Captain Festus.

"George, here, defeated them all single-handedly!" praised Claude.

"Well... not exactly", admitted George, "But it's a long story. Most of them are still alive; they need tying up before they wake. But how come...?"

"You'd better untie us", Festus cut in. "There'll be time enough for explanations once those pirates are secured."

It took quite a while to free all those who had been kept prisoner in the forward hold. There were about fifty merchants and servants, along with a handful of the crew whose services had not been required by the Saxons. In all, about half the number who had set sail from Gaul.

Having freed the captives, it was now time to imprison their captors. Fortunately, none of the surviving pirates had yet regained consciousness, so it was a simple enough task to bind the hands and feet of each man and carry them all down into the cargo hold.

After this activity, George was called upon to explain, to an attentive audience, how he had managed to overcome all the Saxons and recapture the ship. Flavius was most impressed that it had been his 'poppy milk' that had saved the day.

"I would never have thought that drugging pirates would have been one of its applications", he chortled to himself.

George secretly thought that the Roman might be less impressed when he discovered exactly how much of his 'poppy milk' had been used.

After relating his story, George was eager to discover what had happened while he had been lying unconscious in the aft hold. It turned out that the little group of sailors and merchants, whom he'd seen resisting the pirates, had eventually been overwhelmed and forced to surrender. The victorious Saxons had kept a number of the crew above deck to sail the ship, while the rest of the survivors had been herded into the forward hold and tied up.

"But why keep you alive?" asked George. "What were they going to do with you all?"

"Sell us as slaves, most likely", ventured Flavius.

"Why are we still following the Saxon ship?" George pointed to the red sail directly in line with the bow of their own boat.

"We were ordered to follow its course", Claude replied, shrugging. "If we alter our heading, the pirates who returned to their own vessel will know that something is wrong."

"Which brings us to the question of what we are to do next", chimed in Festus. "We have been tacking along the south coast of Britannia", he added. "It'll be dark in a couple of hours. The pirates will have a hideout in one of these secluded coves, and I reckon we'll be landing soon."

"We need to reverse course", suggested Justus.

"Yes", agreed the captain, "But as soon as we do, the pirates will come after us. Their ship is faster than ours and they still outnumber us two to one."

"What if we wait till they enter the cove then, once they're out of sight, turn the ship and sail straight for Portus Dubris[1]?"

"That's our only choice, I suppose", agreed Festus. "But I still wouldn't give much for our chances."

George shielded his eyes from the sun's glare; the great orange orb was sinking low on the western horizon. Ahead, the high prow of the Saxon ship was swinging in towards land.

"HOLD YOUR COURSE", yelled the captain, above the pounding of the surf and the cries of the gulls.

All eyes were on the pirate vessel. Another few moments and it would disappear around the next headland. Only the stern was visible now.

"STEADY."

The pirate ship vanished from sight.

"NOW, HARD TO PORT."

Along with the rest of the ship, George's gaze turned to the oarsman as he strained at the huge steering oars. They were turning; the boat listed to starboard. George peered anxiously towards the rocky promontory that concealed the pirate vessel. He wondered how long it would take the Saxons to realise that their prize catch wasn't following them into harbour.

The sails billowed out, catching the predominantly westerly wind.

"SHIP ASTERN!"

The cry was unnecessary; they had all seen the red sail emerging from behind the headland. The race was on; they had a good head start but would it be enough?

"They're gaining!" somebody shouted.

There was no doubt about it: the gap was closing. Over the last hour, the mood amongst the ship's company had changed from one of optimism to what was now a gloomy despondency. At first they had made good headway with the prevailing westerly wind, but this had dropped to no more than a light breeze, and the pirate ship, powered with oars as well as a sail, was catching up rapidly.

Heads turned nervously from the blood red sail of the pursuing boat to the rugged coastline ahead. Somewhere, just

---

[1] Dover

beyond the next headland, they would see Portus Dubris's pharos[1], a guiding beacon that would lead them to safety.

"There!" someone shouted. "The pharos!"

A cheer went up at the sight of the twinkling light, shining in the distance. But the sailors weren't celebrating.

"We're not going to make it", Festus muttered, glancing at the Saxon ship and shaking his head. "We're more than a hundred stadia[2] from the port; they'll have overhauled us before we've gone half that."

The cheers died away as those nearby saw the expression on the captain's face, and an uneasy silence settled over the whole boat. George was suddenly conscious of other noises: waves slapping against the hull, wooden boards creaking, sails flapping in the gentle breeze and, carried upon that breeze, the sound of orders being barked out on the Saxon ship. A line of shields was forming on the starboard side; men were swarming up into the rigging. The pirates were preparing to attack.

George felt someone jog his elbow. "What is it, Juba?"

"Over there!" his friend pointed. "I saw something moving through the water."

George stared at the place that the Berber had indicated. That patch of water looked the same as every other bit of the sea. "I don't see anything."

Juba continued to stare into the cold grey depths. "There! A dark shape just beneath the surface."

"A dark shape? How am I supposed to see a dark shape beneath the surface of the dark water under a dark sky?" shrugged George, bemused. "I can't believe you're interested in fish when we're about to be boarded by a bunch of bloodthirsty pirates!"

"I do not think it was a fish..."

"MEN", called out Justus in a loud voice, addressing everyone on board, "IT SEEMS WE ARE ABOUT TO BE BOARDED, FOR THE SECOND TIME TODAY."

George turned, giving his master complete attention.

"BUT DO NOT LOSE HEART", Justus continued, encouragingly; "I DO NOT BELIEVE THAT THE ALMIGHTY GOD WOULD MIRACULOUSLY PROVIDE A WAY OUT OF

---

[1] lighthouse
[2] Roman unit of distance, equivalent to about 185 metres

THE PIRATES' CLUTCHES ONLY TO LET THEM CAPTURE US AGAIN. HE IS NOT LIMITED TO ONE MIRACLE A DAY!"

"Amen!" agreed Juba.

"SO I ASK YOU, NOW, TO JOIN ME IN A PLEA BEFORE THE THRONE OF GRACE", continued the Roman, his hands held high, his eyes staring into the rapidly darkening sky. "FATHER IN HEAVEN, LOOK DOWN AND SEE OUR PLIGHT; RESCUE US FROM THE HAND OF THE WICKED AND BRING US SAFELY TO BRITANNIA'S SHORE, FOR YOUR GLORY. WE ASK THIS IN THE NAME OF JESUS."

There was a smattering of "Amens".

"SWORDS OUT!" yelled the captain, a look of determination on his round face once more.

Suddenly, the boat gave a sharp jolt as if something had struck it. George lost his balance and fell to his knees, his blade clattering on the wooden deck.

"What was that?"

The pirate ship was still a short distance away. *It couldn't have been them.*

There was another bump, not as violent this time. Everyone stared around, puzzled, and then a wild cry went up from the oarsman. All heads turned to see him pointing and gesturing wildly at something just off the starboard bow.

George craned his neck, with the others, to see what it was the man was getting so excited about. At first, he could see nothing, but then Juba nudged him, pointing a little to the right of where he was looking. A shout of horror went up from behind him; something large and black had broken the surface. The thing, whatever it was, arched its broad back and slid beneath the waves, its pointed tail disappearing into the murky depths.

"It's a sea serpent!" breathed one of the sailors.

No one replied; everyone was staring at the place where the creature had dived. A dread silence enveloped the ship; the pirates had been forgotten. Suddenly, without warning, the sea erupted, as something huge shot upwards, sending water cascading in every direction. Everyone on board, from the least experienced traveller to the hardiest sailor, yelled with shock, awestruck by the sight of this monster rising from the deep. The great creature seemed to hang in the air, its fiery red eyes fixed on the puny humans who had disturbed its slumber. Then, arching its back once more, the monster crashed back beneath the surface, its huge snout parting the waves and its four limbs and tail thrashing the water into a foaming fountain that drenched the terrified onlookers.

"Can you pull in leviathan with a fishhook or tie down his tongue with a rope?" questioned a rather dreamy voice.

George turned around to look at the speaker, a bald-headed old sea dog with a bushy white beard. He was staring mesmerised at the place where the great creature had vanished beneath the waves.

"If you lay a hand on him, you will remember the struggle and never do it again", he murmured, his expression blank, as if the words were springing from a distant memory.

The sea exploded skywards once more, as the leviathan hurled itself into the air, less than a boat's width from the starboard bow. There was a sudden rush towards the centre of the ship, a number of men slipping over in their haste to scramble away from the side. Moments later, a wave crashed onto the deck as the monster returned to its watery domain.

"It's toying with us", spat Festus. "Is this how your god answers pleas for help, Justus? With a demon from the deep?"

Before the silver-haired Roman could reply, yet another booming explosion rang out, rocking the ship from bow to stern. Merchants and sailors alike stared, mouths agape, as the sea monster surged upwards, out of the water, its enormous dark bulk catapulting towards the side of the ship.

Realising just in time what was about to happen, the terrified crew scattered as, with a splintering crunch, the leviathan's giant head crashed down onto the starboard bow, its fearsome jaws opening to reveal a huge pink tongue and two rings of razor sharp teeth, each one larger than a man's hand!

The boat tipped sharply to starboard, under the monster's colossal weight. George slipped on the wet surface, sliding towards the gaping jaws. Dropping to the deck, he fought desperately to halt his momentum. Beside him, others were doing the same, arms flailing wildly, frantically searching for something firm to grip on to.

Fingernails digging into the cracks between the wooden boards, George hung on grimly. Above him on the treacherous slope, Justus clung to the mast with one arm, his other hand clasping the captain's left wrist, preventing Festus from disappearing into the leviathan's gaping maw.

To George's left, a red-headed man was sliding head first, down the sloping deck.

"HECTOR, NO!"

The cavernous mouth opened still wider, preparing for its first morsel. George turned his head to follow his friend's tragic descent; there was nothing he could do to save him. Hector gave a frightened yelp, the mighty jaws snapped shut, and the Gaul was gone.

George closed his eyes; he felt numb. The boat juddered, leaning further to starboard; the Briton's slender grip began to falter. Another cry went up; someone else was sliding to their doom. This time, George didn't look around, but clung on to the sloping wooden boards for dear life. Out of the corner of his eye, he could see a small dark figure edging slowly sideways.

"Juba, what are you doing?" he demanded, frantically, through gritted teeth.

"Got to help", was the breathless reply.

"Help who? JUBA!"

The Berber started to slide; he was out of reach. *Not Juba as well!*

As Juba shot towards the great red, tooth-filled tunnel, he rolled sideways. The monstrous jaws twisted to follow him, clamping shut with a terrible snap. As the mighty creature moved, the boat gave another shudder, almost shaking George loose from his precarious position once again.

There was a cry, from his right this time, and another. Below him, the mighty jaws swung across, aiming to catch their latest prey. This time, the leviathan was too slow and George saw the two men slide harmlessly past its gigantic snout.

Now that the monster had shifted position, the Briton could see a little group of men clustered at the very edge of the starboard bow, below the creature's head and out of reach of its deadly jaws. He gave a little cry of delight: Juba and Hector were among them. Miraculously, it seemed that the leviathan's savage bites had missed his comrades, leaving them to slide safely to the side of the ship.

The group of about half a dozen men were attempting to lift the leviathan's foreleg over what was left of the deck rail, to try and dislodge the mighty creature from its position. Actually it was more like a great paddle than a leg, as long as two men, and it was taking all their combined strengths to move it.

As he watched the group's desperate efforts, a deep rumbling sound emanated from somewhere within the monster. George coughed as wreathes of grey smoke billowed up from its nostrils. A feeling of dread washed over him; something worse was about to happen. The ship lurched once more, there was an anguished cry from above, and George looked up in time to see Justus lose his hold on the mast. He and Festus were sliding directly towards him!

A foot struck him on the head and then he was skidding across the deck, momentum carrying all three of them straight towards the leviathan's snout. George caught a glimpse of a fierce red eye, shining through the smoke, and then the mouth opened, revealing a terrifying cavern, ringed about with deadly stalactites and stalagmites.

For a moment, George stared into the black pit that led to the monster's stomach; he tasted its foul breath. All around him was screaming and flailing and… then the yawning cavern had gone and George found himself shooting through the air. The deck rushed up to meet him and, with a thump, he landed in a mass of thrashing arms and legs. A wave crashed over the top of him, soaking him to the skin. George sat up, coughing and spluttering, and spat a mouthful of salt water onto the deck. Somewhere nearby, a cheer went up; it seemed that the little group of men had managed to dislodge the mighty beast.

As George staggered to his feet, shaken by this latest ordeal, something hit the mast with a clang. He stared upwards; a metal hook had become tangled in the rigging.

"THE PIRATES!"

In all the excitement with the leviathan, everyone had forgotten about the Saxons. Now their boat was alongside and a row of fierce warriors was preparing to board the merchant vessel.

There was a sudden rush to port. Caught up in the stampede, George barely heard the cry from above. Glancing up, he saw a blur of movement as a black-clad figure hurtled towards him. Instinctively, George hurled himself into the air, colliding heavily with the pirate before crashing to the deck, winded.

Gasping for air, George could only watch as, still clinging to his rope, the pirate swung back over the side of the ship. All around him, men were rushing and yelling, but George saw only one, swinging in a slow arc over the dark water. The two men stared at each other, pain and anger etched on both their faces, then the look in the other man's eyes changed to one of terror. A dark mass appeared below the pirate, a red eye shone in the gloom, and two impossibly large jaws opened to receive their victim. The Saxon's mouth widened in a silent scream and then he vanished, engulfed by the monster from the deep!

A wave of terror passed over the Saxon crew. War-cries died in their throats and weapons hung limply at their sides as they stared fearfully into the churning water between the two ships. An eerie silence descended on the scene as the two opposing sides temporarily forgot their quarrel.

Then, with a rush of foaming water, the awesome creature burst forth, leaping high into the evening air before crashing down, this time, on the bows of the pirate ship. Panic ensued as their vessel tipped sharply to starboard, throwing men off their feet and hurling one unfortunate screaming into the depths. George watched in morbid fascination as the great mouth opened and there was a sudden whoosh and a flash of light!

"Their sail's on fire!"

Orange tongues licked up the side of the crimson sail. Somehow, the leviathan had ignited the sailcloth with its breath!

"His snorting throws out flashes of light. Firebrands stream from his mouth", stated the dreamy voice, once more quoting from some ancient text.

"CUT THE ROPES!" yelled Festus. "IT'S TIME TO LEAVE THE PARTY."

Chapter 34 – Homecoming

It had been raining steadily all morning and, from the look of the grey sky, it wasn't going to clear up any time soon. A chilly breeze was gusting off the sea, whipping the rain into the faces of those who were unfortunate enough to be out in it. It was certainly not a day for visiting the beach but, despite the miserable weather, there were quite a number standing on the sand at Portus Dubris[1].

The crowd was made up of sailors, merchants and their servants, most of whom were staring into the leaping flames of the large bonfire that they had recently lit, with the aid of a good quantity of olive oil. They had gathered for one reason: to honour those who had died defending their ship.

Normally, at such an event, the bodies of the dead would be burned on the fire, but in this case there were no bodies to burn, as the pirates had thrown all the dead overboard after the battle. It had seemed right to build a pyre, though, and it gave a kind of symbolic focus to the gathering.

The crowd listened in respectful silence as, one by one, men stepped forward and spoke about their dead friends and colleagues. It was a very solemn occasion; prayers were said, tears were shed, and the general mood mirrored the leaden sky.

Whether by design or some unspoken convention, the speeches were moving in a steady clockwise direction around the fire. A tall, imperious looking merchant, heavily wrapped in a grey woollen cloak, had just finished a rather dull and, George suspected, insincere tribute to two of his servants who had been killed in the fighting, and now it was time for Justus to speak.

"Friends", began the silver-haired Roman, his rich deep voice carrying easily to the far corners of the crowd. "I want to tell you about my son, Brennos."

There were tears in Justus's eyes as he said this, but the broad smile on his face did not falter.

"The first time I came across him was right here in Portus Dubris", the Roman continued. "The dockhands had stolen, or in their words – mislaid, some of my valuable vases, and this big blond-haired lad, who I'd never met in my life before, found them

---

[1] Dover

for me. When I asked him how I could repay his kindness, he said 'Fifteen denarii plus a hot meal every day until I disappoint you.' Well, what could I say? I hired him on the spot. Though if I'd have known then how much he could eat, I would have knocked him down to ten", mused Justus, chuckling to himself.

"Since that day", the Roman went on, "Brennos has got me out of trouble on many occasions. He, with George's help, rescued me from the Bulls of Hades – great beasts with horns like spears and hides like stone!" he added, impressively.

"He saved me from a band of cut-throats", added Cassia, her voice heavy with emotion.

"With a little help from his friends", appended Hector, not to be left out.

"He rescued you from that jealous lover, at the races in Leptis Magna", called out George, cheekily, wishing to silence Hector.

"Eh, what's that?" enquired Justus, "I haven't heard that one."

"And he saved you from that bear, near Lugdunum[1]", countered the Gaul, keen to change the subject.

"True", acknowledged George. "He's saved my life five or…" The Briton looked up into the cloudy grey sky, imagining the grinning face of his best friend. "…Maybe even six times", he finished, smiling to himself.

"As you can see", Justus concluded, motioning to the crowd, "Brennos lived as he has died: risking his own life to get others out of the mess they'd got themselves into."

There was a pause as the Roman reached inside his cloak and drew out a scroll that he had been protecting from the inclement weather.

"As commendable as that is, if it was all I could say about my son, I would still be grieving on this day of remembrance", Justus said, as he unfurled the parchment in his hand. "For Brennos, like the rest of us, had got himself into a mess before a holy God he was unready to meet."

Clearing his throat, Justus turned to the scroll and began to read from it:

---

[1] Lyons

"Very rarely will anyone die for a righteous man, though for a good man someone might possibly dare to die. But God demonstrates his own love for us in this: While we were still sinners, Christ died for us."

The Roman merchant swallowed hard. He was struggling to overcome the emotion of the moment but, unlike those who had spoken before him, he was battling with joy not sorrow.

"About a month ago", Justus continued, wiping tears from his eyes with his left hand, "Brennos made peace with his maker, and so I know that when his time came, he was ready; his soul is safe with his saviour."

As the silver-haired merchant fell silent, another took his place and the round of speeches continued. But something had changed almost imperceptibly: there were fewer tears now, and the occasional scattering of laughter, as someone said something amusing about their deceased friends. Even the rain wasn't falling as heavily as it had been and, as morning drifted into afternoon, it stopped altogether. Finally, as the speeches ended and the fire burned low, an amphora of wine was opened and the group began to toast their fallen comrades.

It suddenly dawned on George that this might not be such a good idea. "Wait a moment!" he called out, "Have you checked…"

Over by the wine servers, the tall merchant, still heavily wrapped in his grey woollen cloak, but looking far less imperious, staggered forwards, slipped to his knees, and collapsed face-down on the beach.

"…the wine?" he finished lamely.

There was a thud as another drinker hit the sand.

George put his hand to his mouth to cover an inappropriate smile. "Oops."

Sixty wooden cartwheels rumbled endlessly over the tightly packed stones that made up the long road from Deva[1] to Eburacum[2]. Bleak moorland surrounded them on either side with no signs of life for mile after lonely mile, save for the occasional rabbit, scampering for its burrow at the sound of the caravan's approach.

The road, though characteristically straight, rose and dipped with the contours of the rolling hills, making hard work for the

---

[1] Chester
[2] York

plodding carthorses. Justus had dismounted from his seat at the front of the wagon and was leading one tired beast by the head. Juba walked at the other side, speaking gentle words of encouragement to the other as if it were a small child.

Hector and Cassia were walking beside the cart, laughing and joking with one another and, George noticed, getting dangerously close to holding hands.

The Briton brought up the rear of the party, observing his friends, his family, but at a distance. He felt as if he was in a dream that was coming to an end; Cyrenaica and the village of Silene seemed but a distant memory. The day after tomorrow, Justus would be turning for home – a four month journey that would take him back to Julia; Juba would do the same, travelling back to his bride to be.

Another peel of laughter erupted from the pair in front; Cassia and Hector were getting on a bit too well for his liking. George felt an ache within, a sense of missed opportunity. Forcing his gaze away from the happy couple, he turned his thoughts to his departed mentor and friend. George hadn't realised, until after his fellow Briton had died, just how much he relied on that friendship; he was missing Brennos terribly.

But that part of the dream has already come to an end, George reflected. One stage of his life was ending; a new chapter was about to begin. Soon he would be home, and although part of him was anxious about what he would find there and how he would be received, another part of him longed to see his mother and Catherine once again. What tales he had to tell them! He had left home a fugitive; he was returning a hero!

Lost in his own thoughts, George had barely noticed that they had reached the brow of a hill. Looking down into the valley beyond, he caught sight of a smallish settlement surrounded by ditches and stone walls.

"Cambodunum!" he exclaimed, unable to contain his excitement.

It had taken them thirty-two days to get here from Portus Dubris. They had had to delay their departure from the port, firstly in order to deliver the captured pirates to the Roman authorities, and secondly as they waited for the return to consciousness of those unfortunate enough to have drunk the drugged wine.

Once everyone was fit to travel, the caravan had journeyed north to Durovernum[1], turned west to Londinium[2], continuing through Calleva[3] and on to Corinium[4]. After that, they had travelled north up the long road through Viriconium[5] to Deva, and now they were finally approaching Cambodunum. George's village was less than five miles away.

They reached the gates of the town as the late afternoon sun dropped towards the western horizon. Hector and Cassia headed into the settlement to buy food while George and Juba helped Justus to set up camp.

As the Briton walked towards the edge of the pine forest that overlooked Cambodunum, in search of dry firewood, he was seized by a sudden compulsion to climb the hill and make his way to his mother's house. *Just one more day*, he told himself, as he headed back to camp, his arms cradling a bundle of fallen branches.

Hector's beef stew tasted so good that George was forced to admit that he would miss the Gaul's cooking. After eating a portion that "Brennos would have been proud of", the Briton lay back beside the roaring fire and listened to his friend's tales of Perseus, a Greek hero who was sent on a perilous quest to slay a monstrous snake-haired gorgon whose gaze turned all who looked on her to stone.

George had heard the story before; he must have heard every one of Hector's stories at least three times, but there was no denying that the Gaul was a master storyteller.

As he listened, his eyes half closed, a feeling of warm contentment flooded over him. George's mind wandered back to the days when his own stories had so captivated Catherine, happy times before everything had gone so horribly wrong, and he dared to hope that those days could be again.

"Wake up, George", called Juba, nudging him, "You are on first watch."

"Eh?" The dozing Briton opened his eyes. He had missed the end of the tale.

A short while later, George paced around the campfire, ensuring that he would not fall asleep during the quarter of the night

---

[1] Canterbury
[2] London
[3] Silchester
[4] Cirencester
[5] Wroxeter

that he was on lookout duty. As he did so, he mentally ran through the story that he was going to tell his mother, Catherine, and maybe even the whole village, tomorrow. It was going to be an amazing tale: sword fighting, duels, ambushes, fantastic creatures, daring escapes, thrilling rescues, trolls, pirates, sea monsters… George smiled confidently to himself; no one could fail to be impressed by such an epic.

The chill of the early morning air nipped at his nose and ears as George climbed the steep path that led through the pine forest. After breakfasting with his companions, he had bid them all a short farewell, promising to look in on them again before the following morning, when they would be leaving for Eburacum. He wondered if his mother, and maybe even Catherine, would come with him to see them off. He felt sure that they would want to meet those who had been so influential in moulding him into the person he was today.

Passing out from beneath the pines, George followed the path as it dipped slightly, leading down to the stepping-stones that he knew so well. He crossed these without difficulty, as the waterway was slow and shallow at this point, unlike further downstream where he had experienced its power and ferocity first hand.

George made his way up the zigzagging path to the base of Lookout Hill. Staring fondly at its heather-clad slopes, he debated whether to scale it now, but decided that there would be time enough for that later; he was going to waste no time on this special day: a day of reunion and redemption.

Hurrying through the narrow valley that lay between him and his destination, George marched up the far side and entered the woods that bordered his home. Listening to the birds twittering in the treetops, it seemed almost unbelievable that the last time he had been here, he had been fleeing for his life through a thunderstorm. A lot had happened in the last seven years!

The trees were starting to thin out. Any moment now, George was going to catch a glimpse of his village, the place that had been home for the first eighteen years of his life. And at last, there it was: the random assortment of round wooden huts, the great hall at its centre, the animal enclosures on the south and west sides and, beyond those, the wheat fields, full of ripening golden corn.

George hesitated. Should he walk boldly into the village like a hero returning from battle? That could be unwise considering the manner in which he had left. Deciding not to risk making his presence known just yet, George skirted the edge of the wood in a clockwise direction, only breaking cover of the trees when his mother's hut was in sight. He would gauge her reception first before putting in a public appearance.

He walked briskly towards the dwelling, his heart beating rapidly. A couple of villagers looked up as he passed, but neither said anything; it was possible that they hadn't recognised him. His heart in his mouth, George knocked at the door and waited. He could hear movement within; this was it.

"Hello, mother."

The woman standing in the open doorway gave a little gasp, her eyes widening in shock, and for one scary moment, George thought she was going to recoil from him. But a heartbeat later, she had flung her arms around his shoulders, burying her head in his tunic.

She held him in a tight embrace, sobbing into his chest, while George awkwardly patted her hair, not knowing quite what to do. Eventually she pulled away, staring into his eyes, tears glistening on her rosy cheeks.

The woman who stood before him had more flecks of grey in her hair than he remembered, and maybe one or two extra lines on her face, but other than that she seemed unchanged by their time apart.

"Where have you been?" she asked, her voice slightly hysterical, as though she were scolding him for staying out late.

"I've been travelling the world", George replied, "And I have something for you."

Pushing his cloak to one side, he untied a leather bag from his belt and handed it to his astonished mother.

"Open it", he prompted, as she stood staring at him, seemingly overwhelmed by his sudden return.

Fumbling with the drawstring, she reached inside the bag and pulled out a handful of the silver coins that lay within. She stared down at them uncomprehendingly.

"They're to replace the silver I stole from you, the night I ran away", George explained.

His mother looked down at the coins in her hand and then up at her long lost son. "Where have you been these last seven winters?" she repeated, her voice shaking with emotion. "I thought you'd died!"

"I joined a merchant caravan travelling through Cambodunum", replied George. *Why do mums always imagine the worst-case scenario?*

"And what happened to Tristan?"

George had been looking into his mother's hazel eyes, but at this question he dropped his gaze. "He was eaten... by a... a... bear", he muttered, a lump in his throat. "The beast killed one of the sheep while we were on watch, and we tracked it to a cave, and..." His voice trailed off; things weren't going quite as he'd imagined.

"Caradog said you'd killed the boy!" blurted his mother.

"What?"

"He said you'd already murdered the old druid and stolen his golden sickle!"

"That's ridiculous! We found the sickle next to the druid's remains; the bear had eaten him too."

"And the sheriff told us that you stole his sword and then, when he confronted you, you attacked him with it!"

George didn't refute this allegation; it was, after all, true.

"Do you think that I'm a murderer?"

George stared at his mother with wide-eyed disbelief. He had returned home, hoping for a hero's welcome; he had not expected an inquisition!

She stared back at him, her tear-stained face looking into his. This time, however, it was she who dropped her gaze. "No", she replied, softly. "I don't think you're a murderer."

There was a sudden clanging noise, and George's mother instantly looked towards the open door, her eyes wide with fear. George turned to see what had made the commotion, but it was only a neighbour who had managed to drop a pot that she had been carrying.

As the woman busied herself picking up the contents of her fumbled pot, George turned back to his mother. He was surprised to find that the fearful look had not left her face.

"You must leave", she urged, motioning towards the door. "If Caradog finds out you're here, he'll have you arrested!"

"But I'm innocent!"

"That won't matter to the Romans. They won't care who's guilty and who's innocent; all they care about is money and power. Now go!"

"But when will I see you again?"

George's mother looked up at her son, tears in her eyes. She shook her head, unable to speak.

"I'm staying on the outskirts of Cambodunum", George blurted out, "By the southwest gate. I'll be there until early tomorrow. Look for a big crimson tent. If you can't see it, ask for Justus Liberius, the merchant. He's a Roman with silver hair."

"I… don't… think", his mother began, choking back her tears.

"Please", begged George.

"I'll… try", she sniffed, unable to meet his gaze. "But please go now; he could be here any moment!"

Having secured this unconvincing promise from his mother, George stared into her tear-streaked face for one moment longer and then exited the hut. As he hurried towards the trees, George couldn't help turning his head for one last glimpse of his mother. There she stood, framed in the doorway of her thatched hut, grief stricken, watching her only son, the son she had not seen for seven years, and dare not see again.

As the noises of twittering birds and scampering squirrels once more filled his ears, George stopped walking and put his head in his hands. What was he going to do now? He had been dreaming about this day for six months, he had travelled from the far edge of the Empire, battled bears, pirates and a sea monster, and for what? *Is this it? I've repaid my debt; am I supposed to just walk away now? Am I never to see my mother again?*

George paced to and fro on the edge of the wood, tears clouding his vision, frustration boiling his blood. *What do I do now?* "Catherine." He spoke the name aloud. She was his only hope now.

George made his way through the thick undergrowth, hacking at branches that hindered his progress. He had often played in these woods as a child, but they seemed far wilder and more overgrown than they had then; it was as if no one trod these paths any more.

Forcing his way through a particularly nasty thorn bush, George reached a place where a number of round huts were visible through the greenery to his right. Pushing the branches apart, he scanned the area for signs of life. Seeing no one between him and the dilapidated dwelling he was making for, George ran for it.

He covered the open ground quickly, reaching his destination without attracting any unwanted attention, but as he crouched next to the rough wall of the hut, George realised that there was something wrong. The wall, that he was leaning against, had bits of wood protruding from it, and the clay that was meant to hold these interlocking branches together had crumbled. Looking up, he was startled to see that the roof was in a worse state than the walls: much of the thatching seemed to have been removed, leaving gaping holes open to the elements.

Numbly, George moved to the doorway (the door had been removed too) and peered inside. The interior was completely bare and smelled damp and musty. It was clear that nobody had lived here for many years.

George slumped to his knees, the weight of his disappointment crashing down upon him. "No", he moaned, "Not Catherine too!"

In all his years of living in this village, George had only ever seen huts abandoned for one reason: after the death of the last surviving family member.

Chapter 35 – An Unexpected Encounter

George marched through the village, his face set resolutely towards home. He had to know what had happened to Catherine, and he didn't care who saw him.

As he neared his mother's hut, raised voices made him slow his pace. A group of half a dozen men were gathered outside. The leader, a tall thin man dressed in a flowing white toga, was arguing vociferously with his mother. It was Caradog; it seemed his mother had been right about the reaction to his visit.

George ducked behind a nearby dwelling. He had to get out of here before they caught him. *What do you think you're doing?* The voice inside his head had an accusing tone. *The hero returns? You haven't changed at all; you're still hiding and running just like you did the night Tristan died!*

George hesitated. A short distance to his right lay the safety of the woods; he could return to Cambodunum, rejoin Justus, go back to life the way it had been. *I've repaid my debt to my mother. Catherine's gone: there's nothing I can do about that.* He took a tentative step towards the trees and then halted again; it was as if an invisible force was holding him back. An image flashed across his mind: a dark shadowy figure with huge fangs, stalking a girl with golden hair… *Help me, George!*

Heart beating like a drum, George took a deep breath, stepped from behind the hut and walked slowly towards the group of men.

"THERE HE IS!" boomed a deep voice.

Cunobelinos, the village blacksmith, was advancing towards him, a large hammer clutched firmly in his big right hand.

"MURDERER!" he cried, lifting the heavy wooden-shafted tool above his head.

His mother let out a scream. George, eyes fixed on the approaching figure, clasped his sword hilt with his right hand and drew the weapon from its sheath in one rapid movement. There was a ringing clang as the iron head of the descending hammer was met in mid-air by the rising blade. Before his astonished foe could react, George spun on his heel and drove an elbow into the blacksmith's gut.

With a gasp of pain, Cunobelinos doubled up and collapsed backwards, his hammer dropping to the ground with a thud. Adrenalin pumping through his veins, George stepped away from his fallen opponent and faced the other five men, a fierce glint in his eye.

"I've killed at least six men in self defence!" warned George, brandishing his sword threateningly. "I can double that if you force me to!"

They were all staring at him now, and George could see both hatred and fear in their eyes.

"You will be brought to justice for your crimes", spat Caradog, but he made no move to attack.

The sheriff's companions stood assessing the situation for a moment and then, apparently unwilling to take on this master swordsman, three of them began to move away. The fourth, a fair-haired lad of about George's age, sheathed his sword and walked towards him. As the young man drew closer, George recognised him: it was Dean, the boy who had teased him mercilessly on so many occasions. Dean nodded his head, in what might have been a gesture of grudging respect, and then continued over to the fallen blacksmith, whom he proceeded to help to his feet.

Muttering darkly, and still clutching his stomach, Cunobelinos allowed himself to be led away. That just left Caradog. The sheriff, seeing that he no longer had anyone to enforce his will, gave George a final murderous glare before departing the scene, his toga billowing out behind him.

George's heart was still thumping wildly in his chest, and his hands were shaking so that he could barely sheathe his sword, but the path to his mother was no longer barred. Looking up, he saw that she was staring at him with an odd expression on her face, a curious distant look that he couldn't read.

"Mother", he blurted out, "Where's Catherine?"

His mother didn't answer at once; she was still gazing quizzically at her son.

"I told you to go", mumbled his mother, uncertainly, ignoring his question.

"But mother…"

"You can't stay here", she interrupted, her tone more forceful.

"Then come with me", he pleaded.

Taken aback, she stared into his eyes, tears welling up in her own. She let her gaze fall. "I can't", she said miserably, shaking her head slowly. "I've lived in this village my whole life, George. I can't leave."

George watched as a large tear fell to the hard earth; his heart was breaking. He moved across to his distraught mother and laid a hand tenderly on her shoulder.

"Please mum, where's Catherine?"

She took a moment to compose herself and then looked up into his anxious face. "Catherine left soon after you did." She sniffed, wiped her eyes and continued. "She told me she couldn't stay here; there were too many painful memories. I'm sorry, George. What happened that night may not have been your fault, but it has had terrible consequences, and we will both have to live with them for the rest of our lives!"

"If you're staying, you might as well make yourself useful", remarked Hector, as the Gaul helped a customer with one of the large red-slipped ware jugs.

"What do you need?" asked George, distractedly.

"Food", replied the Gaul, simply, and then added in a dreamy voice: "A nice joint of pork, with a sprinkling of garlic and sage, in a tangy apple sauce…"

"I'll get the pork", cut in George, before Hector could add further to his wish list. "You can sort out the fancy stuff."

"Barbarian!" chuckled the Gaul as, with a shake of his head, George disappeared into the crowded marketplace.

George was glad of something to do, a task to focus his mind. Since leaving his village, he had been mentally wrestling with the question of what to do next. The decision of which cut of pork to buy was a much simpler prospect.

Battling his way through the crowded market square, George followed the delicious aroma of freshly baked bread. And there, next to the bakery was the butcher's, one of many shops built into the stone forum, distinguishable by the huge chunks of meat hanging from numerous hooks in the ceiling.

"That large joint of pork, please", requested George, indicating the cut of meat he wanted.

The butcher, a plump red-faced man with a bald head and wide nostrils, who bore a striking resemblance to a pig himself, reached up to unhook the carcass.

"My pork's selling well today", he remarked, conversationally. "I've sold half a dozen already."

"Mmm", grunted George, not really in the mood for chatting with total strangers.

"And you'll never guess what my first customer of the day said she was going to do with her joint."

"Nnn", mumbled George, certain that he wouldn't have to guess; he was going to be told regardless of whether he wanted the information.

The butcher plonked the large lump of pork on the stone counter. "She said she was going to use it to poison the dragon!"

"What?"

"Not that my meat is poisonous, you understand", spluttered the shopkeeper hurriedly. "She was going to add the poison herself."

"What dragon?" demanded George, his hands gripping the counter.

"You're obviously not from these parts", continued the butcher, slightly taken aback by George's reaction to his story. "Everyone around here's heard of the dragon. It lives up by the lake; no one goes up there any more. It's supposed to have eaten more than thirty men!" he added impressively. "No, wait, COME BACK! WHAT ABOUT YOUR PORK?"

George raced away from the forum, dodging left and right to avoid the many shoppers, and hared down the main street, in the direction of the town gate, sword clanking at his side. As he sped along the cobbled road, his mind was whirling with the information he'd just received: a dragon in Britannia? Was this the shadowy beast that had haunted his dreams? How had a creature, fabled to exist in the unexplored interior of Africa, suddenly appeared less than three miles from his home? Questions buzzed around his head, with no answers to silence them. Right now, the only thing he knew for certain was that he had to get to the lake. What he would find when he got there remained a mystery, but on a day when his hopes and dreams had vanished like the morning mist, at last this was something he felt sure of.

By the time he reached the camp, George was panting heavily and had a stitch in his side. Locating their large crimson tent, he spotted Marius, Flavius's servant, the man guarding their property as a favour to Justus, who was becoming increasingly short-handed.

"I'm just borrowing a horse", explained George, reaching for a saddle.

"You've not lost anyone, I hope", chuckled Marius, remembering the last time George had needed to 'borrow a horse'.

"I hope not", replied George, enigmatically, as he untied the coal black steed from its tether.

George sat astride his mount and surveyed the body of water below. Waves rippled across its cold blue surface in the stiff afternoon breeze, but nothing stirred on either shore. *Now what?* No, wait, there was something moving at the eastern end of the lake: a tiny figure, walking slowly, burdened with a heavy bundle on its back.

George pulled on the reins and nudged his steed into action. Keeping the figure in view, he rode, at a canter, to a point overlooking the eastern end of the lake. Below him, a narrow river flowed out of an opening in the rock, feeding into the lake. Glancing upstream, George spotted a waterfall some distance away, its churning white water showing up clearly against a green background of bushes and shrubs. It crossed his mind that this must be the same river that he had jumped into all those years ago.

Urging his horse onward, George rode around the end of the lake, dismounting as the ground became gradually steeper. Here, the undulating nature of the terrain meant that he temporarily lost sight of his quarry. Leading his coal black steed by the reins, George made his way, as swiftly as he could, down a steep and stony down-slope, suddenly nervous that something horrible might befall the woman before he could reach her. He still had no idea why she would want to poison a dragon, or what a dragon was doing in these parts at all!

Struggling to haul his mount up out of the dip, covered as it was with dense patches of heather, George emerged triumphant onto the brow of a low hill. From here, the land fell away down to the water, giving him a perfect view of the whole length of the shore. Crouching a short distance from the trees at the western end of the lake, was a young woman with long golden hair. She was bending over something on the ground, presumably the pig's carcass.

A sudden movement to his left caught George's eye. Turning, he jolted with shock, stumbling backwards, and let out an audible gasp. The reins of his mount dropped limply from his outstretched hand as he gaped in horror at what could only be the dragon.

When George had heard the word 'dragon', earlier, it had conjured up images of the creature he had seen in the ship's hold at Alexandria. That dragon had been a curiosity; the thing he was now looking at was a monster!

It was huge, easily twice as tall as a man, standing almost upright on its two powerful hind legs, its long thick tail, with its wicked spear-like point, swaying threateningly behind it. George had seen many strange creatures on his travels, but none had filled his heart with the level of dread that he felt right now. The great green scaly monster was moving stealthily towards its prey: not the lifeless pig, but the poor girl who had carried it up from town!

"GO! GET OUT OF THERE!"

George charged down the grassy slope, crying out and waving his arms wildly as he ran. The young woman looked up in surprise, her frightened eyes alighting on the source of the danger. With a scream, she jumped to her feet and fled inland.

"NO!" yelled George, nearly losing his footing on the uneven ground. "THE TREES! HEAD FOR THE TREES!"

At full stretch, George's left foot plunged into a hollow and he tripped, tumbling over and over, his world spinning and bumping, his stomach lurching as he plummeted over a bank and hit the springy turf with a painful thud.

George stared up at the clouds revolving slowly in the cold grey sky. A dark green shape appeared at the very edge of his vision; there was a flash of yellow in it. He turned his head groggily to one side, focusing on… the dragon's eye!

Crying out, George staggered to his feet and stepped backwards, reaching for his sword. Suddenly, the ground beneath him gave way and he was falling, a shower of leaves filling the air.

George's descent came to an abrupt halt as he hit the hard rocky earth at the bottom of the narrow pit into which he'd fallen. He was covered in a pile of earth and twigs. Spitting soil out of his mouth, he struggled to rise, but quickly dropped back as a set of savage talons appeared above him!

A sprinkling of earth and stones cascaded down upon the hapless Briton as the monstrous foot quested for its prey. Yelling with fright, George again reached for his sword, but his right arm was pinned to his side in the narrow confines of the hole.

The gigantic scaly foot was getting closer; its cruelly curved claws were a mere handbreadth from his face! George sucked his breath in, flattening himself against the pit floor.

The foot was gone. George stared up at the sky visible above and let out a ragged sigh. Next moment, the light was gone, blocked out by two enormous jaws!

The great mouth snapped shut less than a foot above him. It disappeared from view... then the gigantic scaly snout was back. George yelled wildly! He could see dozens of finger-length, dagger-like teeth; he could feel the monster's rancid breath on his face. A gobbet of foul smelling saliva landed on his neck.

The dragon's head withdrew once again. George stayed frozen to the spot, not daring to move a muscle. Gradually he became conscious of screaming - the girl he had tried to save. *Why is she still here?*

A dark shape moved over the surface of the pit. *The dragon's tail?* He could hear the beast's heavy tread; it seemed to be moving away. George hesitated for six or seven heartbeats. Another scream rang out, more desperate than the last. He sat up, spitting more soil out of his mouth and scattering stones, leaves and twigs in his wake. Reaching upward, George grabbed the lip of the pit and hauled himself to his feet, his head back above ground level.

Turning to his left, he spied the beast, moving uphill at a surprisingly quick pace for such a huge animal. Beyond it, the young woman stumbled towards a dark opening in the hillside, the distance between her and her nightmarish pursuer diminishing at an alarming rate. Yelling at the top of his lungs, George threw himself out of the hole, which had so nearly been his tomb, and charged after the dragon.

George raced up the stony incline, his parched throat burning from the double exertions of running and shouting. Ahead of him, the monster stooped, lunging for its prey. With a shriek, the girl vanished into the darkness. The great beast thrust its snout into the cave, snapping its immense jaws. A terrified cry told George that, mercifully, the beast had missed.

The Briton slowed and came to a stop, panting heavily. It was possible that the young woman, whoever she was, had reached a place of safety, but it had just dawned on George that he was in a very different position.

Controlling his breathing with difficulty, he began edging sideways towards the trees. *Don't turn around! Don't turn around!*

A thunderous roar rent the air in two! George's heart missed a beat; he lost his footing, slipping on a loose rock, and gashed his right knee. Staggering to his feet, George drew his sword clumsily, his hand shaking. The dragon had turned to face him, crouching on its haunches; yellow eyes blazing, mouth open, claws outstretched.

As he stared up at the green monster, two thoughts flashed across George's mind: that he had heard that roar, or something like it, before, and that the sharpened steel blade that he was holding was unlikely even to make a mark on the dragon's thick scaly hide! The great beast took a step forward, its terrible eyes fixed on the puny human who stood before it, and then without warning it lunged at George, who was forced to jump sideways to avoid the gaping jaws.

Regaining his balance, George swung at the beast's head, but he was too slow: the dragon had reared up on its hind legs, towering high above its adversary, preparing for another strike. George backed away, sword held aloft, sweat dripping from his brow.

"In here!" cried a woman's voice. "It's your only chance!"

Her voice, like the dragon's roar, seemed strangely familiar; it was as if this had all happened before...

Momentarily distracted by his thoughts, George was taken by surprise as the monster leapt at him. With a wild cry, he ducked, swinging his sword upward. Next instant, it was jarred from his grip and he was knocked to the ground.

Head reeling, George looked up to see two huge clawed feet, one on either side of him. On hands and knees, he scrambled between the monstrous legs, dodging out of the way as a mighty foot kicked out at him. Swerving right, he staggered towards the figure beckoning desperately to him from the cave entrance.

"LOOK OUT!"

There was a blur of movement; George hurled himself forward. Something struck him in the back, propelling him into the darkness, where he hit the ground hard, his mouth filling with blood.

Chapter 36 – A Dragon's Tale

A terrified shriek echoed off the walls of the cave. George felt something brush against his right boot. He turned his head and immediately let out a yell; the dragon had squeezed its huge head through the narrow opening, and its scaly snout was hovering a few inches above his leg!

The monster opened its immense jaws to snatch him up from the cold stone floor. Desperately, George scrambled forwards on hands and knees just as the great drooling mouth slammed shut!

He had reached the far wall of the little cave, a mere eight to ten feet from the entrance. But would that be enough? The dragon's bulk blocked out all the light; he could sense the long neck snaking towards him through the blackness, imagine the great jaws opening to receive him. The blood ran cold in his veins as he waited, pressing himself as close to the rock as he could, his injured back rubbing painfully against the uneven stone.

Light returned; the monstrous head was withdrawing from the cave. The entrance was just too narrow to allow the great beast to reach him. George inched away from the jagged rock wall and stretched out his cramped legs. As he did so, the dragon gave a bloodcurdling roar, which sent him scurrying backwards. In the silence that followed, he could make out the sounds of its huge clawed feet padding away.

"Are you all right, George?" asked a shaky voice in the darkness, a voice that he knew.

"Catherine?" His own voice was unsteady.

"It is a long time since I have gone by that name. My friends call me Catalina: that's my Latin name", she explained.

There was a short pause. George was trembling all over; he could hardly believe that he was still alive, and now to find that the golden-haired woman was Catherine…

"Thank you for saving my life."

"Th…that's all right", stammered George, grateful that the darkness covered his shaking limbs.

"Are you hurt?"

"Not badly", he answered, uncertainly running a hand down his bruised back, where the dragon's tail had caught him, and licking his cut lip.

There was another awkward silence. George desperately sought for something to say.

"I looked for you at the village", was all he could think of. "My mother said you'd left soon after…" He stumbled, not wanting to bring up the subject of Tristan's death. "…soon after… I did", he finished lamely.

"Yes", she confirmed, "I couldn't stay…"

George gritted his teeth; he felt like this conversation was teetering on the brink of some yawning chasm: one more false step and they would plunge over the edge!

"I live in Cambodunum now."

"Oh."

"But tell me about yourself, George. What have you been up to for the last seven years?"

"It's a long story." George felt a ray of hope; they were edging away from the chasm.

"Well, I don't know about you, but I'm not quite ready to go back out for round two yet."

There was warmth in her voice, even a trace of mirth. He hesitated; this all seemed a bit too good to be true.

"Well, go on, George; it's not like you to shy away from telling a good story."

In the darkness, George pinched himself on the arm – no, he wasn't dreaming – and, without need for further prompting, launched into his epic tale.

It was as if they had been, somehow, transported back into childhood: George, the boy with the wonderful imagination, who told such amazing stories, and Catherine, the girl who hung on his every word: drinking in the graphic descriptions, thrilling to the chases, gasping at the near misses, and wondering at the exotic beasts encountered.

Catherine was particularly interested in George's newfound faith, interrupting his account several times for further details, but George didn't mind in the least. He had a warm cosy feeling inside, despite the chill air of the cave, and the spectres of the hostile villagers and the deadly dragon were banished, for the moment, to the dim recesses of his mind.

Describing the events that led up to his duel with Primus, over Cassia, George became conscious of silence from his audience, and suddenly wished he had left that episode out altogether. As he retold this part, and later, as he gave the account of his date in Ostia, George realised how foolish he had been. He imagined that Catherine would be thinking something very similar. Reaching the dramatic rescue in the woods, he was relieved to hear the occasional gasp of astonishment once again.

Arriving at the sea battle with the pirates, George recounted the tragic events of Brennos's demise. As he recalled his friend's death, George's eyes filled up and a lump appeared in his throat; tears ran down his cheeks and onto his neck. Wiping them away with the back of his hand and sniffing heavily, he pressed on. Suddenly, he felt the touch of slender fingers on his arm. Startled, George lost his thread.

"I don't understand how a dozen pirates could fit in a single amphora?" Catherine questioned, a few moments later, withdrawing her hand.

"Err… what? Oh, no… I meant drinking from, not hiding in", recovered George, flustered. "They had all been drinking from the drugged amphora."

After this little wobble in the narrative, George successfully wowed Catherine, once more, with his escape from the pirates, and the monstrous leviathan, and then decided to end the story there. He had no wish to mention the conversation he had had with his mother, or the hostile reception he had received in the village; both of these topics were bound to lead to the subject of Tristan.

"And that's all there is to tell, really", he concluded. "We travelled north with the caravan, arrived in Cambodunum last night, and I went to the village this morning to return the silver to my mother. And then, as I was about to buy dinner for my companions, the butcher told me of some mad woman who was trying to poison a dragon with his joint of pork! I couldn't miss that now, could I?"

There was movement beside him in the dark; Catherine had risen to her feet.

"That's the most incredible story I've ever heard!" she remarked, walking slowly toward the cave entrance.

"It is true", commented George, anxiously, as he, too, rose stiffly to his feet.

"I know", replied Catherine, earnestly, and then she giggled, "I think that's only the second true story I've ever heard you tell."

George was a little taken aback by this revelation; he had always imagined that the gullible orphan girl had believed all his stories.

"What was the other?" he asked, out of curiosity.

"The one about you stealing that egg from the market."

"How did you know that one was true?"

She didn't reply to this, but stared silently out across the water.

Joining her at the cave mouth, George surveyed the land around the lake; there was no sign of the dragon. With an unspoken agreement, they ventured forth from their refuge, casting anxious glances at the nearby wood and at the surrounding hills: still nothing.

Not daring to speak, the pair moved away from the dark opening in the hillside, heading for open country. Spotting his trusty blade lying undamaged a short distance to their left, George picked it up, dusted it down, and slid it back into its sheath, before moving off. They had just begun to climb the grassy slope that led up from the lakeshore, when George spied movement to his right.

Catherine let out a cry of alarm as he grabbed her by the arm, turning to face the dark shape that he had spotted out of the corner of his eye. It was only his horse. George relaxed, releasing his grip on Catherine, feeling a little embarrassed at his jumpiness.

"I thought it would have eaten my horse", he said.

"And I thought it would have eaten my pig", she replied, bitterly, looking back towards the lake.

"The one you poisoned?"

Catherine nodded grimly. "I've tried everything I can think of to get rid of that dragon, but nothing works. I've attempted to poison it before: using scraps of meat coated with stuff that my master puts down to kill rats, but the dragon just ate the meat, quite happily, and walked off. Then I spent days digging a pit, covering it with brushwood and leaves, but I hadn't really appreciated the sheer size of the monster; the hole wasn't nearly deep or wide enough, I…"

"Was that the one I fell into?" interrupted George, grinning.

"Yes", she replied apologetically. "That was a waste of time; I doubt if even one of the dragon's legs would fit in it!"

"Not right to the bottom", chuckled George. "It saved my life!"

"When I saw you fall in, I thought you were dead for sure", continued Catherine. "I was so relieved to see you reappear."

"What did you use to poison the meat this time?" asked George, interestedly, as he closed in on his reluctant steed. "Was it belladonna?"

"How did you know that?" she exclaimed in shocked tones.

"Flavius, the merchant I mentioned, told me all sorts of interesting things about herbs and plants", he replied, grabbing hold of the reins as he did so. "Belladonna is one of the most poisonous plants known to man, but despite this, it is also used, by women in high society, to make their eyes look more attractive."

As he said this, George found himself looking into her grey-green eyes; she was a very beautiful woman. He supposed he must always have known this, but somehow it hadn't really registered until now.

"You are very knowledgeable, George", she said, shyly turning her head away.

George, feeling mightily pleased with himself, flashed Catherine a smile as he helped her up onto his coal black mount, and then climbed up behind her. Flicking the reins, he directed the horse forward at a brisk walk. From being one of his darkest days, this was turning out to be one of the best of his life.

There was one thing that threatened to spoil it, though, something that made him feel uneasy, a question that nagged away at him. Eventually, when they had rounded the far end of the lake, he asked it. "Why are you so desperate to kill this dragon?"

Catherine didn't answer. Unable to see her face, George had no idea whether the enquiry had upset her, or if she had just not heard it. He couldn't imagine why it should upset her, but the unexplained feeling of unease persisted.

"Shouldn't the town authorities send some soldiers to deal with the dragon?" he asked, trying a different tack.

"They did", she replied, in a rather choked voice.

"The dragon killed them all – a dozen men – the last sacrificed himself so that I could escape into the cave."

George laid a comforting hand tentatively upon her shoulder.

She continued, her tone determined: "I vowed then, that I wouldn't allow anyone else to risk their life on my behalf; I would find a way to kill the beast myself, or die trying."

"But why must it be you?" George persisted, although the voice in his head was screaming at him to drop the subject.

Catherine didn't reply at first and, for a moment, he feared that he had pushed her too far, but after a short pause she sighed deeply and spoke again: "Let me tell you a story, George", she said.

Her tone of voice was different: resigned perhaps. He had no idea what was coming next, only an uncomfortable feeling that he wasn't going to like it.

"Twelve, or maybe, thirteen winters ago, a retired Roman soldier, named Vitus, sat fishing on the lake below us. It had been a successful trip, and he was just returning to the shore, his boat laden with the day's catch, when he noticed a strange blue-green object nestling in the reeds by the bank. On closer investigation it proved to be a huge egg, leathery to the touch…"

"My egg!" interrupted George. "I mean, the egg I stole from the market in Cambodunum."

Catherine nodded her head slowly and then continued: "Marvelling at his find, Vitus retrieved the egg and took it home with him. He laid it on the hearth, and set to cooking some of the fish he had caught, for tea. Before the fish were quite ready, he was startled by a crunching sound. Unsure where the strange noise had come from, Vitus looked about him anxiously, finally noticing that the giant egg now had a small crack at one end. Staring intently at the cylindrical object, the ex-soldier let out a cry of shock as a piece of shell became dislodged and a long green snout emerged! He watched, spellbound, as the scaly creature chewed its way out of the leathery casing using tiny needle-sharp teeth. It had soon nibbled a sizeable hole, and was able to wriggle its long lithe body free, which included about a foot of tail. There it stood, on the hearth, upright on its two strong hind legs, tail balanced behind it, staring up at him with piercing yellow eyes. Opening its mouth, it let out a number of screeching noises. The spell was broken; Vitus suddenly realised that the strange hatchling was looking to him to provide for it: it probably thought he was its mother! What did the newborn baby require? Food? But what did it eat? The fish were, by now, sizzling away madly in the pan, and so, uncertainly, he removed the smallest one with a fork and dropped it onto the stone hearth. Immediately, the lizard-like thing bent down and stuck its snout into the tender meat, pulling it to pieces with the aid of tiny sharp claws on its short forelimbs."

"But", began George, interrupting again, "The merchant said it was an ostrich egg."

"What's an ostrich?"

"A huge flightless bird."

"This was no bird", dismissed Catherine, with a wave of her hand. "The merchant was mistaken. In fact, when Vitus's daughter, Drusilla, came home and saw the creature, with its three-toed feet and pointed tail, she was convinced that it was a demon! She refused to have it in the house, so after tea, her father tied a rope around its neck and walked it back to the lake, where he set it free. However, the kindly Roman felt somehow responsible for the strange little lizard, and every time he went fishing up at the lake, he would feed it some of his catch. This went on for about a month, during which the creature almost doubled in size, and then, one day, it just vanished."

"Did he ever see it again?" George wanted to know.

"Not until…" replied Catherine, slowly, as if she was choosing her words carefully, perhaps not wanting to give away the story's ending "…the day he died."

Engrossed in her tale, George hadn't realised how far they had come. He now noticed that the trees were thinning out and the ground was beginning to slope away from them: they had reached the edge of the pinewood; his time with Catherine was almost over.

"Where did the creature go after it left the lake?" George pondered, as they dismounted at the head of the steep track, and began to traverse the slope on foot.

He was merely thinking out loud, and fully expected Catherine to have no idea of the answer, but in this he was quite wrong.

"It climbed into the hills to the south", she replied, confidently.

"How do you know that?"

"Do you remember that Samhain festival when the wolves attacked our village?"

George remembered it only too well. He nodded.

"Can you recall those terrible sounds just before they arrived?"

"You mean the wolves howling?"

Catherine gave a little shake of the head, her brow furrowed. "No, they were different, like the call of an eagle, perhaps, but deeper."

George cast his mind back to that awful night; now that he thought about it, there had been noises similar to what Catherine was describing. He nodded slowly.

"That was the beast from the lake. It chased the wolves out of the area, leaving itself as the only predator for miles."

They had reached the town gate now. George hesitated, wondering whether he would be expected to say goodbye at this point, but Catherine beckoned him on.

"My workplace isn't far", she said.

Pleased at this extension to their conversation, George led his mount past the watchful eye of the sentry at the gate, and down the street, which was fairly quiet by this late hour of the afternoon.

"So where did the lizard go next?" George was intrigued.

"It found a cave in the hills and used it for a den."

Catherine's voice quivered slightly as she said this, and as she turned away, George caught sight of a tear. Unsure what had prompted this response, he followed in silence, waiting uneasily for her to continue.

Catherine paused for a moment, closing her eyes briefly, seemingly fighting some internal struggle. Next moment, her eyes were wide open and her face wore a determined expression: she had begun this tale reluctantly, but having started, she was going to see it through, no matter how painful.

"The beast started to take sheep from the village enclosures", she continued, her voice heavy with emotion. "It would break in at night and then drag the carcasses back to its cave. Then, one winter, the old druid was out collecting mistletoe nearby, and the savage creature devoured him!"

Her words were tumbling out uncontrollably now, her voice becoming hysterical; there was no stopping her. She was like a ship speeding uncontrollably toward the life-stealing rocks. "The monster continued to poach the village livestock, and after one such raid, two boys took it upon themselves to track the sheep-thief down. They happened upon the druid's remains and found the nearby cave. On entering it, they stumbled across the dragon and…"

Catherine's voice choked off in a violent sob. George stared at her, horror struck: the strange lizard, which had hatched from the egg he had stolen, was the dragon? And it was the dragon that had killed and eaten Tristan? He could hardly believe it, and yet it made sense: when he had fought that bear in Gaul, something had not seemed right; he now realised that the animal had sounded different. The roar that had echoed through the cave, on that fateful night, had had a low rumbling quality to it, not unlike the bear's growl, but there had also been a harsher, higher pitched element, reminiscent of a bird of prey, just like the cries he had heard on the night of the wolves, and, of course, the far louder, terrifying roars that he had lately experienced from the fully grown dragon.

It all fit; he could see it now: his theft of the egg, his greed, his desire for recognition, had unleashed the terror that had slain his friend! And it wasn't just Tristan; there was the druid too, and the Roman fisherman. The dragon had obviously outgrown the cave and decided to return to the lake, where the pitiless monster had devoured the man who'd mistakenly hatched it and cared for it. And how many more innocent victims had followed? Catherine had mentioned a dozen soldiers who had been murdered by the beast, and the butcher had talked about it eating more than thirty men! *And it's all my fault!* The full horror of it struck him like a physical blow: he was responsible for all those deaths, just as surely as if he had murdered them himself!

George turned away, overcome by the burden of guilt that now rested squarely on his shoulders. Figures passed him in the street, but he didn't see them, not really; it was as if he was caught in a fog of emotion, lost in the horror of what he had done. Across the road, a door opened. He was vaguely aware of a young woman emerging from the building opposite and rushing up to Catherine. Her shrill voice sounded in his head, as if from a great distance away.

"Catalina, what's the matter? Where have you been?"

The words on a neatly painted sign that stood next to the open door read: 'Claudius's Fine Tunic Emporium'. With difficulty, George focused on the two women: Catherine was distraught, her head buried in her companion's shoulder. The other woman, Roman in appearance, with long brown hair and matching brown eyes, cast him an accusatory glance, identifying him as the cause of her friend's grief.

George just stood there awkwardly, one hand hanging limply at his side, the other clutching the reins of his horse. He had thought that he'd regained Catherine's friendship. No, it was worse than that: he had dared to believe that she would fall in love with him! How could he have been such a fool? To think that, after he had blighted her life, and the lives of countless others!

"I'm sorry", he mumbled, barely audibly, and then, clearing his throat, he tried again, his voice louder and more distinct: "I'm sorry."

Catherine gave no sign that she had heard, but remained sobbing inconsolably into her friend's shoulder, while the Roman girl continued to glare at him over the top of her friend's blonde locks.

"I can't bring Tristan back", George stated, his voice shaking with passion; "The only thing I can do is take vengeance on the beast that took him from you."

Resolved, he turned on his heel and strode away. No one else was going to die on his account; he had been running from this destiny for seven years, but he wasn't running any more: one way or another, this was going to end now!

Chapter 37 – Seeking Death!

George marched determinedly through the cobbled streets of Cambodunum, the borrowed horse clip-clopping behind him. His objective was now very clear: slay the dragon or die in the attempt! His pace slowed as he neared the sentry, standing guard at the town gate. The objective may be clear, but as to how he was to carry it out... *The 'die in the attempt' part will be easy enough*, he mused sardonically.

The enormity of what he had vowed seemed to grow with every step, bearing down upon George like a great weight. Finally, he came to a stop in the middle of the road. *How can I hope to defeat a beast that can kill a dozen Roman soldiers at one go?* His shoulders slumped dejectedly: it was one thing to talk about slaying a dragon; it was quite another to actually do it! Had anyone ever achieved such a victory before? Or was it like a rabbit taking on a fox: destined to end only one way?

George stared through the open gateway ahead of him; his destiny lay out there. He had cheated death seven years before, but no one could outwit the reaper for long. Death stalked him now, leering at him from beneath that dark cowl, knowing the young man would soon be in his irresistible clutches.

These morbid reflections forced a sudden shiver from George, as if a chill breeze had just blown through his very heart. But even as he stood there, trembling before the town gate, a ray of sunlight burst through the clouds, filling him with inner warmth once more: those years had not been wasted. He had made his peace with God – the old George had died – he was a new creature now, no longer the lying selfish cowardly thief that he had been. Oh, those things were still within him, buried, sometimes rising to the surface on dark days, but in essence he was a completely different person. Death no longer held any terror for him; it could have no more hold over him than it had over his saviour.

He would not have to answer for his crimes, he was certain of that, but that did not release him from their consequences. George pondered this for a moment. Was it his destiny to die at the claws of the dragon? His life did seem to be drawing to a natural conclusion: his time as part of Justus's travelling family was over, Brennos was dead; his feelings for Cassia were dead. He had returned home, but he could never truly return: he could not go back to living with his mother, even if the rest of the village would let him. *And Catherine?* George sighed: that friendship was broken, never to be repaired. One by one, the ties that held him to this world had been severed; now it was time to take his leave.

But I'm going out fighting, screamed a defiant voice inside his head, a voice that reminded him of Brennos. What would his old friend, and mentor, have done in this situation? Would even heroic Brennos, the mighty Bull slayer, have been stumped by this seemingly invincible foe? George's mind raced back to the terrifying encounter with the 'Bulls of Hades': *Those beasts had tough hides, yet one was slain.* How had his friend administered the killing blow? George had not seen the actual stroke, but he knew what must have happened: Brennos had galloped in, javelin held high, and then launched the weapon into the mighty beast...

"That's it!" he yelled out loud, causing a passing slave girl to drop her basket of bread. "Thank you", he added, speaking into the air, as he bent down and helped the frightened woman to gather up her fallen goods.

With a hasty apology, George yanked on the reins of his bewildered steed, and headed back in the direction of the market and, more specifically, the weaponsmith's shop.

Brennos had once explained to him the principle of memento, or was that momentum? *Some Latin word!* Anyway, the idea was that an object hurled from a charging horse would fly with the speed of the horse, as well as that of the thrower's arm, causing it to strike its target with far greater force than if it had been propelled from a standing position.

If he could hit the dragon with a javelin, driven by the speed of a galloping steed, it might just penetrate the beast's scaly armour. It was his best chance, in fact his only chance, of victory.

Nearing the forum, George's nostrils were, at once, assailed by that familiar delicious smell of freshly baked bread. It crossed his mind that he had not eaten anything since breakfast. At the same time, it occurred to him that although he had been past this bakery on many occasions, he had never sampled any of its produce.

I'm going to rectify that, he decided. *It's no good going into battle on an empty stomach!* Certain that Brennos would have approved of that sentiment, had he been here, George stepped up to the stall.

"I'll have one of the white breads… and one of the brown", he requested, eyeing the stacks of neat round loaves hungrily. If this was to be his last meal, he was going to enjoy it!

Reaching for his money pouch, George got a sudden shock: all he had were five silver coins, the money that Hector had given him to buy the joint of pork with. This was more than enough for the bread, but he had intended to buy at least two javelins from the weaponsmith's. It had completely slipped his mind that he had, that very morning, given all his worldly wealth to his mother!

Feeling downcast, once more, George paid for the bread and moved a little distance away from the shop. He packed the round brown loaf into his saddlebag, for later, and started munching on the white one. It was crusty on the outside, but soft, warm and crumbly on the inside, and he couldn't help but savour the delicious taste, despite his predicament. He didn't regret buying the bread; he was sure that a javelin would have cost considerably more than five denarii in any case.

Standing in the shadows of the forum's stone archway, devouring the white loaf, George wondered what to do next. He needed a javelin, preferably two or even three, but how could he get them? He knew that Justus carried a stock of them in his cart, but there was no way the Roman would let him borrow them to face a lethal dragon on his own. His friends would insist on sharing the danger, and he could not stand to see any one of them lose their life on his account; the dragon was his responsibility, and his alone.

As the Briton pondered this, a voice wafted across to him from the bakery: "…I'll not be needing more than a dozen of those for tomorrow, Quintus. I've never known the inn so quiet!"

George stared across at the short fat man, leaning against the stone counter of the baker's shop. He had a little less hair, and a little more belly than George remembered, but there was no mistaking the jolly innkeeper of the Boar's Head: "Caddy!"

Startled, the stout landlord turned and looked straight at the young man standing beneath the archway. The puzzled frown on his chubby face turned to dawning recognition: "George? It is you! How long has it been? Five years?"

"Seven."

"No, really?" Caddy stared at him in astonishment. "You must come over to the inn and tell me all about what you've been up to. I take it you're travelling with the caravan?"

"I was", replied George, feeling awkward. The innkeeper was obviously genuinely overjoyed to see him, and yet he would have to disappoint the man; George knew that if he were to set foot in the Boar's Head, his resolve would crumble.

"Is everything all right, George? Are you in trouble?" A look of concern furrowed Caddy's wide brow.

George hesitated; he had spent less than two weeks of his life in the company of this man, and yet he knew that Caddy would do anything for him. He felt guilty that the innkeeper had given him so much and all he had ever done in this relationship was take. And here he was, about to ask for more. *But who else is there to ask?*

"Do you remember when I told you that my best friend had been killed by a bear?" George began.

"Aye", confirmed Caddy, nodding his head.

"Well I was wrong. I found out today that a dragon killed him."

"The monster that lives up by the lake?" Caddy was wide-eyed with astonishment, his mouth dropping open in the manner that George remembered well.

"I have vowed to Catherine – that's my best friend's sister – that I will slay the beast or die in the attempt!"

The innkeeper looked at the young man before him, a horrified expression on his round face. "Then, George, you will die", he gasped. "No man could kill such a creature! They say it is armoured from head to tail with impenetrable scales! They say it can snap a man in two with one bite! They say it fights like the devil himself! It killed ten men in one encounter!"

"Twelve", corrected George, managing to keep his voice level with difficulty; just talking about the dragon caused his heart to beat faster. "But I think I may have a way to defeat the beast."

"What can I do to help?"

"I need javelins", replied George. "I paid off my debts this morning", he explained, "And now I don't have enough money."

The kindly innkeeper needed no further explanation. "How many do you want?" he asked, reaching for his moneybag.

"Well, I need one… and maybe a spare", added George, hesitantly, unwilling to put his friend to any more trouble than was absolutely necessary.

"You shall have three", insisted Caddy, "And all my prayers!"

George opened his eyes and looked about him. The sky overhead was the grey of early morning, with a sprinkling of stars still visible in the half-light. To the east, the first rays of dawn were painting the clouds with a crimson hue.

It took the Briton a few moments to remember where he was: outside in the open country with no tents or dwellings nearby. He had decided not to return to the caravan, last night – there would have been too many questions – and hunting the dragon after dark would have been foolish in the extreme. So he had ridden about a mile from Cambodunum, in the direction of the lake, and camped out beneath the heavens.

He rested for a while, comfortably warm beneath his old green travelling cloak, head resting on the small leather backpack that doubled as a pillow, staring as the great red orb rose majestically from below the horizon.

The world slowly changed from the violent contrasts of reds, oranges, greys and blacks, to peaceful greens, browns and blues. Dewdrops glistened on the grass, a blackbird chirruped from the bough of a nearby pine, and a bee buzzed contentedly as it got to work on a patch of red campion a few feet away from George's resting place. Here, all was peaceful and bright, free from worry and care.

Sighing deeply, George pushed aside his cloak and stretched, yawning widely. The business of the day hung heavy upon him, robbing the Briton of the fleeting joy he had felt at the sunrise. He nibbled at the brown loaf, appetite gone.

Stowing the remainder of the bread in his pack, George fastened his sword-belt and then approached his mount. The animal was busily tearing up mouthfuls of grass, blissfully unaware of the peril that it was about to face.

That was my last sunrise, George mused, morbidly. *Now let's get this over.*

"Catalina, you mustn't." Drusilla stood barring the door to the street, her arms folded. "You know how angry Claudius was, yesterday, when you went missing for half the day. If you aren't here when he arrives, he will throw you out! You will have no money and nowhere to stay."

"If I don't go now, a good friend will die", Catherine replied urgently. "If I have to sacrifice this job to save him, then so be it."

Drusilla continued to scowl, but moved away from the doorway.

"Thank you", acknowledged Catherine, stepping out onto the cobbles, and pulling her shawl across her shoulders, as she felt the chill of the early morning air. "Hopefully this won't take long and I'll be back before Claudius gets here."

What a fool I've been! Catherine berated herself as she hurried towards the town gate. *I should have gone after him last night. What if I'm too late? I'll never forgive myself!* Never forgive? Wasn't that what she'd said to George when he'd come to tell her of Tristan's death? *I have forgiven him, haven't I?*

She had been trying to forget that night for seven years, but seeing him again had brought it all back. Catherine brushed a tear from her eye. She mustn't lose control again; she had to persuade George not to face the dragon, and that wouldn't be accomplished by bawling her eyes out.

Reaching the gate, she stood to one side as two horses entered, pulling a large covered wagon. She glanced at the driver, a bald man sporting a large golden earring. How had George described his travelling companions? A silver-haired Roman and his daughter, a red-headed Gaul, a dark skinned Berber... She was pretty sure there hadn't been any bald men in there. Squeezing past the cart, she headed for the brightly coloured tents beyond the town's perimeter.

Turning anxiously as another cart passed, Catherine caught sight of a stocky red-haired man, with a neatly combed moustache, standing over by a large crimson tent.

"Excuse me!" she called, somewhat breathlessly. "Do you know a man named George?"

"Why certainly", responded the red-head, in a thick Gaulish accent. He gave a sweeping bow. "How may I be of assistance?"

"May I speak with him?"

"Alas, there I cannot help you", replied the Gaul, dramatically. "He vanished at midday yesterday. He took a horse and rode away south, and that was the last time anyone saw him."

Catherine gave a little moan of despair; she was too late. George had not returned to his friends. *He must have set out to find the dragon last night!*

"I know where he is", Catherine stated, hurriedly. "He's gone to fight the dragon."

"Did you say 'dragon'?" Hector stared incredulously at her.

"It's a long story", she replied, "But unless George's friends come to his rescue, it's going to have a tragic ending!"

It was still early morning, about the third hour, when George arrived at the far side of the lake. So far, there had been no sign of the dragon. He anxiously scanned the shoreline again. At this end, coarse grass and thick bushes grew almost to the water's edge, while at the wooded western tip, a narrow strip of shingle ran down to the shore. Between him and the trees, the ground was open and relatively flat; there was nowhere for the great beast to hide.

Keeping his eyes on the dark woods ahead, George unfastened his pack, to which he had tied the three javelins that Caddy had bought him. He drove first one, and then a second, into the soft ground, where they stood, their wooden shafts quivering, their sharp metal points buried in the turf. Carrying more than one was unwieldy; if he failed to bring down the beast at the first attempt, he would return here for a second, and then a third. George tried to suppress the feeling that if he missed with his first strike, he was unlikely to get a second chance, let alone a third!

Unfastening his cloak, George threw it to the ground, dropping his pack on top of it. He was ready now, or as ready as he was going to be, unencumbered save for the javelin in his right hand and the sword at his left side.

George rested the shaft of the javelin on his horse's neck, steadying it with his left hand as he clenched and unclenched the fingers of his right. He had been waiting for at least an hour now, and there was still no sign of the dragon. How long would he have to sit here?

He scanned the surrounding hills, checking that the great lizard wasn't sneaking up on him, and then went back to his vigil of watching the woods. Knowing that the arrival of the monster would spell almost certain death, George was in no hurry, but part of him still just wanted to get it over with.

George eased his mount forward; perhaps he needed to get closer, tempt the beast out. The pace of his heartbeat had quickened; he had covered about half the distance to the trees. He could make out the entrance to the cave now. Glancing toward the shoreline, George noticed that the pig's carcass had gone. Puzzled, he scanned the surrounding ground, looking for any signs of the meat. What could have happened to it? Had the dragon eaten it after all?

A sudden thought occurred to him: *If the dragon did eat the poisoned meat, it could be lying sick and helpless in the wood!* George spurred his horse forward; if the poison had weakened his foe, he might have a chance of killing it. He had to hurry, though, before the fearsome monster could recover.

Ducking beneath a low branch, George entered the wood. The trees were widely spaced in here, not like in the pine forest overlooking Cambodunum. Even on horseback, it was easy enough to negotiate between the gnarled trunks. It was going to be difficult to find his quarry, however; the heavy boughs overhead, thick with leaves, blocked out a great deal of the light, and the uneven rows of trunks stretched as far as the eye could see.

Underfoot, a carpet of twigs and dead leaves put paid to any hope of following tracks to the creature's lair. *I bet Juba could find it, if he was here.* But the Berber wasn't here, and although George could have used his help, he was glad that his friend was safe. Juba had something to live for: a bright future awaiting him, back in Cyrenaica; George did not.

Juba stared down at the body of water below, keen eyes searching for his friend.

"Do you see him?" Hector asked, shielding his gaze from the sunlight.

The Berber shook his head forlornly.

"The dragon has its lair in the woods at the western end", Catherine informed them, her voice shaking with anxiety.

Justus turned their steed toward the trees, but Catherine laid a restraining hand on the Roman's arm. "No, we need to approach from the opposite shore", she explained. "It's the way George will have gone. He may be watching the woods from that side, or he could be up by the cave." She pointed vaguely at the narrow rocky slope across the water from them; the dark opening was invisible at this distance.

"What if he's already entered the wood?" Hector enquired.

Catherine swallowed hard, the knot tightening in her stomach. "If he's gone in there, God alone can help him!"

George continued deeper into the murky wood, the eerie silence of his surroundings broken only by the crunching of leaves, the cracking of twigs beneath his horse's hooves and, of course, the pounding of his heart. After riding a considerable distance, he came to a place where sunlight actually broke through the leafy canopy: a small clearing, bordered on one side by an uprooted trunk and, at its far end, a beautiful covering of bluebells.

As George stared at the pretty flowers, something else caught his eye: in the middle of the purple patch, lying broken and discarded, was a rusting breastplate! He stiffened, tightening his grip on the javelin in his right hand; here at last was evidence of the dragon's presence.

A few paces beyond the clearing, a sword hilt poked out from beneath a thorny bush; a little further on, a helmet, stained black with dried blood, lay in a patch of nettles. Beyond that, a pile of gnawed bones offered silent testimony to the ruthless efficiency of his foe.

Following this macabre path, George battled the cold hand of fear that clutched at his insides. He wiped beads of sweat from his brow; he was getting close now, he could feel it.

George turned sharply in the saddle; something had stirred between the trees over to his left, he was sure of it. His mount gave a snort and pawed the ground; had the horse caught a scent? George stared intently through the greenery, every sense on heightened alert. *What's making that low rumbling noise?* Straining his ears to pick up the faint sound, George was forced to yank on the reins as his steed veered away to the right; something had spooked it.

Bringing the black stallion under control with some difficulty, George forced his way through a curtain of low-hanging, leafy branches, and found himself in a second clearing. Immediately, he froze, his heart stopping for an instant before hammering away violently within his chest. Lying curled up on the forest floor, not ten paces away, bathed in the warm rays of the late morning sun, was the dragon!

The thing was enormous, its bright green scaly bulk covering most of the glade. The great lizard lay on its side, powerful hind legs drawn up to its belly, its huge head resting on the pointed tip of its colossal tail. The dragon's eyes were closed, and its mighty chest rose and fell with deep, rhythmical, rumbling breaths.

Neither George, nor his steed, moved a muscle. Man and beast remained motionless, staring wide-eyed at the slumbering giant before them. It truly was an awesome sight; George couldn't help but admire the majestic creature. Everything about it was built for speed and power, from its huge well-muscled legs, to its sinewy forearms, with those cruelly curved claws. From the deadly jaws, filled with razor-sharp teeth, to the savagely pointed tip of its whip-like tail, the dragon was a perfect predator, equipped with weaponry unsurpassed by any gladiator. And yet, the beast had a striking beauty to it also: the dark green spines on the back of its skull adorned the great head like a crown, and the impenetrable emerald scales glittered with a faint bluish tinge as they shimmered in the sunlight.

What am I doing? George suddenly snapped out of his trance. *This thing murdered Tristan! And it will eat me too, if I give it chance to wake up!*

The dragon didn't look sick, so it either hadn't eaten the pig or was immune to the effects of belladonna, but he had caught it napping. This was his chance, while the creature was vulnerable; he had to strike now!

Cautiously, George swung his left leg over the saddle, and slid off the horse's back, landing noiselessly on the hard earth. Tiptoeing, spear in hand, he advanced on the monster, carefully avoiding a broken branch that lay in his path. He was three paces away from the terrible lizard now; two, one.

He paused, javelin held high, ready to strike. *But where should I strike?* He surveyed the creature's armoured hide. *It must have a weakness.* Should he aim for the heart? The belly and chest of the dragon were of paler hue than the rest, and covered in what looked more like tough leathery skin than scales. Would the iron point penetrate there? Possibly, but how was he to get to them? The great thick tail blocked his way. Should he risk stepping over it, or take aim from here? *But what if I miss the heart? I won't get a second go at this!*

Uncertain, George turned his attention to the beast's head; perhaps he should attempt to decapitate the dragon with his sword. He glanced down at the creature's thick muscled neck. *Will my blade be able to cut through that?* George doubted it. *What about the eye? If I thrust my javelin through its eyelid, it'll die surely.* But the nagging doubts continued. Could he be sure of hitting the smaller target?

As George stood there indecisively, staring at the scaly green eyelid, it flicked open! The Briton gave a yelp of fright, and then, panicked into action, thrust his javelin at the bright orb.

He was too late; the dragon shifted its great head in a heartbeat, catching the wooden shaft in its fearsome jaws and biting it in two with a sickening splintering crunch!

Stumbling backwards, unarmed and terror stricken, George took the only course of action he could: he turned and ran. With an ungainly leap, he launched himself back into the saddle, overbalancing slightly in his haste to depart the scene. The black stallion needed no urging; it shot off through the trees like an arrow from a well-strung bow, almost unseating his rider in the process.

George clung on for his life, frantically reaching for the reins as he slid sideways. The leather straps eluded him and, in desperation, he grabbed a handful of the flowing mane, as his mount galloped madly between the unevenly spaced trunks. Behind them, the sounds of the dragon's heavy tread grew steadily louder; the beast was outrunning his horse!

Hanging on grimly to the stallion's mane with his right hand, George stretched his left arm towards the reins, desperate to bring his frightened steed under control before it threw him off. Even as the tip of one finger made contact with the leather straps, his mount swerved under him. For a moment, George hovered, leaning way over the horse's left flank, his gaze fixed on the ground, which had become just a blurry jumble of colours and shapes. Then his steed swung the other way, bundling him back into the saddle, and he grasped another handful of horsehair; he was at the mercy of the animal beneath him!

Ducking to avoid a low branch, George pitched forward, both hands buried deep in the mass of flying black hair in front of him. Trees whizzed past on either side; they were going flat out, but still the sounds of pursuit increased. Surely he was imagining it; the dragon couldn't be gaining. George risked a quick glance over his shoulder; the creature from his nightmares was a mere two lengths behind them, its mouth half open in anticipation of a kill, revealing rows of terrible daggers!

Hastily turning back, George barely had time to take in the fallen log in front of them, before his stomach was plunged to the soles of his feet as the stallion took off in a desperate leap. For one horrible moment, horse and rider seemed to hang suspended in mid-air, and then the front hooves made contact with the earth, knocking George flat against his mount's neck.

Something struck him on the cheek: *the reins!* He made a wild lunge for them, his right hand closing over the leather. Even as he did so, a heavy thud behind him told George that the dragon, too, had leapt the felled tree.

He could feel hot breath on his back, smell the stench of rotting meat; the dragon was almost upon him! In desperation, George tugged at the reins, forcing his mount to swerve right. As they turned sharply, something hit him in the face, knocking him backwards in the saddle. Reeling, his forehead stinging painfully, George hauled on the leather straps in his hands, pulling himself upright as a great grey trunk loomed large in his blurred vision.

Horse and rider shot between two ancient oaks with a handbreadth to spare. Behind them, a loud crack and a snarl was evidence that the dragon had fared less well.

Moments later, they sped from between the outer trees, back into the glaring sunlight, hooves thundering along the even stretch of turf that separated the lakeshore from the rolling hills beyond.

"Down there!" called Juba.

Everyone turned in the direction that the Berber was indicating. Far below them, at the wooded end of the lake, a lone horseman was riding along the shoreline.

"George!" cried Catherine, relief flooding out of her.

Next moment, her heart was in her mouth; the dragon was emerging from the trees.

"By Mercury!" swore Hector. "It's huge!"

The black stallion galloped on, passing the two remaining spears, which were still sticking out of the ground, bearing his crazy master away from the battle that he could not win. It would have been so easy just to let himself be borne away, to take the path that led to life; instead, George yanked on the reins, bringing his mount to a halt. It was possibly the hardest decision he had ever had to make. Fear gnawed at his belly, voices screamed inside his head, telling him to flee, to save himself, but he refused to listen.

Four pairs of eyes watched disbelievingly as George turned his reluctant steed to face the terror that approached.

"What is he doing?"

"He's going to charge!"

"No, George!" gasped Catherine, tears obscuring her vision.

Catherine's tear-stained face rushed into George's mind; he owed her this. For the last seven years, the dragon had dominated her thinking; she needed to move on, to be free of this burden. His thoughts turned to Tristan: the foul beast had stolen the best years of his friend's life, and now it was going to pay. More faces appeared: Caddy, Brennos, Julia, Cahina, even the great troll with whom he'd conversed. All seemed to be urging him onward, to fulfil his destiny. George bowed his head resolutely. As he did so, his thoughts slipped back to a story Justus had told seven years earlier, the story of Samson: the hero whose sacrificial death had bought freedom for his people.

"Lord Jesus, let my sacrifice bring peace to Catherine."

Raising his head, George looked steadily at the advancing monster, paused for a heartbeat, and then spurred his horse forward.

Chapter 38 – Death and Glory!

Breaking into a canter, George bent low over the neck of his steed and grasped the shaft of the nearer javelin, wrenching it from the springy turf. Hefting the weapon to his shoulder, in one swift movement, he balanced it on his right palm, holding it steady as they increased speed to a gallop.

The legendary George rode forth to battle, teeth gritted in determination, sunlight glinting off the point of his spear, as he charged headlong at his mighty foe. Looming ahead, growing larger with every stride, the great dragon broke into a run, thundering towards them on powerful hind legs, tail held out behind it, counterbalancing the fearsome head, which stretched out on the long neck, straining to reach its latest prey.

With gigantic strides, the beast ate up the ground between them. The gap was down to thirty lengths, now twenty, now ten. George drew his right arm back, ready to launch the javelin; the dragon opened its jaws, ready to receive him.

The horse faltered, veering right; George released the iron-tipped weapon, slipping sideways as he did so. The spear struck the great lizard a glancing blow, skimming off the hard scales. George made a despairing lunge for the reins, as the panicked stallion turned, grasped thin air, and fell.

THUD. He landed hard on the dry ground, rolling over and over in the coarse yellow grass. Fighting for breath, George struggled to his knees, head swimming from the fall, and promptly collapsed sideways. Gulping a lungful of air, he rose again, more slowly this time, and peered dazedly about.

In one direction, the cool blue waters of the lake sloshed against the bank. Turning slowly left, he could make out a black shape moving away along the shoreline: his horse, but where was the…?

A roar erupted from somewhere close behind; George spun around, drawing his sword clumsily from its sheath. The dragon moved in for the kill, flexing its evil curved fore-claws in anticipation. George stood swaying slightly, trying to bring his nemesis into focus; it would surely be the last sight he would see!

The dragon arched its neck, towering high above the insignificant creature before it, and then lunged. George swung, gripping the hilt of his sword with both hands. There was a dull clang, followed by a fierce snort. Reeling backwards from the force of the attack, George, momentarily, locked eyes with his opponent, and noticed a thin trickle of red appear beside the right nostril on the dark green scaly snout.

In that instant, two thoughts flitted across the Briton's confused mind: *It is mortal; it can be killed*, and, *I just hit it with everything I've got, and all I did was give it a nosebleed!*

George backed up, looking for a possible weakness, somewhere he could hit the monster and actually do serious damage. The beast crouched, ready to spring, its great yellow eyes fixed unblinkingly on its prey.

With a snarl, the savage creature charged at George, who, with a cry, leapt sideways as giant jaws snapped shut over the patch of ground he'd just vacated. A flailing foreleg swung through the air, aiming for his head, and he barely got his guard up in time. Two feet of steel collided with six inches of claw. The man was thrown backwards by the force of the blow; the dragon gave a howl, which George suspected was born more of anger than of pain: now it had a bloody nose and a broken nail!

Stumbling to his feet, the beleaguered Briton raised his sword once more, waiting for the monster's next assault. He knew he was moments away from death, but a strange calm had descended upon him, almost a resignation to his fate.

The mighty dragon whipped around with lightning speed. George threw himself to the ground as, with a whoosh, the deadly tail swung over him, missing his head by the narrowest of margins.

Rolling sideways, George crouched on his haunches, staring up at the fearsome beast, trying to work out which of its many weapons it would employ for the next attack. The dragon turned slowly, its great head moving from left to right, piercing yellow eyes scanning the surrounding ground for signs of its opponent's body, momentarily unable to locate him. In a few heartbeats it would acquire him again; this could be his final chance!

Leaving himself no time for second thoughts, George charged forward, and as the scaly back rotated away from him, revealing the leathery underbelly, he struck, thrusting the point of his blade upwards with all his might.

There was a splintering crunch, followed by a bloodcurdling howl. Next instant, George was forced to leap backwards as the enraged monster aimed a savage kick at him. Anticipating another strike, he raised his sword defiantly, only to discover, to his horror that the blade had broken off at the hilt!

George stared dumbstruck at the now useless weapon clutched in his fist: the sword that had served him so well in so many perilous situations, travelling with him across thousands of miles; the blade given to him by his father, now broken in pieces by the dragon's granite hide!

The blood turned to ice in his veins; he stood defenceless before a monster that could kill him with a single blow from any one of its four limbs, tail or jaws! There was no hole to fall into, no cave to hide in; this time he really was going to die!

Anxiety gnawed at the pit of Catherine's stomach as she stumbled through the thick grass and dense patches of heather, trying desperately to keep up with her taller companions. It was maddening to know that, just a short distance away, George was facing death alone when, if only he'd kept riding… *But he can't; he's keeping his promise to you.* The last words that she'd heard him say flashed across her mind: *"I can't bring Tristan back; the only thing I can do is take vengeance on the beast that took him from you."* This was her fault. *Why did I have to go and make him feel so guilty?*

The ground rose sharply in front of her. Gasping for breath and battling a stitch in her side, Catherine staggered after the others, who were struggling to haul their mounts up the incline. They were within a few feet of the top of the low hill that lay between them and the lakeshore. In a few steps they would know whether their rescue attempt was in vain.

Catherine shut her eyes and clenched her teeth, praying hard; she could scarcely bear to look. When she did, she found that with each step, the land below unfurled like a scroll, until the whole of the lake, up to the woods at its farther end, was visible. It didn't take her long to locate the dragon, some way off along the shoreline, and there was George, on foot, fighting for his life!

"Let's go, gentlemen!" called Justus as, with a well-practised movement, he swung himself into the saddle, gripping a javelin in his right fist.

Hector and Juba followed their master's lead, without hesitation, despite the looks of apprehension clearly etched on both faces. For a moment, fear grasped at the hearts of all three, seeking to conquer their resolve, then friendship triumphed, and the horsemen galloped headlong down the grassy slope, leaving Catherine to watch helplessly from the hilltop.

The dreadful yellow eyes were fixed upon him once more, the neck was arching, the terrible jaws opening. In his mind, the fight was over, he had given up, but survival instinct took over: George hurled the sword hilt into the dragon's face, dodged right, and ran.

The ground shook as the mighty beast whirled around and set off in pursuit. He could not hope to outpace the dragon on foot; he had barely managed to stay ahead of it while on horseback! The thunderous footfalls grew rapidly closer, as did the snorting from the monster's nostrils. In a couple of strides it would have him!

George sprinted towards the lake, his shoulders hunched, as he anticipated the giant jaws clamping down on his exposed back. Ahead of him, a line of low dense bushes bordered the dark blue expanse. With a terrified yell, George leapt over the barrier and plunged into the icy waters, barely able to gasp a lungful of air before disappearing below the choppy surface.

A chill spread throughout George's body, as he grasped at the gritty stones and slimy weeds of the lakebed, pressing himself to the bottom like a limpet on a rock. He opened his eyes, staring fearfully upward through the murky water. The lake was only about four feet deep at this point; should he swim deeper or lie still? Would the dragon come in after him?

There was a muffled explosion, and George found himself being carried upward by a sudden force that rocked the lake bottom: the dragon had come in after him!

Desperate not to break the surface, George dipped his head, spread his palms, and pulled downwards through the water, heading further from the bank. His chest was tight, his cheeks bulging; a few bubbles escaped from his mouth. Would the dragon see them? Had he given away his position?

He turned left and right, gazing toward the surface, but couldn't see a thing; swirling sand and grit, stirred up from the lakebed, obscured his vision. George's lungs had reached bursting point; he twisted from side to side, no longer able to lie still at the bottom, his need for air overcoming all other considerations.

Unable to hold his breath any longer, George wriggled to his feet, throwing back his head to take in the life-giving air, but he had gone deeper than he thought; murky water still surrounded his head. Panicking, George launched himself upward, crashing through to the sunlight just as his lungs gave out.

Gasping and coughing, as he swallowed some of the lake along with the badly needed air, George floundered, anticipating a sudden strike from the beast that hunted him. Water ran into his eyes, momentarily impairing his vision. He gulped more air, preparing to dive below the surface once again, but where was his foe? Treading water, he turned away from the bank; had the dragon gone deeper? Was it somewhere below him, preparing to surge upward and seize him in its jaws, like the monstrous leviathan?

A faint cry penetrated George's water-filled ears. Surprised, he looked up, turning his head in the direction of the sound. It was then that he caught sight of the dragon: it had left the lake and was heading east along the shore. George's feeling of relief was tempered by another cry, louder this time: the monster had fixed its gaze on another human prey. *No!* Striking out for the bank, the determined Briton had just one thought on his mind: *No one else must die for me!*

A rather bedraggled George emerged from the bushes at the lakeside, sopping wet, his arms and legs covered in scratches. His sodden tunic felt like it had lead weights attached to it, and his calcei, the soft leather boots that he wore, squelched uncomfortably as he walked. He was, of course, fortunate that the leather straps had not become unfastened during his recent swim. In fact he was more than a little fortunate to be alive at all, but George had no time to dwell on this for, less than two stadia[1] from his position, three horsemen had boldly engaged the dragon.

Frantically looking left and then right, George located his coal black steed: it had fled to the edge of the woods. He charged after it, flapping and squelching, while shouting and waving wildly, but this seemed to unnerve the beast further, for some reason. The horse tossed its mane and trotted away towards the trees.

A thunderous roar erupted from somewhere behind him, followed by several yells. *I don't have time for this!*

---

[1] Roman unit of distance. One Stadium is equivalent to about 185 metres

Forcing himself to calm down, George slowed to a walking pace and halted, allowing a loud sigh to escape from his lips. His heart was pounding and his mind racing, but despite these feelings of anxiety, and the need for action, the Briton closed his eyes, breathed deeply, and whispered a silent prayer.

When he glanced up moments later, the black stallion was no nearer, and the savage snarls and terrified cries had not ceased, yet an inexplicable sense of peace now rested upon him; even his pulse had slowed somewhat.

George gave a whistle, beckoning the horse over with slow easy movements. At first there was no response; the frightened animal just stared at him with its big dark eyes. Then it took a tentative step in his direction, pawing the ground.

Ignoring the increasingly panicked shouts, and the voices in his head that screamed at him to hurry, George continued to motion calmly to his reluctant steed. Slowly, steadily, the black stallion trotted back to its erstwhile rider.

Swinging himself soggily into the saddle, George patted the animal on the neck and then urged him forward. Mount and rider cantered back along the shoreline, heart rates quickening once more at the anticipation of battle. Directly ahead, the last remaining javelin stood forlornly in the grass. Passing just to the left of it, George leaned out over the horse's right flank, seized the shaft and yanked it out of the ground. Righting his balance, he lifted the weapon to his shoulder, and spurred his steed into a gallop.

Speeding towards the fray, George caught his first close-up glimpse of one of the mysterious horsemen. "Justus!"

The white-robed Roman wheeled around the huge scaly monster, brandishing a spear in his right hand. A few lengths further off, a slim dark-skinned rider seemed to be having trouble controlling his mount. The frightened creature reared up, neighing wildly, almost throwing Juba from the saddle.

As he drew ever nearer to the conflict, a chestnut coloured mare, without a rider, galloped madly away from the pursuing dragon. *Where's Hector?*

George spied what, at first sight, looked like a bundle of clothing on the ground; there was a mass of bright red curls at one end.

"HECTOR!"

Was he dead? Anger arose within George, white-hot anger that burned deep within; this beast had murdered Tristan, alienated Catherine, and now killed one of his faithful friends, his close family. The dragon was going to pay!

A hideous spine-chilling scream echoed across the valley. George turned, staring wide-eyed at the scene of carnage that was unfolding before him: the dragon had sunk its savage teeth into the fleeing mare. Blood sprayed out from the unfortunate creature's punctured hide as the terrible knives bit deeper. Then, with an awful display of brute strength, the mighty beast lifted the horse fully off the ground with its powerful jaws! There was a horrible crunching sound, and the monster dropped the lifeless animal back to earth with a soggy thud.

Gritting his teeth with determination, George steered towards the evil green assassin. It had turned its malevolent gaze on Justus now, and was following the Roman's every move, as he dodged and weaved, looking in vain for a chink in the dragon's scaly armour. The Briton was now directly behind his target, less than thirty lengths away. He galloped on; twenty lengths separated them now. The monster snapped at Justus, its gigantic head missing the white-robed figure by the narrowest of margins. Fifteen lengths away and still the scaly beast had not noticed his approach. George cocked his arm back, preparing to launch the javelin on its way. This was it, this was his last weapon, his last chance; he had to make this blow count or surely his death would be in vain!

The coal black steed carried its rider ever nearer to the deadly dragon; close enough to make out the individual scales on its impenetrable hide, joined together like plates of armour with no gaps in between; close enough to see the black slit at the centre of its evil yellow eye, as the beast turned its head to face him.

Something moved at the periphery of his vision, a green blur whipping towards them at great speed. George threw his arm forward to release the javelin, and then his horse was swept from under him by the beast's mighty tail!

The firm, reassuring back was gone, replaced by sky, then ground, then sky again, as he somersaulted through the air with gut-wrenching speed. He hit the earth with a sickening thud, patches of light and dark revolving before his unfocused eyes, pain bursting upon him in great waves.

George lay on the ground, unable to move, unable to breathe, watching the clouds above as they spun madly round and round. Darkness crept over him, starting from the corners of his eyes, and spreading until only a narrow corridor of light was visible. He fought to hold on, struggled against the shadows, but the pain was too great, the blackness too thick.

Images flitted across his mind, people he'd met on his travels, far away places he'd seen. Only one lingered: his mother, her sad eyes staring down at him. *Rest, George. You've done all you can do.* Then his mum was gone, replaced by a younger woman with blonde hair. She was sobbing uncontrollably, hands covering her face. Would she forgive him now? If only he could see her one last time…

Dimly aware that something, or someone, was standing over him, George attempted to focus, shielding his gaze from the blinding sunlight.

A savage bloodcurdling roar echoed through the dim recesses of George's mind, shattering his peaceful dreams, if that's what they were, and hauling him roughly back to the present. Something was standing over him, but it wasn't Catherine, it was the huge dark form of the monstrous dragon!

Horror-struck, George attempted to rise, but his movements were sluggish; even as he lifted his aching back from the ground, he knew that he had no hope of dodging a lightning strike from the creature that had unhorsed him, and he no longer had a sword or javelin with which to defend himself.

The dragon arched its neck, preparing to plunge its deadly fangs into the vulnerable prey that lay before it. A woman screamed, but whether in reality or within his subconscious mind, George couldn't tell: dreams and reality were starting to blur. Overcome by pain and fatigue, he collapsed into the grass, closing his eyes, hoping for a quick death.

The fingers of George's left hand fell limply upon something smooth and wooden, lying discarded on the ground. In an instant, he had opened his eyes: *The javelin!*

The dragon thrust its head downward, mouth opening wide to reveal a great red pointed tongue ringed by yellow dagger-like teeth. At the same moment, using his last vestiges of energy, George whipped his left arm across his body, grasping the shaft with his right hand. The powerful jaws began to close, blocking out the daylight, sealing him in. Knives punctured his arm; hot blood ran along it, dripping down onto his legs. Pain racked his already battered body. Blood flowed freely from his head, his shoulders, his hands; the screams faded along with the remaining light...

Chapter 39 – A Legend is Born

The coarse yellow grass was splattered with blood; it was everywhere, staining the ground where George had fallen. Catherine ran on, her throat burning, her eyes blinded by tears.

"Why?"

Why had God taken first her brother, and now George, from her?

Stumbling as she reached level ground, Catherine stopped long enough to wipe her eyes with the backs of her hands. Brushing long blonde locks out of the way, she stared at the battlefield before her. Immediately ahead, Juba had dismounted and was helping a dazed Hector into a sitting position. To her right, George's coal black stallion lay battered and broken. Some distance beyond that, the remains of the chestnut mare littered the turf, and between them, a little way to the left, was the dragon.

Catherine stared at the huge scaly monster. It stood unmoving above its fallen victim; it didn't seem to have shifted position since the kill. There was something very strange here. She took a step closer, noticing that the beast, though still upright, had sunk to its knees.

"Wait!" ordered Justus, alighting from his mount, putting himself between her and the motionless brute.

The Roman held out his sword and stepped cautiously forward. Catherine followed, keeping in step with the merchant. Both had their eyes fixed on the dragon, anticipating its sudden turn and strike. They were less than ten paces from the monstrous lizard now, and still it made no move to stop them.

Silently, they drew alongside the gigantic creature. Its huge head was bowed low, barely two feet from the ground, its deadly jaws half open, exposing its great red tongue and rows of cruel curved teeth. Beneath the gaping maw, lay the lifeless blood-bespattered figure of George, his eyes tight shut, his face set in a painful grimace and, in his clenched fists, the wooden shaft of a javelin.

Both of them stared along the length of the shaft: the butt of the weapon had been rammed downward with such force that it had sunk into the turf just to the right of George's hip; the other end of the javelin disappeared into the cavernous mouth.

"It's gone right through!" marvelled Justus, in an awed voice. "The spear point is sticking through the top of its skull!"

"He's killed it", sniffed Catherine, wiping her eyes. "You did it, George."

She bent down to his blood-smeared face; a tear fell from her eye and landed on his pale cheek.

George opened one eye! "Those angels are taking their time", he said, his voice croaky.

"You're alive!"

"Not for long", replied George, weakly, surveying his blood-soaked tunic.

"That's the dragon's blood", clarified Justus, joyfully, looking George up and down. "Well, mostly", he amended, spotting a gash on his servant's upper right arm, where one of the beast's razor-sharp incisors had punctured the skin. "In its attempt to devour you whole, the great lizard has impaled itself on your spear!"

"I can't believe it", stated George, in a dreamy voice. "I released that javelin before I was thrown from my horse, and yet it landed right by my hand. It was as if Jesus had sent an angel to place it there."

"I have no doubt that he did", confirmed Justus, thoughtfully.

At that moment, Juba approached, supporting a rather wobbly Hector. "Brennos would have been very proud of you", the Berber announced, reverently.

"It's a pity he couldn't see this", agreed Hector, wistfully.

"He wouldn't have wanted to", contradicted George, shaking his head and coughing. "He vowed to eat his own loincloth if he ever saw a real dragon!"

"And this is a genuine 'three camel' dragon", nodded Juba, smiling broadly.

"As I said", laughed the Gaul, "It's a pity he couldn't see this."

Between them, the companions managed to tug George out from beneath the great green hulk before it finally collapsed to the ground, and then Catherine got busy washing and bandaging his various wounds.

"I'm sorry I cried back in town", she told him, as she wrapped a linen cloth around his arm. "I haven't talked about Tristan's death with anyone, and it just brought it all back to me. I have forgiven you though, really I have."

"Thank you", replied George, wearily, "That means a lot to me." *More than you'll ever know*, he mused, closing his eyes as he felt the warming rays of the midday sun on his face.

While the Briton's wounds were receiving attention, Justus had been hacking away at the giant carcass with his sword. Now that he was properly patched up, George examined the Roman's handiwork. The merchant had severed the dragon's mighty neck so that the colossal head could be carried using the javelin as a pole.

"It's for the parade", he told a bewildered George.

"What parade?"

"You'll see", was the Roman's enigmatic reply.

With only two horses between the five of them, and the heavy burden of the dragon's head to carry, it took some time before the triumphant group arrived back at the gates of Cambodunum.

"By Saturn!" swore the guard, as they entered with the beast's head held high.

"We are taking this to show the governor", was Justus's only explanation, and staring at the hideous apparition as if his eyes would pop out of his head, the sentry let them pass.

Unsurprisingly, the party attracted a great deal of attention from those milling about in the town's streets. By the time they had reached the forum, their following had swelled to quite a procession. In the lead, Justus climbed the marble steps of the basilica confidently, passing between the huge pillars that supported the roof, and entered the impressive building. The guard on duty made no move to block his entrance, or even to question him, but just stared open-mouthed at the monstrous head dangling from the pole carried by Hector and Juba.

George, with Catherine by his side, trailed the audacious Roman straight into the government building. Puffing and panting, the pole-bearers struggled up the last few steps and gained admittance also. There followed a deep booming, as the imposing double doors slammed shut behind them; it seemed that the guard had sensibly elected to bar the inquisitive crowd.

The atmosphere inside the basilica was in marked contrast to that outside. In here all was peaceful and tranquil; the heat of the afternoon sun replaced by the cool of wide airy halls, and instead of dusty cobbles, glossy tiles of black and white paved the way to the spacious interior.

Except for the squeaking of boots on the polished surface, no one made a sound, not even Hector, who had been continuously muttering about the weight he was being asked to carry. It seemed to George that silence was expected in a place like this, and that to speak here was to invite punishment. He was pretty sure that they weren't supposed to be wandering through these corridors unattended either; he just hoped that Justus knew what he was doing.

Up ahead, another set of double doors, similar in design, but smaller than those they had entered by, barred their path. To the left of these, an officious looking man with wispy hair and a hooked nose, sat behind a large wooden desk piled high with parchments.

"No appointments after the sixth hour without prior agreement", declared the man, without looking up from his work.

"I think an exception can be made in this case", insisted Justus.

The clerk glared up at him, annoyed at this disturbance. "By Vulcan!" he swore, squeezing his reed pen in sudden fright, and inadvertently covering the nearest parchment in black liquid.

Flustered, he began frantically dabbing at the ink puddle, which continued to spread unchecked across his neatly lined accounts. Taking advantage of this distraction, Justus pushed open the heavy doors.

"This is the governor's office", whispered Catherine to George, as they strode into the large, magnificently furnished room beyond.

Passing a collection of expensive looking vases, on the left, and a marble statue, on their right, the companions strode purposefully towards the enormous table at the far end of the room, behind which sat an immensely fat toga-clad Roman.

"By Vulcan!"

"Yes, your clerk was saying", began Justus dryly. "I expect you will want to record that on this day, George here", he motioned with his hand, "Has slain the mighty dragon that was terrorising the occupants of this town and those of the many surrounding villages."

"Dr…dragon?" spluttered the governor, nervously eyeing the nightmarish visage draped on the pole.

"The one you didn't believe existed", muttered Catherine bitterly.

"Yes… of course… Err… well done."

"Perhaps a reward would be in order", suggested Justus.

"A reward?" The governor seemed uncertain for a moment, and then recovered. "Yes, certainly. Quintillus!"

The flustered clerk appeared at the door.

"Quintillus, I'm declaring the rest of the day a public holiday. Make sure that everyone is notified, won't you. If anyone needs me, I'll be at the baths."

"I told you there'd be a parade, didn't I?" remarked Justus as they marched through the streets at the head of a cheering crowd, all straining to get a look at the famed dragon's head, and George, the hero who had slain it.

George, wearied after his exertions, and a little embarrassed at all the attention he was receiving, smiled weakly and waved once more. A roar of approval rose from the gathered throng.

"Never mind waving", complained Hector, "You should take a turn carrying this thing; it weighs more than Juba's moneybag! My arms will stretch past my knees if we keep this up much longer!"

"You can set it down at the end of this street", laughed the Roman merchant. "We're going to pay a little visit to the Boar's Head."

Justus, who seemed to be running the town for the day, certainly had the whole parade stage-managed. They had arrived outside the now familiar inn with its faded sign.

"Juba, if you could keep an eye on the dragon while we're inside", remarked the merchant. "I'll send Hector out to relieve you presently. Oh, and I'm expecting a delivery, by cart", he added cryptically.

"Mind your knuckles on the step, Hector", quipped George, as they entered.

Caddy was pottering around, whistling tunelessly, and wiping down the empty tables; it had been another quiet day. He looked up as the door opened.

"George!"

The Briton winced as he found himself embraced in a bear-hug. "I didn't think I was going to see you again."

"These are my friends", introduced George, when he had recovered: "Justus the merchant; Catherine, the lady I was telling you about, and Hector."

"Hector de Massilia", interjected the Gaul, feeling that his introduction was somewhat lacking.

"And waiting patiently outside, is my good friend Juba", continued George, ignoring the interruption. "He is guarding something I would like you to see."

Caddy pulled open the door inquiringly, and stared, his jaw almost hitting the cobbles.

"Slain with God's help, and your javelin", remarked the Briton, grinning widely.

The stout innkeeper was speechless.

"Perhaps you would like to hear the tale", suggested Justus. Then spotting a cart heading towards them from the marketplace, he motioned in its general direction: "A small reward for your kindness, on George's behalf - a dozen amphorae of Gaulish wine."

In the time that it took for Caddy to regain the power of speech, the Boar's Head had become packed to the rafters. It seemed that half the citizens of Cambodunum had turned out to hear George's account of the dragon slaying! The stout innkeeper was soon busy pouring drinks and taking meal orders, while Mrs Caddy and the kitchen staff struggled to keep up with the demand. Aidan was rushed off his feet, serving food to the merry throng, and feeling sorry for his former work colleague, as well as wishing to escape the constant questioning, George got up and gave him a hand.

"This dragon slaying of yours is very good for business, George", remarked Caddy, opening a fresh amphora of wine. "I don't suppose you could do it on a regular basis?"

"I'm afraid dragons are pretty thin on the ground in these parts", replied George, plonking a full tray of food on a nearby table. "If you run out of meat, though, I expect Hector could fetch some dragon rump."

The Gaul set his mug down with a bang. "If you think I'm going to parade through the streets of this town with a dragon's backside dangling from a pole, then you're as stupid as you look!" he blustered.

"And now", announced Justus, interrupting, "We must be moving on."

"Where to?" George enquired.

The Roman didn't reply, but just winked at him and gave a knowing smile; he was obviously thoroughly enjoying his new role as parade organiser.

George said fond farewells to Caddy, Mrs Caddy and Aidan, and then they were on the march once more. Many who had followed them earlier, remained at the Boar's Head, seduced by the warm friendly atmosphere and the roast peacock in its deliciously creamy herb and apple sauce. But some continued with them even beyond the gates of the town, where Justus, after a brief conversation with Catherine, and a quick check to make sure that his daughter was coping in their absence, turned southward.

At first, George thought they might be heading back to the lake, perhaps to view the dragon's carcass, but it soon became apparent that they were, in fact, making for his village. He looked across at his master anxiously; so far Justus had had everything under control, but now? The Roman could have no notion of the strength of opposition that they were bound to face on arrival.

He turned to Catherine. "I'm not sure this is such a good idea."

"I am", she responded, without hesitation.

George did not share her confidence. She had not been present at his recent visit; he'd not exactly received an open invitation to return! By the time they had climbed the last hill, all the peace and joy that George had experienced since his miraculous defeat of the dragon, had ebbed away, his spirits sinking like the sun in the western sky.

In stark contrast to the Briton's sombre mood, Justus oozed enthusiasm as he strode confidently into the midst of the huts, ahead of Hector and Juba, who rode close behind, bearing the grisly trophy aloft. Reaching the large wooden building at the centre of the village, the merchant knocked boldly on the door.

Moments later, a familiar figure, tall and thin, clad in a white toga, emerged from the great hall.

"By Juno!"

"By Jesus, actually", responded Justus, his voice calm and measured, "But I'll let George explain the details."

"George?" The village blacksmith joined Caradog at the entrance, his muscular arms folded defiantly across his barrel chest. "That murderer is not..." He broke off, his mouth agape.

"George is not a murderer", Catherine's shrill voice rang out in the silence. "This dragon..." she pointed at the bestial head, "...is the murderer. This is what ate my brother; this is what killed the druid. And today", she continued, her voice quivering with emotion, "George has triumphed over this monster and avenged their deaths."

"That's all very well", replied the sheriff, tearing his gaze from the monstrous jaws, "But Governor Porcius…"

"Governor Porcius has declared a public holiday in George's honour", interrupted Justus, smoothly.

"He has?" Caradog was stopped dead in his tracks.

"He has."

"Well, in that case…" The sheriff's expression turned from storm to sunshine in the blink of an eye. "Let a banquet be prepared." He clapped his hands authoritatively. "You will be our guests, of course", he added, smiling benevolently at the little group.

For the next hour or so, the village became a hive of activity: oak tables were carried into the nearby meadow, with logs arranged for seating; wood was gathered and a bonfire lit; a couple of calves were slaughtered and spit roasted, while industrious women prepared an assortment of bread and cakes.

Throughout all this busyness, George sat in a daze; he could hardly believe what was happening. Only yesterday he had been assaulted and hounded from his home, and now, here they were holding a feast in his honour, and a fine feast at that, especially considering the lack of preparation time.

As the sun set behind the western hills, the villagers and their guests ate and drank, and George, who felt as if he were living in some kind of dream, told his tale from beginning to end. Everyone listened with rapt attention and, as fantastic as the story was, no one disbelieved a word. How could they, when he had eyewitnesses to back up his claims, and the dragon's severed head staring balefully back at them from its perch by the fire? And when it was over, several locals came over to congratulate the hero. Dean and his wife - a heavily pregnant Sylvia - both shook him warmly by the hand.

"How tall did you say that old troll was, George?" Dean enquired.

"Nine feet."

"Well, well." He gave George a mischievous wink, and George grinned back at him, remembering the tall story he'd once been ridiculed for.

Even Cunobelinos gave him a bone-crushing handshake. "Maybe you should enter the javelin contest this year", he suggested.

"No", laughed George, "I can't throw straight to save my life, and believe me, I've tried! I could try the wrestling though", he mused.

The big blacksmith patted his belly, winced slightly, and muttered, "I'd better just stick to the javelin from now on, then."

Loudest amongst his growing ranks of supporters, was his mother. "To think, my son – a hero!" she exclaimed, giving him a big hug.

Before he had time to get too embarrassed, though, she had pulled away. "You're all sticky!"

"He's not sat in another cake, surely", chuckled Dean.

"It's your arm; it's bleeding!"

"I'll live", responded George.

But that wasn't good enough for his mother, who insisted on washing his recent injuries with water that she'd heated over the fire.

"Ow, mum!" he complained as a hot cloth was squeezed over his arm.

"Don't be such a baby!" she scolded.

Watching the scene with fascination, Juba gave one of his amazingly broad grins. "No one should have to take on a dragon and their mother in the same day", he remarked.

It was a balmy evening, early in September. A cool breeze ruffled the surface of the lake, as one man sat gazing out across the water. Hundreds of people had visited this spot in the last couple of months, all of them eager for a look at the remains of the mighty beast, the beast that he had slain. He was a hero; people had composed songs of his mighty deeds.

George glanced over at the dragon's carcass, lying some distance to his left. Scavenging birds, animals and insects had done their work well, and there was little flesh left, now, on the imposing skeleton. He wondered how long it would take for even the bones to disappear.

George shook his head and stared out across the lake; he was no hero. But for divine intervention, he would have departed this life without laying a scratch on the monster. Why had he survived when other far more worthy souls had perished? And what was he supposed to do now? He had returned home, he had achieved his goal, but now that the general euphoria had died away, all he felt was a sense of emptiness. It was a hollow victory; it couldn't bring back Tristan. The evil creature had digested his little friend long ago; there was nothing left of him now, except maybe a pile of bones lying forgotten in a dark cave.

Something rustled the grass behind him. Startled, George turned in the direction of the sound, and was relieved to see a familiar young woman approaching, a playful grin on her pretty face. He looked away. The friendship he and Catherine had rebuilt together over the summer was very precious to him, and ordinarily he would have been overjoyed to see her, but today he just wanted to be alone with his thoughts.

"You shouldn't be out here at this time."

"Why not? This lake is perfectly safe now", she argued, sitting down alongside him, "And besides, I have the legendary George to protect me." She slipped her arm through his.

George continued to stare morosely across the cold grey surface of the lake.

"What's the matter?" she asked, concern in her soft voice.

"I was thinking about Tristan", he replied uncertainly. Up till now, he had been unwilling to broach this subject for fear of reopening old wounds.

There was a moment's silence, and then Catherine spoke. "I've been thinking a lot about my brother these past few weeks", she said, "And now that I'm no longer focusing on avenging his death, I find myself dwelling on pleasant memories of him, for a change."

"The thing that sticks in my mind is the prayer he offered up just before we entered the cave", ventured George, unhappily. "He asked God for the strength to defeat the beast within…"

He paused, wiping the corner of his eye, and then blurted out: "Why did God ignore that prayer? He helped me to slay the dragon; he could have saved Tristan seven years ago!"

"You said yourself that God helped you defeat the dragon", responded Catherine, slowly but firmly. "That was the answer to Tristan's prayer.

"It took seven years for God to get the message?"

"No. It took God seven years to prepare you to fulfil that task."

"But what about Tristan?" George wanted to know. "God didn't protect him, did he?"

"He did something better", replied Catherine, a trace of emotion in her voice, "He called my brother home."

The pair sat in silence as the last light of the setting sun dyed the lake a deep red.

"I wish God hadn't called Tristan home", George muttered into the stillness, "Or Brennos; I've got so much to tell them."

"They are in a place of wonder, a land with no horizons; they are in the presence of the Almighty", whispered Catherine, in an awed voice. "I think they may have a few stories to tell you when your time comes."

George contemplated this, his eyes drawn to the great crimson orb that was slowly dropping below the trees at the lake's western tip. The way Catherine described the afterlife made him almost wish he were there, that the dragon had killed him with its last gasp. But it hadn't; he had survived.

It was as if Catherine had read his mind. "So you've travelled the world, slain the dragon and claimed hero status; what's next?"

"I don't know", answered George, uncertainly, conscious of the gentle touch of her hand on his arm. "Justus did say that if I changed my mind about staying, I could catch them up before they sailed back to Gaul."

He glanced at Catherine, and for a fleeting moment, thought he detected a look of disappointment on her face. He turned away.

"It's too late to go after them, though; they'll be halfway across Gaul by now. And I wondered if maybe it was time to settle down", he pondered, dreamily, "But the only one I'd really like to settle down with is you."

"Is that a proposal?" she enquired, sounding slightly shocked.

George's brain caught up with his mouth; he couldn't believe what he'd just said. "I suppose it is", he acknowledged, a little taken aback by his own boldness.

Next moment, he found that he was looking right into Catherine's beautiful eyes, and her soft warm lips had touched his own.

It had all happened rather suddenly, and George was still struggling to keep up. Even as they embraced, he found himself mentally replaying the last few sentences. He had always found communicating with women to be a confusing business: they rarely seemed to say exactly what they meant, and often interpreted his words in ways other than he intended. But despite this inherent difficulty, George was fairly certain that he had just asked Catherine to marry him and, although she had not actually said 'yes', he was almost sure that she had accepted!

Printed in Great Britain
by Amazon.co.uk, Ltd.,
Marston Gate.